MW01227679

Also by Peter R. Talley:

Orbs of Avalon: Tales of Urban Magick and Horror

The Chalk Princess

The Cerulean Sphere

Lost in Darling City: Tales of Magic, Mobsters, and Monsters

Learn more:

Website: www.PeterTalley.com

Facebook: Peter R. Talley – Author

Twitter: Peter R. Talley (@petertalley14)

BEYOND
THE LEVEE
AND OTHER
GHOSTLY TALES

EDITED BY PETER R. TALLEY

This is a work of fiction. The characters, incidents, and dialogue are drawn from the authors' imagination and are not construed as real. Any resemblance to actual events or persons, living or dead, is entirely coincidental.

Copyright © 2020 Peter R. Talley
Cover design: Caedus Design Co.
Embedded cover image: "Untimely"
by Shannon Elizabeth Gardner

Published in 2020 by Peter R. Talley
through Kindle Direct Publishing

All rights reserved. No part of this book may be reproduced, scanned, or distributed in any printed or electronic form without permission. Please do not participate in or encourage piracy of copyrighted materials in violation of the author's rights.

ISBN-13: 9798669936402

TABLE OF CONTENTS

"Untimely" by Shannon Elizabeth Gardner

BEYOND THE LEVEE AND OTHER GHOSTLY TALES

A DEEP SPRING CLEANING

BY SALINDA TYSON

"They're asleep."

Two shadows poised at the foot of the bed, listening, staring.

"How strange," the smaller shadow said. "Snoring, tossing, turning. Alive."

"Do they sense us, mama? Could they see us?"

"I don't think so, dear." The larger shadow seemed to brush the smaller one's hair and shoulder. "I believe they are quite blind and deaf to us, unless an ouster comes, but we are fading. The walls nearly caught me fast last time I passed through them."

"Oh, the walls. Old walls, new walls. Why did they change the walls? It is our house."

"Fashion, perhaps. But it is their house now. Not ours since 1892, when we died of the pneumonia."

"What horrible memories. Coughing, coughing, my ribs sore … and coughing blood." The smaller ghost shuddered.

The larger one kissed her forehead. "All done, child, only memories are caught in this room. She in the bed—she has changed this room completely."

"Look. See where she's put the mirror—"

"Do not go near the mirror!"

The smaller shadow drew back. "I won't. I promise."

The two silhouettes wafted like smoke, exploring the room now so strange to them, reaching toward the bed, table, chairs, and curtains with wispy, insubstantial fingers.

The pair drifted like mist to the window, peering out at a moon-silvered lawn.

A shudder vibrated through the walls. "Uff!" A portly gentleman dressed in the style of the late 1920s stepped through the wall into the room. He doffed a misty top hat. He was always the first to greet them, staring through them, blinking, then nodding at them. A big, bulky, fierce man with a bristling mustache.

"Ladies." He smiled a Cheshire cat smile, settling his hat on his unruly hair. There was something shadowy at his neck.

The old house, built before the Civil War, swarmed with generations of ghosts, or memories of selves who had lived there before spirits moved into the beyond and dissipated into sheets without expression or memory.

The eldest ghosts, unless they had come to a bad end in the house—just turned into vapors and drifted away into the beyond where even a truly talented medium could not contact them. Younger spirits, flappers and card players, materialized around midnight in a haze that flowed through the left-hand wall like a tide. Glasses glinted and clinked. An aroma of alcohol hung in the air.

Older ghosts were mere suggestions sketched in the air. Stuck in the room, but slipping away past memory and form.

The small shadow cocked her head. "Sometimes their dogs or cats see us, sense us, bark or hiss. But they mostly don't, just stare with those glowing eyes. Why?"

"Animals recognize us as beings from the between, because their senses are keener."

A memory of a clock struck half past midnight. Flappers and card game vanished like a magician's trick.

Half past midnight: A sudden scream invaded the room. A female form rose from a huddled heap in the middle of the room, looked down at her dead self, and hovered, rising toward the chandelier, but reaching toward the crumpled figure on the floor. The thin sound of her weeping went on and on, like the heartbeat of the floor, the walls, the room itself.

In the bed, the couple sighed, the man shifted, turning his back to the woman. She grabbed the covers, yanking them fully over her. An edge of the quilt brushed into one haunt, flinging it back into the wall.

But the woman woke. She glanced around, ran her fingers through her hair. She flung her feet over the side of the bed, thrust her feet into slippers, shuffled to the window where the moon blazed gold above the treetops. She stiffened and turned suddenly, as if catching movement from the side of her eye.

She padded back to the bed, shook the man, George, by the shoulder.

"What the—" He threw the covers off and sat up, his hair a mess.

"I feel that feeling again," she said. "Cold, creepy … something is or was in this room."

"It is cold. Baby, we need to turn the thermostat up. That's all."

She snorted, shook her head. "We need to call the exorcist, the house cleaner, the banisher, the ouster. It's ghosts. That's why Pooka and Sylvester won't come in here. Animal instinct. They know. With the history of this house, nobody with a superstitious bone in their body will buy it. You know that. Death in a house is bad vibes, bad mojo."

"I'm not scared of mojo."

"No, but losing what we've put into this house scares you!"

George reached for his glasses.

"Point taken, okay."

"So, I'll call the house cleaner, the ouster?"

George stuffed his feet into his slippers and joined her at the window. "Don't tell friends we did this, okay?"

"What? Mr. Engineer Scientific Guy doesn't want folks to know he indulged in non-logical, non-scientific activities? Consulted a woo-woo practitioner?"

George laughed his endearing laugh. "Does it say woo-woo practitioner on their card, by chance?"

Susan slapped his shoulder.

***

The ouster was a middle-aged woman whose black hair had a white streak. She carried a carpet bag ("Mary Poppins?" George sniffed until Susan shushed him.)

"Just call me Mabel." She insisted they not show her the haunted room, but toured the house, immediately picking the bedroom.

"Yep, this is the spot, hot spot, cold spot." She nodded, set down her bag, and asked for a table. Round table, more natural, more holistic, she said. From the bag, she pulled a full container of Morton's salt. "Salt is salt," she commented. Next came a sage smudging bundle, candles, feathers, and a ball of red twine.

"How much do you charge?" Susan asked.

Mabel frowned. "Charge, smardge. No money. This is spiritual work. Got it? No silver crossing my palms."

The couple shrugged. "Okay."

"Stay while I work," Mabel said. She lit the candles. "Sit around the table."

They sat in the center of the room, lights turned out.

14

Mabel talked while she worked, like a doctor narrating an examination. First, a black cloth draped over the ornately framed mirror. "No mirrors," Mabel tsk-tsked. "They tend to hold ghosts back." She smudged all four corners, including George and Susan, waving the sage bundle around them back and front. She swept the room clean, muttering in all the corners, scooped the dust and took it out the kitchen door, buried it in the yard in the spot near where their labradoodle Pooka hid bones. Pooka barked, but calmed instantly when Mabel said, "Spirit work, dog. You understand, descendant of Cerberus?"

In the room she opened the window, then laid a circle, sprinkling salt through pinched fingers with unerring precision as she turned inside the circle. Inside the circle of salt she laid the red string.

"Now for a spring cleaning, a deep cleaning, eh?" Mabel joined them at the table, lit the circle of candles and incense. "So, you know about the woman murdered here, of course?"

Susan and George exchanged a look.

Mabel shrugged. "Public libraries are great for research. Old newspapers filled me in on the story. Two sisters, one widowed but with a young daughter, lived here. The older sister's estranged husband came to the house one night and shot her. Her sister and niece witnessed it." She sighed. "That's why this room's haunted." She bowed her head and gestured for them to hold hands. "That's why it's so full of sorrow, why it needs to be cleansed."

Susan squeezed George's hand. "Makes sense."

He nodded. "So, what's our part?"

Mabel folded her hands. "Think about all the troubled ones who have lived in this house, this room. Focus on wishing them at peace." She pressed her hands flat on the table.

"Spirits who linger in this room, in this house. Hear me, no matter how you came to be bound here. It is time to depart. It is time to go to the other side, into peace and light.

***

Voices chorused in the room, penetrating the house as it had been in the 1880s, the 1890s, the 1920s, and the present, a weird harmonized echo that pierced and stitched together generations of time.

"Hear me," Mabel said, her voice calm and low. "Hear me and attend."

Susan and George could not describe afterwards what they saw—a blur of shadowy figures twisted into ribbons of smoke and swirled like motes in a beam of sunlight. It seemed a great invisible broom swept all emotions and words ever expressed within these walls, all anguish and joy, all suffering and terror, into a heap, collecting it, and sending it through the open window into—the beyond.

***

The murdered woman, her face tear-streaked, glided to her sister's side and smiled wistfully at her niece. The shadow mother touched her girl's hand. "Child, the mirror is covered. See the black sheet? You know what that means. We must leave this house for good."

The man in the top hat turned out empty pockets, fingered the noose around his neck, smiled his Cheshire Cat grin, and wept as he swirled into the ouster's gathering. Pushed through the open window, the long-captive spirits surged like tide onto the lawn. There figures of mist and fog beckoned.

"The fog men, child, guard the borders between our kind and the living. Don't be frightened. This is what needs to happen. This is the way we must go." She took her daughter's and her sister's hands. They stepped forward, at peace.

***

Mabel bent forward until her forehead touched the table. She sighed, raised her face. Moonlight silvered the lawn. Brisk air stirred the curtains in the open window. She rose slowly—arthritis kicking in her knees—shut the window and studied her clients.

"Nothing like spring cleaning, now, is there?" All three smiled.

BODIES BURNING INSIDE THE GHOST VACUUM

BY RICHARD D. BROWN

The fog men are coming
They pass by the sheets that sway in the moonlit night.
The vapors are rising,
All this chaos is causing quite a fright!

"But do not worry!"
The town's crier exclaims.
"The ouster will be here shortly,"
The crier goes on to further explain.

The townsfolk sit in their house
Waiting for the ghosts to subside
In the meantime,
They play games with their families
And hope they don't die …
Of starvation.

While this onslaught of ghosts is nothing new
The problem is they get their food fresh
Gives them something to do.
And this current uproar
Happening unexpectedly
Forces the townsfolk to stop hunting reluctantly.

"But,"
As the townsfolk think to themselves,
"it's better to be safe than sorry
I'd much rather be alive with my worries
Than taken apart
By something that scares me."

As they watch through their windows
With caution and in shock.
The ouster comes
With a book and a clock.

He checks the time and sees
It's rather early.
He thinks to himself,
Somewhat arrogantly,
That the exorcising of these demons
Should be a breeze!

He meets with the fog men
Who explain
How the problem started
As they hold their head in shame
While they openly admit that
"We're the ones to blame."

"What do you mean?"
The ouster asks.
To which the fog men reply,
"We were playing a game,
Slacking on our tasks.
When Dave threw a ball
Which hit a flask.
Which fell down and made a mess
Hitting the release button, I guess.
To come to think of it,
We're not sure how they escaped
But we know we are to blame.
Because it is always our fault when something goes wrong.
Our job is to protect the lands
From the living and the dead
After all!"

They look so sad.
So defeated and in shame.
The ouster looks at them and says,
"You're right.
You are to blame!
But what's done is done.
We have more important tasks to adhere to
Now, tell me …
What do you all think I should do?"

The fog men stand silently in thought
They have been caught
Between a rock and a hard place.
For, here is a question
They cannot answer.

They look up and then down
Side to side.
Finally, Dave speaks up.
Saying,
"I don't know …
You decide.
You're the ouster,
This is your domain.
I refuse to allow me
Or my team
To accept any more of the blame.
Like you said,
What's done is done.
We called you to fix it …
Now then,
Have fun with it!"

The fog men march off
Disappear in the shadows.
The anger that comes from this
Serves as ammo
To the lone ouster
Who now struggles
To figure out how to
Capture the ghosts as easily as he'd like to.

Then,
As he's thinking,
A vapor appears
Out of thin air.
With a tip of the hat,
The vapor asks,
"Hello, how are you sir?"
Before flying off to scare
Some townsfolk
Who,
I guess,
Got fed up with hiding.
Or perhaps they were bored,
Their intentions unclear.
Whatever the case,
They were trying to kill a deer.

It was an odd occurrence
All of it.
The townsfolk to the vapor.
But it was something that the ouster would hold dear.
For, this was the first time
That a vapor came near
And spoke to him
In words that were clear.

Still,
This doesn't solve the problem
Of the ghosts running amok.
He has to do something, he knows
But he feels ever so stuck.
He thinks and he thinks
Nothing comes to mind.
All that he is doing
Is wasting his time.

He looks at the clock
It's a quarter to midnight
If he doesn't find a solution soon
There's no telling what the ghosts will do!

He notices from afar the sheets
Sitting quietly.
They look comfy in their white cloth
Content with their untimely death.
He wonders if the two of them can work together
For the time being
So that he can clear out the vapors and stop the screaming
From the townsfolk who
Keep on leaving
Their houses to get food
But aren't succeeding.
Instead, they are being
Scared back off into their houses
Where they are kneeling.
Asking God to rid their town of the ghosts
So that they can keep on eating,
Serving their families,
And stop pleading.

For begging grows tiring
After a while,
Except for those
Who are in complete denial.
Like "Old Man" Reaving—
That's his name—
Who stays sitting
Believing
That if he keeps asking
God will send down blessings upon him
So that he may keep receiving
The gift of life
He has worked so hard for
Over the past twenty years.

The sheets deny the offer from the ouster
Because they know they'll be sucked up too
In his little ghost vacuum
Soon enough.
And they're enjoying being outside.
It's a breath of fresh air
From the darkness inside.

This all results in the ouster
Shouting from the top of his lungs
"OKAY, GHOSTS …
I'VE HAD IT.
YOU'VE ALL HAD ENOUGH FUN."
He quiets down a bit as he says this next,
"I was hoping it wouldn't have to come to this."

And he opens the book,
Turns to page six-hundred and sixty-six
Without any more hesitation,
He begins to chant.
"And you can take this,
And YOU can have that!"

The spell he's casting is meant to be
One that freezes the ghosts for eternity.
Except it seems as if he has said something wrong
As he hears the sound of a gong
Ringing from an unknown location.
Next thing he knows,
He feels a marvelous vibration.
The other townsfolk feel it too
They're all thinking the same thing,
"Ouster, what did you do!?"

The next thing anyone knows
Is that they are being engulfed in flames.
From head to toe,
All the humans are being burnt alive.
The ouster doesn't understand.
He tries to look at the book as he's dying,
But it doesn't work as his body is too busy flailing.
Eventually, every living body turns to ash
As more sheets and vapors appear in the aftermath.

FIN

IN THE LAND OF DREAMS

BY CARI ENGLAND

As darkness rained down on my subconscious, I prepared myself for the descent; a descent into an unknown realm, into a shadowed world within reality. Every night, as my mind craved the absence of thought, my consciousness was pulled beyond my reach, leaving any chance of rest lost to the other. Each nightmarish outing dropped me into the center of a mirrored existence, my being called by the haunting cries of the stranded.

This plane held an ever-present, oppressive atmosphere; a low-hanging fog masking any signs of life. It felt like a lifetime passed while my eyes adjusted to my murky surroundings. I had become accustomed to this world, the land of dreams I entered every time I closed my eyes. A land filled with silence, the loudest absence I'd ever heard.

My fear kept me dormant each time I entered their domain, unwilling to glance into this world: the beyond, the in-between, a limbo for those who had nowhere else to go. They stayed suspended in darkness, calling out to anyone who would listen. Three hours of sleep a night left me there for an eternity until my present would draw me back.

Tonight, the silence was different, the void buzzing with intensity. Through the thick, misty air, shapes began to separate from their surroundings; motionless, formless beings suspended in dread. They were the quietest of everyone here; I called them vapors, the only name that seemed appropriate for the indistinguishable beings. I had never ventured past these mist-like apparitions, wanting nothing more than to return to my reality. But this venture was unlike my previous entrapments, and I was compelled to move forward. Weaving through the floating forms, the air around me chilled with each step; the darkened expanse vibrated with the unknown. The further I drifted into this haunted world, the more the atmosphere shifted. There was something else here with me, something aware of my presence.

Every instinct screamed at me to stop and wait for my soul to be pulled back to a world of light; however, my curiosity propelled me forward. A presence separated from the overbearing blackness, more solid than the vapors that occupied the space around me. Darker figures split off in every direction, moving faster than my crippled gaze could follow; they disappeared the second I laid my eyes on them. While my fear was ever-present in this land, I had never felt as though I was being pursued—until now. Quickening my pace, the quiet world was never broken by a single sound; I was being hunted in a sea of silence.

There was nothing, no noticeable changes at any point in this dreamscape. I could have been running in place and not been able to tell the difference. The air around me lightened as more figures became distinguishable; the surrounding fog taking the form of individual beings. It transformed before my eyes, the vapors remaining in their territory as the fog-encrusted humanoids sprang to life. There was no ounce of welcome in their soulless expressions as their eyeless gazes searched the monochromatic world for an intruder.

Something loomed just visible in the distance, a structure of some kind; this was my only hope at evading the fog men that pursued me. I pushed myself as fast as my lead-laden legs would go, sound finally finding me in this abyss. Like the rustling of thousands of giant wings, the foggy beings flew through the misty wasteland converging on my location. The onslaught of echoes brought me to a sudden halt, though, when I froze, so did the incoming creatures. I took a tentative step toward the unidentifiable mass in the distance and, as I moved, so did the misty masses. With every breath I took, their gruesome faces shifted in my direction; I had little choice in what to do next.

After one last steadying breath, I bolted for the only structure visible in this nightmare. The faster I ran, the louder their approach became until a howling overtook the atmosphere. Finally, a building loomed over me, the door standing wide open. My adrenaline hurled me through the opening; I sprang to my feet and threw my weight against the door just as the foggy depictions converged on the structure. Once again, silence greeted me.

With immense relief, I turned around to be met by a twisted illustration of a familiar space. Displayed in a colorless palette, my home sat bathed in a dim light; the ominous fog swirled around the rooms in a thick blanket. This darkness pressed against my eyes, distorting my perception. As I moved further into the room, whispers followed me; I could feel their eyes on me but couldn't see them. The fluttering breaths grew with every passing second, their unnerving pitch rising to an eerie screech.

The stagnant air that encompassed me crawled closer with each inhale, my surroundings springing into being with dread. Facing the room, I found the walls pulsating with life; mist slowly seeped through the walls of the familiar space, quickly obscuring any ounce of detail that occupied the room around me. The fog men began to form in front of me, their desire to keep me contained becoming clear. I raced from the room, narrowly escaping my otherworldly pursuers.

In a flash of darkness, I was back in the expansive field of mist. Through the shapeless, sorrowful vapors darted the dark masses of the dream land's guards. Everywhere I turned, their ominous presence inched ever closer until I was surrounded. Their dreadful gazes emanated power, a dark force of protectors. With nowhere to run, I braced myself for what was to come; with unyielding speed, they all converged on me, plunging me into purgatory.

Gasping for air, I flew upright in bed, my blankets twisted around me from a sleep fueled by nightmares. I was home. Closing my eyes in relief, I felt the air around me harden. Whispers filtered into my ears, their sinister omnipresence taking over the soft morning light that streamed into my room. Looking up to the shadows that faced me, they had no intention of allowing me to leave their embrace.

GHOST QUEEN

BY PETER TALLEY

Far below, light is dimming
From far beyond, life is unsown
The river Styx is ever flowing
Witness the reaper of flesh and of bone

In distant hall, the ghost queen is waiting
Enter her court, kneel by the throne
Cast off your sheet of fear and fetter
We are together, yet forever alone

Spectral debate, dreams are fleeting
What has become of your destiny?
Where is the light? Where is the fire?
There is no angel, nor devil for thee

Ponder your fate, moaning in terror
Listen and grasp for what was lost
In this moment you are unwanted
Cherish the notion, weigh not the cost

BLACK ROCK LIGHTHOUSE

BY J. TONZELLI

Built in 1865 and standing 190 feet above sea level—with 237 steel steps from top to bottom—the Black Rocks Lighthouse of Avalon Shores was once quite a sight. For six years, it had the honor of being the tallest lighthouse in the continental United States (until it was unseated by the 207-foot-tall lighthouse of Cape Hatteras, North Carolina, in 1871). The name of Avalon's famous structure derived from the black basalt jetty rocks painstakingly positioned into a ring around the lighthouse's base to combat erosion.

A man named O'Shaughnessy designed the lighthouse, and then oversaw its construction over a period of two years. His passion for architecture was unparalleled, and outmatched only by his passion for the sea, so when the United States Lighthouse Board recruited him to design the lighthouse for Avalon Shores, he was ecstatic. He began sketching immediately, envisioning a two-tone black and white façade.

O'Shaughnessy was a native of Ireland, but unlike most of his emigrating countrymen, he brought with him to America a very moderate wealth. Using this wealth, he arranged to import bricks from an old church that had once stood in his native Kinsale. The church had been a touchstone of the small town for generations before it collapsed, falling victim to shifting soils following a season of freak heavy rains. Despite its unfortunate end, O'Shaughnessy had considered the church to be good luck, and felt the inclusion of its bricks would bless his lighthouse in some way. Per his request, an Ireland crew imported his bricks and sent them sailing across the open ocean. Upon their arrival, hired craftsmen carefully sanded, painted, and seamlessly weaved the bricks into the construction design of O'Shaughnessy's dream project. Specifically, these bricks would comprise the three equidistant black rings that O'Shaughnessy envisioned in the otherwise white lighthouse.

The finished product was majestic and immediately became the pride of Avalon Shores. Construction ended mid-winter of 1865, though its official unveiling would not take place until the spring of 1866. It was a major event in the town. The mayor made a rousing speech, which gracefully cloaked the small town's dependence on the ability to safely export goods with images of salty dogs sailing majestic waters, the sun on their backs. When dusk fell, the bright lamps at the lighthouse's top were illuminated, and when the white light rode the gray clouds across the sky, a brief hush fell over the crowd. And then applause rang out. That night, O'Shaughnessy served the inaugural first shift as lighthouse keeper, smoking his pipe and keeping an eye on everything before the sun rose that morning.

Black Rocks Lighthouse stood like a sentry for over seventy years, receiving occasional and routine renovations. Engineers installed brighter lamps to keep up with increasingly strict regulations, new internal steps replaced the older rickety ones, and, not the least important, technology was upgraded in every way possible in the control center at the lighthouse's top. O'Shaughnessy died before any of this had occurred, however; he succumbed to a heart attack at sixty-three.

On October 16, 1925, an immense storm, the likes of which most Avalonians had never seen, rampaged their shores. Waves fifty feet high crashed across the rocks of the beaches and the lighthouse itself. The structure once thought sound began to buckle under the weight of the water and the strength of the wind. The lighthouse's creaking and groaning could be heard almost a mile away in every direction. The two-man crew working her that night abandoned the place and ran for safety, knowing her destruction was imminent. Their attempt to alert the coast guard that the lamps of Black Rocks Lighthouse would soon extinguish had little result, as power across the seaside town failed, including the phones. The groaning that emanated from the suffering lighthouse—which the two men later described as eerily similar to moans of human pain—intensified. Soon after, the two men became the only witnesses to the lighthouse's collapse into the angry seas. The waves greedily swept the fallen bricks, including the ones O'Shaughnessy once considered lucky, into the unseen depths of the waters.

The town was devastated for all manner of reasons. The lighthouse, while not having brought considerable wealth to the town, had certainly made things more comfortable for everyone. Not only did its bright lights allow for easy post-sundown dock deliveries, but had also proved a popular tourist destination. Officials scrambled to begin plans to erect a new lighthouse in its place, but looked upon rebuilding on the original foundation with great doubt, afraid to lose yet another lighthouse to a merciless storm. Further, entire portions of the jetty were now missing, and the falling bricks of the lighthouse had done considerable damage to its concrete base. It was decided that the area would be cleaned up as best as possible, but would never again serve as the base for a new lighthouse—not without a considerable amount of money, time, and ingenious engineering.

Two weeks later, a small clipper ship just off the coast of Avalon Shores became lost in the dark. The captain of the vessel had only his sextant to guide him through the black waves. As he unknowingly drifted closer to the hidden rocks of Avalon Shores, a ring of light whipped across the night. And then another. The captain looked with panicky eyes and claimed he saw Black Rocks Lighthouse, and upon doing so had discovered just how close to his vessel's destruction he had strayed. He very quickly repositioned the course of his vessel, giving Avalon Shores a wide berth. The man later admitted he had been awake for almost thirty hours straight, desperate to make a timely delivery of smelt after his vessel had suffered a mechanical problem, which is probably why his claims of seeing the black and white lighthouse were laughed off and disregarded. The man stuck to his guns, never changing a word of his story, even after the town explained to him that the lighthouse had collapsed two weeks prior.

Some of the townspeople enjoyed this tale, amused as if it were no more than an anecdote to tell at dinner parties, while others simply said the man had mistaken his dates and had seen the lighthouse prior to its collapse. But that all changed when multiple reports began steadily rolling in—reports that the lighthouse's glow could be spotted from way out in the water. The idle amusement in the claims ceased almost overnight—especially when it wasn't just strangers or sailors passing through, but members of their own town claiming to see the lighthouse standing stoically, as if it had never tumbled into the waves. Despite the many eyewitness accounts that poured in, there was no constant presence of the lighthouse—in physical form or otherwise. The only time it ever seemed to appear was when someone at sea was in distress.

Soon, pride wafted through Avalon Shores once again in regards to their lighthouse. Though stories of the "ghost lighthouse" traveled far down the shores in both directions, outsiders never gave it any serious consideration, so it remained a secret exclusive to the town. Avalon citizens stopped talking about it and simply let it be.

As time went on, construction began on a new lighthouse, roughly a hundred feet from the previous location and further from shore. It included a reinforced base with twice as many basalt rocks as before, ensuring its stability. With a larger crew, and newer technology to aid in their construction, the town was confident they could have a new lighthouse up and running in less than a year.

One night in early May 1926, another vessel appeared in the midnight horizon. It was a dark, foreboding vessel with antiquated carvings and an ominous design. Manning the vessel was a pirate named Donovan, one of the more bloodthirsty sailing the ocean at that time. He and his crew were lowly creatures, not stopping at merely robbing and pillaging other ships. No, the men were a band of murderers, taking sick pleasure from ending the lives of those who crossed their paths. Oftentimes these men would storm a ship or a small seaside town to murder and mutilate, leaving would-be treasures and valuables behind. They were not out to profit. They were only out to kill.

On this May night, as they sailed closer and closer to Avalon Shores, light they assumed to be coming from the nearby lighthouse flooded across their ship. But according to the lone survivor of the vessel, he claimed it was:

... the brightest light we had ever seen—brighter than the sun. It was so bright that our flesh began to warm, and even sweat. The light blinded us; we could not see a foot in front of our noses. For several minutes, we stumbled across the decks, our hands covering our eyes. Any man who dared look into the light had his eyes burned out in seconds. Our ship struck the rocks.

We went down in less than three minutes. The men's bodies were smashed repeatedly against the rocks by the tide, and those who survived the thrashings sunk below the waves. After that, the light vanished. Though I didn't deserve to be spared, I washed up on shore. Before I passed out, I remember thinking, "Where the hell is the lighthouse that left us blind?" Because there was nothing there!

The lone survivor of the crash later confessed that the men were scouting out Avalon Shores, planning to invade and kill a bulk of the town before the week was out.

Construction of Avalon Shores' new lighthouse—rechristened as simply Avalon Light—completed earlier than anticipated. There was little fanfare around the event this time around. Instead, the town installed a memorial plaque just outside the main entrance of the new lighthouse.

The plaque is still there to this day, and it reads:

"She shone her light to those in peril;
and with it she vanquished the darkness."
In Memory: The Black Rocks Lighthouse
1865 – ?

ASH WEDNESDAY

BY PETER TALLEY

"I'll be with you in a minute," said the unshaven man in response to the knock at his office door. He shuffled the papers on his desk into a makeshift pile and hid the bottle of gin. It wasn't easy for the man to tuck his shirt back into his trousers before the door started to open.

"Detective Watts?"

"I haven't been called that for a while," said the man. He was half-finished with fixing his tie when he saw the woman. She wore a wet, red rain coat and held a black umbrella. Her eyes twinkled with dark excitement. He knew her from his time in Darling City. She went by many different names but it was always the same type of trouble.

"I'm in need of an ouster."

I definitely haven't heard that term used in ages, thought Watts. "I'm rusty," he admitted. "Maybe you should look up another gumshoe?"

"Maybe I should," considered the woman. "The thing is, Ziggy, you owe me. Who got your family out of Darling City?"

Zachary "Ziggy" Watts crossed his arms and gritted his teeth. A promise of safe passage was made in exchange for a favor. His wife and newborn daughter were the last to escape the city before a great catastrophe. After they relocated it was as if the metropolis ceased to exist.

The problem was that Ziggy could remember his time in Darling when everyone around him forgot.

"Let's cut to the chase," said the woman. "You owe me a favor."

"What's on your mind?"

"First off," she asked. "Do you know what day it is?"

"It's Wednesday, right? The day that comes after Tuesday," said Watts. "That's one mystery solved."

"You don't sound so sure," said the woman. "The day of the week doesn't matter much, Detective."

"Then why'd you ask?"

"Today's Ash Wednesday," she said looking around his office. "It's important to keep these things in mind."

"What's it to me?"

"It's the day I hired you for a job. Your final job," she said with a sly smile. "If you complete this task you'll be able to retire in comfort." She leaned over his desk and raised both eyebrows to entice the man. "I promise I'll make it worth your while."

"Consider me reluctant to even think about taking your case," said Watts.

"I can tell you're interested."

"They thought I was crazy," said Watts. "It drove me to drink. You cost me my job and my family."

"Your little Runa is safe because of our arrangement."

"My family won't speak with me."

"That's true," said the woman. "They believe you're dead."

"What?"

The woman in the red rain coat waited for her words to sink in before she added, "Ruma's lived a happy and healthy life. She's a great-grandmother."

"Why does she think I'm dead?"

"Because you've been deceased for over sixty years."

A screeching sound from the street below his office window startled Watts. It was as if a train derailed from its tracks and crashed into a pen of terrified animals. When he looked out the window, he saw that the city around him was different. Color was missing, streets were empty of traffic, and a fog drifted and consumed anything it touched.

"What's with the faceless crew?" asked Watts. He saw four fog men huddled together on the sidewalk. Their bodies were swirling tornadoes of white, gray, and black mist. They each wore the same style of fashionable trench coats and fedoras, as if they were in uniform. "I'm guessing they aren't your bodyguards."

"It's Ash Wednesday, Ziggy," said the woman. "It's the other day besides All Saints when my kind can directly affect the spirit world. I stitched you back together. Those guardians want to keep you leashed."

I never figured out what they were, thought Watts. *What if they were souls I exorcised? I made a lot of money as an ouster back in Darling. Knowing my luck, these ghosts have been waiting for me on the other side.*

"You've been trapped inside this office for a long time, detective. Let me help you."

"How's that again? I don't want your job and I certainly don't need your help," said Watts. "I don't even know your name."

"Call me Ashley. As in, Ash Wednesday."

"That's rich," said Watts.

"I like that," she said with laughter. "I was going to go with Price for my last name. You're a clever man, detective. You may call me Ashley Rich if that will make things easier."

"So how are you going to help me? Do I earn a harp and halo if I'm a good boy?"

"How's your left foot? I sense you're in pain."

"It's my gout acting up," said Watts. "I'm fine."

"Are you?" asked Ashley with concern. "Ghosts can remember pain but we both know this is different. Lying isn't going to heal the effects …"

"I don't want to be a sheet," said Watts. "My damn toes have fused together. Yeah. I know what's happening. My past profession clued me into the 'what's what' with the afterlife."

"Ousters imagine they know it all," said Ashley. "What you don't know is how fast it will spread. Confinement in this rathole of an office bought you time. I can give you more."

"What's the case?"

"So you've accepted? Or are you trying to change the subject?"

"We're negotiating," said Watts. "I'm curious why I'm your guy. What do I have to do? Why am I special?"

Ashley smiled.

It doesn't mean I'm taking the gig, thought Watts.

He smiled back and noticed the woman's shadow. It made him grin. "Nice wings," said Watts. "But angels don't get a discount."

"You know I'm a fey," said Ashley. "That's why *we* need you, Ziggy." She wiggled her nose and the butterfly wings of her shadow disappeared. "Avalon's interested in the spirit world. It's supposed to be a junction point, not a destination in the Beyond. We need a ghost to investigate where we can't."

"I wouldn't know where to start," admitted Watts. "If what you say is on the up and up, I've been out of the game for sixty years." He shrugged it off nonchalantly and said, "I might've been an ouster back in Darling, but I gave all that up trying to stay sane."

"We don't have much time," cautioned Ashley. "You have until sundown tomorrow to find answers. After that, I can't heal you. Ash Wednesday lets us break the rules. You can move about freely and get rewarded. Take advantage of it, Ziggy. All you have to do is find out who's calling the shots. We want to find out if we are in danger of war."

"Shit, I don't even know how I died."

"You died by brain aneurism," said Ashley. "Why you haven't moved on isn't my concern."

"It feels like I've been taking a long nap," said Watts. "I wake up and here you are calling in a marker. Forgive me, Miss Rich, but something smells fishy."

"You're a smart one, Ziggy. Keep playing it smart. I'll heal the cursed foot and your slate is clean."

"Can you point me in the right direction?" asked Watts. "Give me a name. Where am I supposed to go?"

"Micah Roth," said Ashley. The room got cold when she spoke the name of a man they both knew from Darling City. She walked to the window and pointed to a building across the street. "He's listening to our conversation, Ziggy."

"No deal," said Watts. "I have rules against mixing it up with magicians."

"You're on the same side."

"I don't give a shit," said Watts. "A man has to have standards. I won't work with a magician and, besides, you know I don't do partners."

"You're a magician too," reminded Ashely.

"I'm a ghost," smirked Watts.

"He's the only lead you're going to get."

***

Ziggy Watts waited inside the lobby of his building. He looked out past the glass of the revolving door into a world that was barely familiar. At street level, the taller buildings that should've towered above were lost in the bleakness of a foreboding sky. The clouds hung low over the structures with an oppressive judgment that discouraged the detective from leaving.

Across the foggy street was a ghost dressed in overalls and a baseball hat. Watts could tell they suffered from the same ailment. It wouldn't be long before they both lost their sanity and appeared as featureless mannequins. This ghost looked worse than Watts, with missing fingers that made the ghost's hands look like flippers.

Poor bastard, thought Watts. *At least we still have our faces. ...*

One of the fog men from earlier suddenly pressed itself against the window next to the revolving door. Its gloved hands slid down the smooth glass. It waited for Watts to recover from the fright before it howled hard and shook the window.

Now how am I going to get past you? thought Watts. *I need a distraction.* He cracked his knuckles and moved closer to the window. *Where's the rest of your quartet?* Watts looked past the fog man and saw the other three. The identical figures were interested in the ghost across the street. They turned in unison to stalk their prey. The ghost in the ball cap noticed and tried to run. He disappeared around a corner but the fog men relentlessly followed. *He's not going to make it,* thought Watts. *Thanks for your sacrifice.*

"It's you and me, buddy," said Watts to the remaining fog man. "Let's see how you like my tricks." The ouster slammed the palms of his hands against the glass. A fizzle of spectral energy within his fingertips flickered outward through the window and into the fog man.

C'mon, thought Watts. *I'm still an exorcist.* He concentrated on finding a connection to the fog man but quickly realized it wasn't like any ghost he had ousted. *What the hell are you?* He tried again and this time located a core energy source. *It feels like a bundle of knots! What happens if I give them a tug?* Watts imagined his fingers reaching into and through the fog man. He grabbed hold of what felt like cold barbed-wire and pulled tightly until the creature howled in agony. It only took a moment before the fog man was rent apart.

"It worked," said Watts. "I've still got it."

Ziggy ran for the revolving door. He rounded his way through the vestibule and was outdoors within seconds. The air smelled funny to the ouster. It was heavy and reminded him of mildew. He watched for any threats and saw his target on the far side of the street. It was the tumbler known as Micah Roth.

It was a wrinkled and weary ghost that waited for Watts near the statue of a headless statesman. Micah Roth was significantly older than the last time Watts saw the magician. His beard and hair had whitened. The years mustn't have been kind to Roth, for his fingers were broken into twisted, odd shapes that would prevent him from working tumbler magic.

"We can't talk here," said Micah. "Follow me." He started walking in the opposite direction and led Watts to the entrance of an alley. "Through here is a passageway to a safe area further into the ..."

"It looks like a trap," said Watts. "Maybe I'll take my chances with whatever's out here."

Micah Roth raised his voice slightly. "We do it my way or not at all." He grimaced at the ouster and continued, "If you want out, tell me now."

"I'm from Darling," said Watts. "I remember what you did."

"Good," said Roth. "It isn't a coincidence that you're here. We're connected." His weak attempt to smile faded when he asked, "Will you follow me?"

You damned an entire city, thought Watts. He nodded in agreement. *You betrayed your friends.*

"Believe what you wish," said Micah Roth. "What I've done is impossible to explain."

"Get out of my head," said Watts.

"Nothing would please me more," said Roth as he continued down the alley. "We, however, are connected. You should know something, Zachary. I also remember you."

"I was small potatoes compared to the gang you called friends," said Watts. "What the hell were you thinking when you opened that portal?"

"Consider yourself fortunate that we both called Orin Ames a friend."

The two found themselves in front of a rusted steel door. The unsecured padlock was easily removed. Micah tossed the heavy object to the ground and slid the door open. It squeaked loudly before getting stuck halfway along its track.

"How did you escape?" asked Watts.

Micah ignored the questioned and squeezed through the partially opened doorway. Watts shrugged and followed behind the grumpy magician. It was darker than either expected. They continued forward until they saw a solitary lightbulb dangling from the ceiling on their right.

"We go this way," said Micah. "Use caution. I can sense we're being surrounded."

"What are we up against?" asked Watts in a whisper.

"Phantoms," responded Micah. "They will mostly be vapors but that doesn't mean we're in danger."

"Oussssster," hissed a nearby voice.

"Be afraid," said another. "We see you."

"Sssstay with me," beckoned a woman's voice that echoed inside Watt's mind.

"How do they know me?" asked Watts. "Did I send them here?"

The lightbulb dimmed the closer the two got to it. Micah reached up and tapped the bulb with his broken hands. He sighed as the glass sphere swung back and forth without any further response.

"The way's been sealed," said Micah. He wanted to speak again but was distracted by the sound of his own voice. "Time works differently here. Keep your thoughts positive or we're going to be in trouble."

"You said this place was safe," said Watts.

"I wasn't allowed to finish ..."

The glow from within the lightbulb went out. An eerie stillness soon permeated the room. Wailing cries from formless vapors filled the darkness as a sudden rush of stale wind slammed into Watts. He wasn't sure what happened to Micah Roth but he quickly realized he was now alone with the angry phantoms.

***

"Daddy, Daddy!" shouted Ziggy's daughter. Ruma ran toward her father with a welcoming smile and outstretched arms. She appeared as a child. Ziggy wept at the sight of the innocent girl he loved. It didn't matter how this was happening. His heart was full of warmth as she leapt at the surprised ouster. Ziggy hugged her tightly and yet felt her dissipate into stardust the moment they touched.

"Zacharias Watts," boomed a deep voice from high above. "You have been judged worthy of an audience."

45

Am I on trial? wondered Watts. He craned his neck and looked up at a balcony. Hooded figures draped in thick, billowing fabric stared back.

"Where's my daughter?"

"She is well," said a ghost from next to Watts. He wore an ashen-colored toga and spoke slowly in a thick Italian accent. "We wanted you to understand the importance of the situation."

"Are you the man in charge?" asked Watts.

"You stand in the symposium hall of the Senate of the Dead," replied the ghost. "We are equals," he said as his cold hand reached and rested on Watt's right shoulder. "My name is Jude. I am here to provide answers."

"Before we get too chummy," said Watts. "I'd like to see my family."

"All in good time," reassured Jude. "First we must speak with the senators. You've were expected many years ago. They wish to discuss what delayed you."

A ghostly woman in a black veil consulted a skeletal being that was dressed like a rock star. When finished whispering, she addressed the large, circular, tiered room. "This soul before us seeks rest. He was suspended in time by our enemies. The fey of Avalon have once again insulted our practices and attempted to thwart our efforts in protecting our home. The Spectral Realm will answer with …"

"Scythes, substance, silver, and sand!" roared the assembly of senators.

"Yes, venerated senators," said the ghostly woman. "No longer shall we stand idly by and let forces outside of our borders dictate what it means to be deceased."

The crowd cheered.

"There will be no further debate. There will be no censure. There will be only judgment!"

"What is she talking about?" asked Watts.

Jude held his index finger to his lips and indicated it was a time to remain silent.

"Zacharias was delivered to us," spoke the veiled woman. "His name means 'Yahweh has remembered.' Here is our answer, dear senators! Avalon mocks us as their own throne sits empty of a monarch. Now is the time to carve out their heart. We must expand our borders and ensure the fey never try to reclaim what we've forged out of sacrifice!"

"Silver is the color of inevitability! Silver is the color of death!" shouted a ghost from the audience. It was Micah Roth. He leaned against the rail of the balcony and watched as Ziggy recognized the company he kept. To his right was Orin Ames. To his left was Buster Morelli and Tommy Bates.

"Holy shit," said Watts. "Fallen magicians."

Jude eyed Watt suspiciously and said, "All are welcome here." He leaned in closer and whispered, "You have a chance to change your fate, ouster. I suggest you take it."

"I don't give a shit about politics," said Watts.

All occupants of the circular, tiered room stared in awe at the ouster in the center of the room. The veiled woman's pale hands clenched the rail of the balcony. She leaned over the edge, which briefly exposed what was behind her veil. A visage of malnutrition, fear, and outrage glowered downward at the ouster.

"He meant no offense," said Jude.

"And none was taken," said Orin Ames. "Ziggy is an old friend. If the enemy sent him, it is because they wanted to rattle us."

"I don't know what kind of mess I stepped into here," said Watts. "I'm not one of you. Let me see my family and I'll do whatever you want."

"As I said," said Jude. "We wanted you to understand the importance of the situation."

"He smells of sheet," said a senator with wide eyes. "Is he infected?"

"That's why I'm here," said Watts to the assembly. "I've been promised healing."

Members of the senate laughed at Watts until the woman in the veil raised her hand and stated, "You've been lied to, Zacharias. The fey have no way to heal this affliction. We shall all suffer from the same impairment if we do not move on."

"Well, let me move on!" shouted Watts. "Where's my pearly gates? Tell Saint Pete I'm ready to sit on a cloud."

"We can't do that," said Orin Ames.

"Oh, don't tell me I'm stuck with these guys," said Watts. "I'm no magician. These jackasses used to shit on what I did for a living."

"We know what you did," said the veiled woman. "You act as if you were an exterminator of vermin when in fact you were damaging our efforts. The *service* you so proudly offered severed memories, caused madness, and destroyed souls."

"I was paid to solve a problem," said Watts.

"Tread carefully," suggested Jude. "What you did is looked upon as a serious crime by the senate."

"So what's you part in all of this?" asked Watts. He decided to bring Orin and the other magicians into the discussion. "Is this your plan, Orin?"

"Certainly not!" said the magician.

"Don't look at me," said Buster Morelli, who was dressed in battered army fatigues. "I've been telling these morons to cross over since I got here."

"We've atoned for our sins," said Micah. "There's purpose here. We want to do our part to make this pocket realm into a kingdom."

"Think about it," said Tommy Bates. "It is a second chance for us and a way to snub the fey. They shouldn't get to call all the shots. Who put them in charge, anyways?"

"I don't know your story, friend," said Watts to Tommy Bates. "What I do know is that picking a fight with the fey sounds like a bad idea."

"I'm like you," said Tommy. "I could speak with the dead. My friends and I were living it up after we discovered magic. Isn't that right, Bus?"

The solider agreed, "It's true. Magic was the reason you guys made it back from the war." He now addressed Watts and said, "I wasn't so lucky."

"We came back changed men," said Tommy. "We saw the horrors of war and learned how to cast magic. We were big freakin' deals back in our day!"

"Until the fey pushed back," said Orin. "It happened in Darling City."

"It happened everywhere," said Tommy. "I was the first casualty in a new war. I was supposed to be a warning to stop using magic. Instead, I started a goddamned split between my friends and they fought back."

"It was amusing," said Jude. "Avalon's princess was missing. All of the border kingdoms sought to take advantage of this chaotic time."

"An opportunity presented itself to the senate," said the veiled woman. "We were quick to offer sanctuary to these betrayed magicians who were larger pieces in a game they didn't understand."

"We wanted you," said Jude to Watts.

"He's speaking the truth," said Orin. "It was disappointing to learn that you were already compromised. You made a bargain for the safety of your family. The problem is that fey are accomplished liars."

"You've been haunting the same office, suspended in time, cursed by the same being who claims she can heal you," said Jude.

"She promised retirement."

"We can guarantee so much more," said the veiled woman. "Avalon delivered you from Darling City. The senate will deliver you, your wife, and your daughter to a greater reward. You will be reunited. We have that authority. Return to the fey with our response and we will send you to paradise."

"So you have the keys to the kingdom?" asked Watts. "Then why are all of you standing around here? This place doesn't seem so great to me."

"Your family chose to wait," said Jude. "Upon their deaths, I personally informed them of your bargain. You were never insane. The truth is that Zachary Watts was a hero."

"He should be again," said Micah Roth. "I'm ready to take you back across."

"That is, if you are ready," said Orin.

"What do you want me to tell Ashley Rich?"

A door opened at the far end of the symposium hall. Senators in the circular, tiered room awaited their ruler. The brightest of light shone through as a massive, cloaked figure appeared. It walked from the light toward Watts and grew larger as it came near. It held within its bony fingers a wide, rectangular box.

"Scythes, substance, silver, and sand," replied the cloaked figure. Its face was a skull of ivory bone, which possessed several sharpened teeth. The epitome of death extended the box forward and said, "Take this sickle. Defend my senate."

***

"I'll be with you in a minute," said the unshaven man in response to the knock at his office door. He shuffled the papers on his desk into a makeshift pile and hid the bottle of gin. It wasn't easy for the man to tuck his shirt back into his trousers before the door started to open.

"Detective Watts?"

"I haven't been called that for a while," said the man. He was half-finished with fixing his tie when he saw the woman. She wore a wet, red rain coat and held a black umbrella. Her eyes twinkled with dark excitement. He knew her from his time in Darling City. She went by many different names but it was always the same type of trouble.

"I'm in need of an ouster."

I definitely haven't heard that term used in ages, thought Watts. "I'm rusty," he admitted. "Maybe you should look up another gumshoe?"

"Maybe I should," considered the woman. "The thing is, Ziggy, you owe me. Who got your family out of Darling City?"

Zachary Watts smiled at the woman and asked, "Would you like a drink?" He bent over and reached under his desk for the silver sickle inside the opened, rectangular box. "I've got some gin around here," he said before flipping the desk forward.

Ashley Rich effortlessly shoved the metal desk to the side of the room with a swipe of her black umbrella. It created the perfect opening for Watts to slash the sickle deep within her chest. A spray of colors fountained from the fey's body as she stumbled backward in shock.

The true form of the woman in the red raincoat was sickly and alien. Worn wings of faded grandeur drooped sadly from her shoulder blades. Her beauty was nothing more than an illusion that stained the room in streaked rainbows. She was dying. Her frail hand reached out to touch the angry ghost.

"Silver is the color of inevitability," said Watts. He tore the sickle from Ashley's chest and swung the curved blade again. "Silver is the color of death!"

As the fey's head flew from its body, a final spurt of color burbled forth and onto Ziggy. He felt drenched in spectacular colors that burned and drowned his soul. For a moment he thought he heard Ruma crying, and then all went silent. Death had finally come to collect him and send him home.

IT DANCES NOW

BY JUSTIN ALCALA

"We are all captives to the darkness. It's only when we embrace our prisons that nightmares root and evil blooms."

The American Civil War thundered for two years before the maelstrom of Gettysburg struck. It was a sticky July day when forces from both sides assembled. Over one hundred thousand Union troops settled in the low ridges to the northwest of town. Commander George Meade knew there weren't enough surgeons to care for the throngs of injured, but it wouldn't stop him from engaging Robert E. Lee. This battle could be the turning point for both armies.

The few surgeons on staff included Cecil Gibbs. The young, weatherworn man was distinct from his colleagues, with his chiffon hair, willow eyes, and an ashen complexion. As a child, Cecil was bedridden from polio, and his twisted physique showed it. As hard as life had been, Cecil wouldn't let it hold him back and dove into medicine as soon as he had the strength to walk. Still, as determined as Cecil was, his demeanor was odd, even for surgeons' standards.

His parents died of consumption when Cecil was just a boy. Cecil had no other family besides his neighboring aunt. The state allowed her legal guardianship of the boy, but the mile between the two estates caused her visits to be few. Cecil was fortunate to get a feeding a day, and it was brief with little conversation. The decade of isolation caused the boy's mind to warp and contort his character. He was a recluse by society's standards, and Cecil learned to cultivate peoples' uncertainty for him into a shield.

Day one of battle saw too much bloodshed. A clash of calvary corps was cause for thousands of wounded and dying. His surgeon table pooled a pond of crimson as slick as sunlight on a wet street. The number of men slopped before him overwhelmed Cecil. One by one, Cecil cauterized, stitched, and carved up soldiers. His hands were stained red, and his saw dulled. Young boys no longer able to walk brought back shattered memories. The shock of screams and gurgles haunted Cecil's mind. Watching limbs jerk, eyes flutter, and life leave men's eyes branded Cecil for decades to come. And as the hours went on, the surgeon broke.

When Cecil returned from the tent alleys, his tear-stained eyes glittered and a crooked smile smeared across his face. He was someone different. He picked up his tools with an eagerness set aside for the devil. Where cries once rang, Cecil now heard singing. Where the surgeon's tools once grated, only violins strummed. Before long Cecil was immersed in a symphony, and he was the conductor.

By dusk of day two, the injured had tripled, and Cecil the surgeon was no more. His colleagues declared that Cecil had gone mad. He grinned and cackled as they put new meat before him, and began unnecessarily sawing limbs. Union command ordered Cecil removed from his surgical tent, but he disappeared before anyone could arrest him. It's said it that Cecil had been spotted limping up Cemetery Ridge, a tall silhouette lumbering along with its arm around Cecil's shoulder.

On the dawn of day three, infantry holding Culp's Hill brought injured men from the woods. These poor souls survived their initial wounds, mostly gunshots and artillery shrapnel, but were hastily cared for by a restless field surgeon that seemed to have sprouted from nowhere. While survivors initially were relieved, they became horrified when the medic bound them to a tree before sawing off limbs. The maniac didn't stop until there was nothing left but a torso and head. Worse yet, Confederate soldiers along the battlefields were being found in the same state. Cecil was using the chaos of battle to mask his murder spree. Something had to be done.

Allan Pinkerton was the head of Union Intelligence. His spies reached across Union and Confederate lines and across Gettysburg. Their aim: Win the war by capturing battlefield intelligence and reporting it to command for better use. When news of Cecil reached the proper authorities, they sent dispatchers to Pinkerton agents with orders to remove themselves from the front lines and seek the madman. Of the handful of agents informed along the lines, only one responded.

Oliver Lamb joined the Union Intelligence a year into the war. He was known for his no-nonsense, incorruptible attitude. Unlike some agents, Oliver felt his place as a Pinkerton agent was a calling from higher authorities. He didn't flaunt his divine duty, nor did he ever speak of it. He just knew it to be so. Oliver dutifully removed himself from his post as a Union scout and investigated.

Now to say it was challenging to dodge fighting while hunting Cecil was an understatement. Skirmishes broke out from hills above, craters below, and everywhere in between. Men died just as often while drinking tea as they did on the front. Nevertheless, Oliver was a master tracker, and he stalked each of Cecil's steps. Oliver found the discarded limbs Cecil had heaved into piles along hills and bushes. Oliver interviewed bystanders. Oliver even tracked Cecil's foot trail.

Only, whenever Oliver uncovered a detail, he found it strange that there was always proof of a second culprit at hand. A sharpshooter recalled a tall man in black with Cecil inspecting casualties along Barlow's Knoll. A victim recollected an assistant with Cecil just outside of peripheral vision. Oliver even found a second set of large footsteps that walked along Cecil's boot prints as he made his way to Oak Hill. Cecil somehow had a partner.

Oliver was a steadfast man, however, and after hours of dodging canons and gunfire, he finally found Cecil along Herr Ridge. Oliver crawled through the muck, sneaking up on his mark. The surgeon wrung the blood from his hands along a creek. Oliver crept closer only to find Cecil's latest work, an unconscious boy no older than sixteen butchered along a tree limb. Oliver knew he was dealing with a broken man, and would only have one shot. Oliver removed his revolver from its holster. He cleared his throat.

"Cecil," Oliver announced, pulling back the hammer of his firearm. "It's over." Cecil stared at his reflection in the stream.

"Is it?" Cecil inquired, his voice hoarse.

"It is," Oliver confirmed. He kept a safe distance like you would from a wounded cougar.

"It only made me stronger," Cecil sighed.

"What?"

"Not having a body," Cecil confirmed. "I had polio as a boy. It empowered me as a man."

"Are you sure about that?" Oliver asked. It was rhetorical, and Oliver didn't wait for a response. "Come on. To your feet."

Cecil slowly reeled around. His eyes were bloodshot with tears strumming down his cheeks. His once-pale complexion was blush with scratch marks along his neck. Cecil stared down the barrel of Oliver's gun. Oliver swallowed the lump in his throat before raising the revolver high. A man as desperate as Cecil was capable of anything.

"It's not why I did it, though," Cecil confessed in a monotone voice.

"No?" Oliver asked while using his open hand to reach into his pack. He'd hung a pair of manacles along the side pouch and blindly tugged at them while keeping his aim on Cecil. He could feel the bindings release from the straps.

"It made me do it," Cecil said bluntly. Oliver didn't know if he should indulge the mad man any longer, but he thought it could help diffuse the situation without violence. Oliver palmed the now unsheathed manacles and hurled them at Cecil's feet.

"It?" Oliver said as he watched the cuffs roll onto Cecile's boots. "Who is it?"

"It doesn't have a name," Cecil confided. "It doesn't talk about itself either. All it speaks about is what it wants me to do."

"And it told you to mutilate these people?"

"Not mutilate," Cecil argued, "cleanse." Oliver had heard enough.

"Put on the manacles, Cecil," Oliver ordered. Cecil shook his head.

"I don't hear it any longer, though," he moaned. "I was," he stuttered, "I was its mother, but it dances to its own music now." Cecil frowned while taking a step forward. Oliver noticed the saw in Cecil's hand for the first time.

"Put on the damn restraints," Oliver roared. "You still get a trial, Cecil." Cecil shook his head hard while hurrying forward.

"You know where to take this," Cecil lamented, lifting the weapon above his head. "So wash me."

"Cecil, maybe you have some sense about you, but if you do, you're keeping it secret. Now," Oliver seethed through clenched teeth, "last warning. Put the manacles on."

Cecil took a step forward like a sailor taking his first steps on shore. An errant smirk rose from his lips as he picked up his pace. Oliver aimed, hoping Cecil would stop, but the madman only sped into a sprint. Oliver fired three times. The first shot went wide, but the second bullet found its target, striking Cecil in the shoulder before the third hit him in the heart. Cecil fell to the ground. Oliver paused and watched as Cecil lay motionless, his eyes staring at the sky. Oliver approached and kicked the saw from Cecil's hand. It was done.

As Oliver searched Cecil's body, he found the pages of a journal crushed into the surgeon's coat pocket. Oliver unwrinkled the parchment and placed them neatly in his back pocket. When he was done, he searched the nearby area for the second culprit. Although the elevens on his neck stood like wild grass, there was never any evidence of an accomplice near Cecil's makeshift lair. Folks had been mistaken. There was only one crazed man, a surgeon that blamed his sinful deeds on an unseen conspirator.

Oliver would petition for a nearby Union garrison to help bring back the corpse of Cecil and his victim. They commended the Pinkerton agent for his diligent work, but amidst the hell, command wished to sweep the incident under the rug rather than give out a medal or commemorate the intelligence officer. Oliver understood, and by evening, found himself on a new assignment. Luckily, the battle would end after that third day. Oliver celebrated with the Union forces on their victory and followed the limping army as they advanced on General Lee's heels.

In his haste, Oliver had forgotten to turn in Cecil's last journal entries. On a night when the moon beckoned the dead, Oliver examined the papers by the campfire. In charcoal were drawings Oliver couldn't understand. A well-drawn man of Cecil's likeness stood above a stack of wounded men. Rendered in the backdrop was an emaciated figure nearly twice as tall as Cecil. Its flesh was sable, and it was absent of any distinguishing features beyond a maw of shark-like teeth locked in a bemused grin. The figure's leg kicked out, its hands reached outward, and one hand clasped Cecil's shoulder. The demon seemed to dance behind Cecil, watching the surgeon's work.

Months later, Oliver joined General Sherman's march south. It was a harrowing trek, but it helped Oliver keep his mind away from his encounter with Cecil. Along the way, Oliver received reports from passing Pinkerton agents that Confederate soldiers were found mutilated along the roads only a few days south. Intelligence said that a rebel soldier with a case of the rattles stretched out a murder spree throughout Fulton County. He blamed a creature that whispered to him in the night, a black figure with teeth like a lion. The confederate soldier was later found and hung for his crimes.

Still, as Oliver continued to keep his ear to the ground, he learned that the horrific attacks went on, even past the war. A matriarch would kill her family in Dekalb or a man from the swamps would terrorize a low-country village in Chatham. Each time, they'd always claim to have an accomplice that could never be found. Oliver remembered what Cecil had said. "I was its mother, but it dances to its own music now."

PASTORAL CARE

BY PETER TALLEY

The morning cry of dawn was moments away as the sunlight barely revealed itself upon the highest point of a bell tower. A lone structure sat at the base of the valley. It was a countryside church unfamiliar to the early-morning wanderer. The roof appeared weathered and the windows caked with dirt from a stiff wind.

A brief moment of hesitation crossed over the young Southerner's pale face. Molasses-colored eyes examined the church's door handle. He pulled on a corner of his overcoat to conceal the ivory-handled revolver within his belt holster.

The abandoned countryside church's door opened easily. As the Southerner took his first step in, he was surprised by the elderly pastor at the far end of the building. The elderly man, dressed in black, cautiously examined the brown-haired wanderer.

"You are welcome here," said the pastor. "Why do you seem so surprised?"

"To be honest," said the Southerner. "I wasn't certain what was going to happen. You see, I haven't been inside a church for years."

The pastor smiled and beckoned the man to step further into the church.

"I seek refuge," said Sutter. "I'm also terribly hungry."

"As you can see, this building hasn't much to offer to a weary traveler."

"I don't require much in the ways of hospitality," said the Southerner. "At best, I was hoping I could rest my feet for a while."

"You walked all this way?"

"My horse ... died," admitted the Southerner.

"Please take a seat and rest," said the pastor. "I'm sure you can purchase another horse in town." He walked down the main aisle to greet the Southerner. "We haven't had a visitor like you before."

The Southerner grinned at the shorter man and replied, "I reckon you haven't."

"You can stay as long as you want. I'll appreciate the company."

"Thank you for your graciousness. I wish I had something to give in return."

"How about your story? What brings you to this part of the country?"

"Oh I don't know," said Sutter. "I'd like to think a humble man like myself could get lost while searching for his freedom. You don't want to hear my story. I'm just another simple man looking for answers."

"I see," said the pastor.

Sutter eyed the man suspiciously and asked, "What do you see?"

"I won't pester you, stranger. I'm not here to judge. Enjoy your rest."

"Hold on," said Sutter. "Don't leave it there. If you have something to say ..."

"Only an old man's curiosity," joked the pastor. "I didn't mean to pry. You just sound far from home."

"In more ways than one."

"What answers are you seeking?"

Sutter stretched his arms out on the back of the pew and sighed.

"Why don't you tell me what you're doing here?" asked Sutter.

"What do you mean?"

"You don't live here," said Sutter. "I didn't see any parsonage or horse carriage nearby."

The pastor nervously shook his head.

"Did I frighten you?" asked Sutter.

"Why? Do I frighten *you*?" questioned the pastor defensively.

"No more than any man of the cloth," answered Sutter. "I do find it odd that you're all alone in this place of worship. I know it isn't Sunday morning but forgive me for saying that this place looks mighty worn-down."

"They've built a new church in town," said the pastor. "It was easier for the congregation to move rather than make repairs after last season's storms."

"I see," said Sutter.

"It looks to be another beautiful morning. That's my favorite part of being an early riser."

"I'm more of a night-owl."

"I suspected as much," said the pastor, taking his place by a window. "How long have you been on the run?

"I thought you weren't going to pass any judgements?"

"You want sanctuary in my church? Well if so, I'm going to need to know to a little more about you, stranger. Are you a criminal?"

"Heh," laughed Sutter. "I knew you saw my gun."

"I hadn't," said the pastor. "Bringing a weapon into the house of God, however, doesn't do much for your cause."

"My cause?"

"You aren't going to find any answers with that."

"Listen to me, you old fool. I didn't want to come here. I was running out of options."

"I suppose it was better than you ending up on the Johnson's farm. They've had enough problems with coyotes."

"I'd think twice about kicking me out."

"Oh, you can stay," said the pastor. "I'm not afraid of you."

"You should be," said Sutter. "You don't know what I'm capable of when I'm hungry.

"I know what you are," said the pastor.

"A sinner? I surely am."

"You're a vampire."

Sutter Kincade stood up fast, drew his ivory-handled pistol, and pointed it at the elderly man. He revealed two sharp fangs when he flashed a predatory smile. His secret was known and now the pastor had to die.

"They told you I was coming!"

"No," said the pastor. "As you pointed out, I'm here all alone. I haven't seen a living soul in months."

"How'd you know I was a vampire?"

"It was fairly obvious. I've heard stories of your kind coming to town. I'm guessing that's why you're passing through? You probably have business with the monster who brought the railroad to our town."

"I'm here for revenge."

"Also not helping your cause."

"I don't need answers from the likes of you!" Sutter pulled back the hammer of his revolver and snarled, "Shooting you would be too easy."

"Are you going to shoot or bite my neck?"

"I told you I was hungry," said Sutter as he rushed toward the pastor. When Sutter leapt at the elderly man, he realized too

63

late that he'd been fooled. The feral vampire passed through the apparition of the pastor and slammed hard against the wall of the church.

"Get behind me, Satan," laughed the pastor. "You never even checked to see if I had a heartbeat? Were you that frightened of walking into a church?"

"I was more afraid of the rising sun," growled Sutter. "I don't like being played for a fool."

"Who does?" asked the ghost. "Why don't you tell me about this revenge plot? We're stuck together until the sun sets. I can see you're a troubled soul. Maybe I can help you find some peace?"

FOOTPRINTS

BY R. YOUNG

She stood at five feet nothing in her stocking feet; the boots she wore didn't add much. Heels were for pretty girls who didn't need to move fast and kick hard. At least, that's what she told people. The truth was that heels hurt like a bitch and she didn't see any reason to put herself in pain. Whoever thought stiletto heels could be used as some kind of weapon had no idea how hard they were to move in.

She removed them in the corner of the room, pointing the toes toward the wall as she always did. The lightbulb that hung from the ceiling on a wire rocked gently in the breeze from the window. Her office was tidy, small, and sparse. The meagre earnings she earned as a paranormal investigator covered the rent, but it was a close-run thing.

"You always do this," Caliban said, his voice low, with the hint of a threat running through it that was ever present.

"A lady has her secrets," she said before slipping behind the screen so she could change. She could see his silhouette pacing backwards and forwards across the room. He moved from one corner to the next, keeping to the shadows.

"One day I'll get to see what lies beneath that awful coat you wear."

"Who says I wear anything underneath?"

"You're a terrible flirt, Lavender. Remember who you're speaking to," the threat remained in his voice, but he was being playful, friendly even.

"It went well today."

"Child's play."

"That's not what the family thought."

Caliban made a noise that might have been agreement, but was more likely disdain.

She took her time. Having Caliban by her side all day wore upon her; teasing him like this had become a routine. Today had been a hard day. Routines helped.

"You're tired."

"You're not?" she asked.

There was no response. She stripped off her clothes until she was standing in her underwear and glanced down at her stomach. Scratches marred her skin which hadn't been there before this afternoon. It didn't bother her. Injuries were normal and she would be fooling herself if she didn't acknowledge that she'd been lucky. It could've gone worse. It should've.

"Will they be okay?" she asked as she pulled on a pair of trousers. They were too tight.

"Shouldn't you know?"

He was a bastard. Calling him anything nicer would have been untrue and inaccurate. "Caliban, be more supportive."

"Why would I be supportive? Caliban, do this. Caliban, do that. Caliban, make me look good."

"I did not," she buttoned up the blouse, "ask you to make me look good."

"No, but you would've been upset if I hadn't."

It irked her that he was right. She grabbed the coat from where it hung over the top of the screen and shrugged into it, doing up the double-breasted buttons before stepping out into the room.

A knock came at the door. As she turned to look at it, she could see the frame of a person, female judging by the build, through the frosted glass. 'Footprints investigations' had seemed like a good name two months ago; now she wasn't so sure.

"Come on in," she shouted.

The door rattled, the frame too tight due to swelling in the humid weather, but eventually it gave way and a woman walked in who instantly made her feel inadequate. She was tall and wore heels. Her clothes said money but her perfume was too strong and her eyes flitted around the room. It wasn't the gaze of someone fearful; it was a rapid assessment of the space she was in.

"Lavender Mains, paranormal investigator. How can I help?" Lavender said, lifting her fingers before realising the homburg she wore, mainly to look more like a detective, was hanging on a hook by the door.

"Ms. Mains, nice to meet you," the woman said. Her voice made it clear that it wasn't nice to meet Lavender at all. The words were as far removed from the tone as could be.

"Sure, why don't you take a seat and tell me what brings you to my humble place of work." The temptation to say something smart and uncalled for was there, but she ignored it. She couldn't afford to annoy anyone who might be in the mood to pay her money.

"I've heard good things about you."

Another lie. A definite lie. There might be people out there who had good things to say about the Footprints agency, but Lavender could count them on one hand. You don't build up a reputation from a couple of months of scaring away ghosts, especially when half your clients refuse to pay the full bill.

"That's nice of you to say. We always aim to please."

"We?"

Caliban had vanished at the first knock at the door.

"My associate has stepped out for a moment. So, Miss?"

"My family is looking to resolve a quite grisly affair. Before I continue I would like to be assured of confidentiality."

"Client confidentiality is important to us. Anyone we are working for can be assured of our discretion," Lavender said. She moved around the desk and took a seat, feeling very conscious that her bare stocking feet didn't quite convey the professional image she was aiming for.

"Do I need to sign something?"

"Are you hiring us?"

The woman nodded. "Yes, of course. Money is required," she said with what Lavender could only assume was contempt. At the same time, she reached into a small handbag that hung from her shoulder and pulled out a wad of bills.

It took significant willpower not to stare as the woman placed the money on the table with gloved hands. "I'm not sure what you charge but I imagine that is quite sufficient for our needs. I will, of course, pay more should you actually achieve anything."

"Well, I guess you're a client now. Miss?"

"The story is quite a simple one. We had some staff who were involved in things of a ... shall we say ... unsavoury nature. Something occult. Frankly, I would have paid it no mind except they made rather a mess of things and it resulted in a death. There was talk of a haunting of some kind but it seems to have been resolved when the contents of the house were sold. It was ... well, the haunting was of quite a perverse nature. Peeping toms and ... Never mind. I wish to find the items that were ... I'm sorry, this all sounds quite ridiculous, I realise."

"Nothing's ridiculous here."

"No, of course. I mean, I know this is all real but it just seems so ..."

"Beneath you?"

"Yes, exactly. How good of you to recognise it. I know that might seem callous, arrogant even, but it is exactly that. If it wasn't beneath me, why would I need to hire someone like yourself?" As the woman said it, she looked Lavender up and down.

"The items?"

"I'm not sure what it was. There were clothes, jewellery, and some furnishings."

"Your name, please?"

"Lady Gilead."

Lavender put her hands on the table and smiled. "Lady Gilead. I mean no insult when I say this, but it will help a great deal with the case. Did you ... did you have relations with this creature that haunted you?"

"How dare you!"

The colour in the woman's cheeks said everything Lavender needed to know.

"I'm sorry, Lady Gilead, but I cannot bring back your paranormal lover. That's not the way these things work. I would suggest you give up trying to reclaim this ... ghost. In my experience—"

"In your experience? You're nothing more than an upstart. How old are you, anyway?"

"Is that relevant?"

"I'll have you know—"

"Excuse me. I need to put on my boots."

"Boots? I have paid you. I expect you to take my concerns seriously."

"Oh, I am, don't worry," Lavender said as she stood up and pulled the boots on one at a time.

"The name of your ghost?"

"How would I know?"

"It was Caliban, wasn't it?" Lavender asked.

Paranormal Investigator Mains grinned her teeth whiter, brighter, pointier than before.

"Hello, my dear," the voice that came from within the little woman was low, with a hint of a threat running through it.

The colour drained from Lady Gilead's face. "Caliban?"

"It's over, my Lady."

"The ... those were my grandfather's boots?"

"No. These were always my boots ... and they're made for walking."

WINDOWS ARE MIRRORS MIRRORS ARE WINDOWS

BY LAUREN BOLGER

If night is an ocean,
a pool of unknown,
Marinate us in black
& settle in our centre.
Look close and see your reflection
Look closer and see your future.
An inverse. A world in wait.

Fate is a ravenous thing
what lies asleep in daytime;
now roused and ready to eat.

Headlights floated across the old motel. Lucy Daestrom grinned at Annie Hobbes as she pulled into the parking lot with their rental, a white Infinity SUV. The contours of Annie's face were touched by faded yellow neon. The rest obscured in shadow. Like a muddy gold nugget, Lucy thought. She laughed quietly as Annie eased into park.

"Fun party," her low, gravelly voice was acrid, gleeful. She pressed her lips together, holding in more laughter.

"Which party were you at?" Annie sighed. She reached down wearily and killed the engine. The locks clunked loudly in the quiet car.

The whine of neon intensified through the cracked window. Lucy smoothed out her bangs between pointer finger and thumb in the console mirror, her tongue pressed against her upper lip in concentration. She couldn't see her freckles, but she felt them burning in the dark, mocking her.

"Are you coming inside, or …?" Annie's voice sounded terse.

"I was waiting for you," Lucy looked Annie dead in the eye and smiled. Annie's face hardened.

"I'll go first, then," Lucy relented. She grabbed the door handle and it slipped, banging loudly back into the door. "Oops." She tried again with success. She leaned out, tumbling loudly onto the pavement.

The contents of her purse clattered across the busted gravel. Lucy doubled over in laughter. She looked up at Annie, who continued glaring at her.

"You are so fucking embarrassing," Annie flung open her door and slammed it closed. She came around to Lucy's side, hastily collecting the lip gloss and makeup compacts.

"Well, this is ruined," she admonished Lucy, opening a blush compact. The cake of blush was cracked. Half of it crumbled to the ground when she held it up for Lucy to see.

Lucy laughed some more with her mouth closed. It escaped through her nose in obnoxious snorts.

"Why did you drink so much?"

"I'm not drunk," Lucy insisted. More snorted laughter.

"Ugh!" Annie balled up her fists and pressed them to her forehead. She examined Lucy between the heels of both hands. "Seriously! Why did you embarrass me in front of my friends?"

"I dunno. But I'm so excited to spend the night in the Bates Motel. Drifting to sleep to an airplane-engine lullaby."

"We're on a budget."

"What budget?" Lucy's hand shot out towards the car. "Look at that shit you rented! Look at your outfit! I mean sure, we did fly here as, like, the dog and cat of an unknowing coach passenger ..."

"Yeah," Annie admitted. "I wanted my friends to think I was at least a little rich." She shook her head. "But none of it matters since you made a scene and we left early." Annie stormed off, jamming her hand in the pocket of her black romper, digging for the key.

"I could've stayed. You're the one who made us leave early," Lucy followed, joining the handles of her small purse. She transferred it to one hand, pulling at the back of her hunter green skirt'that'd crept up her thighs. She followed Annie up the cement stairs to the second floor. She reached for the bannister, but thought twice when she noticed the red rust that ravaged the weathered old metal.

"Yeah, because you made a scene," Annie growled, trying and failing with the key at the door with the crooked "9." She flipped the teeth down on the key and retried.

Lucy looked down the long cement catwalk. There were no lights on the second landing, and outside it was black as pitch. Her eyes were still adjusting. She could swear she saw someone watching them from the corner of the building. She couldn't stop staring. The black outline was still there.

She turned away, distracted when the lock scraped loudly out of its chamber. She glanced down the catwalk again as Annie opened the door. The face was still there. Then it seemed to just ... cease to be. Lucy's heart banged in her chest.

"Annie," Lucy whispered loudly. She rushed into the room, bashing the door open into Annie's arm.

"Ow," Annie cried out. "Shit!"

"Ah! I'm sorry!" Lucy hovered her hand protectively over Annie's arm.

Annie bit down on the corner of her lip, squeezing her eyes shut, pressing her arm against her side. "It's ok," she whispered through a sharp inhale.

"Is there anything I can do?"

"No, I think I'm ..." Annie crossed the room and rummaged through her suitcase. She opened and closed her left hand. "The pain, like, shot down my arm into my fingers." She stood still a few minutes, holding her arm. She sighed. "Can I have ice?"

Lucy turned away, staring at her reflection in the full-length mirror by the door. She tightened her ponytail. She hadn't made much of an effort to look good, yet she felt herself wishing she had. She hated the feeling of being stuck inside her skin. She pictured herself stepping out of it like Annie's black jumper. She wondered if Annie ever felt that way. *Doubtful,* she thought, frowning at her freckled face. It frowned back at her.

"What's the matter?"

"Just wanna look good for the organ harvesting goon waiting for me at the ice machine."

"Are you too scared to go?"

"No."

"I mean, I don't mind. I could go. You didn't break my legs. Yet."

"No no ... I'll go."

"Lucy ..." Annie paused for a minute, mouth open in a sly smile. "Are you even drunk?"

"No."

"What were you drinking so much of at the party? It had a lime in it."

"I was making myself ginger ale," Lucy set her purse on the table by the big picture windows. "I didn't know anyone. I was bored. … I'll go, okay?" she said, ripping the curtains shut.

"You actually burped. As loud as you could! On purpose!"

"The seltzer was really bubbly. Nobody heard me."

"Just because nobody looked doesn't mean they didn't hear you. They were being polite."

"Polite? To pretend you didn't hear a noise?" Lucy scoffed. She laughed bitterly.

"They were trying to give you a moment to yourself as you … degassed yourself!! How can you pretend it's them? You were a rude asshole from anyone's perspective. Rich. Poor. Drug addict. Waitress. Whatever."

"If you're so repressed that you look like a deer in headlights when someone burps, you're broken. Anyway, I'm not the ONLY one …"

"Yes you are. You were the only one acting like that. Everyone else was—"

"What about Kara?" Lucy challenged.

"Kara?"

"Excited eyebrows lady?"

"Cora," Annie corrected.

"It's like … the same fucking name!" Lucy threw up her hands.

"Cora is passive aggressive. She sandwiches insults carefully between compliments, so you can ignore it. There's not a chance you actually believe what you're saying to me right now," Annie shook her head. "And I can't believe you've been acting drunk all night. That is so weird."

"I can't."

"Can't what?"

"Ignore Cora. When she's being a bitch."

"Funny. Everyone else manages to pull it off. You were so weird to Cora."

"Oh, I love your nails!" Cora grinned maniacally. Excitement (or sarcasm) leapt in the glossy sheen of her eyes.

"Thanks! They're press-ons!" Lucy glared back, chewing her gum loudly. She held her stare until Cora rolled her eyes and stalked off.

"Well they *are* press-ons!" Lucy extended her fingernails at Annie. "I thought she might want her chauffer to take her to CVS and buy her own set!"

"Just shut up."

"I'm telling you. She looked at me like she wanted to rip my fingernails off and pocket them! She's scary," Lucy watched Annie's reaction.

"That's nightmare fuel," Annie replied. She was starting to smile. She looked away, hiding it.

"You're not like them, you know."

"Are you still getting me ice?" Annie said to the wall.

"You're better than them." Lucy pushed on, watching Annie in silence until her gaze was returned. There was a flash of recognition in Annie's eyes, then …

"THE ICE!" Annie shouted, her eyes bugging out playfully.

"Okay, okay! Christ!" Lucy pulled on a sweater. She scooped the ice bucket off the table, opened the door, and slipped outside, peeking at Annie with one eye, the other obscured behind the door.

"Fucking go!" Annie shouted.

Lucy grinned at Annie and shut the door, plunging herself in darkness. She heard the wind rustle bare tree branches. The cold breeze wrapped itself around her. She heard the TV flip on from inside. Some yammering news station. The glow of the TV flashed through the curtain on the other side. She shuddered and looked down the dark corridor. The night was silent, except for buzzing neon.

She stood, blinking, waiting for her eyes to adjust. Once she could make out the iron banister to her left, she began walking quickly to the corner, where she thought she'd seen the face.

Her heart felt ready to burst as she neared the corner. *Like ripping off a bandage,* she thought, steeling herself. She held her breath and rounded it quickly.

Another short landing, and a little alcove. A shelter from the elements with soda, snack, and ice machines. A green metal sign was legible in the dim halogen: ICE AND VENDING.

Lucy stood in the dark, stomach tumbling. Same as she'd felt seeing the face peek out. It'd been right where she was standing. She hastened toward the lit area, hugging the empty ice bucket.

The smell of old, wet metal hovered about the place. She stood there holding in the blue plastic button, letting the ice drop down. She was bent over a little, waiting for the bucket to fill. She leaned further left, studying the snack machine.

They never stock this thing, she thought. A couple of bags of off-brand cheesy popcorn and some gum. *Didn't they change this gum label years ago?*

A sudden scuffing noise sounded behind her. She turned quickly, letting go of the bucket. The ledge wasn't wide enough to hold it. It tipped and fell to the ground. Ice skittered everywhere.

"Fuck!" Her heart was hammering. She picked up the bucket. She moved to gather the fallen ice, but stopped herself. *It'll melt.* She pushed herself up from a kneeling position off the concrete. *Or maybe it won't. I can't stay here.*

She leaned toward the ice machine again. Her hands shook, so she pressed the bucket against the ledge to steady it. *I'll get a couple cubes and then book it back.* She turned to the snack machine and saw the reflection in the glass; someone standing directly behind her.

She screamed, and she felt a pair of hands grip her shoulders. She threw the bucket. She ran, crazed, almost tripping over herself, rebalancing against the iron banister. She turned and booked it down the corridor.

She was five doors away. Three. Almost there. She didn't feel anything following her, so she turned to look behind her. Nothing was there. She started to turn back to the room.

Her breath stopped in her throat. There it was, in the neighbor's window. Standing behind their curtain. A gray-black figure up against the white of the drapes. Its back was facing her, but she could see it had long brown hair. It was naked. Covered in a crinkled, leathery hide.

Lucy's breath came in small gasps. *It has to be something else. A crazy old lady. A Halloween decoration.* She backed up against the bannister. It turned its head slowly to face her. It didn't have eyes, just deep creases where eyes should be. It slammed its palms against the glass. The pounding of its hands shook her. Demanded that she keep moving.

She screamed again, and ran two more doors down to her room, left hand shielding her eyes from the windows. She grabbed for her key. Wedged between her hip bone and underwear. No pockets in the godforsaken stupid skirt.

Her hands trembled horribly. She pulled it out and tried to grip the key. She gave up and pounded on the door, desperate to reach the room with the jabbering TV. The warm, normal place with someone she knew.

"Annie, help!" she sobbed, slapping the door with an open palm.

"What the hell?" she heard Annie exclaim, in muffled alarm behind the door. Lucy heard something drop, and footsteps come quickly.

"Was that you scream—" Annie opened the door. "Oh. My god." Annie stood there, mouth agape, in her plaid pajama pants and t-shirt. The TV blared on, lighting their shapes, and the shapes of the beds, in the dark room.

Lucy stumbled inside, shutting the door quickly behind her. She started to cry.

"Lucy, what happened?"

"There's something out there," Lucy whispered, locking the door. She sat in the chair by the window, dropping her head in her hands. She looked up. "It was there when we came up the stairs. But I told myself it was nothing. Then it was in the reflection of the snack machine. It touched me. It ... followed me back here."

Annie took a reluctant step forward, peeking out the curtains. She stepped back and crossed her arms.

"Lucy ... are you ... sure that's what you saw? Was it a guy?"

"No ... not a person." Lucy was expecting the fear to subside. But getting inside had changed nothing.

The loud bang sounded again. Like the hands on the window outside.

"Get away from the window!" Lucy hissed. She grabbed Annie. They stumbled quickly behind the second queen bed, tripping over each other. They collapsed there together, crouching down on the scratchy carpet.

"You're scaring me," Annie's eyes were wide and wet. Lucy held a finger to her lips. All they could hear were the quiet "s"s from the newscast. Lucy pictured horrible things happening in the dark. She couldn't not know. She had to see.

She looked toward the curtains. Something caught her eye. It was moving slowly, out of the big wall mirror by the door. Its two hands had already touched down on the floor. The head emerged. Then the torso. The gray ghost was pulling itself into the room. The head was moving slowly back and forth. Scanning the room. Looking for her.

She couldn't duck down. She couldn't look away. She had to watch. To know where it would go.

It turned to her, and the head stopped moving. It knew she was there. She watched, suspended in place. Once the ghost pulled itself out, it crawled quickly. A desperate scramble as it made its way along the wall to reach them.

"Lu-cy," Annie whispered. Her voice divided the syllables in whispered gasps. Lucy's eyes were stuck on the ghost. She grabbed Annie's hand as the thing passed the foot of the bed they were sitting behind.

It was there. On all fours. Directly in front of them. Staring.

"Oh god, oh god," Lucy said as she breathed in.

A loud keening wail emitted from the gray ghost. She watched its jaw open. As the wail deepened and grew louder, the jaw dropped further down. Lucy stared into its mouth, almost mesmerized. The flashing white of the TV played across the side of its face, further darkening the cracks that crawled across its skin.

It crawled closer, head tilted like a curious child. Its face impossibly close to hers. It smelled like vomit. Acrid and sour. She gagged, covering her mouth and nose. She heard Annie's muffled crying behind her, and reached her arm back to comfort her.

It crawled onto Lucy now, pushing on her shoulders. She pressed on its chest with all her strength, trying to push it off. But it was much stronger. It tipped Lucy back, and climbed on top of her.

"Lucy, no! Lucy!" Annie cried from behind her. But it moved over Lucy's face, and went for Annie.

"Why," she begged for a reason. "Why Annie?" as she watched the jaw drop wide, like a snake, swallowing her friend.

Annie'd screamed until her head was submerged by the gaping mouth. Lucy screamed for Annie after that. She pulled on Annie. On her arms, which had gone limp after a few minutes of fighting.

Lucy followed as it crawled back to the mirror, its bulging stomach dragging on the floor. She continued grabbing at it. Climbing and pulling on it. But once it got Annie, it was done.

Lucy stayed on it as it climbed slowly into the mirror. She watched the ripples radiate outward as it entered, making the glass seem like water. She thought she'd be able to follow. Until her knuckles crashed into the mirror. She wrapped herself lower and lower down the ghost's body as it went through. Until she was desperately gripping its ankles. Finally, her head bashed into the mirror. Her brain lurched violently in her skull. Giant white stars blinded her, then left her in blackness.

***

Lucy sat straight up from oblivion. Her eyes felt swollen. The sun was streaming in through the window, making her blink. She turned and saw an EMT in a dark blue jumpsuit, leaning back to give her space.

"I thought she was—" the EMT started to mumble to someone else in the room.

"I guess she's not. And I would know," a man said, then chuckled in the doorway. "Just got a text. I gotta go." He turned and walked out.

Lucy saw the word CORONER on the back of the man's jumpsuit. "You thought I was dead?" She looked up at the EMT who was watching her uncomfortably. "Why?" She felt embarrassed by the attention, and confused. "I'm not. Annie is," Lucy said. She scrunched her face and touched her hands to her swollen eyes. No tears came.

"You've been here a couple days. We didn't know what to expect. We need to bring you in. To hydrate you. Do you remember feeling sick? Did you take any ... controlled substances?"

"No. I must have passed out. I was ... upset. My friend is gone."

"I'm so sorry ..." the EMT said. "Can you stand?"

On their way out of the room, Lucy noticed the outline of a "6" faded into the motel room door. The door number must have come undone from its position and swung down, looking like a 9.

For some reason, this made her picture her reflection frowning at her in the mirror. The mouth stretching open. The howling. At the time she thought it was subhuman. But it wasn't. It was ... backwards. Like a horror movie sound effect. The rise of the scream at the end instead of the beginning. It had sounded like Annie's voice. ...

Lucy's legs gave out. She felt the EMT grip her roughly to steady her, then lower her down, watching her intently. She sat on her legs on the cement catwalk, weakly holding the EMT's arm. Trying not to sleep.

"I ... I saw it ..." she stammered. "I know what it's like when we die."

HARVEST

BY PAM BISSONNETTE

Cold. Why am I so cold?
The ambulance barreled its way from Jackson Prison to the local hospital. As the ambulance rounded corners, straps held Jake in place.
"I don't think this guy is gonna to make it. Too much blood loss."
"Yeah. I reckon. Had it comin' though."
"Yeah? What'd he do?"
"Knifed his wife."
"Shit!"
"Been doin' time for a lotta years I hear."
"So he finally got what was comin' to him."
"Yeah. I reckon."
"Seems like a lotta trouble to save a murderer."
"He's an organ donor. All he's good for now."
Jake fell numb as the thought shot through him. *I'm dying.*
Images flickered through his consciousness: Mary home late again smelling of booze and cigarettes; his suspicion and rage; the knife in his hand and blood on the floor; years of drudge and remorse in prison among inmates as wounded as himself; finally the fight—David's explosive anger and the fear in Alex's eyes.

This can't happen. I have to do something. Then Jake's blood spurting on David, on Alex, on the floor.

The ambulance pulled up at Jackson General Hospital and was met by people in white coats who loaded Jake into the ER.

People clustered around. Brisk hands and fingers touched him. After some minutes, a person announced DOA, date and time.

DOA? But I'm not dead.

A man barked out, "He's an organ donor. Prep him."

His body was stripped and washed with some kind of pungent antiseptic. A cart was wheeled in with several vessels and instruments. And then they began to work.

NO! I'm not dead! Not dead. Not—dead.

But Jake couldn't move. Couldn't shout.

A scalpel in a gloved hand moved close into his field of vision.

His mind screamed. *NO!*

His eyes were the first to go. He expected pain and loss of sight, but strangely, he perceived without pain as they sliced into his face. The terror of experiencing his eyeballs lifted out of his head and placed in a container paralyzed him.

Then they cut into his chest and abdomen. One by one, they gently lifted out organs and carefully placed them in vessels. Fear, revulsion, and disassociation shot through him. They disassembled him, like a toy robot he took apart as a child.

Finally, they sewed up the incisions in the body. They attempted to make it more seemly after having robbed it of its organs: its dark hair smoothed, its eye sockets bandaged, its frame swathed to the neck.

It—my body is now an It. Long ago Jake had signed an organ donor card. But I didn't think it would be like this. He wept without eyes. *I must be dead. I—am—dead.*

Jake drifted apart from his body like smoke from a quenched candle wick.

They wheeled the body away. Jake didn't follow. No point. *Not me.* People came to sanitize the ER, clean away the last debris of his life. *Where to go? Where to be?*

The ER gradually faded into the opacity of an all-encompassing, disorienting, gray fog. Alone, with nothing but his self. And what a pitiful self. A bungled life. A wasted existence. *It would have been better if I'd never been born.*

A groundswell of remorse, guilt, and self-loathing surged through him as he recalled his anger, his distrust, his jealously and hurt pride when he lashed out at Mary in rage. *I deserved prison. I deserved death! No way to atone. Ask forgiveness. But then why would she forgive?*

All those long prison years of remorse and guilt, the hard-won humility and self-control. They fueled Jake's seeking escape from himself. It didn't matter that self-reproach had eroded his anger. Or the horror at what he'd done had burnt out his violence. He could not undo his evil, or escape the suppurating ulcer of his unmerciful condemnation of himself.

Is this hell?

Jake remained suspended in the gray fog for an indeterminable amount of time. It reminded him of a time scuba diving, suspended in dim murky water with the novelty of weightless movement in three dimensions in absolute silence except for his own breath through the regulator. There was no way of knowing which way you were moving, or which way was up or down except by watching your bubbles. No bubbles here.

Eventually the fog thinned and faded away by stages into sunless bright white light to reveal an orchard that expanded in all directions in neat rows on a carpet of white clover. It rolled up and down mild hills and valleys to the horizon in every direction. Some trees were old and gnarled, some young whips, some laden with fruit, some with only blossoms. The blossoms were shell pink, five-petalled, and emitted a sweet, soft fragrance. The red round fruit grew in clusters of five. Damaged or rotten fruit had fallen to the ground and fermented, releasing a cider vinegar odor. Here and there bundles of pruned branches lay between the rows. The trees wore headdresses of arrow-pointed, forest-green leaves with trunks clad in smooth bark the color of rich mocha, except for the patriarchs whose skin had split, warped, and peeled. Fluttering leaves whispered in a slight breeze.

Where am I? What is this place?

Jake wandered along the rows. The orchard formed an expansive, uniform pattern that masked any sense of direction or distance. Jake could have walked for hours or days, over acres or square miles. He drew close to a young tree with smooth bark, lithe limbs, and delicate blossoms. He placed a hand on its trunk. He could have sworn it quivered at his touch, or maybe it was just the breeze. *I have hands? I have legs and feet?*

He ambled further into the orchard when a figure with a broad-brimmed straw hat, overalls, and flannel shirt, carrying a full bucket of fruit, strode toward him. Instantly alert, Jake stopped and waited for the figure to approach.

"I've been waiting for you." His voice was neither deep nor high, but a mellow, mid-range tone.

"Who are you?" asked Jake.

The figure set down his bucket, took off his hat, wiped his brow with the back of his sleeve, and smiled at Jake. "I'm the Harvester."

"Is this orchard yours, then?"

"You might say that." The Harvester's eyes twinkled.

He was hairless, with an ageless face showing traces of feminine softness around his mouth and eyes. Hands hardened and browned with work had a slender fineness that reminded him of his mother's.

"Why were you waiting for me? How did you know I'd be here?"

"Everyone comes here," said the Harvester.

So all the dead come here.

The Harvester picked up his full bucket. Gestured for Jake to follow. They walked through the orchard. The Harvester would occasionally stop to pull a blemished fruit from a limb and drop it on the ground. Or take a pruner from his belt and snip off a diseased limb or spur. Or prop a limb so heavy with fruit it might break. Eventually they stopped at a mature tree with a healthy crop of fruit in the peak of ripeness. On the ground beneath the tree were many rotted, shriveled, and squashed fruit, and an empty bucket.

"This is your tree," said the Harvester.

"My tree?"

The Harvester put down his full bucket and began to pick the tree's fruit to carefully place in the empty bucket under the tree.

"I don't understand."

The Harvester continued to gently pick the fruit. Place it in the bucket. "You chose to donate your fruit."

"Fruit?"

"The fruit of your tree, your life."

"My life!" A surge of regret and horror jarred and spiked as his consciousness cast back to the moment that he'd let define his life: to the emotions reflected in Mary's deep brown eyes of pleading as she clung to him; confusion as he pushed her away; pain as he pulled a knife; terror as he stabbed her; hatred as her blood seeped out, until her eyes drained and dulled into death.

"My life has been a waste—worse—evil. I killed my wife in a rage. I didn't deserve to live—but I did—for years—in prison. I have nothing to give."

The Harvester took out a bandana and wiped his brow, then continued picking.

"Why am I here? Please—talk to me."

The Harvester left off picking and leaned against the tree trunk to face Jake. "You have a great deal to give. Why do you think not?"

"Didn't I just tell you?!" Jake slumped down onto the ground. He could not shut out a vision of Mary's blood running, mingling together with his own. The pain of remorse, guilt, and self-loathing burned unrelenting, intense, searing.

I can't stand anymore of this. Please, just let me die, really die. Oblivion, so I don't have to remember. I don't want to be conscious anymore.

The Harvester looked intently at Jake as though he knew what Jake was thinking. "Oblivion? Consciousness is the greatest gift. It was too hard and took too long to evolve. Too rare and precious in the Universe not to conserve."

"Then I'm here forever—hating myself."

"Only if you choose to be." The Harvester sat down with his back against the tree trunk. "Who are you? Not your name, not your past life, but who you are—now—really."

Jake considered for a long while.

Who am I? The real me? I'm obviously not my body. My mind and memories? I'd give anything to be unconscious of these, to be free of the anger and violence that shaped my past. Of what am I conscious now? Right now—I'm a man who regrets existence.

"I'm an angry, violent, jealous, distrustful, proud man who lead a terribly wasted and hurtful life."

"Really? That was what you were, but who are you now?"

Jake had no answer.

"What about the decades in prison where you eventually became an instrument of peace? A humble man of compassion toward inmates and guards? You gave your life to protect a young man you barely knew." The Harvester gestured toward the rotten fruit on the ground. "Don't let the detritus of your life define you."

Jake picked up a soft fruit off the ground. He squeezed until it disintegrated into pulp. "The only thing that kept me going all those years was to chip away at the person I hated. God knows there's plenty of time and opportunity in prison to do that! But I can't forget what I did. And there's no one who can forgive me."

"You can forgive you," said the Harvester quietly.

Forgive. How is that possible? So I gave my life to save someone after taking the life of another. I deserved to die! But do I deserve to die now? End my existence so I can escape self-pain?

"Even if Mary appeared and forgave me, I still couldn't. I despise myself, and nothing will change that as long as I'm conscious. I've been living with this pain most of my life. Never a bit of happiness or joy. Nothing good to look forward to. And now to exist this way forever with no escape ..."

"Jake, look at me. Now, in the present, you're a good man. You used the tools given you to transform."

"Tools?"

"Guilt. Remorse. Self-loathing. You should be grateful for each one of them. Without these goads you'd have been incapable of changing, of evolving. But you don't need them anymore. Let them go."

But Mary ... "I cut short the life of my wife."

"Like you, she needs to learn how to forgive. You've given her that opportunity."

The Harvester stood, took the pruner from his belt, handed it to Jake, and gave him a hand up. "See these suckers? They rob the tree of nourishment and produce no fruit."

Suckers sprang from around the base of the tree and from individual branches. Jake worked his way around the tree, cutting them off, thinking about what the Harvester had said. *Is this truth? That I'm a better man than who I was. I should be grateful for my pain. Forgive myself.*

With each sucker he cut away he felt a little lighter, a little calmer, and a little more whole. Not quite comfort, and a far cry from joy or happiness, but better than the familiar pain. Jake finished and handed back the pruner. A pile of barren suckers lay on the ground among the rotten fruit.

The Harvester pocketed the pruner, picked a fruit, and bit into it, juice running through his fingers.

Jake finished harvesting his tree. As each fruit joined the others in the bucket, he experienced a tendril of solace and belonging. The last fruit he palmed and eyed closely, inhaling its sweet aroma. He bent to place it in the bucket but then hesitated, glancing up. The Harvester nodded.

Jake bit into the ripe fruit. Its sweetness filled his mouth; juice ran down his throat. Gratitude flooded him. His eyes met the Harvester's. Jake finally understood.

The Harvester picked up his own full bucket. "I'm ready. Shall we go?"

Jake was thoughtful for a while. "I'm not ready. I still have some—work to do, I think."

"Come along when you're ready." The Harvester handed Jake the pruner and his broad-brimmed straw hat. He hoisted his bucket, turned, and walked down the row of trees until Jake lost sight of him in the bright white light. Jake put on the hat and stowed the pruner in his belt.

A slight breeze rustled the leaves through the otherwise quiet orchard. The sweet smell of blossoms blended with the faint scent of vinegar. He strolled alone through the rows of trees, but he didn't feel alone. He carried his bucket of fruit and felt very much alive and whole. Occasionally he pruned a sucker, or a sickly branch or spur, or plucked a damaged fruit to drop on the ground. He worked his way through the orchard until he saw a figure in the distance. A dark-haired woman in a blue chambray shift wandered haltingly in Jake's direction. Her head darted from side to side like a wary doe, until with a start she saw Jake and abruptly stopped. He couldn't be sure, but she looked a bit familiar. He approached and then realized why he was here.

"I've been waiting for you."

"Who are you?" asked the agitated woman.

That question again. Who am I?

"I'm the Harvester."

JE REVIENS

BY DAVID ANTROBUS

There was a moment as they climbed the logging road when Max thought they were in trouble. They had rounded another corner when Jasper hunkered in confrontation and bristled and growled with what, to Max, felt like excess zeal. Max stopped and squinted, his heart jackhammering past normal exertion, eyes fixed on the gnarled and twisted stump beside the road up ahead. For that was all it was. Not a black bear. Especially not a murdered hiker. Just a storm-blasted old stump.

His released breath was all the border collie needed to also relax, and the two companions continued their path over the loose, broken shale logging road that switchbacked all the way to the mountain's summit. Although it felt like midsummer heat still, it was in fact late morning on the day after Labour Day, and as a consequence he'd barely seen another person since they'd parked the Jeep a couple hours earlier, down in the rainforest shade. His boots and his dog's paws kicked up the sweet, dusty berry scent of a late Canadian summer.

Max was hot. His water bottle was below halfway, already tasting like lukewarm sweat, and he knew Jasper was possibly more thirsty than he was. He decided to keep going to the next large buttonhook in the road, a good distance up ahead but clearly in the cooling shade of a stand of cedars, after which he'd make a call about continuing.

They trudged on, the gradient climbing, everything blasted and bare. Jasper, his blacks and whites blurring into greys, slunk wary and busy. Max too stayed on high alert, watching all things. Bone-dry coyote shit like scorched braids. Faded du Maurier filters. A gleaming black corvid feather beside a rusted can of Molson Canadian. Spent and flattened shotgun casings. All light-peppered with the dust of a parched season. A tiny infant forest sprouting from the descending incline to their right, baby spruce and fir like hopeful stubble on an ailing face. Beyond, the hazy valley entire, with its veiny, shimmering roads, swayback barns and bright pastures, its silt-gagged sloughs and cedar-shingle roofs, tree farms and dikes, and all the critters—women, men, children too—that made of this flood-prone land at least a temporary home.

Reaching the shade and breathing hard, Max knew he'd already made his decision. There'd be no great vistas today, no panoramic views of the faraway delta and distant Pacific and its scattered and sparkling island emeralds set in liquid sapphire. Sad, but there would be other days; the summit could wait. No, he'd underestimated the sheer fatigue factor of this early September scorcher, and needed to head back the way he'd come, find shade and water.

Laughing out loud, he yelled, "Not today, Jasper, old friend!" then was immediately chagrined by his note of hysteria in so muted and lonesome a place. Jasper sat quietly panting, accepting of all outcomes.

Out of nowhere, Max recalled the stupid fight he'd had with Becky earlier, and how, if he got into trouble here, she'd likely be as indisposed to help him as she'd ever been. He hadn't even told her his destination. Dumb. Despite the heat, his skin rippled with the chill waves of portent. The gist of their blowup was already trivial: something about a landlord, a truck, a cord of beech wood, and a conversation they both agreed needed to happen.

Labour Day. He thought about that. Only yesterday, his peers and neighbours had been up here, dirt biking and shooting, swimming and four-wheeling, making a holy hellacious racket and leaving their thoughtless scraps and heedless scars across a big and tolerant land. Never seemed right to him that on account of our bigger brains we had carte blanche to make the deepest gouge. But yeah. Labour Day. He heard a story not long after he arrived in Milltown Falls about another Labour Day long ago, back in maybe the seventies or some other sepia-washed time. A town gives up its secrets in small parcels, usually, so this particular one Max had garnered from various local folk, yet mostly distilled by a gaunt, cadaverous man named Swampman Jacques in the Fisherman's Catch pub one night, down by the big river.

Like so many tragedies, it had begun as a lark. Everyone was gathered on the southern shore of Devil's Lake, and partying had commenced in earnest. One or two groups sparked up joints, a couple forty-pounders were cracked open and, at some point late on a clear galactic night, someone decided that releasing the parking brake in a camper would be a laugh riot. Short version: it wasn't. Two passed-out teenagers slipped into the lake that night, right around midnight, and never came home. Witnesses claimed to have heard the underwater screams and even what might have been clawing sounds as the van dropped into the depths. Yet even the cops knew it hadn't been done out of malice, and while the victims' families could never fully quiet their outraged grief, most of the town circled the wagons and left it alone in terms of blame, chalking it off to dumb adolescent idiocy.

Although the victims themselves were less sanguine. Legends were built on swimmers who felt the pull of the restless dead beneath a surface suddenly flyblown, about hikers who glimmered then darkened from existence, fell off the world's radar, soon after passing the turnoff for the lake.

If you've ever taken a dip in Devil's Lake, you'll know. You'll recall how warm it felt when you stepped along its shoreline shallows, your feet growing sore on flinty grey quartzite, your torso soft and frail as you waded into its hotspring heat. Was your dog there too? Did you register the infernal drone of the deer fly before you ducked your head and breaststroked toward the centre of this shadowed lake? Mostly to escape the damnable fly? Held your breath only to meet the same winged demon, who'd waited, who hadn't for a second been fooled. While your dog plunged in, his earnest smiling head bobbing toward you, to save you, since that was his only ever job, to make you safe as a lamb. There's a point where your lower torso feels like it belongs to another creature, where the warm surface smile turns instantly to cold rage, somewhere near your heart, and your dangling parts sense their imminent uncoupling.

Local legends be damned. Max was feverish with the day's heat and his own exertion, his skin streaked with riverscapes of silt drawn from dust and sweat, and as his hot, dry boots had crunched their way down the logging road, the legendary chill of the lake had become a siren for him. When he reached it near midday, it was deserted. And silent. A diving raft lay still at its centre. As he waded in, he felt a note of disquiet when Jasper balked and whined, but it was brief, and soon the collie had overcome his rare hesitance and joined his companion, both making for the raft in the middle of the lake. Forested, almost sheer slopes rose on all sides; abysmal, umbral, in defiance of a bright hot day, only the shallowest of membranes managed to absorb the smallest daubs of warmth. The cold below that surface was anaesthetic, immobilizing. Max kicked out and Jasper still whined occasionally, his limbs pistoning overtime to keep up.

A moment before they reached the platform, Max felt something brush his leg. A fish? He instinctively recoiled but felt the same whispery touch on his other leg. He stopped swimming, trod water, and looked down. What he saw almost stopped his heart: a white grasping limb and, attached to it, further down in the depths, a silent screaming face. The limb's icy fingers grasped his ankle. Insanely, in the temporal dilation of trauma, Max could clearly see a watch on the wrist of that terrible pale limb, one of those old watches that used to play "The Yellow Rose of Texas" every hour on the hour and, God save him, but he thought he could hear that song now, so weak and watery, with the watch face showing 12:00, and the cold iron grip of the bleached and slime-covered hand was pulling him down into the endless dark, and now Jasper was snarling and launching his sleek body below the surface and frenziedly biting the thing that assailed his master, and Max tried to help, he did, but the cold had him now, and he wondered why he could no longer see the light of the surface, and whether he had fallen asleep by the shore, and this was all a ...

***

It was the appalling howling dog that had alerted them. Even before they rounded the corner, hidden by stands of dark silent fir and red alder, their hackles rose at the sound, both boys strangely aware that whatever awaited them here would likely dwell forever in nightmares yet to come. Reaching the lakeshore almost reluctantly, their every instinct urging them to go home, to leave now and phone this in, they stopped and stared.

A naked man lay on the rocky shore, clearly dead. Bloated and bluish, his corpse was a latticework of lacerations. Bizarrely, he was encircled by a tree limb—what appeared to be a twisted branch of white birch—and even more perplexingly, someone had placed an old-style watch around one end of it. But worse still was the dog and the sounds it made—like all the loss of the world distilled into a late summer lakeshore snapshot; the sound of eternal sorrowing. Between howls, it would lower its head, and they saw that its muzzle still dripped with fresh blood. The boys backed away, watching that baying creature as they did so, and long after the emergency people had come and gone, had asked their serious questions and swabbed and scrubbed away the scene in a way memory never could, the two boys agreed on one thing in particular—that up until that grim and awful day they'd neither seen nor heard of such a thing as a pure white border collie.

BOWL CUT

BY PETER TALLEY

It used to be painted white, thought the man standing outside of the small, one-story building. *Maybe I'm remembering it wrong? I wonder what happened to the old barbershop pole?*

"Can I help you, sir?" asked a woman. She wore a puffy winter coat and matching earmuffs that made her appear younger.

"Megan?" *I can't believe it,* thought the man.

"Yeah? I'm sorry," she hesitated. "I usually don't open for another hour. You're lucky I saw you from my window."

She still lives in the old house next door.

"That's fine. I was actually out for a walk."

"In this weather?"

"I needed fresh air," admitted the man. "I didn't know if this place was still open."

"We've been slowly remodeling. I really do need a better sign."

"You probably don't remember me," said the man with a nervous laugh. "I used to wait on this street corner for the school bus."

"Jim? Oh my God! It is you!"

"No," said the man. "I'm Keith. It's okay. Jim is my older brother."

"Oh, shit. That's right! I'm sorry," said Megan with a smile. "How long has it been?"

Thirty years, thought Keith. *Thirty long years.*

"It's good to see you," said Megan. She fumbled with her keys because of her mittens. "Damn, it's cold out. You should come in and have some coffee." She unlocked the blue door to the shop and stepped inside. "We can also see about giving you a haircut."

"Oh? Does it look like I need one?"

"Isn't that why you're here?" asked Megan. "Give me a minute to turn up the heat and get the coffee on."

Keith closed the door behind him and stamped his shoes clean on the floor mat. He watched as the woman continued her morning routine. It wasn't until he saw the coat rack in the corner that he felt comfortable, since so much of that room had been remodeled.

"You kept that?"

"Where else are you going to hang your coat?" shrugged Megan. "I thought about putting up hooks near the window. I want my shop to look modern but I just couldn't throw everything out."

"I remember sitting over there and reading comics. It was nice of your grandpa to let us come in on the cold mornings."

"I hated those things," said Megan.

"There was this horror comic I couldn't get enough of," said Keith. "The cover really freaked me out."

"Oh, God," said Megan. "Was it the one with the melted face? I used to slide it under the stack without looking. It was so fucking scary." She paused and laughed nervously before looking over to the corner where the table of comics used to be.

"I'm sorry. It's crazy how that memory came back so strong. I haven't thought of them since I was a kid."

"I'm sorry for bringing it up," said Keith. "It was that cover though. I can still close my eyes and see it staring at me with the goopy eye."

"Yeah. Didn't they make a TV show off of it? Hell, I don't know. I hate scary stuff."

"I wonder whatever happened to those old comics," said Keith. "Do you think your family still has them in a box? Comics like that could be worth something nowadays."

"They were the first things to go after grandpa passed," said Megan. "I think Dad sold them off at a garage sale."

"Well, that's a shame. I would've enjoyed seeing them again."

"So what brings you back here? The last I heard you graduated high school and joined the Army."

"That's true," said Keith. "I enlisted for college money."

"How'd that go? What was your major?"

Keith stared into the mirror awkwardly and didn't answer.

"Oh shit," said Megan. "I'm sorry."

"Yeah. I never got around to going. It's no big deal. After my time in Iraq, I felt like college was a waste of time."

"I can see that," she said with a soft smile to break the tension. "I went to beauty school after a year at the community college. I thought I wanted to go into teaching but I just couldn't make it to those early classes."

"I think you would've been a great teacher," said Keith.

"Thanks. How do you want your coffee?

"Black," said Keith. "I can't drink it any other way."

"So what brings you back home?" asked Megan. She poured creamer into her mug and stirred until the light brown contents swirled.

"You wouldn't believe me," said Keith.

"Try me."

"Well I wanted to get back in touch with family. I haven't seen my mom since Jim died."

"Oh my God! I didn't know! What happened?"

"It was an accident," said Keith. "He was cleaning a gun and it went off."

"Oh, shit."

"It wasn't suicide," said Keith.

"What? No! I didn't think that."

"Sure you did," said Keith. "That's what everyone thinks."

"I'm sorry."

"It wasn't your fault," said Keith. "You really didn't know he died?"

"No. Did it happen here?"

"Yeah."

"For some reason I thought you both left town. I'm sorry I didn't know. I would've reached out to your parents."

"Dad was already gone," said Keith. "He died from a heart attack."

"I'm sure your mom is glad you're back home."

How the fuck would you know?

"So what happened with your family?" asked Keith.

"Not much," said Megan. "Do you remember my sister, Dana?"

"Yeah?"

"She got married a few years back to Tom Zimmerman."

"I don't remember him," said Keith.

"Really? I thought you rode the same bus."

He did, thought Keith.

"Are you going to let me cut your hair? I could fit you in right now but I do have an appointment in a few minutes."

"I'm lucky you opened early," said Keith. "Sure. I could go for a trim. You just can't use Darrell's bowl."

Megan laughed and shook her head.

"Please tell me you threw it out with the comics!"

"Trust me, Keith," said Megan. "I don't give bowl cuts."

"Thank Christ! We used to joke Darrell had two bowls."

"I heard," said Megan. "One for the boys and a bigger bowl for men!"

He made us look like morons.

"Should I sit down?"

"Please make yourself comfortable. Let me grab you a cape. I don't want you getting itchy."

"Thanks," said Keith with a larger than life smile. He waited for Megan to turn away before he grabbed her shears from the counter.

"Here. Put this on …" was the last thing Megan said before the shears punctured the side of her neck. She stumbled backward against the counter as Keith tried to stab her again.

"Darrell would tell us ghost stories," said the madman. "Your grandpa was a sadist! He enjoyed making us look like stupid …"

"Shut up, boy," rattled a voice from beneath Keith's feet. "Shut your filthy mouth!"

Keith froze in terror at the sight of the old barber rising from the floor. The blood from the shears dripped onto his shoe, but all Keith could do was stand mute and watch as the ghost of Darrell Miller approached.

"You've murdered again," said the barber. "You filthy little fucker! I'm going to enjoy watching you burn."

"I've always felt you judging me," stammered Keith. "You made me ugly!"

The bloody shear passed through Darrel's chest without connecting to anything. Keith kept swiping anyway, growing angrier with each slash until the barber's fist caught him directly under the chin. The sudden punch dropped the madman into the pool of Megan's blood.

"You shouldn't have come back here," said Darrell. "Why didn't you listen to your shrink?"

"Screw you, old man!" shouted Keith. He stood up and slashed again at the ghost. This time the shears sliced into the old barber and made the ghost howl in pain.

"You didn't have to hurt her."

"Worry about yourself," said Keith. "I'm taking you down!"

"But I'm here for you," said the barber. A swift motion knocked the shears from Keith's grasp. "You're out of time."

"What?"

"You heard me. I'm taking *you* down to hell." Darrell pointed to the two bodies on the barbershop floor. "You're dead, son."

"Why? What did you do to me?"

"I claimed your life," said Darrell. "Believe it or not. I asked for the privilege."

"You don't understand what I've been through!"

"I know you had a hard life, son. That doesn't given you an excuse to be a fuck-up."

"Back the fuck off! This is all your fault! You made me read those comics. You showed me that it was okay to be different."

"You can't pin this on a bad haircut or a scary comic," said Darrell. "I didn't make you enjoy the killing. That's on you."

"They wouldn't listen! No one ever listens!" Keith shouted and the mirrors in the small shop shattered. "You don't get to judge me!"

"The world broke you and I've been sent to reap you," cackled the old barber. "Welcome to the fire!" He reached out with his right hand and said, "I'm taking you where you'll be loved. Come on, Keith. It's time to come home."

The two spirits swirled about the room like a tornado and, in a flash of red, vanished from the world.

Megan's vision blurred as she tried to unlock her cell phone to call for help. She'd lost a lot of blood and was in shock. The door to her shop opened. She could see her first appointment of the day. It was an elderly woman who screamed.

THE VOICE

BY J. TONZELLI

The old woman was very sad and lonely after her husband died. He had been her whole world, and her whole reason for existing. The couple had three children, now grown, none of whom kept in touch, except on holidays—and even that only resulted in a courtesy call. Essentially, the old woman was alone. Sometimes it was so tough that she wondered how she would get through each day.

But that all went away the day the voice came.

"Hello?" it asked, sounding small, young, and faraway.

At first, the woman thought it might have been coming from her television, which had earlier aired a news report about a missing child, so she did not think it strange.

"Hello?" the voice asked again. "Is anyone there?"

The old woman muted her television, realizing that the voice was coming from somewhere in her house!

"Hello?" the old woman asked back. "Can you hear me?"

"Yes!" the voice called. "Please … what's happening?" The voice wavered, in and out, as if caught in a swaying wind.

The old woman was beside herself. After all this time, she finally had some company. "What's your name?" she asked.

"Carl," answered the young-sounding voice. "I don't know what's happening. It's so dark here."

"How old are you, Carl?" the woman asked.

"Twelve," he answered. "I'm twelve. Or ... I guess I was? Am I ... dead?"

"I don't know, Carl," the old woman said. "What do you see?"

"Angels," Carl answered. "I see angels. They're everywhere."

"Stay with the angels, Carl," the old woman firmly said. "They will take care of you. They will keep you safe. Do you understand?"

"I want to go home. I want to see my mommy."

"I'm so sorry, Carl, but you can't go home. You're with the angels now."

There was silence for a moment.

"Who are you?" asked Carl.

"My name is Regina," answered the old woman. "I can hear you. I'm in the living room in my house, but I can hear you!"

"How long am I going to be here?" the voice called.

Regina could tell that Carl was upset, and understandably so, but she had worked as a schoolteacher for many years until she retired. If she knew how to do anything, it was being caring but firm with young children.

"I don't know, Carl," Regina said. "You might be there forever. That's how it works. There's no going back."

She could hear Carl begin to softly cry.

"You should do your best to forget about your family and your life, Carl. It will only make it harder. You cannot go back to them. Do you understand?"

Carl cried some more.

"Don't cry, Carl. Don't be sad. I'm glad you're here. My husband died recently and I have been so alone. Now that you're here, you can keep me company. Tell me about yourself. What do you like to do for fun?"

"I don't want to be dead," Carl said, still crying.

It was remarkable how well she could hear the boy. Even though his voice continued to fade in and out, like someone playing with the volume on a television, she could even hear the boy sniff his nose as he cried. It broke her heart to hear him so upset, but she was grateful to have companionship.

"Go on, Carl," she softly ordered. "Tell me about yourself."

And after a while, he did. Carl told Regina all about his life—how he had played baseball, and staged battles with army men against his older brother, Patrick. Likewise, Regina told Carl about herself—how she collected figurines she bought at yard sales, how she was currently trying to continue her lifelong goal of reading a biography of every former United States president. She also talked of her deceased husband—how much she missed seeing his face.

Carl's voice remained in Regina's house for weeks following, and while he would sometimes become upset, the two grew to know each other quite well. Regina sometimes wondered if anyone else could hear the voice, or if she were the only one. Without ever receiving any visitors, she had no way to answer that question, but she felt somehow chosen to be the receiver of the young boy's voice and she was grateful.

One day she finally had her chance to find out, for someone had knocked at her door. She opened it to reveal it was her daughter, Heidi.

"Hi, Mom," she said and pecked Regina on the cheek. She brushed past her and walked into the house.

"What a nice surprise!" Regina said, though she wasn't sure she had meant it. She had gotten so used to having only Carl's company that it felt wrong for anyone else to be there. "What brings you by?"

"Bob and I have run into a problem," she said. She walked into the living room, flung off her coat, and tossed it on an armchair. "We're redoing the bathroom in the guest room and we found these really nice tiles we like, but we can't afford it right now because of Kasie's piano lessons. We were hoping—"

"Hello?" Carl's voice called suddenly. It was shallow and tinny, almost impossible to hear.

Regina's eyes went wide, and she hoped that Heidi hadn't heard Carl's voice.

But Heidi had stopped in midstride at the sound and was looking at her mother questioningly.

"What was that?"

"Oh, nothing," Regina said. "You were saying about the tiles?"

Carl called out again: "Is someone else there?"

"Carl, shush!" Regina finally shouted. "I have company!"

"Who's Carl?" Heidi asked, looking perplexed. "Who are you talking to?"

"Just Carl," Regina said, relenting. "He's been talking to me ever since your father died."

"Is that right?" Heidi asked, looking alarmingly at her mother. "And what does ... Carl say?"

Regina shrugged. "All kinds of things. That he sees angels. He likes baseball. His favorite food is pizza."

"And you talk to Carl ... all the time?"

"Why, sure!" Regina said, smiling, actually enjoying getting the chance to talk about her new friend. "Watch this!" She stepped into the center of the living room, and with a loud voice, said, "Carl, my daughter, Heidi, is here. Why don't you say hello?"

Heidi rolled her eyes. "Okay, I was afraid this was gonna happen with you being here all alone. Why don't we—"

"Hello, Heidi!" Carl said. "You have a real nice mom!"

Heidi's eyes bugged open. "Who is that?" she demanded.

"I told you!" Regina said. "It's Carl!"

Heidi was beside herself. "Who is Carl? Where is his voice coming from?"

"He's with the angels!" Regina answered. "He must be ... you know ..." She pointed upwards toward the heavens and then whispered, "Upstairs."

"Carl?" Heidi called out. "Carl ... where are you? What do you see?"

"I see angels! And bright light!" he answered.

Heidi's mouth fell open. News reports about a boy kidnapped in the area began flashing in her brain like lightning. "Oh, Mother, tell me you didn't!" Heidi shouted as she began running up the steps to the second floor.

"Where are you going, dear?" Regina called behind her, her own voice light and fluttery. "Are you going to look for the angels? I hope not—you'll only disappoint yourself!" She laughed to herself.

Heidi ignored her mother and made her way up the rest of the stairs. She ran down the hallway toward the last door that led to the attic. She'd remembered her mother's angel figurine collection from her youth. She remembered that the collection had grown so extensive that her father had refurnished part of the attic with white walls and handcrafted white shelves to display them. He had even installed bright lights above the shelves to illuminate them with heavenly light.

"I'm here, Carl!" Heidi called out and opened the door.

The attic was empty. The lights Regina's husband had installed were resting in piles on the floor, dismantled and poking out of cardboard boxes. There were no white shelves, no angel figurines, and most importantly, no little boy.

Carl's voice called out again. "Heidi?" it asked. It sounded wavy and inconsistent, as if it were coming from very far away.

"Yes, Carl! I'm here!" she called. "Where are you?"

"I'm with the angels!" he called back. "Your father is here, too! He wants me to tell you something! He wants you to stop acting like a spoiled brat and pay for your own goddamned bathroom tiles!"

THE VISIT

BY BARBARA AVON

My heart is covered in soot. Black, like the coal in Kringle's bag. Sin didn't discolour it. It's painted in hues borrowed from the very sad, the horribly bad, and the formidably ugly. Upon my death, the pink will return and it will drift skyward.

The asphalt feels cool against my face. My breath crystalizes before me; still laced with mirth. The office party was typical of Davis, Davis, and Sons. A monumental buffet was meant to entice V.I.P. A threesome in monkey suits played soft jazz. The libations flowed freely, served by a kid fresh out of college, vying for an entry-level position within the firm. It was all very grotesque.

On the advice of our superior, we left early; before midnight. "Keep 'em wanting more, boys. That's the road to success." We made our escape with full bellies and even fuller Rolodex, intent to climb the corporate ladder rungs until our feet bled.

Where is Gary?

It's too quiet. I should be hearing sirens. I should be seeing hallucinatory red and blue, behind my half-closed lids. I see nothing but her face. The sad one.

"Does it hurt?" she asks me.

"I don't feel much."

"No. I mean, does it hurt? To remember what you did to me?"

My eyes pop open. She sits before me Indian-style in the same acid wash jeans and pink neon sweatshirt she wore on our only date. Her sixteen-year-old hair is styled sky-high. Her eyes are lined in navy. She wears a smirk I've never seen before. She was always timid. It was easier that way.

"Well, Tom?"

"I'm dying, aren't I?"

"Not yet. First, you have to remember what you did to me."

"I don't understand," I tell her. My arms and legs feel deflated, like a goddamn sex doll that's lost its groove. I wonder, again, where Gary is, and if he's fused together with the steering wheel of his new Porsche.

"You do. You remember. You took me to your special place. The place where you took all of your sweethearts. Tommy's Lair, the girls called it. Like it was some fucking honour to be invited into your parents' basement."

She starts to cry in a most beautiful manner—quietly, and with a slight smile poised on her lips.

"It's funny, because I never told you something, Tom. I never told you that I didn't even like you. I just wanted to be done with it. I just wanted it to be over. You didn't even kiss me."

I want to object, but I can't see my breath anymore. The half-syllable is invisible. She ignores the panic in my eyes, put there by the realization that dead men don't breathe.

"Pink Floyd played in the background. That was kind of cool. The bed. Oh God, the bed, though. It was merely a soiled cot. I remember thinking how grey it was. You poured your dad's liquor down my throat. The good kind. You told me I deserved it. You told me I was special. But you know what

Tom? I knew you were lying. And I enjoyed every fucking second of it."

"You're wrong. It wasn't like that."

"Liar!"

She looks away, down the icy street. We had taken the back roads home. I don't remember why. I don't even remember her name. I strain to listen and can hear a chain jingling, or a dog collar. Lassie, to the rescue.

"They're coming, Tom. Don't worry. They're coming."

I try to raise my head, and succumb to the mind-numbing pain. There is nothing but darkness, and an indelible feeling of emptiness.

"Hey. Wake up."

A guy in a suit is using my head as a soccer ball.

Gary.

A fire sears my throat. I want to lick the pavement beneath me, but my tongue won't reach.

"You're … you're okay …" I manage to tell him.

He raises a bottle of Jack to his lips. The party, it seems, isn't over.

"What are you doing? Help me."

The pinstripes in his expensive trousers blur together. He's wearing black jeans, and the black leather jacket he never took off. Even in the blistering heat, that jacket was like a second skin. He's the tough kid from an even tougher neighbourhood. The horribly bad.

"Don't worry, Tommy. They're coming."

"Who? Who is coming?"

My head hurts from twisting my eyeball towards the sky. I wish he'd sit down, but nothing could ever keep Gary down. He was always itching to go somewhere, and do something. He was always searching for the elusive escape route.

"I saw Old Man Watson today. Said he'd beat the living shit out of me for stealing smokes from his stupid store."

The sky shifts. I can't see it, but I can feel it. Old Man Watson crawls past me, with one arm inching his brown, emaciated shell forward.

"I'm dead, aren't I?"

"Not yet. So I told the bastard to shut the fuck up. Then I shot him. Pisssshhh ... dead in the eyes," he says, threatening me with his fingers.

The horror registers in my eyes. I want the sad one back. Misery loves company.

"I'm just playing with you, Tommy. What the fuck, man! I don't own a gun."

Gary does a little dance, and breathes into his hands. His breath on the air is comforting. I still can't see my own, and I'm a little worried about that.

"Cold as fuck out here, eh?"

His long, blond hair is greasy, making it look yellower. He runs his fingers through it. Blood covers his hand. He shows it to me.

"Guess we got ourselves into some trouble. Eh, Tommy?" he says, wiping his bloody hand on dead cow. "What's going on? Why aren't you talking to me? Fuck," he swears, spitting on the ground, "you always did think you were better than me, Tommy. You always made me feel like a piece of shit."

Jingle. Jingle. Jingle.

I want to ask him if he can hear it, but the crease between his eyes grows deeper. A cavern of disgust lies there.

"What are you talking about? You're my best friend ..."

"Shut up! This is all your fault! Just like Ma," he says wistfully. "She could never shut up. I kept telling her, and telling her to just be quiet. He wouldn't be mad, if she'd just be quiet. Did I ever tell you that I'm the one who found her? Eh? Hanging from the rafters like a fucking pinata."

His laugh echoes endlessly. I want to cover my ears, but I'm a goddamn cripple. His words are the salt in my wounds.

"I ... no, Gare. You never told me."

"Well, I'm telling you now. Dad never killed himself, either. Just a bit of rat poison in his morning Frosted Flakes. Just a pinch. Less than a pinch. Remember that, Tommy. You don't wanna kill them all at once. Too messy, that way. Too many unanswerable questions."

He walks over to me. He crouches before me. I want to flinch, but it's like I'm glued to the road. The sticky sweet taste of the whiskey sears my wind-burned lips. It dribbles down my chin, and neck. It itches, and I can't fucking scratch.

"Is that how you did it?"

"Did what?"

He stands tall. His shadow is non-existent. "To the Sad One." A second swift kick to the head, and I'm lost in blackness.

It's starting to feel nice here. It's like sleeping, but someone opens the shutters. The blackness dissipates. There's the scent of apple in the air. It's the scent of her perfume. I can see her, on bended knee, begging me to stay. Discarded wrapping paper surrounds her like some cruel joke. I had kept my gifts simple; vulgar, even. A blender served as my parting gift. I left her my heart, too, but she didn't know it. I loved her then, I love her, still.

"I love you too, Tom."

I struggle to see through a purple haze. Saliva drips from my mouth. Maybe it's blood.

"You ... you still love me?"

"Of course."

The tears freeze before they can fall. She looks like an angel, sent to whisk me away. I need my body back. It's shattered, and I need it back, to be able to hold her, and kiss her, and tell her I'm sorry.

"I know you're sorry."

She sits very close to me. Her hand inches toward my face, but she doesn't touch me—a well-deserved torture.

"I really hate to see you this way. You were so handsome when we first met. Do you remember?"

"The ... video store."

"Yes. I knew you were following me. I almost ran away. Then we reached for the same movie. It's amazing how the human touch can make everything different. You became real, when our hands touched. And not just some creepy guy following me."

My laugh is trapped inside of me. My lips won't curl into a smile.

"I'm scared, Amy."

"Don't worry, Tom. They're coming."

"I ... I hurt you."

"Yes."

"The firm. My work ..."

"I know. Work was always your number-one priority."

"I was wrong, honey. I want you to know that."

She hides behind her long, dark hair. Her cheeks are painted cherub-red. Her full lips scream for a kiss. She jerks her head toward the darkness.

"Did you hear that?"

"Chains?"

"Yes."

"I hear them. They're getting louder."

She grows frantic. Her words pollute the air between us.

"I have to tell you something, Tom. The night before we broke up, on Christmas Eve. Remember that I was out with the girls? I didn't mean to, Tom. It was stupid. Tracy had fed me too many shots, and, I don't know. He was charming, and a very stupid mistake."

The formidably ugly.

"You're wrong," she says with a profound sadness. "It's not me, Tom. You're the ugly one. You're the one who took Gary's keys. You're the one who made love to the bottle. While you were driving, for Christ's sake. Jesus Christ, what were you thinking, Tom? What were you thinking swigging from that bottle as if it were your mama's breast?"

"No ..."

"Yes. Poor Gary. I can see half of him," she says, staring somewhere behind me.

"No. No. No. ... It was him. He was driving."

She looks at me like Sister Mary Margaret used to when she knew I was fibbing, and would warn me about burning embers.

"It all ends here. They're here, Tom. They're here," she whispers.

She vanishes before my eyes. She doesn't fade. She vanishes. The jingle is deafening, yet muffled beneath a chorus of growls.

I can see myself stumbling towards the Porsche. I can see myself reaching into Gary's suit jacket and taking his keys. I see myself pushing him into the passenger side seat. He's singing a Christmas carol off key; wasted, done. I can see myself pulling the bottle of Jack Daniels from inside my coat. I had snatched it on the way out. I had given the kid a large tip to keep his mouth shut. I remember the impact, and the tree that came out of nowhere. I can hear Gary's scream that sounds just like my own, as Cerberus takes a large chunk of my face between its fangs.

My heart is covered in soot. Black, like the coal in Kringle's bag. Sin discoloured it. It's painted in hues borrowed from the very sad, the horribly bad, and the formidably ugly. Upon my death, its beat silenced, it will drift Underworld.

LOVE IN THE LILACS

BY IAN M. RYAN

Introduction to Life Now

I woke up to the usual smell of lilacs in my room, as I welcomed her with lilacs every morning. I was only 27 at the time and she was 25. Her heart was mine and mine was hers. We had been dating for three years when we decided to move in together and, yes, it was difficult to go three years without being with her in my house. My parents passed away when I was 25 and she helped guide me through the darkest and toughest years of my life, until she passed away. Now I feel like I see her and hear her everywhere I go.

I spend my days in the garden, keeping it upscale and making sure I still have the lilacs to bring into the house every morning. I can still picture her smiling as I hand them over to her. I haven't been working; I have no motivation now that she's gone. I know I have to get back to work, but these past two months have been heartbreaking and a time where I've been nothing but alone. I went to my brothers' houses and my sister's, trying to mask the pain of losing someone I loved so dearly. Nothing would help, nothing will bring her back to me and I can't accept that she's gone.

After I'm in the garden I go back inside and look at old pictures of us. She was thin and had long, blonde hair. She wore contacts but it didn't take away from the beautiful blue eyes she would hide behind the first time I met her. She held back the tears and held back the lack of hope that she had, because the last relationship she was in brought her down so much. She was abused, both physically and mentally, and it tore me apart to hear her say that she was hurt by this man. I used to see it in my dreams, that's how vividly she remembered it when she told me about these events. These events controlled her and hurt her; I couldn't stand that. As our relationship progressed, I saw that hurt smile turn into a loving one. I saw it with our families, with our dog, and with the children that she taught. She had everything going for her, until she didn't.

I still remember this picture. She was wearing the surgical mask in the hospital because they told us that she was harmful to the people who had not been sick. I remember going into that hospital room every day knowing each day could be my last with her. The virus took her from me in four days. It broke her down, inch by inch. I hated seeing that same pain in her eyes as the pain from the abuse she took. However, I knew that this was a deeper abuse, one that took her life. I still hold that same hatred energy toward the outside world because this happened to her. People told me they were sorry for my loss, and that it would get better with time, but no time will ever bring her back to me. No sorry will ever take back the tears I've cried every day for the past two months, nothing will ever bring her back. ...

The Destruction of Lilacs

I woke up that next morning, May 1, with a pain in my stomach, a stabbing right through my gut. I rose out of my bed almost unconsciously to see a woman running out of my backyard with dirt on her, the same dirt that's in my garden. I sprinted down the stairs to see what had happened, and I discovered something that broke my heart. My lilac garden was shredded. It was in ruins. I was devastated. This was my wife's favorite flower; how could someone destroy that? Each flower bed was destroyed. There was no chance for them re-growing, the roots were pulled out of the ground. Maybe that lady just didn't like lilacs, but my wife loved them, and I knew what I need to do.

I went to Lowe's to pick up more lilacs for my garden, and I also asked about security cameras for my garden as well. I picked up a few after talking to the salesperson and I was on my way. Today would be dedicated solely to figuring out what I wanted to do with my garden. I set up the flowers the exact same way I had them. My wife loved them that way. I set up the cameras above and all around the flower beds. One above the lilacs, and one in each corner of the backyard. If someone was in my yard, I would get a good look at them and they would hear about what they're doing. Purple lilacs were symbols of eternal love, and my love for my wife was in fact eternal. I headed inside for the night and was hoping this would be the end of the trouble in the garden.

What Happened?

A few weeks went by and I was happy and content with how my flower bed was. However, the first day of the month of June, I woke up with the exact same pain in my stomach again. A pierce and a pull, again I rose to see a woman running out of my backyard. I raced down the stairs and found my flower bed had been destroyed again. I couldn't wait to see who had done it. I picked up all five of the cameras and watched the footage. I couldn't believe what was being brought to my eyes. A girl in a white dress, a white princess dress. The same one Katie wore in her casket. I watched this figure look at the flowers, and watched them rip out of the ground and tear apart in the air. I saw the tears falling down her face. It didn't look like she wanted to do it. She looked at the camera and rushed toward it. I saw her mouth moving so I turned up the volume on the camera.

Her voice—it was infiltrating my mind. I couldn't believe what I was hearing. The tears came down my face as I listened to the words she was saying to me. How could this be? It was almost a conversation; she knew what I would say back to her. ...

"Liam, why are you still bringing me flowers every day? Darling, you need to get on with life. It's been three months."

But, Katie, life without you is dull and it's boring. I need to bring you these flowers because I miss you. I love you forever. Lilacs are symbols of eternal love.

"Flowers are material things; you loved me deeper than the flowers. Lilacs are a flower that symbolizes earthly love and passion. If it truly means that much to you, why don't you bring me new flowers, something that shows more than earthly love ...?"

Lilacs are your favorite, Katie. They smell beautiful and they are beautiful. Just like you.

"There is a world full of beautiful flowers out there, Liam. You found me. You can find another beautiful flower with a beautiful smell and one that fits the garden. Think about the color yellow. You'll be waking up soon. I have to run! I love you eternally, Liam."

Choices

I took Katie's words to heart. I knew I needed to make a change for her. If she was pulling up these flowers, it was because she needed a change. Something to make her happy. Something that made her feel loved beyond the love I had for her on earth. I took down my cameras, since I knew it was only Katie. I knew she would be back again to talk to me. I'd been going back to work with an empty flower bed when I came across a beautiful flower bed on my walk home. I went up to the door to ask what kind of flowers they were and when I knocked on the door, a beautiful woman walked outside. I asked about the flowers and she told me they were primrose and blue lilacs. The flower bed brought me happiness and took away much of the tension I had. This new woman told me the lilacs are a symbol of happiness and tranquility and the primroses are a symbol of eternal love. My jaw dropped. I couldn't believe what I heard. I knew what flowers would fill the garden now. The beautiful woman handed me a note card and told me good luck with my garden.

As I was walking back to my home, I looked at the note card. It had her phone number as well as the names of the flowers. Her name was Jenn. When I arrived home, I was shocked to find my flower bed filled with primroses and blue lilacs. I flipped over the card from Jenn and it said, "Katie told me I would find love in the lilacs." I felt a cool wind sweep past me and saw my wife rise into the sky and disappear, smiling down upon me. I will always find love in the lilacs.

DOWNWARD SLOPE

BY PETER TALLEY

It was a late Saturday afternoon near the middle of February. My sister and I trudged our way to the top of the snowy hill at the edge of town. I was responsible for pulling our red plastic sled.

"How much further?" asked Jillian through her scarf.

"I'm telling you, it will be worth it."

"I'm cold."

"Me too," I said. "We're almost to the top."

"I want to go home," said Jillian. "It's too cold out!"

I remember the thermometer in the garage showing it was in the teens. What we didn't plan for was the wind. If I was smart I would've turned us around and forgot about the stupid dare.

"You made it," said Rory. "We thought you were going to chicken out."

"I told you I'd be here," I said to the bully in the puffy, blue coat.

"Why'd you bring her?" asked Rory. "You know she can't take your place."

His friends laughed at us. I didn't respond. I looked over Rory's shoulder and down the other side of the steep hill. We called it Cemetery Run because at the bottom was a mostly-forgotten graveyard. Dad said it was from the first settlers of the area. During spring you couldn't even tell there was anything in the field except for tall prairie grass and weeds. Wintertime was different, though. You could see the weather-worn crosses if you squinted carefully. They were slightly a darker color of white than the snow. The best and worst part of sledding down this hill was that you gained a lot of speed. If you didn't fall off your sled, you still had to duck underneath a wooden fence, and hope you wouldn't slam into a gravestone.

"Come on, chickenshit," said one of the other boys. I think it was Artie but I wasn't really paying attention. "I'm freezing. Let's get on with it!"

I lined up the sled and looked at Jillian. I wish she hadn't come. She folded her arms and shivered in the wind. I couldn't tell if she was more mad at me or just cold. I put on a brave smile and said, "It'll be okay."

"Stop stalling," said Rory. "Get on the sled!"

It was stupid that I bragged about doing this run before. I hadn't. The thought of sliding that fast scared me. I don't know why I let Rory push me into this mess. Was he calling my bluff? I don't think so. I really think he just wanted to see if I was brave enough to do it again. Nobody ever made it as far I bragged. I told them at recess that I could beat my old record. If I didn't prove it, I was going to be known forever as the kid who lied.

"He's going to do it," said Rory.

"You know he is," said Jillian. "He's no chicken!"

"We'll see how far he gets," said Rory. "I'm betting he falls off halfway down."

"I bet he cracks his head open on the fence!" said another kid.

I took in a deep breath of cold air and shoved off before I had to hear anymore smack talk. The problem was that I didn't move an inch. The damn snow was too deep where I placed the sled! The crowd behind me laughed and before I could say anything I felt Rory give me a hard kick in the back. I lost my balance as the sled turned to the side and rocketed down the hill.

I was horribly off track, and the sound of my sister screaming from behind didn't help. I tried to correct the course of the sled but it was too late. I was going over rough patches of ice and feared that at any second I was going to be launched into the air.

"Oh shit!" I shouted as I bounced and damn-near flipped over. The midpoint of the hill was where I felt the sled starting to shift. I was going into a spin that was going to make me go down the rest of the hill backwards! At the last second I threw all of my weight to the left and regained control. The impact on my tailbone, however, brought tears to my eyes.

I heard Artie yell, "He's going to make it!"

My fingers tensed as I grabbed the sides of the sled tighter than before. I wanted to keep my eyes open but the cold tears, fear of crashing, and wind made me want to shut out the world. I blinked and at the last second I saw that I was headed straight toward a fence post!

"Watch out!" shouted Jillian.

I wasn't to going to wipe out this close to the end! I kicked my right leg into the ground and used the heel of my boot to push away. The idea worked! I was now about to go under the fence. I leaned backward and felt the tip of my nose scrape against the bottom of a wooden fence rail.

I saw a headstone fly by out of the corner of my eye. Above me were gray clouds and a blurry sun. I would be lucky if I could skid into a stop without hitting one of the old stones. A sigh of relief escaped my mouth as the sled finally came to a peaceful rest. I made it further than the lie I told. I actually won! In the distance I heard the sound of crunching snow.

I screamed at the sight of a terrifying, blue-skinned woman leaning over me. She wore a Pilgrim's bonnet and held a spiteful expression of anger engraved on her withered face. I couldn't move. I felt her cold hands through my coat as she grabbed my shoulders.

I tried to scream, "Help," but no sound came out.

The woman's foggy eyes made me feel dizzy. I tried to scream again and break free from her icy grasp. It didn't work! Her cracked lips smiled and then her mouth opened. I felt the remaining warmth of my body rush out of me and into her as I struggled helplessly.

I awoke a week later in the county hospital. My parents and Jillian were at my side. They said I was lucky to be alive after the accident. I couldn't remember what happened. Anytime I tried to think back on the moment, my head would pound and I'd get a bloody nose. I never went sledding again. Now that I'm a parent, I forbid my kids to go out alone. I know it isn't safe out there. The cold woman exists and I won't let her finish what she started those twenty years ago.

THE OLD MANSION

BY LEONOR BASS

There were times she recounted the events which led her to her madness and tried to erase them from her mind, to replace them with something different. But the voice kept creeping inside her head, whispering, repeating her name until she closed her eyes and cried herself to sleep—as if that were enough.

In the whiteness of her room hung a picture of what had caused her life to be destroyed. What she thought to be destiny, good fortune, was the sole thing that had changed her whole world. She stared at it as a reminder of everything she had lost, including her own sanity.

The Old Mansion, she had called it. Beautiful, imposing, a bit dark in color and at times obscure, but perfect for her. She had made the decision to move into it despite the advice of many and the harrowing stories she had heard regarding the true nature of its abandonment. Although she never listened, there was still something in the back of her head, a voice of reason that kept telling her perhaps living there was not a good idea.

And it truly wasn't.

If she could only explain, put into words how everything had begun, maybe her own madness wouldn't be haunting her. If only they would listen—how the voice crept into her brain in her sleep; the way the house spoke to her and screamed her name for so long she often covered her ears. She would pretend the dovelike voice was just part of a nightmare, until that nightmare drove her crazy and made her beg for it to stop. The neighbors had called the police when she lost all control of her actions and the blood from her wrist stained the bathroom floor. She didn't want to die. She just wanted silence.

"Are you ready to talk now?" the doctor spoke.

Aline's eyes were still stuck on the picture before her; she wanted to ignore the question. Her session always included a retelling of her problems, and her only problem was The Old Mansion.

"You won't get better unless you solve what is troubling you, Aline. That's what I'm here for, you know."

"You want to talk about—the voice?" Aline whispered. Without looking into the woman's face, she could tell she wore a blank expression. To her doctor, each conversation was mandatory. To Aline, it was mind-wrecking.

"Is she—back again?" the doctor asked.

The question made Aline whip around—it seemed the doctor was questioning her sanity, the facts she had exposed so many times. The voice was real. The voice was there. Was that so hard to understand?

"She'll never believe you."

"You don't understand. She never leaves. She's always there. SHE'S ALWAYS HERE!" The desperation began again. The palpitation, the sweating in her palms, the eagerness to bang her head against something hard so the voice would stop talking, but each time she tried, someone was there to make her sleep. Sleeping never helped.

"Tell me, Aline, tell me so I can help you," the doctor encouraged her. Her voice was so soft, so soothing that it made Aline feel the calmness that she needed. Made her believe she actually cared about her for a moment and she wasn't another woman locked in a mental institution.

"She—she's always whispering. Always calling my name—" Aline whispered. She had talked about it for so long it seemed her words had lost all meaning, like reciting a script by heart but every word came from her desperation to be understood. "She's telling me things—she wants me to do, and—I don't want to do them."

"What does she want you to do?"

Aline remained in silence. If she could explain everything the woman told her and what the voice wanted to force her to do, she would remain in the mad house for the rest of her life.

"Things—that sometimes I don't understand." Aline turned her back toward the wall once again. The picture of The Old Mansion seemed to come to life every time she looked at it, as if it were speaking to her too, calling her home.

"Is she talking to you now?"

Aline was barely listening. Her mind, body and soul were back to the picture on her wall. She heard the whispering back in her ear, calling her name, muttering words that made no sense, until the murmur became so clear to her that it made her shiver.

"You'll never get out. She'll never let you leave."

"Get rid of her, Aline. She thinks you're crazy."

"She's telling me the truth. You think I'm crazy," Aline whispered. She could feel the doctor moving uncomfortably in her chair, and the beating of the doctor's heart became clear to Aline, like a song in her ear.

"I don't—" the doctor spoke again, but Aline turned around abruptly, making the young woman jump from her seat.

"STOP LYING!" Aline snapped. "I can hear you. I can hear her telling me everything. You won't let me leave. You all think I'm nuts—but she's here. She's in my brain. She's in my blood—she's everywhere."

"Aline, you need to calm down," the doctor spoke, her voice trembling with fear. "Just take a breath."

Aline felt nothing except her heart pumping in her chest, perspiration dripping down her forehead and a void in her soul. She had no control over her body, as if she had been replaced by someone devoid of sentiment and guilt. She didn't care about the woman in front of her, of her fear, or the tears running down her cheeks.

Aline only cared about what the voice was telling her— what she was ordered to do.

"To be free, a soul needs to be taken. Now, it's your turn."

The screams were muffled by Aline's own hand. The doctor struggled to release herself from Aline's strong grip, but was unsuccessful, and her attacker felt the eagerness to put an end to her life. She was in control now.

"To be free, a soul must be taken," Aline whispered, her hands wrapped around the doctor's neck, squeezing hard, never letting go.

The doctor's body fell to the floor at Aline's feet, and she stared at it with a twisted smile on her face, like it was a marvelous masterpiece. Her job was done; her soul rejuvenated and her heart at peace, it was time to go home. The Old Mansion awaited, and so did the innocent souls the voice commanded her to take.

THE AUSTIN INTELLIGENCE

BY RICH HOSEK

"There's a woman in your office, Mr. Bythewood."

"How did she get in there?" Mr. Bythewood asked.

"I don't know. She was here when I arrived," his assistant, Ms. Blackstone replied.

"What does she want?"

"She didn't say, but she looks very rich."

Mr. Bythewood considered the situation. He was the head of one of the most successful investment firms on Wall Street, and it wasn't unheard of for him to receive inquiries from wealthy people who valued their privacy as much as the returns on their investments. But rarely did they do so in person. Regardless, he would have a word with Junger in security.

"Hold my calls, Ms. Blackstone."

"Yes, Mr. Bythewood," the assistant replied. She sat down behind her desk and started opening the mail.

Mr. Bythewood turned the knob on his inner office door and pushed it open.

Standing in the center of the room was a strikingly beautiful woman. Mr. Bythewood judged her to be in her mid-thirties, but with plastic surgery these days, she could easily have been older.

"Good morning, Ms. …" He let the greeting hang in the air between them, hoping she would volunteer her name to complete it.

"You can call me Lina, Mr. Bythewood," the woman said.

"How can I help you, Lina?" Mr. Bythewood asked as he made his way past her to his desk. "Are you looking to make an investment with our firm?"

She nodded. "Perhaps. But I'm a very cautious woman. I like to do my due diligence before I hand over my money to anyone."

Mr. Bythewood smiled. "You want to know about the Austin Intelligence," he said as he sat in his chair and reclined.

Lina again nodded.

"Well, I can't tell you much more than you already know. It is proprietary technology. Trade secrets and all."

"I want to see it," Lina demanded.

Mr. Bythewood waved his hand in the air above him. "It's a cloud thing. Spread out among thousands of servers in dozens of data centers across the globe."

It was Lina's turn to smile. "You and I both know that's not true."

Mr. Bythewood became suddenly nervous. "What do you mean?"

"I mean," Lina began, "that your whole story about a distributed artificial intelligence is a load of—to put it politely—poppycock."

"Oh, I can assure you that the Austin Intelligence is real," Mr. Bythewood said.

"I didn't say it wasn't real," Lina explained, "just that it wasn't a cloud-based AI."

Mr. Bythewood smiled again, this time nervously. "I'm not sure I know what you mean."

"Do I really need to spell it out for you?" Lina asked.

"Please, I'm curious what you think you know."

Lina walked over to a leather couch and sat down on it. She placed her hands on her knees and stared directly at Mr. Bythewood. "Let's begin with your founder, Leonard Austin. He was a singular genius, a man who had the innate ability to see trends in markets and stocks, identify opportunities in derivatives, and apply what can best be described as an uncanny knack for timing to buy and sell at the precise times to maximize returns."

"Yes, Mr. Austin was indeed a bold innovator in the investment field."

Lina nodded. "And he did all that from a wheelchair, without the ability to move on his own, unable even to speak."

"He faced many challenges," Mr. Bythewood agreed.

"He built this company from nothing."

"He had some help."

"From you?" Lina asked. "You did nothing but exploit him. This company is worth nearly ten billion dollars, but Leonard Austin's net worth at the time of his death was a little over two million."

"Mr. Austin was well compensated for his services as a financial analyst."

"Leonard may have had a mind for financial markets, but he did not have a head for business. You took advantage of that. You recognized his talent, and you built this business around him. But you wouldn't have anything if it hadn't been for him."

Mr. Bythewood shrugged. "And he wouldn't have been anything without me. There would be no BA Investments without my foresight."

"And then he died," Lina said.

"Yes, it was very sad, but he was very sick. The doctors said it was a miracle he had lived as long as he had."

"Yet your firm continues making the kind of bold and lucrative deals you were known for when Leonard Austin was alive."

"Because of the Austin Intelligence."

"Which you claim is an AI that was trained via proprietary algorithms to mimic the decision making of the original Leonard Austin. In fact, it does more than manage your investments, it runs the company, everything from payroll to managing your real estate holdings."

"What's your point?"

"The thing is, your AI appears to be much more advanced than any other expert system. It seems to rely on … intuition, acting with a human-like imagination to see opportunities that other AIs, which apply traditional pattern recognition, miss."

"What can I say? That's why people choose BA Investments. We're just better."

"I want to see him," Lina stated plainly.

"Excuse me?"

"I want to see Leonard Austin."

"Mr. Austin is dead. I was at his funeral. I saw them lower his casket into the ground and cover it with dirt."

Lina looked at Mr. Bythewood, staring deep into his eyes. It unnerved him. "You may have buried Mr. Austin, but he's still working for you."

"Don't be absurd. You said yourself that he died."

Lina rose from her seat and started pacing. "When Leonard Austin was first diagnosed with ALS, the doctors didn't think he would live more than six months. But even though the disease rendered his body useless, his mind still worked."

"Yes, I know all this. I was more than just his business partner; I was his friend."

"Then you know about the system he utilized that allowed him to use a computer."

"Of course. It was a prototype system that used machine learning to interpret his brainwaves and translate them into actions on his computer," Mr. Bythewood explained. "Everyone knows that."

"But what they don't know is that, after Mr. Austin died, the interface continued working."

Mr. Bythewood's face became pale. He clenched his jaw and dug his fingernails into the leather surface of the blotter on his desk. "That's ridiculous," he said unconvincingly.

"You may not be aware, but Leonard's neural interface is configured to send regular diagnostic information back to the device's manufacturer. And according to the analytics, he's still hooked up to it. I want to see him," Lina repeated. "Or should I take my one-point-three billion dollars somewhere else?"

Mr. Bythewood said nothing.

"I can almost see what you're thinking, Mr. Bythewood," Lina said. "You're debating whether the commissions that much money could generate are worth sharing your secret." In her hands was a check. She placed it on the desk in front of him. It was made out in the amount of five hundred million dollars. "There's more if you show him to me."

Mr. Bythewood stared down at the check in front of him. The decision was easy. Besides, ever since it had happened, he had been dying to tell someone. He rose from his desk and crossed to a bookcase behind him. It was completely unnecessary to hide The Intelligence behind a secret door built into a bookcase, but when you have a lot of money, you have to spend it somewhere.

He pulled on a book, and a large section of the wall swung open.

Lina walked past the desk to the open passage and stepped inside the room beyond.

It was an office, not as large or opulent as Bythewood's, but impressive nonetheless.

At the center of it was a desk. Underneath the large, dark slab was a collection of computers connected to each other by a web of cables. On the desk was a system of posts and arms that suspended nine monitors in a three-by-three array pointed at an empty motorized wheelchair. The chair had a halo of sensors attached to the headrest.

Lina smiled at the sight of it. "Hello, Leonard."

She walked toward the chair.

"Whoa, hold on. Stay back. You said you wanted to see. You saw, now step away."

Lina ignored him. She crossed behind the desk and looked at the monitors. A window popped up on one of them. A chat screen.

The word, "Hello," appeared in green letters.

"It's nice to see you again," Lina said.

More words appeared. "Do I know you?"

"Okay, that's enough," Mr. Bythewood said. "You've seen the Austin Intelligence. Time to go."

Lina turned to him. "Why do you call him that?"

"It's not a him, it's an it. The machine learning algorithm in the interface is just mimicking the thought patterns it processed for years. Yes, we tell people it's a massive cloud-based AI because they'd never trust us with their money if they knew it was just a glitching neural interface."

"A glitch?" Lina asked.

"Of course. A happy accident. Serendipity. A billion-dollar bug. What did you think it was? His ghost?" Mr. Bythewood laughed.

Lina did not.

"Look, I'm impressed that that you figured out that we weren't telling the whole truth about the Austin Intelligence, but I hope now you understand why."

"Do you know who created the neural interface?" Lina asked him.

"What?"

"Do you know who built this for him?"

Mr. Bythewood shrugged. "Some computer geek."

Lina smiled, suppressing her anger. "It was built for him by an accomplished engineer who devoted her life to the study of neural interfaces for people with ALS, quadriplegics, and other victims of paralysis. And that woman also happened to be his mother."

"You know, now that you mention it, I did know that. Didn't she pass away a little while ago? I think we made a very generous donation to some foundation or something," Mr. Bythewood said. He became nervous. "Did you ... know her?" he asked.

Lina didn't respond.

"Look," Mr. Bythewood said, regaining his entitled indignation, "this neural interface is the property of BA Investments."

"You're wrong, Mr. Bythewood."

"I have documentation. All personal property of Mr. Austin reverted to BA Investments upon his death."

"No," Lina told him. "You're wrong believing that it's the interface that's running the computers. Do you have any idea how the human mind works?"

He shrugged. "Not exactly. I mean, who does?"

"It comes down to electrical interactions, and all electric currents create an associated electromagnetic field, and the neurons inside our brains create sequences of pulses that we call brainwaves. It is those waves that the neural interface detects and interprets, translating them into actions on the computer. It does this by creating a symbiotic electronic field that resonates with the mind's activity."

"I know that part," Mr. Bythewood said.

"Without the presence of brainwaves, it's just a funny-looking hat. But when Mr. Austin died, this device trapped those electronic signals in place. So, even though you removed his body, the part of him that persists beyond the lifespan of his physical self remained in place."

"What do you mean, the part of him that persists? Are you talking about a soul?"

"I am."

"And you think that it's trapped in that chair."

"He is."

Mr. Bythewood crossed his arms. "Look, all of this is very entertaining, but the fact remains that this chair, this computer, and all of the financial analysis it provides is the property of BA Investments. You can invest with us or not, but you're going to have to go now."

"I see that you've added redundant power supplies to keep the interface going, but did you know that the symbiotic field can be overloaded with the presence of a second set of brainwaves?"

"What is that supposed to mean?"

"It means that if a second 'soul' were to come within sufficient proximity of the device, it would break the containment effect and release Mr. Austin from your cruel imprisonment."

"That's ridiculous."

"Is it? Leonard loved doing what he did. For him it wasn't a job; it was a challenge, seeing the patterns and discovering how to unlock their potential. You gave him an opportunity to pursue his passion, and you did make him comfortable. I am grateful for that."

"But when he died, you should have let him go. I imagine he's been so thrilled with the fact that he can work all day long without any rest that he doesn't even realize that he's dead. Did you know that, in addition to his physical challenges, he was autistic? That's part of what makes him so good at what he does."

"Look, I don't know what you think you're trying to pull, but if you damage that interface in any way, I'll—"

"You'll what? Sue me?"

"You think a ten-billion-dollar company doesn't have an entire floor of lawyers in this building?"

"Oh, I'm sure you do, but I'm afraid they won't be able to help you."

"And why is that?"

"Do you know what Leonard Austin's mother's name was?"

"Why do you keep answering my questions with more questions?"

"Her name was Angelina Austin."

Mr. Bythewood shrugged. "So what?"

"Lina, for short."

It took a moment for the revelation to hit Mr. Bythewood.

Lina took a step toward the chair.

"I'm warning you, you don't want to mess with the Intelligence," Mr. Bythewood said sternly.

She turned back toward him. Only now, instead of being a woman of thirty-something, she was older, a woman in her sixties. She reached toward the chair with an age-spotted hand.

The monitors attached to the computer flickered.

Then Mr. Bythewood gasped as he saw a figure materialize in the chair.

It was Leonard.

"Hello, my son," Lina said.

"Hi, Mom," appeared on the screen with the chat window.

Lina smiled warmly. "You don't need to use that thing to speak any more, son."

"I don't?" Leonard asked, this time with a voice that appeared to come from his mouth.

Mr. Bythewood's knees buckled, and he almost fell to the floor.

"No, you don't need any of it anymore. You're free." She held her hand out to him.

Leonard lifted his own hand from the arm rest and took hold of his mother's. He smiled, excited. "Are we going somewhere?" he asked.

"Yes, but there is one thing I'd like you to do before we go." She placed her hand to the side of his face in a motherly gesture. Something unspoken passed between them.

"Okay," Leonard said, then he looked at the array of computer monitors as a flood of information scrolled by and windows popped open and closed. "All done."

"What's done? What did he do?" Mr. Bythewood asked.

Leonard spotted Mr. Bythewood leaning against the doorway. "Hi, Mr. Bythewood. Did you meet my mom?"

Mr. Bythewood nodded.

"Stand up," Lina said to Leonard.

He reacted with surprise that such a thing was possible, then leaned forward and stood up.

"Come, Leonard. There's so much I want to show you," Lina said.

In the blink of an eye, they were gone.

The computer monitors went blank.

Mr. Bythewood took a moment to regain his balance and push back the blackness that threatened to engulf his consciousness. Leonard was gone. The Austin Intelligence was no more.

He stepped back into his own office. The check Lina had left was sitting on his desk, but when he went to reach for it, it too disappeared. An apt metaphor for the future of his company, he thought. Without the Austin Intelligence, he was nothing.

Ms. Blackstone entered and looked around, confused. "What happened to your guest?" she asked.

Mr. Bythewood sat down in the tall-backed leather chair behind the hand-carved walnut desk and sighed. "I'm afraid, Ms. Blackstone, that your services will no longer be required."

Ms. Blackstone smiled. "He's gone, isn't he?"

Mr. Bythewood was confused by her question. "Pardon me?"

"Mr. Austin. She came here to take him away. I'm glad. You're right. My services are no longer required. I no longer need to watch over him. My job here is done."

Ms. Blackstone promptly disappeared just as quickly and completely as Lina and Leonard had done moments earlier.

"What the hell," thought Mr. Bythewood. "Is everyone who works for me actually dead?" A horrifying revelation crossed his mind. He reached out with one hand and pinched the skin on the back of the other hand, digging his nails into the flesh as hard as he could. "Ow!" he exclaimed in pain.

Then, relieved, he flipped open the sleek laptop on one corner of his desk. Its operating system recognized his face and he clicked on an icon in one corner of the device's desktop that simultaneously began selling all his holdings in BA investments, transferring all of his domestic assets to an off-shore account and putting in a request to prep the company jet.

Only, that's not what happened. Instead, the funds were sent to various charities and foundations. Even his offshore accounts were emptied and deposited among several children's hospitals.

Mr. Bythewood sighed in despair. This was just the beginning, he knew. Without the Austin Intelligence—or rather, Leonard—managing their clients' portfolios, the investors would flee. There might even be lawsuits from clients and stockholders, federal probes, stories on TMZ.

A new email message appeared in his inbox.

It was from Leonard.

"Thank you for helping me build this incredible fortune, Mr. Bythewood," it read. "All of the people who will be helped by your generosity will forever grateful. It was fun working with you. See you on the other side!"

My Bythewood closed the lid of the laptop.

"Sooner than you probably think, my boy," he said.

He opened a drawer in his desk where a gleaming pistol lay, loaded and waiting for just such an occasion as this.

THE DRIVER

BY PETER TALLEY

Our city cemetery is only three blocks outside of town. It sits on a hillside that overlooks corn and bean fields for about as far the eye can see. There isn't much to see here besides a large, white-washed, stone cross that sits near the top of the hill. A few trees accompany the gravestones. There aren't as many as there used to be, though, after that tornado blew through the county a few years ago.

I've heard talk of building a new housing development to the north of the entrance, but I doubt it will be anytime soon. From what I've heard, the city isn't too keen on people trying to dodge city taxes yet still getting the benefits of city water and trash pickup. I don't know. I like the idea of our town growing. I sometimes dream about what I could do with some land of my own. I could see my family in a larger home. It would be something to pass down to future generations and keep them from moving away.

I like driving out to the cemetery on peaceful mornings such as this one. I've been doing this for years. I was given the job shortly after moving to town. Working for the local funeral home has been a great way to serve my community and make some easy cash. I have plenty of stories I could share with you. The biggest perk has undoubtedly been the privilege of driving the funeral coach. You probably call it a hearse. Don't worry about it! There was a lot of terminology I had to learn, too, after taking this job. When I first started, I didn't know the difference between a coffin and casket, and I had to learn that it was far more respectful to refer to my boss as as funeral director rather than a mortician or undertaker.

It takes a special kind of person to be successful in this field. I, however, don't do a lot with the business. I'm more of an extra set of hands when times gets busy. Everyone deserves a vacation, but that doesn't mean people will stop dying. I'm mainly called upon to help with removals or gravesite burial services like the one I'm at today. I help the pallbearers load up the casket, fold up the accordion-like truck, and take my place behind the wheel. There are times I take a passenger with me, but usually it is a solitary drive from the church to the cemetery.

I can't tell you how many services I've helped with over the years. Most of the time everything goes smoothly. I follow behind the funeral director, who is driving the clergy and immediate family. It is a slow crawl to the outskirts of town. I try to keep my eyes on the road ahead but, all too often, I find myself looking through the rearview mirror, over the casket, to make sure the procession of vehicles is keeping up.

At the burial site I'm not much needed after helping to unload the deceased. Afterward, I sit and wait, like I'm doing now. The funeral director does most of the work by lining up the pallbearers and giving them instruction on how to place the casket above the grave. Most people don't know about the vault crew. They've usually been busy on the scene during the funeral service, digging the grave and setting up a shelter and chairs for the family. It also is pretty customary for them to have the dirt that needs to be refilled into the grave out of sight. I really get a kick out of working with those guys. During the gravesite service, they are known to sit on the far side of the hill, until the last of the mourners have left to head back to the church for a luncheon or to go about their lives. Then it's my job to make sure there aren't any complications with lowering the casket, sealing the vault, and picking up the area.

I can't believe today's funeral is going to be her last. I'm going to miss this old car. The boss has decided it's time to retire her. I think she has a few more miles left in her, but I'm not in charge of these kinds of things. Apparently they've already picked out a newer model. I guess the onboard GPS and satellite radio will be a nice touch.

I've always said that I prefer a good funeral to a wedding. First off, they are more permanent. I also think they really make you think about what's important in life. The service is definitely for those left behind. I've seen joyous, sorrowful, and downright ridiculous moments while working in this profession. What gets to me is seeing the younger generations trying to understand what is happening at the time. They don't really understand why the people in the fancy clothes are so sad. Mostly they are just uncomfortable having to stand still and wait for the clergy to wrap up their prayers.

I'm used to this being a fairly routine procedure. I've loved doing this job. It definitely isn't easy knowing that today will also be my final time visiting this cemetery. In the distance I see a face I haven't seen for nearly ten years. She smiles at me from the top of the hill, where there is a bright burst of light.

The driver-side door to the funeral coach opens and I see a younger man in a suit. He stares at where I'm sitting. I recognize him as the funeral director's grandson. I know he doesn't see me, and that's okay. I slide out of the long, black funeral coach and smile at the young man. It is his turn to take the wheel.

ROOM-MATE

BY PAUL WORTHINGTON

The need to relieve himself had first reared its ugly head a couple of hours ago. It was the same routine every night. The need to pee had crept in insidiously just after a plate of microwave noodles and a protein shake. The first hour was always the easiest and could be largely ignored whilst watching the latest uncompromising police drama on the television. Checking various social media outlets was also a great way to eat up a good twenty minutes, but distractions could only keep the call of nature at bay for so long. There happened to be a drain just by the back door that would make a prime location for a spot of alfresco urination were it not for the many overlooking windows.

Ralph shifted positions on his battered old sofa, the leather squeaking and the aged wooden frame creaking with each placement of his 170-pound frame. Multiple positions were tried and tested but none could banish the ache that throbbed within his abdomen. Like a car tyre that has been hooked up to an air compressor for too long, his bladder felt as though it were about to explode. Ralph could take the pain no more; he had to relieve himself, and quickly! He had sat with his legs crossed tightly together for so long that it felt as though he had already wet himself, such was the extent of the sweating in his crotch. If he didn't go soon he'd pee his pants for real!

A glance at the wall-mounted clock that was the shape of a beer bottle revealed it to be just after 9:15 p.m., which was far too early for his usual bedtime, but Ralph's situation was far from usual. There was no way that he was going to the toilet, coming back to the sofa and then returning to the bathroom before bed … not a chance in hell!

Ralph's problem had been going on for two months and showed no sign of ever going away. To avoid frequent visits to the bathroom he had changed gyms, going from a rundown, blood-and-sweat gymnasium to a shiny, newly built example. After his training session and a cleansing shower, he would sufficiently empty his bladder and save himself two bathroom trips later that evening. Ralph did not enjoy one pre-bed trip to his own lavatory; he was never going to enter that terrible place twice in one evening. Eighteen minutes past nine or not, Ralph was going to quickly pee, wash up, and then hurriedly brush his teeth … hopefully setting a new world speed record in the process.

At that point the stalling began! The first part of the nightly routine involved turning off the television, replacing the cushions on the sofa in a symmetrical manner, and then making sure that the front door was locked as he passed to the kitchen. There he would finish the glass of that day's chosen beverage and then swill the glass with a cascade of crisp, cold water. Once the back door had been secured with the key and the ground floor lights turned off, Ralph stood at the foot of the staircase and gazed up at the dim sinister light given off by the sub-standard forty-watt bulb. The sense of foreboding had to be suppressed, beaten back with a mental stick as each step propelled him toward the first-floor bathroom!

The bedroom doors had been left wide open while the brilliant white, panelled bathroom door had been firmly closed, as had been customary lately. Ralph stood just outside the bathroom door, just as he had 24 hours ago, pausing while he plucked up the courage to enter.

In the mornings, Ralph once again resisted the urge to pee until he was safely out of harm's way and in work. Before leaving, teeth were cleaned with a backup toothbrush and paste that had been secreted down in the kitchen. Before bed, he couldn't pee anywhere else, which forced him to visit the bathroom from hell!

Nimble, factory-worker fingers wrapped reluctantly around the chipped and scratched chrome-effect handle, but it took at least five seconds before any pressure was applied. Slowly, he pushed open the creaking door, unleashing an imagined waft of cold air that enveloped him like an avalanche of snow. It must have been the knowledge of what lay within that brought on the shivers and forced out the goose bumps.

A brief fumble just inside the door frame yielded the pull cord and a short, sharp yank brought illumination to a fairly spacious bathroom. Ralph aimed squarely for the toilet as he entered but he could not physically prevent his eyes from flitting to the far corner for a split second. As usual all he could see were the plain white tiles.

Every muscle in his body that had been tense for the last few hours fell into blessed relaxation as his bladder forced out every last drop of urine. In another act of stalling for time, he flushed the toilet and stood there until the sound of the tank refilling had ceased. Once the silence returned there was nothing else for it, he had to stand at the sink in front of the mirror where his nightly ordeal would begin!

The tap squeaked as water began to gush into the sink and the low hum of the gas boiler could be heard coming from the adjacent room. Ralph concentrated his gaze firmly down at his hands as he massaged soap into them, meticulously covering every millimetre of skin up to his wrists. Only once both hands had been rinsed clear of suds and he had reached for the towel did he finally look at his own reflection. Obviously, Ralph saw himself staring back.

Ralph's eyes flitted to the far corner again—not the actual corner, but the reflection and there he was … Ralph's uninvited room-mate! A mournful-looking, bulbous-eyed old man with scraggly white hair down to his shoulders but none on the top of his head. Gaunt in the face, he stood in the corner staring straight at Ralph, his eyes and expression filled with sinister hatred! He stood statue still whilst glaring at Ralph through the reflection. His pale, gnarled hands hung limply at his sides, jutting out from the tattered cuffs of a black coat. The shirt underneath was an off-white, almost cream, and had a rounded collar, giving him the appearance of someone from the late 1800s.

Halfway through brushing his teeth, Ralph craned his neck around and checked the actual corner but no apparition could be seen; only through the mirror did the ghost appear. Ralph had never seen a spirit before but he'd always imagined that it would be ever so slightly translucent. The old man, however, was not. There were no fuzzy edges or see-through parts; the unwanted visitor appeared just as real as Ralph himself.

As usual, the creepy old man just stood completely still for the entire duration of the bathroom visit. Just a stare that could freeze a glass of water, a stare that lived with Ralph even when he wasn't in the bathroom … even when he was asleep!

The staring eyes haunted him but there was no way that he could avoid looking into them; unable to resist, he found himself hypnotically drawn to their gaze. He waited in vain for the apparition either to threaten him verbally or to lurch toward him with arms outstretched, but it just stood indignantly in place.

Breakthroughs almost always happen by some one-in-a-million turn of events, a total mistake that changes things forever.

A few pints after work one evening carried Ralph home with a renewed vigour and a swagger that had deserted him in recent weeks. A good dose of Dutch courage propelled him around the house and even into the bathroom with no thought of the voyeuristic spirit that lurked within.

It was the very next morning and under a cloud of thick hangover fog that Ralph realised that he had spent the first normal evening at home for a good few months ... and it had been pure bliss. It didn't take him long to deduce that the magic ingredient had been a few tall glasses of golden lager. A new medicine—a remedy—had been found and, boy, was Ralph willing to partake! Each evening he drank cans on the sofa or pints at the pub and then he was able to tolerate the lodger in the bathroom with ease, and he could sleep. Ralph's waistline and general health suffered a little bit but such matters were not at the forefront of his motives.

Every sports fan's dream came true one Saturday in May when the action began at 1:00 p.m. with an international rugby match that was closely followed by another. Five-thirty heralded the start of a football cup final and then, to top things off, at 8:30 a night of world championship boxing was scheduled to take place. Ralph arrived at his local pub with his friends at about noon where they stayed, enjoying the sport and downing a ludicrous amount of alcohol before passing out or wobbling home.

Horrendously worse for wear, Ralph stumbled almost blindly home at 1:30-ish. Once home, he slammed the front door as he fell back against it and then proceeded along in bumper-car fashion. A takeaway was placed on the dining table where it stayed, still in the foil containers and the plastic bag. He had intended to devour the unhealthy, but undoubtedly tasty, meal but found himself gripped by nausea, an unwanted but all too common side effect of consuming too much booze. The first pile of multi-coloured vomit landed on the living room's laminate wood floor. To avoid a repeat, he hurried unsteadily to the toilet.

Ralph knelt at the white porcelain toilet as though it were an altar and he were praying for forgiveness, although not even the almighty could stave off an early-onset hangover. He retched until his hollow, empty gut shook from the strain, indicating that he had nothing else to give. With all dignity lost, he crawled along the bathroom floor and, using the sink, he hauled himself to his feet.

There in the reflection staring back stood the other man of the house, just like he had always done. There was no fear but instead Ralph was filled with rage and the compelling need that naturally accompanies drinking alcohol to seek out or instigate a confrontation of some sort. He swore that the old man's expression had changed to a smirk and accused the spirit of enjoying seeing him suffer. The booze took over and all rational considerations left through a window like escaping steam!

Ralph shouted and screamed at the ghostly reflection, barking bile and vitriol through gritted teeth while his hands danced threateningly. The blank, neutral response that he received only added fuel to his rage until his rant reached a shuddering crescendo. With all of his might and the deepest bass tones of his voice he bellowed, "You don't belong here, old fart! This is my goddamn house!"

That ill-advised challenge insulted the apparition that clearly still considered itself to be the rightful owner of the property. The expression changed to a deep scowl and the thin lips tightened around gritted teeth that gnashed with anger.

The sudden movements shocked Ralph, who spun around in horror to see if the ghoul had become visible without the need of a mirror. … It hadn't. When Ralph returned to the mirror he let out a little "Aaaargh" because the ghost had taken a few steps forward and now stood much closer, a sinister leer on its grotesque face. Ralph spun around again, this time swinging punches and kicks as a last line of desperate defence. Unfortunately he could only swipe each blow harmlessly through thin air.

When Ralph met his reflection once more he now stood side by side with the vengeful spirit. This time he was too afraid even to scream! The eyes seemed more bulbous and bloodshot than ever, giving the ghost an unsettling, manic appearance. Ralph watched helplessly in horror as the old man turned to face him before wrapping both pale grey hands snugly around his throat and then proceeding to throttle the life out of the foolish, drunken man!

As soon as the corpse hit the tiled bathroom floor, the old man smiled contentedly before vanishing from this earthly realm once and for all. The next tenants would not be troubled by the ghost of an elderly gentleman glaring at them in the bathroom mirror … oh no! The next residents were going to have to put up with Ralph's vengeful, malevolent spirit stalking the bathroom mirrors for years to come!

NIGHT MARCHERS

BY WENDY WILSON

Kai smiled as the wheels of the jet touched the tarmac. He knew it was fundamentally impossible, but he could swear he smelled the plumeria blossoms native to his island home. It had been too long since his family had all kissed him goodbye as he left for the mainland and university.

"What are you sniffing?" asked the pretty blonde girl next to him. "My nose is all stuffed up."

"Hawaiian flower with a distinctive scent." He turned to the girl. "Can't wait for you to meet my family."

Remy smiled. "If they're anything like you, I know I will love them."

The family was all gathered at the gate, waiting for their prodigal son and the woman he had brought. Mom and Dad and his sister were there, along with a few aunties waving from the back of the group.

"Where's Apono?" Kai asked his father.

"Your brother stayed at the house, said there was enough of a crowd. You know him; he keeps to himself a lot."

"Yeah, I was just looking forward to seeing him."

Remy's face was glued to the window the whole trip to the family compound south of Kona. The absolute beauty of the ocean as it ducked in and out of view on the winding, tree-lined road made her speechless. She turned to Kai.

"I knew Hawaii was pretty but to think you grew up here! Why ever did you leave?"

"Had to find you, didn't I?" Kai joked. "No, seriously, only some colleges have the courses in ancient history I needed. Lots of history here, but to get a degree I had to go off-island."

***

When the cars made a right turn toward the ocean, they traveled another twisting path and ended up at a gated driveway where Remy could see a compound of several smaller buildings surrounding a central large house.

"Home!" called out Kai's dad and they all piled out and a round of hugs and chatter ensued, with the family that had stayed at home. Remy looked a little bit overwhelmed, so Kai took her off to the small cottage that had been his as a teenager.

"This is my place. It's set a bit off from the big house so we'll have some privacy. He opened the door to see a large, dark-haired man standing in front of them, a huge smile on his face and a bottle of beer held out for each of them.

"Welcome home, Kai!" he boomed. "Got your favorite: Big Wave."

"Apono!" Kai yelled and ran forward.

The two brothers embraced as Remy watched. Kai was slight and much shorter than his brother, who looked like a traditional Polynesian warrior, big-boned and stocky. Both had wavy black hair and dark skin and it was clear that they were brothers from the matching smiles to the same tilt to their eyes. They popped open the beer and began to talk.

***

Hours later they were still talking but now it had gone from "What's happening in your life?" to something that the falling darkness encouraged. Their voices lowered with it. Kai broached the subject first.

"So, have you seen them?"

"Yes and no. I hear them sometimes at the new moon. The drums and conches too, as well as the sound of marching." Apono shot a glance at his younger brother. "I haven't gone looking for them but I have tried to talk to Dad and the aunties about them. Dad won't say much and the aunties tell me to run inside and lay down if I hear them, and to not look at them."

Kai nodded. "That's the aunties for you. Dad used to shoo us away, remember? I did some research too. A bit more book-oriented than family tradition. There is some reality in deep myths and what we heard as kids were the processions of Hawaiian warriors."

This got Remy's attention. Her scientific-minded boyfriend saying ghosts were real? Impossible.

"You can't be serious! Ghosts don't exist and, if you heard drums and conch shells, it was the waves and wind. Simple as that." She chuckled. "Don't be going all 'native' on me now."

Neither of the brothers laughed with her.

Lights from the big house slowly flickered out and soon the only illumination was the one lamp over in the corner of the room. The dark crept in as their voices fell with the light. Suddenly Apono grabbed Kai's arm so tight he cried out.

"Shhh!" he raised his index finger to his lips, his head cocked in a listening attitude. "Shhhh, do you hear that?"

Kai closed his eyes to better concentrate.

"I hear something but I can't be sure." He looked at Remy, whose eyes had gone wide as her mouth fell open. "Remy, do you hear anything?" She shook her head, then nodded.

"Ye ... yeah. I think I hear something too. Sounds like flutes or maybe wind instruments. Can't say I hear any drums though."

"What phase is the moon in?" Kai asked.

"Almost the new moon. Dark moon is tomorrow night. That's when the Marchers march."

"Then we have to hurry," Kai said, but wouldn't look at Remy.

***

Dawn broke from over the mountain as roosters crowed their good mornings. Remy sat up and stretched. Kai caught her hand and kissed the veins on her wrist.

"Did you sleep well? We didn't scare you, did we?"

"Well, you got me wondering for a minute there!" A knock on the door revealed Kai's sister, Akamai.

"Are you two up yet? Coffee's on and breakfast is cooking. C'mon up."

***

No one mentioned anything about the Night Marchers so Remy didn't bring it up. The family talked about the island's mythology but avoided mentioning the Marchers until Remy felt like it was deliberate. Kai's dad pulled him to the side. He said he wanted to talk with Kai about traditions and they went off together.

Akamai took Remy for a walk along the property. Akamai proudly told her of the family's long history and how they were pureblood descendants of the original Polynesian settlers of the islands.

"We even have *Ali'i* or, as Europeans say, nobility in our blood. My family has lived on this piece of land for generations going back so far, none of us know how long. Our men were warriors and our women advisors."

"Wow, that's something to be proud of."

"Yes," Akamai mused. "But it also carries a responsibility."

The sun had set and the family gathered around a large bonfire to "talk story" and enjoy the mild night. Kai's dad wanted to know if Remy enjoyed her walks and swim on the beach below the house.

"Oh, yes. It was wonderful! Imagine living so close to such a beautiful black sand beach." She took Kai's hand. "I could love it here." Kai blushed and Remy didn't see the satisfied nods go round the circle. She would do nicely.

Hours later, when the fire had died down and the rest of the *ohana* had gone to bed, Kai, Apono, Remy, and Akaima sat quietly gazing into the dying embers. Remy's head began to nod and she wondered if she had overindulged in the weed that had made the rounds. They had encouraged her to partake of the *pakalolo*, saying to truly belong she had to smoke with them. Never a prude, Remy happily puffed the pipe. But now she was beginning to wonder at the effects. Her head was lolling on her shoulders and she had to concentrate on drawing in breath and pushing it out.

Then, as if far off, she heard voices. Too far away to hear what was being said, and unable to even identify the language, she tried to block them. They persisted.

"I think I need to … to go to bed."

Kai and his siblings smiled at one another.

"One last walk, Rem. We've got something you just have to see."

The three surrounded Remy and guided her through the underbrush that opened up to a path Remy knew hadn't been on the earlier tour. The voices were still there and now, added to them, was the distant throbbing of drums.

"Where are we?" She tried to turn back. The hands gripped her tighter. "Lemme GO!" She flung away from the hands and stumbled away, sweat forming on her brow despite the cool breeze. Kai wasn't telling her something important. A rushing noise began in her ears; her blood pressure was going up.

"Let her go. She's going the right way."

Remy spun around, but the three siblings blocked her path back up and she fell to the forest floor. Dizziness overtook her and the figures in front of her started to spin.

Everything went quiet around her. Distantly, almost softly, and more through her body than her ears, she could sense drums approaching. Time seemed to stand still. The pounding began to get louder. At first Remy thought it was her heart racing but she realized the beating was coming from down the path.

The trees began to shudder in a sudden wind fierce enough to rip the topmost branches off. Now Remy could hear conch shells being blown. How she knew what they were puzzled her, but she knew in the core of her being that the sound was from lips blowing the shells.

Desperately trying to focus her blurring eyes amidst the now-strong wind and piercing drums and conches, Remy once again stood up and tried to break through the bodies blocking her path. Kai laughed with an uncomfortable voice.

"Still think it's the surf and wind causing the noise? Remy? Still think of us as primitive myth-believers? Got news for you. The Night Marchers are real! And they are coming this way!"

"Then we have to run, get away!" Remy clawed at Kai's shoulder. "We can't be here when they march through! We will die!" He flung her away into Apono's strong grip.

"Not everyone dies. Some of us are safe."

"Then protect me! Please!" Why was Kai acting this way? What had gotten into him? He grabbed the arm Apono wasn't holding and pulled her forward, her flip-flops catching in the sand. "You're hurting me!" she cried.

The Marchers were close, only a short distance around a curve in the path. She could see the torches now, red and glowing as if in anger. Shadows ran before the flames, the feet of whatever approached did not touch the ground. The marchers stepped above the dirt path.

Remy slumped between Apono and Kai, all her strength drained. They held her upright. She remembered the one piece of advice if caught out while the Marchers marched: Lay down flat on the ground with your face in the dirt. But the hands holding her refused to let her go.

"Let me lay down! I might survive this!" She pleaded.

"You weren't meant to survive this, Remy," Akamai's voice was triumphant. "We will. We are of their blood. You are not. You will be taken."

Kai put a hand on her back. "In our way, we are partners with the *Huaka'po*. They march to protect, and we honor them."

"How?" Remy whispered as the Marchers drew level with the group.

"By giving them a sacrifice. It has been too long since we gave them one."

Kai pushed Remy into the line of Marchers. Remy gave one final scream of pain and then her body disintegrated. The Marchers turned angry faces to the siblings standing in front of them. From the ranks a voice called, *"Na'u',"* and the others turned away.

"Remind me again, brother, what *Na'u'* means?"

"It means 'mine,' sister." They don't take their own."

SUBMISSION

BY LAUREN STOKER

The door to the waiting room opened silently on its pneumatic hinges from the offices beyond, and a tall, lean woman of indeterminate age entered. The publishing house lobby was one of those scarily modern creations: brushed stainless steel, onyx moldings, tortured metal sculptures, and acres of gleaming black tile. You know the look—the kind of décor that shouts, "Make yourself uncomfortable."

I watched as the woman scanned our motley group dithering in red Naugahyde chairs along the perimeter. She was poured into a black leather, one-piece bodysuit. Her long, black hair cascaded down her back from a high ponytail. Carrying a clipboard, she stalked us in six-inch heels. Not bad-looking, in an Elvira sort of way. Maybe a tad heavy on cleavage and eye make-up, for an upscale office.

Peering through cat-eyed glasses, her volumized eyes checked her sheet before looking up. "Mr. Helmuter? Neil?" she added, in case there was a mob of hopefuls with that last name.

My heart pounded. As I turned in my chair, I prayed it wouldn't make a Naugahyde fart when I stood. I gave her a little finger wave, after making sure my fly was closed.

She checked my headshot: neatly-brushed brown hair, tweed jacket over grey, V-neck sweater, serious expression.

"Ah. Come this way, please." She turned expertly on her stilettos and vanished through the open inner door. I was expected to follow. I did, of course.

It closed with a wheeze like collapsing lungs.

***

I was astonished when I'd gotten the phone call about the novel I'd submitted. Mostly, I just receive form email rejections. But this group had actually called me, and not to berate me for wasting their time. The man on the phone said he'd really liked it. I was psyched.

I'd written a little horror tale that I thought wasn't half-bad, then found their site, rummaging among publishers in that genre. That in itself was an accomplishment. My internet search skills usually suck. Most of the results display everything except what I've queried. But this time my cursor seemed drawn to the site like a compass needle to north.

Their homepage showed a large, swirly, Victorian logo surrounded by appropriately creepy images on a murky background: "MS Ink." Reading their guidelines, I was elated: they seemed ideal for my book—a "good fit." And their address was in Midtown Manhattan.

So, yeah, when I got the call I felt I'd hit the big time.

The man had asked if I could come to New York to discuss the publication of my work in person. What would *you* say? Like I was going to turn that down.

"Sure," I said (Mr. Cool).

I lived only one state away, so no biggie. I could take the train from Connecticut, make a day of it. We set a date and here I was. Clean-shaven in a blue shirt, navy suit, and maroon striped tie, no less.

Cat Woman led me along a labyrinth of somber corridors and into a cavernous, wood-paneled office with an immense desk and walls lined by dark-stained bookcases filled with hardcover volumes. Each volume had a different person's picture on its spine. The more traditional décor was reassuring. It spelled permanence and success.

"Mr. Grimbold will be with you presently," she said, closing the door as she departed, leaving me in silence. Dead silence. The soundproofing rivaled that of a topnotch recording studio.

Such an old-fashioned term, "presently," like Mr. Grimbold would be popping in from another plane or another realm.

I sniffed. There was a disturbing, smoky smell I couldn't quite identify. The dude must be a heavy smoker. Didn't much smell like tobacco, though. More like somebody had burned a whole box of matches.

The room was so dimly lit I remained where I stood. What light there was filtered in through two long windows, heavily curtained in blood-red velvet and giving a restricted view over the street.

An inner door opened from the far end of the office and a man entered. As he did I heard, from another office, someone hollering—in fright or anger, I couldn't tell. Once the door had shut, all was hushed again. He walked to the desk and sat down, switching on his brass desk lamp. "Copy editors, eh?" he said with an apologetic shrug. "The man just can't stand a comma splice. Sorry to keep you."

I recognized the voice I'd heard on the phone. As my eyes adjusted to the half-light, I picked out his name on the brass name plate and the "Editor-in-Chief" after it. I'd gotten his name on the phone, but not his title.

The Man himself called me? Wow!

"Please, Mr. Helmuter," he gestured to the one chair in front of his desk. "No reason to stand on ceremony."

He was dressed in a well-tailored black business suit, white shirt, red tie. It was his hair that was more out-of-norm. Not a hairpiece; I could see the roots of his iron-grey hair springing from his scalp. But, man, what a widow's peak. Like that kid's in *The Addams Family*.

The chair he'd pointed me to was Jacobean: tall and heavy, and carved with twining vines and fantastic beings. Some of the forms looked a bit demonic and disconcertingly frolicsome. I sat, hiding my hands in my lap so he wouldn't see their trembling and doing my best to hide my smirk about the décor. Publishing only horror, it seemed a logical if comical touch to extend that theme into their furnishings.

Grimbold laid his hands flat on his desktop. The nails were unusually long, but well-manicured. "First things first," he began. "Just some formalities. The work is your own and it's original and previously unpublished, yes?"

"That's right," I nodded.

"Quite a good story. Well-crafted."

"Thanks." I swallowed, damping down a gush of gratitude.

"Did you find the online submission software easy to use?"

"Yes," I lied, "for the most part, although a few things were a bit different." I didn't want to let on how mystifying I'd found some parts of their form or divulge that I worked with cranky hardware and geriatric systems. I loathed online submissions but, hey, you gotta do what you gotta do.

"Good, good. And was this a simultaneous submission?" He saw my hesitation, as I attempted translation, and clarified. "Did you submit to any other publishers? It's all right if you did, but if you sign with us, we'd insist on your contacting the other publishers to withdraw your manuscript."

"No, no. Yours was the only publisher I submitted to." I could feel myself blushing at my grammatical gaffe, glad that copy editor couldn't hear me. "I mean, to which I submitted."

The editor nodded sympathetically. "That's fine. Well, Mr. Helmuter, we expect your novel to be ready in time for Christmas." He slid forward a contract to sign. "If you'd be so good ... Please sign here."

Okay, then! Here we go! I signed. I didn't bother to read it as I'd already read their contract from the link he'd sent me after we spoke on the phone.

"And here."

Scribble.

"And here. And please date."

Scribble, date, dot.

"Thank you." He took the contract and dropped it into a pre-labelled folder on his desk. Then he folded his hands and smiled at me.

I sat back in the chair and smiled back, waiting for what came next, mostly because I didn't have a clue. Including some short stories, this was my first thing actually sold.

"Any questions, Mr. Helmuter?"

Like about a zillion, but I didn't want to reveal I was a rookie. The terms and schedule of payments were also covered in the link he'd sent, so I shook my head.

"Excellent!" Grimbold beamed at me, then pushed the intercom on his phone. "Dominata? Could you come in here please? And bring Mr. deSade with you." He clicked off.

The same leather-wrapped woman as before came in, towing a suited Quasimodo with a bad brush cut and enormous hands.

"And now to the binding," the editor said.

Holy shit! Looked like I wouldn't have to battle months of editorial nit-picking. He was already discussing the book cover. *I rock! Might even be the next Dean Koontz.* I allowed myself to relax my shoulders one notch and rested my hands on both arms of the chair.

His two minions stepped up to either side of me and put a hand on each of the chairback's finials. As they did, the chair's carvings animated. My eyebrows shot up as the vines swarmed over my arms and bound me in place.

"What the …?!" I goggled at the carved demons beginning to frolic … up my crotch. They were putting the squeeze on me.

"Is there a problem, Mr. Helmuter? You did submit, did you not? Of your own free will?"

"Well, yeah," I whimpered, helplessly watching the furious forms envelope me. "What the hell is this? It was just a book submission."

"I'll ignore the remark about Hell, Mr. Helmuter, as it seems over-obvious. You also checked the box labeled 'MS' did you not?"

"For 'manuscript,' right? I thought that was required. You know, like if you were attaching something," I said, trying to keep the pitch of my voice below falsetto.

"Ah." He clicked his tongue and sighed, smiling openly now. His teeth were pointed. "So many make that mistake." Grimbold shook his head. "Please don't tell me you also didn't bother to check our corporate information?"

"There are always so many tabs and drop-down menus …" I babbled, struggling.

"I see." Fingers steepled, the editor sat back. "Well, our full name, as you would know if you'd checked our 'About Us' page, is 'Masochists and Sadists, Incorporated.' We're a small subsidiary of Hell, as you might have read. And if you'd scrolled to the bottom of that page, you also would have seen that by checking the 'MS' box on the submission form, you were agreeing to the additional services we perform, as well as exclusive and unlimited rights to your …" he tipped his head, "'content,' as it were."

The minions were now grinning.

"In any event," the editor continued, "you've signed and dated our contract, which is quite binding, I assure you." He paused. "Although I noticed you didn't bother to read it."

"But," I protested, "I did! The link you sent me …"

"Oh, dear. My apologies. That was our standard contract. My staff had missed your checking the 'MS' box when we sent it out. Which contract you sign makes a big difference." He twinkled at my frightened confusion.

Leaning forward over his desk, hands clasped, he cocked an ironic eyebrow at me. "Mr. Helmuter, hasn't anyone ever told you to first read the document in front of you before you sign?"

The twisting and romping vines and demons had reached my throat. As the last of my breath was squeezed out, my vision dimmed, filled with black and red pixilation. A reptilian tail forced its way down my windpipe, choking off my scream.

***

Snow was falling gently past the long, draped windows in the editor's office on The Avenue of the Americas. MS Ink's editor-in-chief stood at his window, looking out at the holiday shoppers going by beneath, burdened with bags of gifts. He always enjoyed this time of year: the good will, the joy, the bright hope to be dashed. Herr Grimbold had his own gift for the literary world this year, as he had every year for the past … Well, who's counting, really? His board of directors would be pleased.

Turning to the bookcase, he slid the new volume into its place on his shelves—another soul brought to the thrill of submission. Neil Helmuter's boyish face smiled out from the spine.

LOOSE CANNON

BY SOPHIE BAKER

Bern was so used to ordering people around that she could not believe it that these people would not listen to her.

"What do you know?" one of the women spat at her. "Nothing. You think you are so smart. What is the circumference of the earth?"

Bern, short for Bernice, said, "What the hell does that matter? Who cares?"

"If you can't answer that, how you ever going to get out of here, waiting on circling the earth? You're stuck in one place." Judy stamped her silver spangled slip-ons, making no noise at all.

"Like I said: Who cares?" Bern looked around for her cigarettes on her porch table, then remembered, *I can't smoke.* That's what she missed more than her husband or her children, taking in long drags on the porch while her husband inside inhaled air supplied by an oxygen tank through a nasal canula. She missed cigarettes more than she did complaining because—guess what?—hovering just twenty feet over her home in Mississippi, she complained all the time, with all the other angry Senate of the Dead and others.

"I knew people should wash their hands. They should have listened to me; I was the best dental hygienist in the office before I got married. All these ridiculous people. I never drove anywhere anyway. Curbside pick-up, having food delivered … big deal. I always got other people to do what I wanted—take me shopping, take me on trips. Morons."

"Who you calling a moron?" She was tripped by a sheet, a ghost who had no facial features.

"How did you do that?" Bern asked as she lost gravity, falling over flat on the red corrugated-tin roof. "How did you make me fall over?"

"You deserved it." The sheet folded long, filmy arms across her chest, sitting on a branch of the prolific pecan tree at the edge of the asphalt driveway.

"How did you make me fall over?"

"Dunno." The sheet leaned backwards, hung upside down from her knees on the tree branch. "Best thing about being dead is you don't have to worry your knickers are showing when you hang upside down."

"Worst thing?" Bern wanted to know.

"You angry ghosts, always finding fault. Complaining. Not these poor people's fault they're dying because of the virus. There's people up here, a whole contingency, whole families died from Spanish flu a century ago. You think they are blaming everyone else? They're mad cos they died too young, out of their time. You? You died when it was your time."

"No, I didn't. I wasn't ready. I had years left. I wanted to see Bernie elected. Too bad these stupid people have COVID. Maybe somebody put a hex on them. I put a hex on my husband's first wife's children, just before I got to this place. See how they like being second-best. I had to fight to get his first wife's clothes out of our bedroom when I was first married. The things I put up with. I lived through a Depression, my Dad was out of a job. These people don't know hardship. Think they are missing out, with colleges and schools closed. College doesn't make you smart; I never needed college, see how smart I am."

"It hurts my ears to listen to you." The sheet raised her arms, patted around her head. "But I can't find my ears. Where are they? Wow, even though I can't feel my eyes, either, I can sure see that. Look at those beautiful roses. Isn't it early for roses?"

"Stop breathing on them. They're mine, Red Knockout roses. I had my husband plant them, water them, mulch them. I didn't have to do a thing except order them from a catalog."

"So, what's this hex you're talking 'bout?"

"Who said anything about a hex?"

"You did."

"Yes, I did, didn't I, and I'm proud of it. I wished bad things to happen to my stepchildren. And they did. One brat's daughter got cancer, and the other's husband had a heart attack, and their children turned on them, treated them like dummies, took things out of their house when his wife wasn't there, said that hoarding gave him a heart attack. Ha, people called me a hoarder. All my beautiful silver, my beautiful paintings. There are still in the house. I can see them when I look in the window."

She refused to admit that she didn't know how to walk through walls, so she held her hands against the window glass and watched a hospice nurse adjust the bead of the oxygen level on her husband's green oxygen tank, smooth his cotton sheets.

"I can't believe I died first. I was supposed to go second."

The sheet shimmied up the pecan tree and peered at the road. There's so few people driving. This street used to be humming. Those poor people, they've lost their jobs, the stock market fell."

"You kidding? I lived through the Depression, my father lost all his money. They're just weak, pansies. You got to be tough. You think I ever cried because my father didn't have enough milk in the fridge? Hell, we didn't even have a fridge, it was an ice box with no ice in it. These people think they have it rough."

"The girl who got cancer, how she doing?"

"She got better. She recovered, completely. They all say it's a miracle. I don't believe in miracles. Not at all. You got to get other people to do your work for you, make them think it was their idea. That may look like a miracle, but, there are no miracles. The only thing that lasts is silver, silver coins, gold, and art. There's no miracles."

"I wish I had another place to hang around, instead of listening to you. If I had to haunt someplace, I wish it didn't have to be near you, but I was born in the slave house right there, next to your house. You talking about milk, I had to wet-nurse my master's babies so his missis would get her figure back. I had to leave my own children to take care of his children. I had no figure after having my babies, some of them my master's babies. You think you got something to be mad about. No use getting mad, it ruins your digestion."

"Don't tell me how to feel. I'm so glad my hex worked on my stepdaughter's children. They don't talk to her now, they hate her. Ha ha ha. Nobody's talking about miracles there. And they thought they loved her. This COVID-19's nothing like the Depression. I lived through that. It started my Daddy drinking. These people don't know what hardship is. I heard it's taking mostly people 60 and over. I got taken too, before I was ready. I'm too young to die, I'm too young to be here."

"You're 80."

"No, I've never been 80. Just shut up."

"Glad to," the sheet turned her featureless face toward the road and watched the non-existent traffic.

MALL SPIRITS

BY PETER TALLEY

Amber was already waiting for me in the mall food court. She smiled from across the long hall of empty tables. I loved how pretty she looked dressed for her shift at the anchor store. These little lunch dates were easily the highlight of my day.

"I remember when this place used to be busy," I said. "Did you see that Jorge's closed down?"

"Is that why you're late?" asked Amber. She rolled her eyes and pointed to the shuttered taco stand. "And then there were three."

"Three what?"

"Options," said Amber. "We've got Chinese, pretzels, or corn dogs. It's a good thing I'm on a diet."

I laughed and realized too late she wasn't trying to be funny.

"I'm sorry I was late."

"What took you so long? She cracked a smile and teased, "Was there a sale I missed?"

"You wouldn't believe me," I said.

"You know how short my break is! What happened?"

"Okay! Do you know Wally?"

"The old guy in the black windbreaker that uses the hallways to exercise before the stores open?"

"Yeah. He was married to Rita. They used to sit over there every morning for coffee."

"What happened? You gotta tell me!"

"I think he died," I said. "I heard one of the mall walkers talking about it."

"Oh shit," said Amber. "That's sad. He had a great sense of humor."

"What's weird is that I just saw him yesterday."

"What's weird about that? He had to be pushing 80," said Amber.

"You don't get it. I think he saw me."

"No freaking way!"

"He looked right at me! What freaked me out was when he called out my name."

"Well you are wearing a name tag," said Amber. "I'm glad I don't have to wear one of those anymore."

"Could you take this seriously? I *really* think he saw me."

"Here we go again with the death sight," said Amber. "What if he did? It's not like you killed him."

"I don't know …"

"What aren't you telling me? Holy shit, Mike! Did you make contact?"

"I told you I freaked out!"

"Did you speak with him? Did he touch you? Oh my God, this is too much!"

"I'm glad you're enjoying this."

"Hey. It's going to be okay." She took my hands into hers and reassured me with a kiss. "Maybe this is a good thing?"

"How can you always be so positive?"

"I died young."

I thought back to that day on the loading dock when I saw Amber for the first time. I hated working at the shitty electronic store, but it beat having to clean toilets. My manager, Roger, sent me to throw out boxes. I was pissed off that he'd denied my vacation request. I was taking my sweet time with the trash compactor and decided to sneak a smoke break.

"You can't smoke back here!" said the cute cosmetic girl.

I tried to act cool but I know I looked like an idiot after she made me jump. Amber bummed a cigarette and we started talking. I learned she went to the other high school in town. We both were working crappy, part-time, summer jobs. It turned out she wanted to see the same band I wanted to see that weekend. You can probably assume the rest. I skipped out on work and ran into her at the show. I got to meet her friends, including a guy named Josh.

"Earth to Mike?" asked Amber from across the table. "What's wrong?"

"You know I don't like it when we talk about ..."

"Dying?"

"Cut it out," I said. "I'm serious. You know it bugs the shit out of me."

"It's been ten years, Mike," said Amber.

"You think I forgot?"

"Why do you always get this way? It was a long time ago."

"What way? How come I can't get angry about what happened?"

"Dying?"

"Yeah! Why do you get to tell me how to feel?"

"Because you're getting angry," said Amber. "What's the point? How is arguing going to change anything? We're dead."

"I just don't get you."

"Mike?"

"Don't you give a shit about anything?"

"You know I do. That's why I'm stuck here. I love you."

The lights around us dimmed. I was brought back in time again. The food court was filled with shoppers and decorated for

Christmas. I couldn't bring myself to see what happened next. I stood up from my chair just as I heard the gunshot.

Then I was in the middle of the mall. It was nighttime and I was along. A few years ago they replaced the fountain that was built with the mall when it opened back in the late '80s. Instead, I was surrounded by the plastic animals of a children's play area.

"Where are you?" I called out. "Look, I'm sorry. Please talk to me."

I saw light from a flashlight coming toward me. I shielded my eyes and realized there was nowhere to run. I raised my hands up slowly and said, "You caught me."

"Is that you, Mike?" asked the security guard.

"Who else would it be?"

"I heard shouting," said the security guard. "I should've known it was you."

"Can you shine that light somewhere else? You know I'm cool."

"Sure, kid," he said. "What were you fighting about this time?"

I glared at the security guard longer than I should've. He didn't flinch. He never has and probably never will.

"I want a quiet shift. Is that okay with you?"

"Yes, sir," I said.

I waited for the guard to move on down the corridor and disappear around the corner to where the toy store used to be. *One of these nights I might remember to look at his badge,* I thought. *He's worked here for years. I really should learn his name.*

The walk back to my old storefront was never quiet. I heard voices coming from the movie theater near the front entrance. The late show was getting out long after the rest of the mall had closed. I shut my eyes and tried to concentrate. If I was lucky I could sometimes smell popcorn. I used to love going to the movies.

I continued my journey to the far side of the mall. I missed the mingling of smells from the candle shop and hair salons that used to be in this area. One of the two bookstores used to be right across from where I stood. In a moment, I would hear a little girl's scream from within the boutique. It used to scare me until I realized it was only from a memory of frightened child getting her ears pierced. People don't realize how many rites of passage took place in this mall.

The eastern corridor isn't much to look at these days. Every one of its 16 bays used to be occupied by a tenant. Kiosks sat in the middle of the long hallway that acted as a median for the vast amount of foot traffic that used to frequent this side of the mall. As of tonight there are two bays that haven't left us due to dwindling business.

In front of me was the anchor store where Amber worked. The two-story building is still open to the public during the day but acts as a discount store. There are rumors they, too, want to seek out greener pastures and build a stand-alone building. What's funny is that, if you know anything about the history, that was a department store way before the mall was built next to it. The owners have changed many times over the years, but they always kept the same nameplate. The family name inspired customer loyalty. I suppose it worked since the old building burned down and they decided to rebuild with the "new" mall.

I smelled smoke. It came before the sound of distant coughing. The gate to the anchor store was closed but I could see motion from within the dimly lit entrance to the women's department. We used to hear ghost stories about the employees who didn't escape the fire. Most of the things people would say turned out to be bullshit. It was more sad than terrifying when you found out the truth. Ruth's burned image would catch you by surprise if you weren't careful. She died after being trapped in a stockroom. I've heard her story. Choking to death on smoke and not being able to see would be a shitty way to go.

"Thanks for waiting," said Amber. She materialized through the gate and looked tired. "Sheila wouldn't stop talking about the new mannequins."

I've heard the same words spoken every night for ten years and it never gets old. This is Amber's memory more than mine. I let it play out because I know no other way to break the loop we are stuck in.

"What?" she asked. "Why are you looking at me like that?"

"You look good," I said. "Want to get some pizza?"

"I've worked a double shift but that's sweet. All I want to do is go home and change out of this skirt."

"You still need a ride home?"

"That would be great," said Amber.

We walked together through the crowded mall to the exit where we were allowed to park. It was the best five minutes of my life because that was the first time Amber held my hand. What I didn't know at the time was how Josh was watching us from inside the arcade. Last night he tried to talk to us. I almost let him.

I didn't like Josh. He was a strange kid. He never took the hint that Amber only liked him as a friend. I knew he was jealous of us. Sometimes at night I felt him following me through the mall. He's always dressed in the same bloody hoodie. I can't see his face all that well but I know he's pissed off.

"You're not supposed to be here," said Helen. The overly cheerful woman in the apron was cutting fudge. I was glad for the interruption. Somehow I was back at her candy store. The colorful taffy wrappers and bright lights made this one of my favorite stores.

"You're not supposed to be here," she said again before flickering away.

"Hey! What are you doing in there?" asked the security guard. "You know this area's off-limits." As the words were spoken I realized the familiar candy store no longer existed. It was dark and I was surrounded by old fixtures and a faded candy counter.

"What's going on? What happened to Helen?"

"Helen who?" asked the security guard.

"You're telling me you didn't see her?"

"I only see you."

"Look, man. I don't know how I got here."

"What is it with you kids?" asked the security guard. "You should be with your girlfriend while you can."

"Have you seen her?"

"Well she ain't here," said the security guard. "Why poke around this place? We don't have a lot of time left. Haven't you heard they're going to demolish the mall?"

"They're going to what?"

"The entire area is going to be rezoned."

"What's going to happen to us?" I asked.

"That's the gossip being spread in the mall office," said the security guard with a shrug. "I knew this job wasn't going to last forever."

"You know you're dead, right? You're one of us," said a voice from next to the former music store. The guard and I both saw the shadowy vapor as it took the familiar form of a man we feared.

"Ghosts can't hurt you, son. They make you hurt yourself," said the security guard. He words reassured me only enough to consider my options.

"Don't make me chase you, Mike," said the shadowy vapor. "You can't outrun my gun."

The security guard scrambled for his radio. It was a scene that would almost be comical in another setting. I've seen it happen over and over, and the sick joke ends when the poor guy is shot in the chest.

I decided to run. I knew it was the wrong move. I should've faced my fear.

The worst part of this nightmare is that I don't even know why. Why did this psycho select our mall? Why have I been running for ten years to a place where I'm scared to go? By the time I think the thought, I am already where I don't want to be. I see Amber. She's terrified. Josh is holding her in his arms. They both are covered in blood.

I don't remember being shot.

Shouting and the echo of multiple gunshots filled the area outside the food court. This defining moment will forever haunt the mall. Maybe it is a good thing that the building is going to be torn down?

THE OBJECT OF THINGS

BY KYLE DUMP

A gray room.

Not unnaturally gray, just gray. Predominantly gray. Mostly gray. The feeling of gray.

A plain room, but honest—spartan. It bore only a bed with a chest at its foot, and a desk with a chair. Dust. Each particle seemed frozen by the late-morning sunlight that poured through bare windows, bleaching the atmosphere and amplifying the gray.

The bed, sturdily framed in cedar, was dressed with a heavy green blanket. Another blanket, heavier and greener, was folded across its foot. The desk's whitewood top was worn by the shifting and shuffling of ink and paper over time, faded to a greenish, grayish beige. Atop it sat three pencils, a pen, a small stack of parchment papers, and an old leather-bound journal.

Outside, a boy daydreamed about a girl, putting off his work and not realizing the trouble it could get him in. It was his room, bathed in mid-morning grays, that held the bed and the table and the book. Not a book, a journal.

The difference between books, journals, and diaries is mostly a semantic one, though it does depend on design intention and utility. Nothing had been printed in this one, yet, which was a mark in favor of it being a journal or diary.

The binding's utility was further informed by the silver clasp that bound the thing closed. It was a knotted rope the width of a thumbnail. The edge curved out gently, for ease of opening.

Black, stamped letters, faded like the rest, spelled the word "Journal" in a tight line near the top-center of its cover, settling all debate and sealing its fate—almost.

It was one of those beautiful, liminal objects often overlooked in life. The ones existing in that space that is both plain and fantastic, beautiful and mundane. Something to be noticed the first, second, or third time one comes across it, but never again—fading into the pattern of things unless used over and over.

Like the whitewood desk, it was well worn. Its spine and covers showed its age. So too did the coiled silver clasp, patinaed by pockets, palms, and time, always time, to a tarnished copper color.

The young man had been surprised when he found, inside, each page was as fresh and clean as the day the book was first bound. A gem! He had picked it up for pocket change from a shop in town and, upon his return home the next day, had immediately begun pouring into it the goings-on of his day-to-day and his innermost thoughts and feelings.

The next afternoon, he returned home from working outside and went straight to his room. When he saw the pages blank again, as clean as before, he knew he had something unique. There was no trace he'd set a single word to it. *What use is it for writing if it does not hold its words?* he thought.

The journal's deceit was in its plainness, really, to obscure the tantalizing thing trapped inside like a fly in amber. Not a fly, a woman.

She had relished the new words as they washed over her when he wrote, despite feeling overwhelmed by the onslaught of another's consciousness once again. It felt fantastic to live in the young man's thoughts, like stretching after a long sit. Usually cramped within the 1-inch of space between the journal's front and back covers, she was set free by the letters laid to ink on her pages, enthralled by the chance of having a new world opened up to her through the descriptions of a new narrator.

Cursed by fate, or something long forgotten, she was the spirit of a young woman. No memory of name or place. She did not know when she'd been bound to the journal, nor why, nor how. She knew only of its confines and her longing to escape them, mixed with vague recollections of owners past, fading in and out like voices from another room.

Her memory was funny, she remembered that much, but even now her thoughts had already begun mingling with those of her master. It was always difficult being sure her mind was her own. The boundaries became fluid quickly.

He tested the book again, after supper.

This time, in place of his intimate thoughts and feelings, the man wrote a single sentence on the first page: "What is this?" The words scratched in slanted cursive. He stared at them on the page for a long time, waiting for them to jump off and run away down the leg of his desk.

The woman waited for more, perturbed at being prodded.

Nothing.

Maybe it has to be triggered by something. He opened and closed the cover a few times to see, but only found the same three words, "What is this?"

He turned to the next page and pressed it hard with his pen, digging indentations into the paper as he wrote, "Where did my words go?"

More staring. More nothing. She could never tell him that.

He flipped the page and wrote it again. Then, again. Each sentence leaving grooves 2 or 3 pages down.

The woman's spirit winced and retreated from his aggression. She was furious and terrified. *How could he want more of me? He just needs to write.*

Write.

Instead, he stared—angry and bored.

Then, after growing tired of staring, he began to doodle: a tree, a dog, a large smiling mouth full of teeth. Half-consciously, he caught himself drawing a naked man, genitals drawn like a misshapen 3 turned 90 degrees. "Make me disappear!" came the words from the angry doodleman.

"WRITE!" she screamed, defiant and enraged by the man and his picture, then vibrated with fury in her paper sepulcher. "Leave me alone and WRITE!" Ink welled up in the lines of the young man's doodles, bolding them and bleeding across the page. The book became soaked in inky black tar. It pooled on the whitewood before the man's very eyes, growing ever more.

He threw himself back, ink licking his palms.

Startled, he stumbled over his chair, but did not fall. Clumsily righting it, he caught a glimpse of his hands, inkless and clean, and shot a look across the room at the journal sitting atop the desk. Both were as clean and unmarked as the day before. The doodle, his words, the words from the other pages, even the grooves he'd made, it was all gone. Replaced by blank pages.

Incredible, he thought, trembling. The hollow taste of adrenaline stung the back of his tongue.

He did not touch the journal for five torturous days after that. The woman moaned for freedom. *I scared him off,* she thought. *I should have been brave. Will he ever return to me?*

It was the morning of that fifth day when she got her answer.

"Is this real?" He wrote after dressing for the day. Then he closed the journal and left for work, not waiting for a response. Returning later, he opened it again only after dinner.

The words remained, unmoved: Is this real?

He regarded them for a few minutes, weighing his wanting to provoke the book again with another crude drawing. He was deciding he definitely did not want to provoke it when, quite subtly … "Hello?" she said quietly, unsure. The lines appeared like a thin whisper on the page.

He was dumbstruck.

"This is real," she wrote below.

Her penmanship was much nicer than his, if it could be called penmanship. The words seemed to simply bubble up from below the surface of the page, as if each sheet of paper were a deep, undisturbed pool.

"How? Who are you?"

Light ink clouds seemed to rise and fall at the page's surface as she thought. "No memory," she replied.

He thought for a moment, then, "Where are you?" He underlined the word for emphasis.

"Trapped in a book." Then, "Cursed."

Reading "cursed" had set him stock still. Cursed.

She had said too much; she knew she had said too much. More transparent splotches rose and fell as she thought. She found herself at a loss. Surely, he would get rid of her now, send her back to wherever he'd found her, leave her alone to long endlessly for sleep so that she might dream she was free. *Brave,* she thought. *Brave.*

What could she say?

"I don't remember my name," she wrote. "I don't know where I was from or who I was. I remember bits and pieces, memories from past owners, snippets of conversation I had as a young woman. None of it remains solid for long." The words poured from her.

She took a beat, organizing her thoughts as they rushed in all at once. The man waited breathlessly, watching the watery ink splotches shrink and grow, darken and fade.

"All I know is captivity."

"Then I'll free you!" he shouted aloud. Then, after looking around sheepishly, he wrote it down.

Naïve. He was a boy, a child in a man's body, ready to jump into the unknown at the slightest peep from a perceived damsel in distress. *I'm certainly old enough to know better,* she thought. Who knew how long she'd been stuffed between her pages? A long time. Sometimes she had glimpses of her life before, milking cows with her mother, a little doll she called Darling that had fallen into disrepair as she grew up.

How strange I should remember that! she mused. *I cannot recollect my name, but I know for a fact the dolly was Darling.*

"Memories are strange," she wrote.

He laughed at the non-sequitur, inspiring his own, "Can you hear me? Can you see?"

"No." The man imagined a sigh when he read her response. "I sense when the book is open. When it's closed. Hands on my cover. I hear through your words, see through your stories."

She explained to him the terrible tightness of her leather-bound cage. How she wished she could move freely, speak, sing. She told him about the loneliness, and he listened. More precisely, he read.

They conversed in this manner into the early morning. Her thoughts and even some of her memories seemed to solidify as they went, but it was incredibly taxing. She was still not sure why, but she knew she was not meant to engage in this way.

The next afternoon, when he sat down at the desk she begged him to tell her a story so that she might relax in it a while.

"About your day, or something made up. Anything," she said.

He obliged, detailing his last daytrip to the shore. She warmed herself, lounging on soft sand in the sunshine.

Things continued in that fashion for weeks. Some nights they would stay up jotting notes to each other. Others, the man regaled the woman with tall tales he'd heard in town, told her secrets, poured himself into her—every thought and emotion—while she recovered from the fatigue of their conversations.

She was remembering more. Were they actually counteracting the curse somehow?

On nights when he simply wrote she still lost herself in his mind, but in the spaces between she was becoming more solid. She could sense more, too, the man pulling his chair out to sit at the desk, the late spring breeze from the window. She hesitated to tell him as much, rightly afraid of his enthusiasm. Naïve.

"This is how we'll break your curse!" he exclaimed, when she finally shared the new developments. He had come in early, taking his lunch at his desk after spending most of the morning daydreaming about her and putting off his work outside.

"Then what?" she replied. "I have no body. I am a ghost."

"First we free your mind. Then, we free your spirit."

"Then?"

He did not reply. He wasn't sure, either. Finally, "Do you remember anything that could help?"

"Help me not be a ghost?"

He scoffed, and she frowned from inside the journal. It was easier to see him now, somehow. She could not explain it.

"Do you remember anything that could help us free you from this book?"

Splotches. She was thinking.

If I tell him he will surely do something foolish. But ... His foolishness had already helped her regain a deeper sense of self than the sullen claustrophobia that had plagued her before. It was unnerving, but she felt hopeful.

"The clasp." The words were hardly an impression on the page. "I can feel it now, loosening from my mind."

"The curse is powered by your clasp?" He examined the tarnished silver rope, weighing it in his fingers as if trying to discern its power.

"Do not be foolish," she wrote, knowing his thoughts.

"Is it foolish to imagine freeing the woman I love?" he responded. Had she a body, the word would have taken her breath away.

Love?

"You can't love me."

"But I do!!!" his ire rose for a moment, then softened. "I love you, Darling. I thought you felt the same."

"And if I did? THEN WHAT?" Each letter was painted with heavy, bleeding lines. "We can never be together." She felt his hot tears splashing on the page, but she did not waiver. "You are a fool."

At that he slammed the book closed and cleared his desk of its contents with a single swipe. The book hit the floor with a thud and, even in his rage, he wondered if he'd hurt her.

Angrily, he swept it up and again examined the clasp. It was a knotted rope. The edge curved out gently, for ease of opening.

His gaze narrowed with intention,

She silently pleaded from her paper prison, "NO! PLEASE!"

He slid his thumb under the clasp, attempting to pry it off. She struggled, feeling the curse rising. She had to stop him. The curse was calling to her.

"STOP!" she shouted. The words manifested from thin air, startling the man. She had somehow spoken aloud, but it was too late. She felt herself disappear.

The journal fell from his hands and then rose suddenly, unaided, hovering. In its eminence, transformed. Spectacular lights leapt across the walls and ceiling like bursts of lightning etching across humid, soup-roiling skies.

She was there in an instant, visible and real, appearing from nowhere. But her appearance was horrifying, impossible for him to comprehend, resembling little more than the shape of a woman. Still, he knew it was her, or it once was. Her form was shrouded in tattered skin and dirty, knotted hair. Fingers pulled to pointed talons. Teeth sharpened to thin daggers.

The curse had made her a monster. Truly dead. Bloodless. Vicious. Her eyes were thoughtless orbs of fog in gaping, ragged holes. She did not know him now. She knew nothing. She knew oblivion. Only the curse compelled her.

She bellowed a sound of scraping and scratching, resembling scaled skin against scaled skin—a thousand snakes pouring from the specter's open, abysmal mouth. Starting at the floor, the noise filled the room like sand, brushing up the man's back as it rose to the ceiling—droning.

He screamed. Tried to scream. It stayed trapped inside. He was incapacitated, enthralled with existential dread at the scene—this pale, ragged demon. His stomach flipped inside him and he choked back the urge to vomit.

The changed woman's horrid pitch seemed to force every particle in the room to join in its vibrational frequency. Rising still, until it somehow seemed to lock in place, finally hitting a level where the environment was able to hold the sound of its own volition. The tone carried solely by thin air, which screamed horrid agitation in the demon's stead.

She cocked her head, dead eyes fixed on the man.

Her once lolling mouth made a sudden furious gesture, a violent baring of sharp, thin teeth. He was unnerved as the sound continued unnaturally, unchanged without her.

She wound herself back like a curling spring, crackling with potential energy. The man's heart thumped loudly in his ears, stretching time between the beats. The demon's spring released with the sort of violent force attributed to a funnel cloud. What followed was something bloody, something intimate—the brutal climax of an old tragedy.

For the barest of moments, they each fought like starving lions, lashing at each other, brawling, both feeling different levels of confusion, betrayal, and rage. It took only a few moments more, though, for the fight to shift into slaughter. Suddenly, she was tearing him to pieces, spraying the gray room crimson red and dark maroon.

He felt everything. Something sharp, poking through the flesh of his thigh. The dull ache of it falling deeply through muscle to bone. Agony and release, at the rending of his arm from his body at the shoulder. Burning, when she slashed and chewed at his face and neck. A sudden cold, as the contents of his abdomen spilled to the floor.

Twisted by the curse, she continued ripping and smashing long after the man had died, bloody claws clasping fistfuls of hair and scalp, needle-teeth stained red. She seemed only to stop at some unseen command that caught her mid-thrash. With it, she rose calmly, arms dropping to her sides. The room was silent. She did not regard her mess.

A sizzling sound electrified the air. The man's gore, spread everywhere—on the walls and the windows, the bed and its blanket—began tracing rivers and streams across the room to the book, like armies of ants marching to the mother of all picnics. Flesh oozed amongst blood, body parts melted, stretching and distorting along the trickling paths.

His remains made their way into the book, spiraling into its pages' depths, where they were absorbed, turning into static charges that flicked along the book's edges and around its clasp. This continued until every trace of him was gone.

With the man's last drop of blood, the mindless spirit followed, falling back into the mundane prison.

And there she sat again, trapped, cramped. And there it sat, an ordinary book, latch cast from silver, cast about the floor, its thumbnail clasp had snapped shut and was glowing just slightly as it radiated heat—errant energy lost in transfer.

The innocent spirit was none the wiser about the chaos she had wrought, the death she had made. She merely hugged her knees to her chest and went on wishing for sleep once more so she could dream about freedom, trying not to fidget.

Outside, the memory of a boy daydreaming about a girl, putting off his work and not realizing the trouble she would get him in. His room, bathed in mid-morning grays—a bed and a table all covered in red ... his memories were already fading within her own, blending into the patterns of her mind. His essence became nothing as it enriched the silver clasp, codifying itself in her bonds.

The Journal's deceit was in its plainness, a thin veil obscuring the oblivion brought by its captive—the deceit of many cursed objects, really. Each's motive unknown. Their burdens felt in secret, leaving no one to tell of them—whispers, distorted memories.

Is this real?

NIGHT SOUNDS

BY LAUREN BOLGER

Some nights
   She wakes up
from a dead sleep
    with the spins.
Her room, concave and bending.

In her stupor, her distorted
black oak dresser and bowed
cool-gray walls suggest
a threshold with no door.
Stretching open.
Wide and hungry.

She bolts upright,
Wide-eyed.
Nothing to cling to
But a mattress edge
and a feeling
of being.

She drags herself across the floor
to the hall, lest she be caught
in the open throat of earth,
and fall
          into
            Its
          belly.

On those nights, she stays up,
vacuuming
dead bugs on the porch.
Crunchy husks
from tiny lives.
Shushing the
vibration in her skull
of a cosmic hopelessness.
(The world is not enough;
The stars are not enough,
if we have to leave them)

She turns on the vacuum.
Relieved, and sighing with
Its faithful hum.
She rolls it; easily, steadily,
Rightmost wheel hugging the baseboard.
Covering the quiet.
Spreading the sound.

Back and forth
Up and down
Til the rhythm and sound
Joins her—electric—
with the night.
She's a cog spinning
with the machinations
of the dark.

When dawn cracks
her patch of black earth,
she is tired again.
Body and soul.

Now—too subdued to worry—
She yanks the plug.

She plods upstairs slowly;
two feet to a step,
But stops halfway up
When she hears a sound.

Her vacuum sound.
Upstairs, not down.
And dampened by … a door?

Or a hum.
Muffled by
would-be lips that aren't.

Something
that was brought awake
  by the world
   sleeping.
   Creeping
  up from the
  y a w n i n g
of her room.

Trying on the sound
of her nighttime maneuvers.
Reaching for her.
Combing her dead-wood floor with wrecked nails.
Longing to hear that soothing hum once again.

PIRATE RADIO

BY PETER TALLEY

My wife and I wait parked by the side of the road for the state trooper to finish his paperwork. Tension is high in our car. The reason I was speeding was to get around a slow pickup truck. I apparently was also following too closely for the weather conditions.

It didn't help that we couldn't find the packet with the proof of insurance and registration paperwork while the trooper stood in the rain. I haven't been pulled over since college, and the fact that my wife thinks this is funny isn't helping.

"I wouldn't want his job," says Helen. "Would you like having to work like that in this storm?"

"He didn't have to pull me over in it."

"Somebody had to slow you down, Mister Fasty McFurious."

"You know I could've got a warning if you hadn't buried the damn packet in the back of the glove box."

"You're right. I totally did that on purpose. I'm so glad you finally caught me."

"What do you think you're doing?" I ask.

"I'm trying to find my phone."

"Can you wait a sec? Here comes the trooper."

The next thing I know I'm being blinded by the guy's flashlight beam. He shines it over on Helen and says, "It isn't safe to be driving that fast tonight. I wrote the ticket for five over. You can pay it online or send it in to the courthouse."

"They have the internet out here?" Helen giggles quietly. We're lucky the trooper didn't hear her.

"Thank you, officer," I say, trying to cover up my wife's ridiculous joke. I take the ticket and the packet from him. I notice that my driver's license is with the rest of the paperwork.

"You should keep those more accessible," said the trooper. "It would've made things easier."

"I'll keep that in mind."

"Are you planning on getting pulled over again?" asked the state trooper with a smug smile.

"That's funny," says my wife.

"No, sir," I say, staring down at the steering wheel.

He nods at us and says, "Have a good night."

I wait for Helen to crack another joke as the trooper walks away. Thankfully she sits quietly and enjoys the snack-mix we bought at the gas station. I start up the car and prepare to pull back onto the two-lane highway. We're soon back on the road with the flashing red and blue lights of the cruiser far behind us in the rearview mirror.

"You didn't have to be such a pussy," says Helen. "He wasn't going to shoot you for speeding."

"It's the goddamn pickup's fault."

"Totally."

"I hate driving at night," I say, waiting for Helen to reply. She sits in the passenger seat looking out the window. "It's so boring. I'm just happy the rain is letting up."

"Can we listen to the radio?"

"I suppose. You know it's going to be religious and country music, right?"

198

"Public broadcasting too," she said.

"You know that doesn't count."

"I know *you* don't like it," she says teasingly.

Helen pushes a button and the car's radio goes right to one of our presets. Unfortunately that radio station is two states away and all we get is static. She dials down the volume and presses the search button. We wait as the numbers on the digital display jump forward to more unintelligible noise.

"Maybe we stick to the CDs?" I suggest. "I've got ..."

"I can't listen to another show tune," says Helen. "I'm sorry, honey, but no."

"Hey, now."

"No!"

"You like it too."

"Nooo!" She jokes while pretending to plug her ears. "I need something that doesn't suck."

A wild guitar solo catches us off guard. The jolt of adrenaline shakes away my drowsiness. As the familiar tune continues, I give thanks that we aren't completely in hillbilly country.

"I haven't heard this song in years," I say as the song comes to an end. "Hopefully we don't lose the station. I think you found us a good one."

"You're listening to Skully X, on Pirate Radio," said the announcer. Cannon blasts rattle our front speakers. I'll admit the corny sound effects make me smile. "Our lines are open. We'll be taking the ninth caller."

"Oh great. He's a comedian," says Helen.

"What do you expect? It's late-night radio."

"We'll see," says Helen. "I'm not holding my breath."

"At least it isn't easy listening."

"Is anyone out there in radio land?" asks the announcer. "We're still waiting for a winner! So if you're out sailing the seven seas, please give us a call."

"I wonder if he's a real pirate," says Helen. "Not like an eyepatch wearing swashbuckler who owns a parrot. I'm talking about a dude that hijacked the airwaves from his mom's basement."

"Well he wouldn't be giving out a phone number that could be traced."

"I'm thinking his station identification seems sketchy. We haven't heard any commercials yet."

"And thank God for that!"

On the other side of the highway is a white stretch limo. I slow down, thinking it is weird for a car like that to be out here in the middle of nowhere. Helen points at it too and says "Hey! Check it out. They have their hazard lights on."

"Fuck it," I say. "We're not stopping." She knows I hate being behind schedule. I can tell it was the wrong thing to say so I quickly try to make things better with, "I saw a sign post a mile back for a town. They'll be fine."

"Next up is a classic that is sure to shiver your timbers," says Skully X. "It's from the ..."

CLICK goes the knob to the radio controls. We sit in a brief and awkward silence until Helen says, "You don't have to be a dick. What if there are kids in that car?"

"I'm sure the driver isn't a kid. Besides everyone has roadside assistance these days."

We drive for ten minutes without talking to one another. I'm thinking about the bullshit reason we are even on this road trip. I can't believe I actually agreed to visit her sister in the new care facility. I'm using up all of my paid time off to vacation at a village for the mentally ill.

"What are you thinking about?" asks Helen.

"Nothing, babe."

"You have that look on your face," she says. "What's up?"

"It's too dark. You can't see my face."

There's no way I'm going to admit how pissed off I am about being on this trip. She knows. We've already argued about it. I love Helen's family, but her sister Linda has always been a sore subject. She ruins holidays by forgetting to take her medication and is always trying to make Helen feel guilty. When I heard Linda got approved to move I was happy for her. I'm not a total asshole. I just know she's going to fuck it up. These kinds of places have waiting lists and it's only a matter of time before my sister-in-law gets kicked out. It's happened four times since our wedding.

"We might need to get a hotel room for the night," says Helen. "I don't want to screw up Linda's schedule. I'm sure she has to work tomorrow."

"What? You're serious?"

"About the hotel?"

"No. I'm talking about us driving all the way here and she can't take the day off? What the fuck are we supposed to do all day?"

Helen shifts uncomfortably in the passenger seat and says, "You know working is part of her living arrangement. If she gets off her routine ..."

"I know."

"Jesus."

"I'm just saying it's really shitty that we have to go all this way to sit on our asses. I don't want to be a jerk but it's selfish. I just wish she could be more responsible."

"That's what she's doing!"

"Bullshit."

"Do you really want to fight about this now?" asks Helen. "I mean, *really*?"

"Look, babe. I'm sorry." I want to say more but I'm distracted by a new light on the dashboard. "Ah, shit. We're running low on gas."

"There's a station coming up. It's in one of those towns you say all look the same. You know, the ones that all start with the letter W."

"It's closed by now."

"We should have enough to coast into town," says Helen optimistically.

"I'd rather try to find a place and not risk it. We'd be lucky if the fumes would even get us close. I don't want to have to walk in the dark."

"It's good everyone has roadside assistance these days," she mocks.

I turn the radio back on and instantly recognize the classic rock power ballad. I turn it up and begin to sing. Helen sighs, reclines the passenger seat, and closes her eyes. I'm about halfway into the second refrain when I realize there's a cow standing in the middle of the highway.

"Hang on!" I shout. The car crosses the center line and I hit the brakes. We skid to a hard stop on the other side of the cow.

"What the hell?" cries out Helen.

"There was a fucking cow in the road!"

She looks over her shoulder and asks, "Where?"

"In the the middle of the goddamn road! Right back there."

"I don't see it," says Helen. She squints while looking through our car's back window and asks, "Are you sure? I don't see anything.

"It's black."

"Don't be racist."

"Wait, what? I can't believe you're trying to be funny. It's dark out and probably blending in."

"What the hell are you talking about? I am funny," says Helen with a laugh. "You're the cow racist."

"I know what I saw!"

"A camouflaged ghost cow?"

"Oh come on," I say. "We're lucky. If we hit that bitch dead on we would've been ..."

"Be swank when you walk the plank! We're going into another long set of classic favorites right here on Pirate Radio."

"Turn that off," I say.

"But first, we have a winner. Hello! You'rrre on the air with Skully X."

"Can you hear me?" asks Helen from within the radio.

"Is this your first time calling?" asks the announcer. "You're our ninth caller. That makes you tonight's winner!"

"Can you hear me?"

"It sounds like we have a bad connection," says Skully X. "Stay on the line. We want to make sure our listeners can hear you."

"I'm trying to reach my husband. He's on the road tonight. We've recently been separated. I want him to know how much I miss him. If you're out there listening tonight, honey. I love you."

"There you have it, landlubbers," says Skully X. "We heeere at Pirate Radio want to thank you for tuning in. Stay safe, keep rocking your boat, and watch out for sharks!"

Static crackles from the speakers. I drive the remainder of the way listening for Helen's voice. The passenger seat never felt so empty. It turns out I did have enough gasoline to make it to Linda's new place. Wiping tears from my eyes, I pull into the visitor parking lot. I decide to sleep in the car. It gives me one more night with Helen. I cradle her urn in my arms and pray that she's forgiven me for driving too fast.

OBSERVERS

BY MARSHALL J. MOORE

"You're not afraid of me?"

She surveyed me wearily through hooded eyes, the unlit cigarette dangling from one corner of her mouth.

"Sorry," she shook her head, giving me an apologetic smile. "I'm not."

"But I'm a ghost." I waved my hand in front of her face, knowing she could see right through my translucent fingers.

"I can see that."

"Then why aren't you afraid?"

She shrugged. "Look at where we are."

I did. A cross hung suspended above the sliding glass doors to the building, flickering neon red. The glass doors were emblazoned with the Rod of Asclepius: a snake curling around a staff. I could no longer feel or smell, but I knew that the air inside those doors must be cold, with an unpleasantly antiseptic sting.

I swallowed. A purely reflexive action, as I had no digestive system. "I see your point."

We stood outside, near one of those upright green plastic ashtrays that had replaced the more solid ones I'd known in life. Or at least, she stood. I floated six inches above the ground.

"Seems like a losing proposition," the girl shrugged. "Haunting a hospital."

I stared at her. She didn't look old enough to have purchased the pack of cigarettes in her hand, or to have that tired, jaded look in her eyes. Her red hair fell just below her jawline in a tangled mop.

"We don't really get to pick and choose," I told her. "If I'd known this was going to be my beat for all eternity, I might have tried to die someplace else."

"Tough luck," she said. I nodded.

We were silent for a moment, the girl and the ghost. A wind gusted through the hospital parking lot, shaking the leaves. It must have been cold, because she shivered and pulled her Army surplus jacket tighter around her.

"You mind if I smoke?" she asked.

"Why would I?"

"Right," she said with a hollow laugh. "Guess not. I'd offer you one, but ..."

"Yeah," I nodded. I reached out and tried to pluck a cigarette from the pack, but my hand passed through it. That earned me another tired smile.

She fumbled a lighter from her jacket and flicked it into life. The dull yellow flame wavered and flickered in the wind. She cupped her hand to shield it, and it drew shadows across the drawn lines of her face. She looked too young to look so haggard.

The cigarette's tip was an orange ember in the night. She closed her eyes and inhaled deeply, then made her mouth an "O" as she exhaled a trail of smoke.

"How does it taste?" I asked, unable to help myself.

The girl looked contemplatively at the cigarette she held carelessly between two fingers. "Like cancer, I guess."

"Nasty way to go," I said without thinking. "Slow."

The orange glow reflected in her eyes was suddenly a flame. "I know that."

She turned, hugging the jacket against her narrow shoulders. I felt a sinking feeling in my stomach—again, a purely psychosomatic sensation. No digestive tract, remember?

"I'm sorry," I said.

"Whatever."

"I didn't mean—"

"It's fine," she said, her tone conveying that it was anything but. "Don't you have, I don't know, a maternity ward or something to haunt?"

"Pointless," I said, floating around to see her face. "New mothers are too exhausted to be scared of anything."

That earned me a smile, though she quickly tried to hide it with a scowl.

"Besides," I said, looking through my feet at the ground below them. "It's been a long time since I've had anyone to talk to."

"What, jumping out and shouting 'Boo!' doesn't count?"

"Not really." That was how this whole conversation had started. Instead of even being startled, she had just stared at me, nonplussed.

"It must get lonely."

I looked up. A small frown dragged at the corners of her mouth.

"Yeah," I admitted. "It does."

"No other specters of the unquiet dead to pass the time with?" She tapped the cigarette, spilling ashes onto concrete. "Talk about who's been sleeping in who else's graveyard, swap stories about how you died, that kind of thing?"

"No," I said. "We're … kind of territorial, I guess. Ghosts."

"Why's that?" She sounded genuinely curious.

"It's … hard to explain."

"Try me."

I looked back at the sliding glass doors of the hospital. "We stay here—on this side of things—because of people. Not places, not things. People we knew, back before."

"Okay." She didn't need me to specify what I meant by "before."

"But the thing about ..." My voice caught in my throat. What was wrong with me today? "... about people, is that they, uh ..."

"They leave," she finished, following my gaze back to the ugly concrete building behind us.

"Yeah," I nodded. "And when they do, they don't stick around for the Casper routine. Only the poor saps who go first make that mistake."

"Like you."

"Like me," I nodded. "So instead we get stuck haunting the places where they left. Marooned, like pirates."

She stared at the hospital. "You lost someone here."

"I did."

She sat down on the curb, kicking her skinny legs out onto the blacktop. Unnecessary as it was, I sat beside her, my posterior a few inches off the curb.

"Does it hurt?" she asked quietly, not looking at me.

"Does what?"

"Being dead."

I shrugged. "Not really. It's ... boring, mostly."

She snorted and took a drag of her cigarette. "You get to fly and walk through walls, right? That's the powers of at least two X-Men just there."

"I also can't eat or drink," I said. "Couldn't taste anything even if I could. Or smell, or touch. All I can really do is ... watch. Just a passive observer while the world spins 'round. Not even anyone to talk to. Except for on very, very rare occasions like this one."

"Why is that?" she asked, looking sidelong at me. "Why can I see and talk to you?"

"You're a sensitive. Like ... a psychic, I guess, only more credible." I gave her a shrewd glance. "I'm not the first spooky thing you've seen, am I?"

Her mouth quirked up in a wry smile. "Nope."

"Heh. I guess we all have our secrets."

"Guess so." She pulled the cigarette from her mouth and studied it intently. By now it was little more than a nub, the tip glowing faintly in the night. "So, the ones who don't become ... like you. What happens to them?"

"Honestly?" I looked up at the night sky. Stars twinkled faintly in the blackness. I wondered how long it had been since I had last looked at those tiny pinpricks of light. "Your guess is as good as mine."

"That's comforting," she said, not bothering to hide the bitterness in her voice.

I looked down at my hands, and through them. I was so used to seeing them as a vaporous, misty white that I had nearly forgotten what color my skin had been in real life. Several shades darker than this, I knew. Definitely darker than the pale girl sitting next to me on the curb.

"I'm sorry," I said, and meant it. "If it's any consolation ... I don't think they suffer. I think they're in a place that's past all that. If they're in a place at all."

"Yeah." She turned, looking over her shoulder at the bright fluorescent lights streaming out through the hospital windows. "That's the one big downside to being alive, you know. The suffering."

"I remember." Images flickered through my mind; faces whose names I could only barely recall. Memories, cloudy and half-formed.

How long, I wondered, until they dissipated completely? How long until I forgot not just who they had been, but who I had been? Already the passage of days and months was confused. How many years would it take for me to devolve into a sheet, roaming the earth with no sense of identity, just an endless hunger and loneliness?

"Sometimes I think that's all life is," she said. The cigarette dropped from her fingers to the blacktop. "Suffering, I mean. You're born, you suffer, you die. End of story. Except for people like you, apparently."

"You don't know that," I said softly.

"No?" She stood, grinding the cigarette out savagely beneath her heel. "Easy for you to say. You're past all of it."

"Exactly," I said, drifting after her as she started toward the hospital. "I'm past suffering. Past joy, too. And sorrow. And love."

She stopped, her shoulders tensing.

"I can't tell the people I love that I love them anymore," I said quietly. "I watched them go, you know. Friends, family. Some of them ..."

I cleared my throat. Stupid ghostly form, suddenly thinking it was a living body after all this time.

"Some of them, I'd fought with. Never had the chance to ... to tell them I was sorry. Or to say goodbye."

I drifted around, until I was in her line of vision again. "You still have time. To make mistakes, and amends. Don't waste it."

She looked at me for a long time, her eyes red and hollow.

"Go," I said, my voice no more than the memory of a whisper. "Say you're sorry. Say 'I love you.' While you still can."

The girl wiped at her eyes with the heel of her hand. Then she nodded, more to herself than to me.

"Thank you," she said softly. She reached out and placed her hand gently over mine, careful not to slip and let her fingers fall through my ephemeral form.

For a moment, I could almost feel her hand on mine.

MORE TO LIFE

BY ALEX BLANK

The air was solid. It grounded, confined trees, kept people upright. Everything looked different, filtered by silence. Isabel walked around the empty park, letting trees sip on her eyelids and fog her direction. She didn't know where she was going, but she dimly recognized her surroundings.

The air had a color. She hadn't realized that before, but it wasn't translucent anymore. Its gray shade was clashing with the outlines of the trees and her own silhouette. She watched herself, as if from a distance, taking one step after another, like a puppet whose moves were orchestrated from the ground upward. Since she died, all the puppeteers were six feet under.

The strings were ones of memory, and each move forward gave her a clearer understanding of where she was and how she wasn't supposed to be there. The town was so small, all of life could not spread out over its premises, all of its happenings had only cramped spaces to work with. She, herself, felt like a cramped space for most of her life.

As she went through the exit and into the street, the texture of the air had shifted and punched her in the senses. She went from tasting the fruit of the soil to inhaling every single breath of the asphalt—the gravel, sand, all of its leftovers.

The street looked the same, if it weren't for the color. When she closed her right eye, she was able to see everyone: mothers with their children, dogs with their leashes, friend groups with third wheels. After closing her left eye, she was left with nothing but their footsteps. She tried to keep both eyes open, to see both realms at once, but she kept blinking, and that blurred the lines of every fence, every smile, every trash can.

It was a town like any other, with no attachments to its name. She could not even remember its name. But she did remember her.

Jane was standing at the corner of the sidewalk, as if waiting for crossroads to choose from. She'd always used to play with last resorts, but now she seemed to be too static for even a single breath.

Isabel covered her right eye. Jane was there. Then she covered her left eye, and the tall figure, with long string-like hair, was still in sight.

Jane wasn't alone, Isabel could sense that. She'd almost gotten thrown off track by the scent of chocolate mixed with vomit as she was getting closer and closer.

Isabel walked toward her, but she felt herself stopping every once in a while, as if someone kept hitting pause on a movie she was in. The pauses accentuated the edges of the figure she was moving toward, her blonde hair contrasting with the solid outline of her body.

Jane had no shadow. The sun was shining, and it was black, but she wasn't tied to any shadowed mimesis, anything to mirror the trace of her.

Isabel remembered the last time she saw her. It was at the supermarket. The latter was running frantically in between aisles, with a shopping cart in front of her. It was filled with junk food. Neither of them had any clue that what Isabel had seen was the deadly stash that would later kill her.

A wallet hollowed. A stomach ripped apart.

As Isabel approached her, she noticed a pool of blood at Jane's feet. It almost looked like red-colored chocolate. Her senses, although dulled, were able to hear a slight sucking sound.

"Jane?" said Isabel. Her voice sounded like water, word-waves clashing against one another. "Is that you?"

Isabel heard, rather than saw, the figure turning around. Chalk fiddling upon the board. It was soothing, somehow.

And then she noticed what was at her feet. A man. Middle-aged; dead.

She remembered him. He used to work at the local grocery store. He was the only one who sold alcohol to the underaged. Although old enough himself, he should have been the one cut off. And now he was.

"Bella?" Jane did not seem surprised; her face was as lifeless as it had always been. She looked as if she didn't notice the man lying at her feet.

"Jane, what is this?" Isabel wanted to tremble, but she was too contracted to do so.

Jane finally looked at the man. "Oh, that. I just—relieved his misery."

"But you're dead," Isabel forced some life into her voice. "How can you even do this? You died. I went to your funeral. I—"

"Yes, and now you have died also, as it appears. Welcome to the club." She moved the man's head with her shoe, as if it were a football, and started walking down the street.

"Did you kill that guy?" asked Isabel.

"I mean, technically, he overdosed slightly. I have simply disabled him from letting it happen again."

"Through, what, killing him?"

"That's what I do now."

"What do you mean, now?"

"Well, there must be a reason why I'm here. I was bulimic, right? I guess that meant I gave a bit of my life while I was still living. So now that I'm here, I had to give a little bit of death, and, apparently, I gave up the setting. And now I'm stuck here."

"I don't understand. So, do others move on?"

"I'm assuming they do. I mean, you don't see that guy," she looked back, at the slowly fading bloodied outline, "walking around, do you? If everyone I killed had come here, I would have been more than dead by now."

"Why do you do this?"

"It's kind of a funny story, really. I was addicted to food, before. And it did not change, only now I'm addicted to ... a different type of food."

Isabel waited for the shock, for chills down her spine. She wanted to feel disgusted or terrified, but the realization poured over her like a discolored Sunday-slump rain.

"Look, this is really not a big deal," said Jane. "I only kill addicts. I know what that feels like; I know the hell one has to go through to survive the day. No one should keep on living like this."

"Then why do you still do it?"

"What do I have to do with it?"

"Everything. You kill addicts because you've convinced yourself they don't—or shouldn't—want to live. But you're really doing it to fuel your own addiction. If it's such a terrible thing to go through, why don't you stop?"

"You know it's not that easy."

"Nothing's easy. But this is not fair."

Jane stopped, as they approached a gothic revival building. It had reflected a light shade of green once, but to Isabel it seemed washed out of colors.

214

"So, tell me, Bella," said Jane, sitting on the porch stairs, "how do you think you died? Why are you still here?"

"Why have we stopped here?"

"You know why. No one's inside now, they're all at the funeral."

"It's today?"

"It doesn't matter. If it hadn't happened today, it would have happened in a year, or five, or ten."

"What are you saying?"

"How long have you been taking those pain pills?"

"I don't know what you're talking about." Isabel remembered how she used to race her brother to the house. Whoever gets here last is dead, he used to say. She was certainly there now.

"Don't give me this crap. It takes one to know one."

"You killed me, didn't you?" muttered Isabel. She wanted to feel something, but the ground held her too closely.

"You overdosed," said Jane. "You could have been dead either way."

"But I could have lived?"

"What kind of life would it have been? Sneaking around, lying, stealing money from everyone you love just to get that one last hit?"

"You're telling me you're feeling better now?"

"I'm not feeling any different. When alive, I was alone. I hated everyone who stood between me and food. And now— I'm also alone, I just don't have to pretend that I'm not. And there is no one standing between me and food."

"So, that's all there is after life? More life?"

"I guess." Jane sounded bored.

"Maybe it doesn't have to be this way? Maybe if you stopped, if you got clean, you would be able to move on and leave this place?"

"Maybe. But I can't be bothered."

"You can't be bothered to truly live?"

"No. I can't be bothered to truly die." Jane stood up and faced Isabel. "Don't you get it? I can't do, or feel, anything to the fullest. I can't even keep food down. I hate feeling full, I always have. I'm stuck in the in-between. I made my peace with that."

"What about me? What am I doing here?"

"Okay, listen, can we stop? I don't know what you're doing here; this wasn't my plan. If anything, you're an inconvenience to me. You have to figure it out on your own. I won't help you."

"You won't help me? You killed me, and now you won't help me?"

"I can't bring you back to life. And the dead are on their own."

Isabel watched Jane walk away. Her footsteps disappeared into the ground, leaving no trace.

She was not like her. Addict or not, Isabel was not like her. She would never steal, or kill, for a drug. She didn't think she would, at least.

She'd been taking those pills for a few weeks. Her grandpa had just died, and she snatched them from his house while no one was looking. But that was different. She did not steal them.

It was going to be temporary. The colors had been too bright, the people too loud, the headaches too straining. She wanted life to turn lighter. But now, in between the uninviting houses, the see-through trees, the expired air—the lightness turned out to be nothing but a blur. She couldn't touch anything, and she didn't want to. The entire world looked like it was waiting for permission to dissolve, yet she was still there, so it couldn't.

She walked up the stairs, and opened the door. It wasn't locked. The house smelled like life. She held it at the tip of her tongue, but she couldn't remember the taste anymore.

She went up the stairs and into her room. It was tidier than before. The books were stacked on shelves, the bed was made. Everything was in its rightful place. It seemed as though she did herself a favor through leaving; the self that would be remembered, the self whose picture was now situated in front of a coffin, the self who had a space of her own. The public self. Not the disintegration she would have eventually become.

Maybe Jane was right, that what she'd been doing was only the start of something. Maybe, in a matter of months, it would have been a room of a stranger, with pills stacked in between shelves and under the bed. No books, no trinkets—she'd have sold them all. She would have become a ghost to the room and to the world.

She lay down on the bed and felt the future. She felt the bed collapsing under her, and the monotone beige of the ceiling drawing circles over itself.

The air was stale and made her float. She couldn't absorb any edge or fabric. From the top of her head to the tip of her toes, she was expanding into the air and shrinking into the sheets.

Was that what dying felt like?

MRS. WAHL

BY PETER TALLEY

It was early evening in the Midwestern town of Cedarton, Nebraska. The downtown business district was winding down its day. Schools let out a few hours ago and families rushed to figure out supper plans before sports practices dominated the rest of their time.

Two boys hid behind an air conditioner unit. They waited nervously for the funeral director to stop talking on his cell phone and climb into the driver side of the hearse. The long, black vehicle pulled away from the brick church, turned a left at the street corner, and returned to the funeral home, which wasn't too far away.

"We got to go now," said the older of the two boys.

The younger boy lingered behind as his brother climbed the steps of the church. He shook his head from side to side and waited to move until his brother noticed he wasn't following along. The look in his brother's eyes told him that it was time to hustle.

"Come on, Lucas. We don't want to be caught," said Brandon from the top step. He tried the handle of the red door and smiled. "See. It's unlocked!"

This is wrong, thought the younger brother. *I don't want to see a dead body.*

"Hurry up!"

Lucas bolted up the steps and joined his brother inside the entryway of the unfamiliar church. The inside smelled different to the boy. It was an older building than where his family attended Mass.

"Do you see it?" asked Lucas.

"Not yet," said Brandon. "Are you scared?"

Yes, thought Lucas. "This is a stupid idea."

Brandon cautiously stepped forward and into the sanctuary. He motioned for Lucas to follow once he confirmed they were alone inside the main part of the church. The older brother led the way down the side aisle.

Where's the coffin? This really is different, thought Brandon. *Grandma said the Lutherans did things wrong.* He looked at the rows of flowers, memorial statues, and photographs. *Oh now I get it. ...*

"I think I heard something," whispered Lucas.

"It's just us," said Brandon. "Us and Mrs. Wahl."

The ceramic urn was of a dark red color with black vines that spread out over the vase-shaped container. It was positioned in the middle of a table at the base of the steps that led to the chancel. Around the urn were numerous picture frames which held the image of the boys' former next door neighbor.

"She's in there?" asked Lucas. "How'd they get her to fit?"

"They cremated her, stupid." Brandon picked up a picture frame and showed it to his younger brother. "Wow. That's us! Do you remember when we played in her yard?"

"Kinda?" shrugged Lucas. "She had really good lemonade."

"Mrs. Wahl had the best lemonade," said Brandon, lost in a memory. "She used to babysit us during summer vacation. We'd play outside all day and watch cartoons in her living room. I really liked playing with her dog. Do you remember the time she set up her lawn sprinkler for us?"

"Not really," said Lucas. "Why did we have to stop going over there?"

"Dad said it was to save money," said Brandon. "I don't know, though. I remember Grandma telling Mom that people at church weren't happy."

"Is that why we started going to Grandma's house instead?"

"Probably," said Brandon. "Mom didn't want Grandma to be angry."

"Ethel is a bitter old busybody," said a woman's voice. It came from behind the children, from somewhere up above.

"I told you I heard something!" shouted Lucas. Upon turning around he saw what appeared to be a soft pink light in the balcony. He tried to act brave as the light hovered its way to the stairs of the bell tower which was directly above the doorway the boys used to enter the church.

"Did you boys come to say goodbye?" asked the light as it slowly descended the stairwell. "I'm happy you're here. I don't want you to be afraid."

"I'm not sc-scared," stuttered Brandon.

"Is it her?" whispered Lucas. "Is it Mrs. Wahl?"

The pink light moved from the bottom step and slid across the back of the church. The warm glow worked its way up the center aisle. As it grew closer to the boys, it shifted and twisted into the form of a finely dressed elderly woman in pearls and a hat.

"Mrs. Wahl?" asked Brandon.

"Hello, boys," said their old neighbor. "I'm surprised you went to all of this trouble to visit me. Would you kindly put the photograph back on the table? People have worked hard to give me a nice send-off."

Brandon replaced the picture frame and said, "We're sorry."

"What for, dear?"

"He means we're sorry for bothering you," blurted Lucas. "Please don't be mad!"

The ghost laughed. "Why in heaven would I be mad?" asked Mrs. Wahl. "I'm very pleased you came to visit one last time."

"Mom said you died."

"Shut up, Lucas," said Brandon. "This isn't real! Ghosts don't exist."

"Be respectful," said Mrs. Wahl. "You're in my church. I sat there every Sunday morning with my family," she said towards a wooden pew. "I took my first communion right where your brother is standing."

A cold shiver went up Brandon's spine when Lucas asked, "Why are you here and not in heaven?"

Mrs. Wahl smiled at the younger boy and stepped closer to the urn. She peered out of the corner of her eye at Lucas and said, "I would like for you tell your grandmother something. Would you do that for me?"

"Yes ma'am," said Lucas.

"Tell Ethel I'm sorry," said Mrs. Wahl. "She won't believe you. It's still important that I tried."

"Why?" asked Brandon. "What did you do?"

"I wanted to be her friend," said Mrs. Wahl. "I tried for many years to make things right. We had so much in common. I'll even admit she was the better baker. We shouldn't have let the community come between us." A brighter glow surrounded the ghost as she turned to the boys and said, "Promise that you'll try to be better than us. It doesn't matter what school or church you go to. Promise that you'll try to be kinder."

Lucas took hold of his older brother's hand. He felt his fear melt away as Mrs. Wahl smiled at the flowers and photographs. She moved about the front of the church within the warm pink light. Upon finishing her tour, she turned to them a final time and dissipated into thin air.

THE FUNERAL

J. TONZELLI

When I was fourteen, my grandmother passed away. She wasn't a very nice person, to be honest, and none of us kids liked her, but she was my father's mom, and he was sad when she died, so we pretended we were sad, too. But we weren't.

Whenever my grandmother came to visit us, she would say the meanest things. She would call my brother fat, my sister dumb, and me she called ugly. She never said anything mean when my parents were around, and even though we were kids at the time, we knew better than to tell our parents the awful things she said. We knew they would never believe us. Luckily, our grandmother only visited a few times a year on holidays, so we never had to really see her.

On the day of her funeral, people gathered around her coffin on the church altar.

"She was a fine person," someone said to my dad and shook his hand. They were sorry for his loss, they said. A lot of people said that on that day.

"Thank you," my dad said and he looked pretty sad.

"I'm glad she's dead," I said to my sister that day. "She was terrible." We were sitting in the back pew reading our grandmother's mass card. Her picture was on the front, and even though she was smiling, the hardness in her eyes gave me chills.

"That's not nice," my brother said. "That's not nice to say about anyone who has died, even if you didn't like them."

"I don't care," I said. "She was mean to us our whole lives. Now she can't be mean anymore."

The funeral eventually ended and everyone began filing out. I waited for the coffin to be rolled out so everyone could follow it to the cemetery, but when it wasn't, I asked my mom why not. She said it was because my grandmother was being cremated, so instead the funeral home would take the body away to do what needed to be done.

The church had emptied out and we were all in the lobby, and I turned and looked back at my grandmother's coffin. I could see the bump of her folded wrists, which sat on her withered chest, and that her skin was sickly white, even from where I stood. Looking at her body, I remembered all the times she was mean to us, and I smirked, but I tried my best to hide it.

I turned back to my mom and said, "Can I go say goodbye one last time?"

"Of course, sweetie," my mom said, and she adjusted the flower pinned to the lapel of my suit jacket. "That's very nice of you."

I walked back into the church as my family all talked amongst each other in the lobby. I strode up to my grandmother's coffin and looked inside. Her face was wrinkled and strange looking—as if it had been re-formed with candle wax. Her dry lips were pursed and closed.

I leaned over to her and whispered, "I'm glad you're dead. You were terrible."

I fell back and knocked my elbow pretty hard on a pew, and I was too terrified to even scream, because her eyes had popped open, and they were frosty and blue, like a foggy street after a warm rain. Her hand curled around the side of her coffin and grasped its rail, using it to pull her dead body into a sitting position. Her head turned robotically, the bones in her neck creaking like dry firewood, and she saw me through her cloudy eyes. She grinned, and the wires sewing her lips closed ripped through her skin.

"No!" I screamed and I turned to run. I heard her climb out of the coffin, and I think it was right when her feet touched the ground when the lights inside the church went off. The only light in the whole place came from the altar's two candles situated on either side of her coffin.

I sprinted down the middle aisle, and in the darkness I could see only the shape of her, lit from behind as she came after me, her burial dress swishing against her legs. I could see loose strands of her hair above her head, and hear her bones cracking as her dead brain forced her dead legs to walk. There was ragged breathing in the dark, and to this day I don't know if that was her breathing or my own.

I made it to the lobby doors, but they were closed. I wrenched helplessly on them and found they were locked. I screamed in terror and beat on the doors, but no one came. I looked through the small windows and saw that the lobby was empty. Everyone had left me.

"No!" I screamed through the window. "Someone help me!"

A hand gripped my shoulder from behind—so hard I thought my bones would shatter. She turned me around and forced me to face her. Her grinning face was inches away from mine, and when she hissed, the smells of the embalming chemicals inside her leaked down my throat and burned my lungs.

"Get off me!" I screamed again and tore away from her grip. I stumbled in the darkness and fell backwards into a pew. I covered my face with my arms and begged to be left alone.

I felt hands grabbing at me again, forcing my arms away from my face, and I fought them as best as I could, but the hands were too powerful. They grabbed my face now, smooth and warm. I opened my eyes and saw my father. He looked very concerned, but there was also a glimmer of a faint, even sympathetic smile. The church's lights were on, and the lobby was filled with members of my large family once again, some of them looking in at me with concern in their eyes. I was crying very hard.

"I know, buddy," he said to me. "I know you're sad she's gone, but don't worry. She will always be with you."

I grabbed onto him and held him tightly, and he held me back as we sat together in the pew. I looked over his shoulder and back to my grandmother's coffin, where she was laying again. Even from where we sat, huddled together in that pew, I saw plain as day that she was smiling.

And the flower from my suit jacket was clenched in her hand.

HIGH-END EXORCISM

BY KYLEE GEE

Exorcising demons had proven to be a lucrative business. My goal had long been to become the best of the best—an ouster—the kind they whispered about over pints of a well-deserved ale. I had never imagined the words "high-end" tagged onto the title. I had been thrown into the exorcism business at a young age, after my dad was possessed by a particularly nasty demon. He didn't make it. As my father's primary caretaker, when the coroner called his death a poisoning, my life in the realm of normal was over. Ambrose, the man who tried to save him, broke me out of jail, faked my death, and taught me everything I knew. He wouldn't be too proud of my present predicament.

"Malorie is supposed to go to Yale like her father," Mrs. Fuller shrieked as I ran into the living room to escape one of the demon's final, desperate ploys for survival. Projectile vomiting, like the sulfur-ridden infant it was. "Young" was the prominent descriptor of this being. I could have done away with it days ago, but then Mrs. Fuller would have left that extra zero off my check.

The wealthy and their children were plastered with sin, an easy target for the most basic of demon spawn. The Fullers were no exception to this. They weren't the most deserving of help, but I enjoyed a medium rare filet mignon and a glass of aged cabernet sauvignon at the end a long week.

"Ma'am, your daughter will be a Fighting Pilgrim in no time once I have the tools I need," I said.

"Handsome Dan," Mrs. Fuller cried.

"Daya," I said, clarifying my name. "And I'm a woman."

It was a clarification I had to make too many times after the demon formerly known as Adramelech burned the hair off my scalp. It didn't help that my metabolism and figure resembled that of a fourteen-year-old boy.

Mrs. Fuller held back her tears long enough to sign the check.

"I'll be back in the morning," I told her, leaving before she could desperately claw at my arms.

"That was harsh," my apprentice, Cooper, breathed out as he followed at my heels.

"Do you think the cost of higher education will go up or down by the time Serena graduates high school?" I asked as I unlocked my Model S Tesla—black. I was nothing if not an environmentalist. My fortune relied on the natural as much as the supernatural.

"She's three," Cooper said, swinging his lengthy arm up to place a chagrinned palm on his temple. "I haven't thought about it."

"Up," I said. "It will go up."

Cooper pressed his lips together in distaste, but he nodded and hopped in the passenger seat.

"We got another call from York," Cooper said as I sped off. "It's getting worse."

I sighed at the prospects of another job when the new sun was only a few hours away from me. "Can you handle it alone?" I asked.

Cooper shook his head, eyes sullen at the idea of sleeping while a good woman suffered.

Lorraine Brooks was arrested in 1995 for riding in a car with her then-boyfriend Luki Holmes, a notorious drug dealer in the state. There were eight kilos of cocaine in his trunk. At seventeen Lorraine was a fan of self-proclaimed bad boys, but she had no clue riding in a car with one would get her forty-five years in prison. That was just the first injustice she would face. A jury of her peers didn't recognize her mental illness. Putting her in prison was a catalyst, landing her in solitary confinement multiple times during her stay in the correctional facility of York.

"Can you get us in tonight?" I asked.

"Serious?" he asked, a sudden jolt of energy hitting his bones. "Yes, of course."

Cooper had an in with Warden Daniels, a superstitious man who had been labeled by many in the local media as "One Flew Fred." Freddy Daniels was many things, but he recognized a possession when he saw one. He thought putting Lorraine in solitary would protect his other inmates. He may have been right, but those tight four walls had only nourished the demon inside Lorraine. She lay supine on her thin mattress when I walked in. The demon inside her didn't bother paying me any attention.

It was too late. It was obvious in each painfully noticeable breath she took in that concrete cell. Her eyes fogged over like my father's had. Her bones bent in an impossible way as I began my fishing incantations. I bit my knuckles. A week ago, maybe there would have been hope. A week ago, when Cooper begged me to consider her case. A week ago, when Mr. Fuller offered me the signing bonus to put a stop to his daughter's benign possession before the tabloids got a hold of another story of Malorie's indiscretions.

I stepped out of Lorraine's cell to get a breath away from the gritty stench of rotting flesh.

"What's the prognosis, Doc?" Cooper asked, adding humor to his tone in order to hide his anxiety.

"Gather the ingredients for a containment exorcism and a blessing of the grounds," I said.

"Containment?" Cooper asked.

"The best I can do is protect the other inmates and the employees," I said clinically. "Maybe I can save Lorraine's soul, but her body is irreversibly broken."

Cooper's eyes narrowed as he struggled for words. "That's not good enough," he finally said.

I shook my head.

"Take my pay from the Fuller case," he said. "I don't need it."

"It won't change anything," I said.

"You wasted a week to get an extra ten grand," Cooper said.

"This is a tier one demon," I said and, even though I wasn't positive, I added: "A week ago I would have told you the same thing."

"There has to be something," Cooper said.

"You never knew your mother," I stated, pulling my own meaning from his desperation.

"She's not mine," Cooper said with bite in his tone at the idea that he could only care for someone with his DNA. "But she's someone's."

"I'm sorry," I said. I really was. Cooper was decent. We needed good ousters. Unfortunately, decency was an easy thing to lose in our line of work.

"Let me have it," Cooper said, even though an hour ago he told me he couldn't handle it.

I nodded. Maybe I hoped I was wrong, maybe I thought failing would teach him a tough lesson. "We bless the grounds first," I said. "Seal off the cell."

Cooper nodded fervently as I took a step back to assist his first leading exorcism. The first, unfortunately, was almost always a fail. We left the prison safe. We left with Lorraine in a body bag. A blanket of exhaustion covered Cooper as we got back in my Tesla five hours later and drove off.

"Breakfast?" I asked, pulling into the truck stop restaurant beside our hotel as the sun reached the top of the sky. It was far from five-star, but occasionally I liked to rough it. It reminded me of the early days with Ambrose—not a penny to my name— not even a Social Security number.

"Shouldn't you go collect from the Fullers?" Cooper asked.

I shrugged.

"Not even pancakes can fix this mess," he said, body sighing, but he got out of my car and I followed.

"They'll plug the leak for a moment," I said. "And the Fullers will probably tag on another zero if I leave them with that low-grade demon for another day."

Cooper shook his head and remained silent as we grabbed a seat. The place was empty; the saggy-eyed waitress only took seconds to get to us.

"Coffee, gentlemen?" she asked stifling a yawn.

I pulled my hood off and stared at her luscious brown locks until it startled some sense into her.

"I'm so sorry, ma'am," she said.

"Coffee would be great," I said. "Irish, if you've got it."

"I don't think—"

"Grant a lady her dying wish?" I asked.

"Uh," the girl's panicked eyes darted around the room until she remembered that she was alone. "Okay."

"And a couple stacks of pancakes," I added, handing the menus back to the girl and waving her away.

"Can you believe that?" I asked, looking back to Cooper.

"I hope I'm never like you," he said, putting his head down on the table.

"Me too," I said.

SALT

BY MARK THOMAS

Ralph wanted to punish the Coulter Street "camp" for vandalizing his car. The case-worker had carefully parked his new Hyundai in a small gravel lot on Yates Street, then descended the metal staircase to a labyrinthian series of shelters under the bridge. It was early December and Ralph was obliged to distribute blankets, socks, clean needles, and cans of liquid protein to a mangled group of people who would rather freeze in the shadows than crawl up the embankment to a registered shelter.

And how was he repaid?

While Ralph was occupied with Crazy Maisie and The Spaceman, some idiot had taken a crow bar and violently scratched the body panels around the lower half of his vehicle. Enough force had been used to crimp the bottom edges of the doors; dozens of shallower abrasions had removed ragged strips of paint and bits of trim.

Ralph longed to demonstrate the connection between bad behavior and well-deserved punishment by tossing every item from their next care package into the black currents of the Springe River. Unfortunately, his supervisor insisted on professional restraint. In fact, Ralph was ordered to go scuttling back to the camp and conduct an emergency harm-reduction survey. He was worried about the steadily declining population. Unbelievable.

Ralph parked his rental vehicle on the platform, secretly hoping this car would be damaged as well. Eventually, his supervisor would have to wake up and smell the futility. Ralph carefully descended the slippery staircase.

Any form of census was ridiculous. You couldn't keep track of the transient population in the "camp." People didn't stay in the dripping, gray garbage-warren long enough to make any sort of accounting meaningful. They showed up, briefly fought to possess the prime strips of mud and concrete, then moved on. Ralph had been faking data for years.

He picked his way around a pile of broken cement slabs, which sprouted twisted rebar spikes like monstrous hairs, and felt the darkness of the bridge before physically encountering its shadow-wall. Ralph paused for a moment and listened to the familiar, resonant hum of traffic, high above. There was a mound of splintered box wood on the hillside, the remains of someone's castle after a violent psychotic battle. Some newspapers fluttered and blew against a wall constructed from upturned wire shopping carts.

He was just thinking that the camp was strangely quiet when he heard someone speak.

"I know." Pause. "What happened to your car?"

Ralph heard the raspy voice but couldn't immediately tell where it originated. He spun around and saw a skinny man with a neatly combed grey beard emerge from a crevice. The caseworker vaguely recognized him. "Sketch?" he said, trying to dredge up the appropriate juvenile nickname.

"No." Pause. "Sketch isn't ... here anymore." Longer pause. "He disappeared." The speech pattern was a familiar tic among residents of the "camp." Their stumbling speech was like a shopping buggy being pushed through frozen mud ruts. It must have been a very specific form of brain damage, although it would be impossible to trace its origins to a specific species of chemical or physical abuse. Ralph wanted to reach into the man's throat and pull the stumbling words out, syllable by syllable. "My name ... is James." Long fingers reached into a jacket pocket and withdrew a touch-screen phone. It was a lot nicer than the Blackberry Ralph had been issued, but he temporarily suppressed his resentment.

"Do you actually have video of someone damaging my car?" The case worker asked.

"Would you ..." the man was nodding "... like to see it?"

"Certainly." Ralph scrambled a little further up the embankment and huddled beside him. James moved his thumb over the screen a few times and it glowed greenish-grey, revealing the dark underside of the Coulter Street Bridge. Ralph could make out the upper portion of an enormous central pier and the network of supports branching from it. A soft voice was pleading, "No ... no ... no," through the speaker, then abruptly disappeared.

"But my car was parked on that little platform near the stairs," Ralph said pointing over his shoulder.

"I know." James sniffed noisily. "Wait," he said.

At first, the image on the screen was static. It might have been a photograph except for the soft pulse of headlights traversing the bridge. Suddenly, a dark mass detached itself from an irregular web of shadows and moved laterally atop a thick conduit until it was midway between the central support column and the bank. Then the shape dropped toward the water like a gigantic spider. Some ambient light illuminated a thick, translucent band connecting the shape to the bridge. The thing paused for a moment, neatly framed within the western arch, then resumed its descent and entered the fast-moving, frigid water with a soft splash.

The band was briefly visible, fluttering and twisting like a piece of tape, then vanished altogether. "Watch," James commanded. Ralph hunched over the tiny screen and saw a ridge of water move toward the near bank. A clump of bare sumac trees shivered as something slithered onto the land.

Tattered clumps of scrub brush vibrated, tracking the thing's movement, but it was too low to the ground to be seen. James gripped Ralph's arm and said, "It's coming." The caseworker looked intently at the screen and saw a creature emerge from a pile of construction debris to scrabble across a bare patch of gravel. For ten or fifteen seconds its form was clearly visible.

"Jesus!" Ralph said. The thing had the general appearance of a large, dark lizard, but its hind limbs were enormously long, like those of a grasshopper. For an instant, those appendages extended high over the creature's head but, mostly, they were pulled tight to its side, pumping like pistons to propel it forward. A blunt, eyeless head swung heavily from side to side and Ralph thought he saw the glint of rodent-like teeth. James' cell phone camera tracked the creature as it disappeared behind the scree of the parking platform. After a few quiet seconds, Ralph saw the roof of his ex-car rock violently in time to shockingly loud gnawing and licking sounds.

"I think," James speculated calmly, "it likes the road salt." Ralph's Hyundai gave a final shudder then the screen abruptly darkened.

Ralph was stunned. The video must have been an elaborate online hoax, a mash-up of stored computer-generated fragments. But to what purpose? "Did someone send you this little movie?" Ralph asked, tentatively.

"No!" James said. "In a manner of speaking, I created it myself."

"What do you mean?" Ralph felt a spasm of panic. Despite the cold, he was sweating profusely.

"I pointed the camera," James raised his arm, "at the underside of the bridge. And ... and ... I formed the monster with my mind!" James smiled and his speech suddenly lost its hesitancy. Words flitted from his mouth like bats. "Anger and resentment crawled out of my pores and formed a cloud that swirled like black mist in the air above me. And that cloud became a shadow, then a ghost that crept through the scrub land and fed and fed. And ultimately that ghost became a living thing, a being that watches over me." There was a definite undercurrent of pride in the bizarre assertion.

Ralph had listened to scores of psychotic delusions over the years; it was an unavoidable part of the job. Of course, none of those previous diatribes had come with video corroboration. Ralph dried his hands on his pants. "But why did you damage my car?"

"I don't control the monster!" James was shocked by the accusation. "Nobody controls what they create." The man's jaw suddenly clamped shut and he stepped backwards gracefully to be absorbed by an intricate pattern of shadows. The case worker watched him disappear. He didn't hear the dry crackling of brush at the river's edge.

While Ralph was watching the glowing cell phone images, the creature had once again descended from the bridge's entrails. Its clear connective membrane was still quivering within the western arch, but the thing itself had crawled out of the black water of the Springe River. It crouched with its blind head lifted up, nostril slits sensing the nearby presence of salt.

AIMLESS

BY CHISTO HEALY

Danni was standing on the side of the road with her thumb out and her bags at her feet. She had come a long way, but she had reached that no-man's-land part of America and she didn't want to traverse it on foot. She had been picked up by two people since she left the cult she had called home. She was born and raised there and her parents were fruit loops just like the rest. If it hadn't been for the internet, she might have been just like them.

She saw, though, that the rest of the world was normal. They listened to music and played games and slept with people their own age. It was just the narcissist and his flock that allowed him to control them. She tolerated a lot for her parents' sake but when she turned eighteen and it became her turn to share that creep's bed, that's where Danni drew the line. It wasn't just immoral. It was gross.

The only destination she had was "out of their reach," and she wasn't sure how far it actually extended, so she knew she had to go far. She wanted to be away from them and to stay away from them for as long as she lived. Sorry, Mom and Dad.

The first lady that picked her up was running from something herself. It seemed like she may have killed her husband. Danni wasn't sure she wanted to know. She stayed with the woman for a day until the guilt that was causing her paranoia became too much. There is no distance far enough to outrun your own conscience, so Danni bid her farewell in Arizona.

After that, she walked for a while until she met a truck driver named Mark. Truck drivers get a bad rep. He was a perfect gentleman. He just wasn't going that far. When he reached the end of the line in Texas, she was back on foot. She walked, lugging the increasingly heavy bags, for four days.

Now the road stretched on for eternity and there was nothing in any direction. She had started this trip in Idaho. If she had to guess, this was probably Mississippi. There were fields everywhere. It was beautiful, but she was also pretty sure it would be easy to die out here. There had been two vehicles so far on this dirt road she had taken off the highway hours ago, and both of them had passed by her without a glance. She didn't want to lift her dress and show leg like they did in the movies. She felt like that was dangerous because it sent out the wrong signals. She was getting far away from an old guy that wanted up her dress. She didn't want to invite another.

She continued down the dirt road until she simply couldn't go anymore. She wished she had been allowed to get a phone, or a job. She was wildly unprepared for a journey like this, and she told herself that she should be proud of herself for making it this far. On the bright side, she was pretty sure that Jeremiah's followers couldn't find her here. She didn't even know where here was. She hadn't seen any signs in a long time.

It was dark and she was sleeping in the grass beside the road, using her bag for a pillow, when she heard an engine. She sat up and smiled at how beautiful the stars were out here. You could see the sky so clearly when there wasn't technology around to ruin it. Home was like that, but home wasn't home anymore. When she looked at the road, there was a car stopped right by her. The engine purred as it idled.

Danni got to her feet and brushed herself off. She already had a certain amount of respect for the driver. The car was definitely old, maybe from the sixties or seventies, and it looked brand new. It was obviously well taken care of. Part of her wondered what they were doing on a dirt road in the middle of nowhere, late at night, but who was she to judge? She had a story of her own.

She gathered her bags and started toward the car. The passenger door opened as she neared. She lifted the seat and threw her bags in the back and then climbed in and shut the door. When the car started moving, she turned for her first look at who was kind enough to pick her up. She almost said, "Wow," out loud, but she bit it back. The driver was a man in his mid-twenties and he looked as much a throwback as his car. He had gelled hair styled perfectly and a v-neck sweater over a button-down shirt.

"My name is Danni," she said. "This is a nice ride. Thanks for picking me up."

"Peter," was all he said back. He kept his eyes on the road.

"You don't have any water, do you?" she asked as she turned back in her seat to dig through her bag. She was pretty sure she had drank the last of her supply but she was so thirsty; she had to at least check.

"No," Peter said.

"Dang," she said, returning to her seat. "I haven't had anything to drink in probably 12 hours, Pete. Can I call you Pete? I'm parched."

Peter just drove.

"Where are you headed?" she asked.

"Nowhere."

"I get that," she said with a huff. "Me too. I just wanted to get away from something but I didn't really have anywhere that I wanted to get to, you know? I'm kind of just wandering aimlessly at this point."

"Yes." Peter turned to look at her and smile. "Aimless," he said. "Just going, unaware of where you are headed."

"Exactly. So where did your journey start? I came from crazy rural Idaho."

"I don't know," Peter said. He turned to face forward again. "I've been going so long, I can't even remember where I began."

"Wow," she did say out loud this time. "Sounds like a long trip. I hope my journey ends before that."

"What if the end of your journey means the end of you?" he asked her. His tone was curious rather than threatening, but the connotation still frightened her enough. She wasn't sure she wanted to know what he meant by the question. Instead of answering, she asked a question of her own. "Do you like music? Maybe we could turn on the radio. Would that be okay?"

He didn't look at her but he did reach forward and turn a knob. Immediately, upbeat surf rock started playing. It went perfectly with the car and the sweater, Danni found herself thinking. They rode without conversation for a while, the only sounds the wind and the music. Then they came upon a gas station, and before Danni could even speak, drove right past it. She looked out the window longingly. "Oh my god, can we go back?"

"No."

"I'm just so thirsty. You can leave me there if you need to. Please, Pete."

"The thirst will stop eventually. Don't worry."

Danni pulled herself away from the window and turned slowly to look at him. "I think I would like to get out now."

"No."

Danni raised her brow. "No?"

Peter shot a quick glance her direction. "I can't stop. I'm not ready."

Danni shook her head. "Just idle like you did before. I'll just jump out and grab my stuff."

Peter's fingers drummed nervously on the wheel. "I shouldn't have done that," he said. "I was just lonely."

Danni frowned. She was starting to believe that she had made a terrible mistake by getting into this car. "I'm sorry you were lonely, and I appreciate you getting me out of nowhere and into somewhere, but I really just want to be on my own again, Pete."

"I don't," he said. "I've been on my own way too long."

"How about you stop at the gas station and I get some water and then we can talk about it?"

"I can't," Peter said, shaking his head. "I idled for a moment to let you in, but I tested fate. If I stop the ride then I go wherever I'm going next, and I'm not ready to find out where that is. I'm sorry."

Danni wondered if he was part of something like the cult she had worked so hard to leave behind. "I don't understand what you're saying."

Peter's fingers continued to drum on the wheel. "You were running from something but didn't know where you were going. Just like me. You have nowhere to go, just somewhere to escape. Me too. We can just keep going, together."

Danni swallowed the lump growing in her throat. "Forever? Without stopping?"

Peter didn't look at her. He kept his eyes on the road. "After the accident, my car was whole again. I was whole again.

242

It was because I wasn't ready. As long as I kept driving, I would stay here in this world. I didn't need to find out if I was going up or down, as long as I kept on driving. You can stay with me. You have nowhere to be. After a while you won't be thirsty anymore. You'll be like me. It'll be okay."

Danny couldn't even process what he was saying. It was impossible. She just needed to get out. The car, the look, the music; it couldn't be. It just couldn't. "I'm not just going to sit here next to you until I die, Peter. I'm not ready to die. Please just let me out."

Peter looked over at her and smiled. "See. You're not ready. You're just like me. We need to stick together."

"I don't want to," she said.

The car picked up speed. She tried to pull the lock up so she could open the door and jump free, but it wouldn't budge. "Please."

He didn't respond. He just went faster. Would he ever need gas or would this car just go forever? There was nothing around but the road and grass on either side. There was nothing even to crash into, but she tried to grab the wheel. Her seat belt got suddenly tight and constricting, pinning her to her seat. "Peter, please. Just let me go."

"Go where?" he said, eyes on the road. "You have nowhere to go. You said so yourself." Danni screamed then. She screamed with everything she had, and there was no one around to hear it.

BE QUIET

BY DANI BISSONNETTE

The house rose out of the tall grass with its gaping bay windows and weathered red brick. Mrs. Crawley had lived there alone ever since her husband died in the Great War. So far as the townsfolk knew, she didn't have any kin. As the grass grew up, Mrs. Crawley receded behind her faded curtains until the mail piled up on her doorstep. The neighbors called the police.

They found her blabbering at the bottom of the staircase, wielding a kitchen knife, stabbing at nothing. "Be quiet!" she yelled, "Be quiet!" her vacant, rheumy eyes stared at a water stain on the ceiling. She was still blabbering when they placed her in the convalescent home and never stopped until the day she died.

The house stood vacant for many years, boarded up, and the children of the town told tales about it and what drove the old woman mad.

On Halloween night, two boys from the town, Jimmy and Kyle, jumped the gate and hurried through the grass to the old house. Kyle carried a hammer.

"My dad says the old woman was rich," Kyle whispered as he pried up the rusted nails.

"The bank would have taken that," said Jimmy.

"Not if they couldn't find it," said Kyle. "Dad says she hid it in the house."

Jimmy pried back the boards as Kyle pulled the nails. Before long, they were in the house. The dust floated through the darkness beyond the front door. Jimmy pulled out a flashlight. "Where do you think she hid it?" he said.

Kyle scratched his head, flicking away cobwebs. "Let's start upstairs."

Jimmy swallowed hard, "What if there are rats?"

Kyle raised the hammer with a sinister grin.

The two of them searched the first floor, door by door, until they found one off the kitchen with worn wooden steps leading up.

"Smells like old socks and mildew," said Jimmy as he followed Kyle.

Two thumps shuddered the floorboards above their heads.

"What was that?" Jimmy stopped. "Sounded like pounding."

"Ain't nobody been up here since the bank boarded up the house," said Kyle as he continued up the stairs.

Jimmy lagged behind as they climbed the stairs to the landing. His flashlight beam sawed back and forth through the dust and the darkness, "Kyle? Kyle, where'd you go?" he called.

Thump. Thump. Jimmy looked up. A dark water stain on the ceiling hung above his head.

"In here!" Kyle hollered, as his head peaked out from a doorway.

"Kyle, I think we should leave," Jimmy said.

"Why? You scared?" Kyle mocked.

"I heard something—I know I did."

"Probably just me, you big sissy. This was the old bat's bedroom, I reckon. Come on and help me look."

Kyle pried at the floorboards with his hammer. The nails squealed as he pulled them out one by one. Jimmy shined his flashlight into the holes, one after another.

"I found something!" Kyle called after the fifth board they pulled up. He threw it across the room at Jimmy's feet.

Jimmy shrieked and backed up as the mummified rat landed on his shoes. "That's not funny, Kyle!"

"You're a big sissy, you know that?" Kyle said. "I should have brought your sister—she ain't scared of dead rats."

Jimmy made a face.

Kyle pried up the last board ... nothing. "Why don't you check the next room?" he asked as he started knocking on the walls.

Jimmy turned for the door and hesitated.

"If you're too damn chicken, you can go home," Kyle said. "I ain't afraid of nothing in this house."

Jimmy muttered something under his breath and walked into the hall. The water stain ... had it gotten bigger? He cast his flashlight beam over the spot. No, couldn't have. Must be the shadows playing tricks on him. Jimmy entered the only other room on the landing. It was a small bedroom, the windows long-since boarded up, and the paper peeling from the walls. On the far wall, toward the back of the house, a small door stood, probably a closet. Jimmy tried the handle. The door was locked.

He walked along the floorboards, strafing his flashlight beam back and forth, until he stepped on one that bent. There were no nails in one end. He pried the board aside. Beneath the old, dry wood, in the little hole, sat an old key. Jimmy reached in and grabbed it.

Thump-thump. Thump-thump. Thump-thump. Thump-thump. It sounded like it was coming from above him. No. No. It had to be Kyle tapping the walls in the next room, looking for treasure.

Jimmy walked over to the little door and tried the key in the lock. It fit. He turned the handle and the door opened. A narrow set of stairs climbed up into the dark. Jimmy swallowed hard. It wasn't a closet after all.

He called across the landing, "Hey, Kyle."

Kyle hollered back. "What is it?"

"I found something," Jimmy said.

Kyle's sneakers swept across the old timbers like cat's paws. Kyle looked up the stairs and smiled. "Maybe she hid her money up here. You think?"

Jimmy shrugged. "I found the key under the floorboards."

"She didn't want someone going up there," Kyle said, rubbing his hands together. "Let's have a look."

Jimmy shook his head, "I heard something up there; I know I did."

"Bwak. Bwak. Bwak," clucked Kyle as he danced around flapping his arms.

Jimmy's face reddened. "Fine, but if there's some old hobo up there with a knife, you can't say I didn't warn you."

Kyle pulled out the hammer and shouted up the stairs, "Any hobos up there, beware! I'm coming up and I'm armed, and my friend is too." He grabbed Jimmy by the collar and hauled him up the stairs.

***

The tiny attic was barely big enough for the two boys to stand up in side by side. Old newspaper insulation and rat dung littered the floorboards and it stank, musty and sour with dust and old rat urine and something else that set Jimmy's teeth on edge. At the back of the attic stood a brick chimney and there was no furniture or paintings anywhere in sight; the bank had removed everything.

"There's nothing here, Kyle. Let's go home."

"Come on, we haven't even looked," said Kyle, starting along the wall.

Jimmy just stood in the center, the boards creaking beneath his feet.

Kyle's flashlight blinked out.

"Kyle?" Jimmy called, casting his beam over the wall where Kyle had been. "Where'd you go?"

He was gone.

Jimmy cast his shaking flashlight beam over the attic ... nothing. "Kyle, quit playing around. This isn't funny!"

Thump. Thump. Thump. Thump.

Jimmy froze. It sounded like it was right behind him.

A hand reached from the darkness and grasped his shoulder.

Jimmy shrieked, elbowing whatever it was in the gut, and ran down the stairs. He tripped on the third to last step and tumbled through the open door, which banged against the wall. His flashlight clattered from his fingers and rolled against the far wall, but in the darkness at the top of the stairs, a figure bent double and wavered in a darker patch of black. Jimmy kicked that door shut so hard the wood nearly splintered. Something metallic pinged and clattered across the floor. Jimmy grabbed his flashlight and ran out of the house.

***

Kyle stood at the top of the attic stairs, gasping for breath. Maybe he'd pushed Jimmy too hard, but the kid was afraid of his own shadow. Kyle sat down and reached for his flashlight. It was gone. He must have dropped it when Jimmy elbowed him. He'd get him back. Kyle felt his way down the stairs hand over hand. He came to the last step and felt for the doorknob. He turned it. The door was locked.

"Jimmy!" Kyle called. "Jimmy, it was a joke. I'm sorry, I was a jerk. Please let me out."

Jimmy did not reply

Kyle tried the door again. No use. He started slamming his shoulder into the wood: Thump. Thump. Thump. Thump.

"Jimmy! Jimmy please!" he begged. "Let me out! I didn't mean it!"

***

Jimmy told his mother what happened the following morning. The police were called and they entered the house, searching for Kyle. The key to the attic door was wedged in the floorboards not three inches in front of the attic door, but when they searched the attic, there was no immediate sign of Kyle. The police searched the rest of the house from top to bottom, but found no trace of Kyle.

In the attic, however, the old chimney had a few bricks loose; it looked like they'd been struck with a hammer. The police pulled them away. Behind the bricks crouched Kyle, covered in ashes and dust, gripping his hammer with bloody fingers. At his feet, a pile of old silver dollars, strings of pearls, and tarnished gold rings lay scattered about. Propped in a corner beside him lay a mummified body in a WWI ARMY uniform.

Jimmy made a statement at the police station.

"Are you going to arrest him?" Jimmy's mother asked.

"No," Officer Selkirk said, looking down at the boy's red-rimmed eyes. "I think he learned his lesson."

"What about Kyle?" Jimmy's mother asked.

"Best leave that up to the doctors, ma'am," said Officer Selkirk.

***

After Jimmy and his mother left, Officer Selkirk placed his report on the captain's desk.

"We got an ID on the body they found in the chimney?" the captain asked.

Selkirk shook his head. "Dentals won't come back for a few days yet, but we're pretty sure it's Mr. Crawley."

The captain leaned back in his chair and whistled through his teeth. "Old Boy's been in that attic some eighty years if it is him."

Selkirk nodded.

"My kids used to go trick-or-treating at her house," said the captain, shaking his head. "All this time she's had a corpse stashed in her house."

Selkirk sighed and flipped through the pages of the file to a picture of the desiccated corpse. "It boggles the mind, doesn't it?"

The captain stared down at his desk for a moment, and then looked at Selkirk. "You and the boys head back over to that house; I want you to dig up the basement. She had a brother, who never came back from the war either."

THE UNLIKELY CRYPT ROBBER

BY BETH STILLMAN BLAHA

"You've never seen a ghost before, have you?"

Maisie blinked at the figure hovering at the edge of the family crypt looming in the moonlight. She couldn't move. It was like one of those dreams where your legs are filled with sand instead of flesh. She shone her flashlight on the crypt's broken door, sitting slightly ajar.

"What's the matter, Maisie?" a girl called out, yards behind her, where she stood safely on the other side of the cemetery gates. "Are you scared?" Giggles from the other girls floated on the cold night air. Maisie exhaled a breath, watching its transparent curl against the night. Transparent as the figure before her. The ancient chain looped around the rusting iron gates far behind her rattled, the naked edges of her ears raw in the December cold.

"Don't listen to them. They're only trying to make a fool of you."

"I-I know that," Maisie said. At least her throat hadn't turned to sand, too.

"No, you don't." The figure's mouth was definitely not moving, but the words came to Maisie's mind. "You believe her."

"I just want to get the ghosts out of my house," Maisie said. "I just moved into the haunted house in town because it was the only house we could afford. Who-who are you?"

"I hear you talking!" The voice came again from behind her. "Who are you talking to?"

"I live here."

"Can you help me?" Maisie's cheap shoes leaked in the cold damp, numbing her toes. "She says that all we needed to get the ghost out of my house was something from your crypt."

"She can't get anything out of your house. She just wants to see if you'll steal from me." The girl floated closer, dark pits where her eyes should have been. Tentacles of cold air reached out from the misty form. "You aren't the first girl she has dared to break into my home."

"She can't?" Traitorous tears filled her eyes. "I'm not?"

"Maisie!" called the girl at the gates, an edge of panic in her voice now.

"She can't, but you can. If you can see me, you don't need her help."

"But you're the only one I've ever seen. I can't see the one in my house."

"Then how do you know it's there?"

"It turns the sinks on, and the lights, and my radio." A tear dropped from her cheek. "I've never been so scared."

"I guess we'll just go home," the girl called, warning in her voice. "Maisie!"

Maisie opened her mouth to call back but the ghost put a finger to her still lips.

"You have ten seconds to show your face!" The worried tone was replaced now by anger. *They think I'm playing a joke on them,* Maisie thought. It felt powerful to think she could make them pretend not to worry about her.

Ten seconds later, the sound of car doors slamming filled the night. The car roared to life, headlights striping the graveyard in shadows. A cloud passed over the moon, the ghost girl fading in the dark.

"But I'm staying the night at her house," Maisie whispered in a panic. "How will I get home?"

"Leave that to me," the ghost girl said as the headlights idled there a moment, waiting for Maisie to rush back, chastened and scared, among the jagged teeth of the crumbling headstones. "She wants you to run back."

The lights swept away from the cemetery then, disappearing around a curve into the night. Maisie gulped back a reply, trying to steady her galloping heart as the cloud moved, the ghost girl almost more lifelike against the bright snow.

"Come in out of the cold," the ghost girl disappeared into the side of the crypt. Maisie curled her numbing fingers around the door and jerked it open, making enough space to slip inside. She wondered what the girls would think if they knew she was sitting inside the crypt when they had been too scared even to squeeze through the cemetery gate.

A sliver of moonlight from a high window revealed a tiny, charred square of stone floor beneath a haphazard pile of partly-burned branches and twigs, a plastic lighter discarded beside it. Maisie coaxed her mostly-numb fingers into starting a weak flame on one of the kindling pieces. It was too far to walk home in the cold, if she had even known the way home in the dark. Her cell phone battery had long since died.

"Other people have spent the night in your crypt?" She said into the dark, not knowing where the girl was. She tried not to think of all the bodies stacked on either side of her, especially not one where the shadows seemed darker near the door. No words came into her head as she crouched closer to the flames. "Hello? Are you here?" Nothing. A wind picked up outside, howling through the stones. She hoped that's what the howling was. The ghost girl had vanished.

***

Maisie must have slipped into an uneasy sleep, because her eyes shot open to the sound of the crypt door scraping open in the gray half-light of dawn. A boy she hadn't seen before stuck his head in.

"Maisie? Are you Maisie?" She nodded, her stiff neck crying out in pain. "Oh, thank God!" He straddled the last glowing embers of her fire as he shook her shoulders, his handsome face in hers.

Maisie didn't quite feel herself. It wasn't that her feet were all pins and needles once she pulled them out from under her, or that her muscles had never been so sore after a few hours propped up against cold stone. No, she had the same physical body, the same stringy hair, and the nose that took up her face. It was the inside of her body that felt fuller, someone sharing the space. Someone else pushing her down, like dunking her underwater, and speaking out of her mouth, seeing a world of color and light through her eyes. Someone braver. She watched just under the surface as the boy dragged her out of the crypt to where the girls from last night stood, bundled in expensive, pastel-colored parkas and heavy boots.

"You're lucky there was stuff in there to make a fire," the boy said to the girls. Now that Maisie could sort-of see the faces together, she could tell it was an older brother who had come to get her.

"Why didn't you come back?" Her ex-friends whined as they stumbled back to the car, Maisie clinging to the boy for support she really didn't need. "That was really stupid."

Maisie grinned. They had pulled a new version of Maisie from the crypt, one that had a chance to set things right with a new energy inside her. One that wasn't afraid of house ghosts or sitting alone at lunch. No, one that was ready for anything. Afraid of nothing.

DREAM PROTECTOR

BY JOHN TIMM

I came again to to see the playground, as I had so many times before. The cracked asphalt playground with the big, wire-mesh fence that protected neighboring houses from baseballs, basketballs, snowballs, and other errant missiles of childhood. Back then, that same big wire-mesh fence also sheltered the children—myself included—from a world of unspoken dangers. Back then, there would have been no question. A fence had as much power as a symbol as it did a barrier. Back then, its mere presence said, "Keep out. Innocence at play."

The playground was barren now. The school it once surrounded gone, long gone, replaced by more asphalt, a large, square patch of a darker color, less cracked, less weather-beaten than the playground surface I came to know during those years. Kindergarten. First grade. Second grade. Third grade. For a moment, I thought I heard the voices of children. It must have been the wind. …

An elderly man approached from the sidewalk. He wore a hat and an overcoat. At first glance, he could have been my father. A fedora with a wide brim and a tan, full-length overcoat, the fashion of another time. I felt compelled to explain my lingering contemplation to him, though not fully certain of the answer myself. "I often dream about the school, and this playground, and my friends ..."

I feared I'd revealed too much already, yet couldn't help but explain further. "I went to grade school here. Grew up down the block over there." I turned and pointed. "Across the street. Third house, the gray one. That was many years, many memories ago."

The elderly man's fixed gaze told me he already knew.

"Do you live around here?" I asked.

"I'm never far away," he said.

What does he mean by that?

I persisted. "No, what I meant was do you live close by—in the neighborhood?"

"Let's just say I'm here when I need be."

I began to feel an uncomfortable mix of irritation and fear. *Time to get out here. Weird old man. Should never have started a conversation in the first place.*

Before I could make a move, the man asked, "Don't you want to know why I'm here?"

I debated a moment with my better judgement, then gave in. "I guess I do. I just wondered if you lived around here so I could ask some questions."

"But do you want to know why I'm here?"

I gave in once more. "Okay, so why are you here?"

"Because I am your dream protector."

"My dream protector? Is that what you just said, 'Dream protector?'"

"It took you a while, but I think you've finally caught on," he said.

"Caught on to ...?"

"—My secret ... and yours."

"Which is ...?"

"We both come here. You come because you dream about this playground, and the school, and your time as a child. I come to protect those dreams."

"Old man, you are crazy. There's no such thing as a dream protector."

"There is. And that is what I am. You may say I'm crazy. But who is crazier, you or I? One of us dreams of a time that is lost forever. There is no school. There are no children. Just a fence and parts of a playground. And one day this, too, will all be torn up and forgotten. But until then, I'm here to help protect those dreams for you. No one else cares about your dreams, do they? But I do." He turned and began to leave, then paused. "I'll always be here as long as you are. When you stop coming, so will I."

So, I am the dreamer of dreams, dreams so compelling they force me to return, time after time, to this same place. Drawn inexorably. And he is the protector of those dreams. Keeping them vivid, keeping them alive. It made just enough sense I could not ignore it. After all, he was the dream protector, not unlike that big wire-mesh fence that kept stray missiles out of the neighbors' yards and, as a symbol, kept us as children safe from the intrusions of the outside world. It made more and more sense as I drove away.

THE SILENT CHILD

BY JESSICA THOMAS

The bookshop smelled as good bookshops do: of paper, earth and old spices. I wandered aisles, fingers trailing over ribbed spines, gold gilding, and the occasional Penguin paperback, the bright orange out of place among faded volumes of Poe, Shelley, and Stoker. I slid Jane Eyre into my hands and, after checking the price (only £1), tucked it under my arm. This was technically all I was looking for—my copy was so well read it was shedding leaves faster than an oak in autumn—and prepared to go, but something made me linger. The shop was cosy, the wind outside was brutal, and I had no cause or desire to hurry home. So instead of turning right to the counter, I turned left and headed up the stairs to the attic.

I was too old for children's books. I knew that, but growing up in a family where video games and sports events were the common diet, I'd spent years starved for stories and attention. So little attention did I attract that sometimes I wondered whether I were invisible as H.G. Wells' man. Soon as I could, I escaped to university, threw myself on the debt-laden road to a degree in English Lit, and loved every moment of it. But assigned reading lists tended to privilege the Brontës and Austen over E.B. White and J.M. Barrie (unsurprisingly), so I had taken to spending my weekends—and meagre income—in

Scribbler's Books, absorbing the stories I had been denied as a child. At Scribbler's I accumulated a collection of which any bookworm would be proud. That shop always had just the book I was looking for. It was rather like being haunted by a coterie of kind, well-read ghosts.

Up in the attic, I navigated through the collection of generously proportioned floor cushions, randomly selected a pile of books, and settled myself down in my favourite spot—a window seat that offered a view of the street below. I did this every time I came; like a tarot reader drawing cards, I let the spirits of Scribbler's show me what they wanted me to read. That day, something felt different. It was a darker collection than usual; instead of bright colours and children conversing with fey folk, I saw crimson leather, forest green covers with gothic lettering, embossed crests, and one with no title at all. This one I studied more closely.

It was the size of my palm and well used, the cover boards visible beneath fraying cloth, and there was a light tingling in my fingers when I stroked the spine—small enough to ignore if I had been the sort to disregard such things. Instead, this frisson of energy propelled me into deeper investigations. As it fell open in my hands, I could have sworn the book emitted the slightest of soft sighs.

There was no date on the inside cover but, having spent more weekends than I could count combing the shelves of various antiquarian booksellers, I guessed early nineteenth century, give or take a decade. I searched for more clues but found nothing—until I landed on the title page. My mouth fell open.

In messy script, someone had crossed out the printed text and handwritten "The Silent Child" with such ferocity the quill had almost pierced the parchment. I passed the pads of my fingers over the letters and felt again that slight tingling, only this time it was unpleasant, sharp, even. It was as though the nib of the writer's pen were poking through and slicing my flesh. With a snap, the glass against my cheek split. I leapt up, felt my head collide with a ceiling beam, and the book slipped from my hands. Vision blurry with pain, ears ringing, I whirled to face the window. The floor swayed. Blood spattered the pane, dripping down in thick rivulets. Gripped by morbid curiosity, I climbed back onto the window seat and peered out, eyes following feather trail down to the pavement where a discombobulated raven lay, his magnificent wings twitching, beak open in a gasp. I shut my eyes, turned my face away, and caught sight of the book, now lying open on the ground. Every spare inch of the page was filled with tiny handwriting. Rough lines crossed out whole sections of type and apparent re-writes crowded the margins. I knelt on the floor and cradled it between my palms. Page after page, neat type cowered beneath the violent outburst of an enraged reader. I flipped back to the beginning and began to read.

Received this advanced edition of the book today 'for my approval.' I can only interpret this gesture as courtesy, the fulfilment of decorum. Butchers of truth, editors have dismembered my text, burned the choice cuts on the altar of economy. What remains is the offal, fit for the Thames. Never mind—I will tell it true, as intended. In this edition if none other. The real tale must be told.

The text which had been so viciously crossed out read like a mother's voice crooning to her young ones, urging them to sit quite comfortably and listen well. It was condescending to say the least—even more so for its contrast to the author's true sentiments.

Heart quickening in my chest, hands shaking, I stroked the page again, feeling once more a tingle of the rage so vehement that it echoed through the parchment, across time.

Stories tell of monsters beaten, of damsels rescued, of fires quenched and hopes restored. The truth is not a story. The truth holds broken hearts and never-ending nights, gentle beasts and impossible things like a child found in the woods by an old man with no one left to love him. Discovered lying pale and cold among poisonous mushrooms and fallen leaves, she was delicate as the fey and more beautiful. Taking her limp body into his arms, the old man carried the waif home and laid her by the fire. For days she lay unconscious. Then, one morning when the woods were wreathed in fog, her eyes opened. In the days and weeks to come, the heart that had long lain languid in the old man's breast began to beat again, as a deep familial affection grew between the two lost spirits.

I jumped, eyes darting to the gooseflesh where some small, cold hand had just taken mine. But there was nothing to see—neither close to me nor anywhere else in the room.

The attic had grown dark and heavy rain was clinking against the pane. The blood was gone but not the memory, and the spider's web of cracks only reminded me of the body, ebony wings splayed as if crucified.

With characteristic gentleness, the old man taught the creature-child to read and to write, and though she never spoke, every word learned became a thread binding them together. Though advanced in years, the man found a peace he never knew. He learned about love and joy and the comfort in closing one's eyes knowing that in the morning there would be a person glad to see them. Little gifts appeared around the place and soon he found himself hunting for them; wildflowers growing between the flagstones, the scent of lavender blooming from a book, his young self reflected in the mirror, the echo of a lullaby once heard but long forgotten. Laughter erupted from wherever the peculiar pair were found, shadows were driven back by sunlight and candles, and for the first time in many years, nightmares and spectres no longer haunted the darkness beyond the window.

It was so dark I could hardly see the page. The temperature had dropped, my breath made clouds in the air, and my fingers had taken on an indigo tinge. This was stupid; it was late, I was freezing and I was going to miss curfew and spend the night on the college steps. But I couldn't leave; something was holding me there, had driven certainty into my bones that if I left off, the book would disappear, the truth lost forever.

Time went by and, though with every morning the old man woke to strength and vigour, what began as a hint in the recesses of his mind could no longer be ignored. As they sat in the kitchen one afternoon, basking in the fire's warmth, his eyes could not help but examine the child resting in an armchair beside him. Where once her face had been full and bright with youthful innocence, it was now gaunt with shadows. The old man's heart ached, all the more since he knew the solution. But the cure brought with it more pain than the prospect of watching her waste away before him.

Tormented by indecision, he took himself to the wood and wandered for many hours until, exhausted, he fell down in the heather to rest. There, his eyes caught sight of a flower, blooming against all odds among the rugged terrain. Battered by the winds, rain, and frosts that frequented that place, a single delicate Columbine thrummed with life and colour so beautiful, so luminous, that he knew he must bring it back as a gift for his dear little companion. Perhaps she would be reminded of the world from which she had come and would return to her old self. With careful hands he plucked the flower and set off home. However, he had not gone five leagues before looking down to find the flower crumpled and wilting in his well-intentioned hands. The man let out a mournful cry and the dying blossom fell to the ground.

The child did not stir as he wrapped her in a blanket and carried her back to the woods. With tears streaming down his cheeks, he lay her in a patch of wild heather at the foot of a giant oak and then locked himself away, lest his resolve fail. Never before had the rooms felt so stark, the hallways so silent, the fire so cold. Then, one day, chancing to look out the window overlooking the wood, he saw a familiar patch of heather, a blanket lying empty in the snow. Never before had such grief and joy been felt in equal measure as they were that night when the old man lay himself down in his bed and smiled the smile of a soul redeemed.

As I write this account, transcribed and assembled from my grandfather's diaries and papers, I sit in the house of which this sorry tale tells. It has been empty for many years but if you were to visit, wander long enough in its halls, you would hear the soft patter of tiny feet upon the stairs, the sigh of a book being lifted from the shelves, and the giggle of a child playing secret games. And during the long hours at that kitchen table, I would swear upon my life that I heard the echo of some larger feet stepping in time to the little ones.

I wiped my eyes and looked up, preparing to close the book. But before I could, something small slipped out from between the final leaves and fell to the ground. I picked it up, turned it over, and felt icy fingers trail down my spine. It was a drawing. A drawing of a child with large, round eyes, rosebud lips, and tangles of soft hair falling over thin shoulders. She was in every way ethereal; somehow too fragile for this world and at the same time, so full of secret knowings that this earth could not possibly contain her. But this was not what cast that cold trickle of fear into my bones. What fixed my eyes on that portrait was that it was, without a doubt, an image of me.

SAGE

BY DANIEL KRUSE

Fifteen-year-old Sage Griffin sat in his room playing his unplugged electric guitar. His mind was spinning wildly and sweat poured off his unlined face. The central theme of his emotional deluge centered on the local Catholic cemetery. Should he go tomorrow night or shouldn't he?

His fundamentalist church had taught him never, ever to believe in ghosts or anything such as spirits.

"There's only one spirit!" Pastor Gabriel Crenshaw boomed one Sunday several weeks earlier. "And that's the Holy Spirit! Forget that and you will burn for eternity. All these occult shows on TV, all the sex—look at the cesspool and decide for yourselves. Good God da mighty, I'd never mislead you and neither would Jesus! Let me hear an amen!"

Sage picked up his cell phone and called his best buddy River Rainier. River's parents were ex-hippies, and there were several people in Somerville, Texas, who never let them forget it. Sage couldn't have cared less. He was leaving the day after high school graduation.

River answered the call. "Sage, buddy. What's up, man?"

"Are we going to the cemetery tomorrow night?"

"Oh, Sage, not that again! Dude, I'm telling ya, there's nothing there. That story was made up when Jamison Jeffries died thirty years ago. All that's in that grave are a bunch of bones and a rusting casket."

"River, man, do you remember what Calvin Conklin said a couple of years ago? He said he went there alone on the anniversary of his death, and he said the energy was incredible."

River cut to the chase.

"Oh, good God, Sage! Calvin lives on expensive grass-fed beef paid for by his dad, potato chips, pot brownies, and bottled water, along with the occasional piece of fruit. He felt the effects of his drugs that night and not Jamison Jeffries' spirit or ghost. I'm not going. And do you know why I'm not going? Because it's all a big fairy tale. Jamison Jeffries … whoopee! Just another blues-influenced wanker."

"He was a great guitar player, River!"

"Yeah, and he cut his career short by doing speed-balls. Anybody that touches dope is a damn fool, Sage. It nearly killed my cousin Seth. Let's face it: Jamison Jeffries screwed up big time."

"Ah, River, I don't do any drugs. Remember? I disapprove."

Sage was sitting on his bed, still holding his phone after talking to River. Sage had many good qualities. He was handsome and had and athletic build, although he never participated in any high school sports. He genuinely liked everyone he met, unless they gave him a reason not to. His world was that of the guitar. People genuinely loved Sage, but they always held their tongues when it came to his parents and their rabid devotion to the Somerville Free Church. In a word, the BBFC was about hate.

You name it and Pastor Crenshaw had expounded on it. Nobody was exempt: pregnant teenaged girls, gay men, lesbians. Pastor Crenshaw threw around all the vile slurs. Sage viewed Pastor Crenshaw as a completely uneducated loser and a genuine hater. He wanted no part of it.

Screw it, I'll go by myself tomorrow night, he thought. But first, he was going to pay someone a visit. Someone who probably believed in the same phenomena as he. The Catholic cemetery was located on the south end of Somerville. There were pine trees and lilac bushes scattered throughout.

Just north of the cemetery stood a medium-size, brown stucco house where a former New York theater person named Charles McPherson lived. Charles name was beside the word "eccentric" in the dictionary. He spent his childhood and teen years in Somerville and settled in New York City where he attended college and worked on Broadway for twenty years. He was a makeup, mask, and custom clothing specialist.

The legend was that he had fallen in love with an actor. They were together five years and everything vanished overnight. Everyone in the "Double B" knew that Charles was gay and they left it at that. He was rarely seen around town. Savvy investing had left Charles financially secure but he had never recovered from his love loss. His hobby for the last ten years had been constructing masks of famous people's faces. He designed them and saw them through to their fruition. The final finishing was done at an artisan's small factory in Europe.

Sage looked up Charles's number in the local phone directory. Apparently, Charles didn't have a cell, but Sage reckoned that maybe he had a land line. He was only slightly nervous as he dialed the number. There was no such thing as a stranger to Sage. It rang once … twice … three times … and Charles picked up on the fourth.

"Yeah, this is Charles."

"This is Sage Griffin. I was wondering if I could visit with you and talk to you about supernatural phenomena."

"Hey, hold on, and not so fast. What makes you think I'm an expert on supernatural phenomena?"

"Well, you do live next to a cemetery."

"Yeah, kid, and it's full of dead people. Nothing more."

"Look, I just want to talk to you for a few minutes and ask you some questions about the cemetery and what it's like living next to one."

"Okay, kid, but I'm not going to sit around for hours. I'll give you a half hour. I'm working on several art projects."

"Can I come over today? Time is running out."

"Yeah, yeah, whenever. I'll be here."

It was already past noon. Sage grabbed his phone and headed to the brown stucco house. It was about a ten-minute walk. Sage knew his folks would never approve of his hanging with an ex-Broadway man, let alone one who was gay.

As he approached the house, he couldn't believe how well-kept everything was. Manicured lawn, flawlessly finished oak doors stained a medium-dark brown, exotic flowers everywhere. He liked what he saw. He walked the winding sidewalk to the front door. He was immediately struck by what he saw hanging on the door. It was a knocker made of stainless steel and cast into the form of the Nazi SS death head. Skepticism flowed through his veins.

He used the knocker and … nothing. Again he knocked three times. Nothing. Just as he was about to knock again, the door opened.

"Mr. Griffin, nice to see you."

Charles extended his hand and Sage shook it. He couldn't believe how firm the handshake was. It was almost too powerful, as if to say, "I call the shots kid."

"Please, come on in. I think we'll sit on the sun porch overlooking the cemetery, since that's the preordained topic of conversation today. So, Sage, what is it you want to know?"

"To begin, did you grow up with Jamison Jeffries?"

"I did. He was a nice guy. Very dedicated to the guitar. He didn't party much back then. That all took place in New York City. He simply could not put the drugs down and they killed him in short order."

"Did you see him play in New York City?"

"Probably about five times. We were not friends but we always acknowledged each other."

"Was he good?"

"Fantastic, if he wasn't loaded. Drugs will kill you, Griffin. Don't do them."

"I don't. I just play guitar and eat and sleep. Very simple."

"Good, good."

"Have you ever heard the rumors about Jamison Jeffries appearing on the anniversary of his death?"

"Of course, and it's total BS. I've never seen the grave or him and I've lived here over ten years."

"Tomorrow night is the anniversary and there's a full moon as well. I'm going. I've got to."

"Hmmm, good luck with that. Well, Sage, our time is up. I must get back to work."

"One more question, Charles. Where did you get the SS death head knocker?"

"It was from an actual World War II SS officer's house in Germany. What I paid for that was sinful!"

"I see. Well, Mr. McPherson, I thank you for your time."

"Certainly, Sage. Good luck tomorrow night. Perhaps the full moon will be your friend and bring you a Mr. Jeffries sighting."

"I'd settle for a ten-second sighting. Anything."

He walked home unsatisfied. Surely someone had to have seen Jeffries over the years.

Someone, anyone. He spent the remainder of the day in his room, preparing for tomorrow's jaunt. He would pack a camera, some bottled water, and a ham sandwich. He would sneak out of the house at 11:00 p.m. and wait in the cemetery. He laid his head on the pillow and listened to "Texas Moon" by The Church. Sleep came fast, void of any dreams.

The next night, he made his way to the Catholic cemetery with all of his things in tow. The moon shone peacefully on the tombstones as he made his way to Jeffries' grave. He checked his watch; it was 11:35 p.m. There were several joints and empty cans of beer lying around the grave. He sat down to eat his ham sandwich, his camera hanging around his neck. The winds rustled through the pines, composing air symphonies.

It was now 11:55 p.m. Without warning, an illuminated figure began moving from the far end of the cemetery. They were about fifty feet from each other. Sage began hyperventilating and wet his shorts as he reached for his camera. He couldn't believe it. It was Jeffries, dressed in black and ready to rock. Sage snapped pictures wildly, barely able to breathe. Jeffries waved and disappeared into the lilac bushes.

Sage fell to the ground and lay there for an hour. It was true. Back at the brown stucco house, Charles McPherson laughed out loud as he removed the LED battery pack from underneath his shirt. He carefully, almost reverently, removed the Jamison Jeffries mask from his face. The kid had gotten pictures too. Sage would be sure to tell everyone and the pictures would be hard to deny. He imagined what would happen when Pastor Crenshaw intervened. There was even a chance that Sage might be hauled away to some mental institution. An uproar, that's what McPherson wanted. Just a good, loud, Broadway-style uproar in an old-fashioned, conservative, Texas town.

PARKLAND

BY PETER PALMIERI

If it had an engine, Leroy Abellard could fix it—it didn't matter if it was a lawnmower or a 25-ton industrial AC unit. By the time he was twelve, Leroy had gained a reputation throughout Terrebonne Parish as a bona fide mechanical wizard. Never had a knack for book-learning. Just the same, at the age of fifty-two, Leroy could boast he had never been unemployed—not counting the six-month stint he spent up at the Dixon Correctional Institute. (Even there, he managed to fix a faulty boiler that had given the maintenance team trouble for years. And Warden Dupree was so pleased with the rebuild of the V-8 on his 1972 Camaro LS he was genuinely sad to see Leroy go.)

So when Dallas ISD gave Leroy the pink slip after yet another shortfall in the city's budget, Leroy didn't fret. He got stewed on spiced rum that night and spent the next day nursing a zinger of a hangover with a time-tested Creole remedy. But by the third day, he was gainfully employed again, working maintenance at Parkland Hospital—graveyard shift.

The first time he ran into them was on his second shift. Leroy was pushing his tool cart in a dim underground corridor with surplus hospital beds parked against one wall when he saw a brightly-lit storeroom off to his right. He slowed as he walked past the open door and noticed two men inside, seated at a folding table playing cards.

"Sorry," Leroy said as he pushed on, startled by their presence.

The man facing him, a nervy-looking white guy with deep-set eyes, nodded at him. The other man, a broad-shouldered guy in shirt-sleeves, didn't even turn around to look.

The following night, he ran into them again. The well-built man caught sight of Leroy this time and waved at him, as though they were old chums. He was older than his partner, handsome in a Technicolor-movie way. Leroy nodded and kept on moving. He couldn't imagine why a couple of white men would be playing cards in the sub-basement of a hospital night after night, but it was no concern of his. "White-collar," he muttered to himself.

Then he didn't see them for a few days. But his first shift the following week, there they were again. This time, the older fellow flashed him a million-dollar smile, called out, and waved him into the storeroom.

Leroy shuffled in, bowing his head slightly, out of habit, having grown up in the South.

"Say, you're new around here, aren't you?" the man said.

"Yessir."

"Well, I'm Jack. This here's Oz," he said, pointing at his partner with his chin. "What's your name?"

"Leroy Abellard, sir."

"Mr. Leroy Abellard—pleased to meet you." Jack spoke in a northern accent, so thick it was almost funny. "I'd shake, Leroy, but I've got such a hot hand," he waved his cards, "I'm afraid I'd scorch your skin." Jack smiled again, beaming, and damn if he didn't look familiar!

Oz scoffed. "You're bluffing. But it is bad luck to press flesh when playing poker."

"Everything's bad luck in your book," Jack said and winked at Leroy. "Say, Leroy, how about you join in for a quick game of gin rummy?"

"I gots work to do," Leroy said.

"Work can wait. No one will be the wiser. Ain't that so, Oz?"

"Damn straight," Oz said through clenched teeth. "But one day the proletariat will rise up. And then the bourgeoisie will take note. And how!"

Leroy settled into an empty chair.

Jack chuckled. He leaned into Leroy and whispered, "I swear, half the time, I have no clue what he's talking about." Jack slapped his cards face down on the table and shoved them into the deck.

"I knew you was bluffing," Oz said.

Again, Jack winked, sending a chill down Leroy's spine, because he finally recognized the man—both of them—and Leroy's old heart started beating so hard now, he thought he'd blow a gasket. But to his surprise, after the initial shock had dissipated, Leroy found himself oddly at ease. He even chuckled after winning a game. At 4:30 in the morning, Jack told a joke about a rabbi and a Catholic priest going to a strip bar that had Leroy doubled over, guffawing. At 6 a.m., Leroy checked his watch, pushed back on his chair, and excused himself.

"Let's do it again!" Jack called out.

"Next time bring cash," Oz said in that nasal voice of his.

An hour later, Leroy punched out, walked into the morning sun, and rode the bus back to his apartment. He showered, ate a bowl of instant oatmeal, and lay in his bed, unable to sleep. At noon, he got dressed, and walked six blocks to the Oak Lawn branch of the public library, where he settled behind a computer screen and spent the next few hours reading about a part of history he should have learned in school.

That night, he played cards with Jack and Oz again, did so for the next few weeks. If a maintenance emergency call came in on Leroy's walkie-talkie, Jack and Oz would trudge along and watch in admiration as Leroy performed his art.

Soon, Leroy began prodding them with questions. "What do you do, Jack?"

"Mostly, I sail," Jack replied. "You ever been to Martha's Vineyard?"

"I mean, for a living," Leroy said.

"You kidding?" Oz interjected. "Jack's never worked a day in his life. His old man's loaded."

"How about you, Oz?" Leroy said.

"I was in the Army."

"What about now?"

Oz shrugged. "I'm here, ain't I?"

It seemed the two were operating under some form of amnesia, that large swaths of their past were inaccessible to them.

"How long y'all been here at Parkland?" Leroy asked one early morning, digging a little deeper.

"Hell! Seems like forever," Oz said.

"Can't you leave? Go where you need to be?" Leroy picked his words carefully.

"Well, that's just it, old boy," Jack replied. "Seems like we're stuck here. I don't quite know how to explain it. I'm not even sure I understand."

"I got nowhere better to be," Oz said.

Jack turned to Oz and said, "We could go sailing round the cape if I could find a way out of here."

Oz chuckled. "If I wanted to sail, I'd have joined the Navy 'stead of the Army."

What astounded Leroy was the deep friendship between the two. Though separated by a vast gulf of age, education, and

274

refinement, it was evident the two genuinely liked each other. More than that—they were soulmates. It was more than a little unsettling.

On a Saturday morning, his day off, Leroy picked up the phone and dialed long distance. His cousin Shontelle was a rootworker who sold herbs and oils and candles out the back of her hair salon in Baton Rouge. Her grandmother had been a Hoodoo priestess. (That stays in the blood.) If anyone knew what to do with Jack and Oz, it was cousin Shontelle.

"What trouble you got yourself in this time?" Shontelle said in her singsong Creole voice when Leroy told her he needed her help.

"It's not like that," Leroy said. "Listen here, for the last month, I been playing cards with John F. Kennedy and Lee Harvey Oswald."

"You already drinking on a Saturday morning?" Shontelle said.

Leroy went on to tell her about his new job at Parkland— "that's where they both died, see?" He told Shontelle how he first ran into them, how he had been spending most nights in their company. He told her about their apparent amnesia and how they seemed to be the best of friends.

Shontelle interjected hums and tongue clicks and the occasional, "Sweet Jesus!"

Leroy finished his monologue with, "And that's about the size of it."

Shontelle waited for a beat and said, "Leroy, they have to move on."

"That's why I called you."

It took Shontelle a week to hatch a plan. She read the Seventh Book of Moses, consulted a Gullah conjurer from the Carolina lowlands, and held a Vudon séance with a high priestess from New Orleans. Then she phoned Leroy, laid it out for him. Had him write it down for good measure. She had him read it back to her twice, word by word.

"The only way they can move on," Shontelle said, "is to gain supreme knowledge. Do you hear what I'm saying?"

"You mean to say, they'll know."

"That's right," Shontelle said. "The truth will shine before their eyes."

"Boy, that's going to be rough."

"You have no idea."

Leroy had ten days to prepare, ten nights before the next full moon. In a canvas duffle bag, he assembled the necessary paraphernalia: frankincense, a gris-gris bag filled with hair and nail clippings, two bundles of sage, a glass candle with a hand-painted cat, the Seventh Book of Moses with the relevant passages underlined in red pencil, the pages dog-eared in a sacrilegious way. On the designated night, he stuffed a live chicken in the bag and smuggled the whole bundle into Parkland Hospital.

Jack was shuffling the deck when Leroy walked into the storeroom.

"You got here just in time," Oz said, leaning back in his chair.

Jack suddenly stopped shuffling the cards. "Why the long face, Leroy?" he said.

"Boys," Leroy said. "It's time for y'all to move on."

In minutes, everything was set. Leroy started reading the incantations. From time to time, Jack had to look over his shoulder and help him pronounce a word. The air came alive with the buzz of static electricity. Leroy felt a mechanical shudder coming from the boiler in the next room, the mark of a power surge. The overhead light bulb flickered, then seemed to burn brighter, emanating a sickly orange glow. At that moment, Leroy grabbed his jackknife and slit the hen's throat, held it upside down to let its blood spill on the floor. The overhead lights went out. The candle flickered and extinguished.

For a minute, the three men sat in cold black silence. When the lights came on again, John F. Kennedy and Lee Harvey Oswald were staring at each other impassively. After a few tense moments, President Kennedy said, "Why?"

"What do you mean, why?" Oswald said.

"Why did you murder me?"

Oswald scoffed. "Hell, I didn't know you, then."

"I had a family."

Oswald raised his voice. "I hated you. Okay? I hated everything you stood for. But things are different now."

Kennedy nodded. "You're right. Things are different now." The president got to his feet, headed for the door. Before stepping into the corridor, he turned back. For a second, it looked like he was going to say something but just shook his head, walked out, and was engulfed by a dazzling light.

"Jack!" Oswald called out. "Jack, I'm sorry."

It was too late, and Oswald knew it. He doubled over and started sobbing. Leroy got to his feet and headed for the corridor.

"Don't leave me," Oswald said.

"You can find your way out now," Leroy said.

"I'm not headed for the light, Leroy. You know that."

"Be that as it may," Leroy said, trying to hide his disdain, "it's time to go."

He walked down the long hallway, kept going until he reached a bank of elevators. A portly man with a gray fedora was punching the call button repeatedly.

"Going up?" Leroy said. Maybe some of that supreme knowledge had rubbed off on him because he could tell straight away that the man was not of this world.

"Been trying to go up for a hell of a long time," the man said.

"What's your name?" Leroy said.

"Rubenstein. Jacob Rubenstein."

"Jack Ruby?"

"That's right."

Leroy sighed. He looked back down the corridor where he had abandoned Oswald and shook his head. "You better come along with me, Mr. Ruby."

LAST GASP

BY CHRIS DEAN

A loud thump reverberated through the starship. After weeks of pure silence any noise would be huge, and Tina crept cautiously from the bunkroom into the corridor. She prayed that this was not her imagination. The atmosphere in the module was thin, stale, and she might be experiencing the first stage of narcolepsy. The mind plays tricks. Isolation and fear had driven her half-crazy and, quite possibly, it was time for those hallucinations to start.

But the sound came again, accompanied by a voice. "... of the rescue ship Jude. Can you respond?" Tina shuffled through the ship in disbelief. She reached the forward compartment where the voice was louder. "We are at airlock B. Controls are locked and we're working to get it open. Can you respond?"

Croaking a hysterical shriek, "I'm here!" she rushed to the communications station and fumbled with the controls. "This is the Ruthr. I hear you!"

"We are opening airlock B. Stand clear of the airlock."

"I'm running out of air." How much oxygen was left? She had lost track of everything. Breathing had been difficult for some time—she knew she didn't have long. "Please hurry!"

"Can anyone respond? Airlock B is frozen and we're forcing a breach. Stand clear."

"Yes, I'm here!" she screamed.

"I repeat, stand clear of the lock."

Why couldn't they hear her? The ship's power systems were low but there was still enough juice for lights and the radio. It made no sense. They were coming in anyway so it didn't really matter. Or did it?

A sense of dread swept through her as she evaluated the implications. Had Riley sabotaged the equipment? The air lock—the radio—who knew what else he could have done? An encrypted message in the computer log would bury her. Did he have access to the main computer in his final hours?

She moved to the entryway and peered past the shadows and spears of the auxiliary lights. There was no computer terminal in the engine room. Riley hadn't had access to anything that would have made a difference.

But Riley had hung on longer than she had expected. As captain he knew the ship better than her. Had he found some way to circumvent the aft bulkhead and escape the engine room? He would have been in bad shape. But he wouldn't have had to go far. Just off the engine room was a service alcove with a terminal. Command control could be activated from there.

Yes! He had sneaked out, sabotaged the systems, and planted an encrypted message. And then he'd slipped back into the engine room so she would never know. When her rescuers got to the computer, they would find out the truth. Very clever for a dying man.

She had to purge the computer records completely. Who knew what Riley could have done? There was clanging at the airlock now. How much time did she have? She had to hurry.

As an astrogater she knew enough about the computers to wipe the files clean in a matter of minutes. On a small ship like the Ruthr it was simple enough. She dumped the master drive and everything else went with it. If Riley had tried to set her up, he had failed. Now the only version of events aboard the ship was hers. Poor Captain Riley went out to repair the fuel leak and drifted off, victim of a faulty tether.

"Stand clear of airlock B. We are cutting a hatch."

The man on the radio was excited now. She heard the hiss of the plasma torch. They would be inside shortly. She spotted Riley's leisure cap on his chair and snatched it up. Would it matter? She put it back, paranoid that somehow this innocuous item would implicate her no matter what she did.

Tina struggled to calm down. If she didn't get it together, she could incriminate herself. She was the disaster victim here, she had to remember that. They'd found her stranded in space, barely alive, and they weren't going to suspect anything. No one would ever know that she had committed murder.

Her act had been a moral one. With only enough air for the both of them for a few weeks, it only made good logistical sense to do what she did. And it had worked; she survived. She'd murdered Riley because it was the right thing to do under dire circumstances. It was a terrible necessity that she hoped she'd never have to do again.

She had eliminated any physical evidence, she was certain of that. Going out in the corridor, she opened the maintenance compartment. This pipe fitting had been troublesome—in order to drain hydrazine from the cooling system she had been forced to unweld and fasten it again. Just an ounce of the fluid in Riley's juice had been enough. There was no way to tell the fitting had been tampered with. She'd even smeared a tiny age-smudge on the side.

The only other evidence was long gone—Riley's body. Hauling it to the airlock had been a difficult task. She slowly shut the compartment as she listened to the hissing of the torch. They were almost through.

Something about transporting Riley through the ship bothered her. It seemed like it had happened so long ago she could barely remember it. She had dragged him to the airlock—

Tina froze. How could she have dumped the body out the airlock? Riley had sabotaged the locks and they weren't working. Had she imagined disposing his body? She rushed to the engine room and stared in shock. There on the deck lay the body. The oxygen deprivation had warped her perception and made her believe she'd gotten rid of it. And now there were people entering the ship. They would see him!

She had to hide the body. Tina searched the room frantically. She found a storage bin that was big enough. She rushed back to the body. When she turned it over, she stood there trying to comprehend what was happening. The dark wavy hair and the vacant blue eyes—no!

"Surprised?"

Edging away from the body in horror, Tina stared at the tall man in the corner. It was Riley—somehow he was there. And the body was a woman. She was the one lying dead on the floor.

"I've been watching you and waiting for this moment for a long time," Riley said. "A month after you killed me you ran out of oxygen."

"No, they're here. They're here to save me," she sobbed. "I'm in here!"

"They couldn't hear you over the radio and they can't hear you now. We're ghosts, Tina."

"No. Please, no."

"It's been thirty years. Why do you think that airlock is frozen?"

She didn't want to believe him, but how could she deny it? Her own body was laying right there. "Why didn't you ever say anything?"

"To you?" Riley winced. "I didn't think we'd have much to talk about. You did murder me, after all."

"Riley, I'm sorry about that." It hadn't accomplished anything. Her air had run out and she had died too.

"Are you? Somehow, I doubt that. Anyway, I had plenty of company. I've been conversing with other ghosts and I've learned a few things."

"Like what?"

"Why I couldn't leave the Ruthr, for one thing. You see, I had unfinished business."

"Unfinished business?"

"Until you found out that you were dead, I was bound to you. Now that you know, I'm free. I should have told you the truth a long time ago. I thought I'd enjoy this more. Frankly, I'm glad it's over."

The hissing of the torch ceased and a section of metal clattered to the deck. The rescuers were inside. But they didn't matter anymore, did they? Tina floated up over the deck. Like Riley, she was free to leave. "A ghost can go anywhere?"

"Anywhere in the universe."

Two figures in spacesuits entered the engine room. After a brief inspection of Tina's body, they retreated from the room. The rescue team left the starship. Riley drifted out into the corridor.

She followed him and watched Riley float through the gaping hole. Grinning, he shot her a wave. Anticipation swept through her as Tina approached the black maw. She had been trapped on that ship for years and she was finally free.

She reached out, but when her hand touched the hole it was blocked by a cold impenetrable wall. Tina tried to push through with both hands. It was impossible to get through. "What is this? Riley, what's happening?"

He'd drifted away and she could barely see him in the black curtain of space. His voice was faint. "Ghosts say guilt is the heaviest burden of all."

Smashing a fist at the cold, invisible wall, she screamed, "What does it mean?"

"What you did to me—I think it marked you, Tina."

"Marked me?"

"I don't think you can leave the ship."

"No! Riley, please."

"There's nothing I can do. I'm sorry." The tiny voice disappeared and the speck of color dissolved into the blackness of space.

He was gone. Tina reached through the hole but her fingers struck the cold wall. She couldn't escape. She would remain adrift between the stars. Trapped by her guilt forever. Tina started screaming. And screaming. And screaming.

LAKE NIASUK

BY IVY MILLER

The bus pulled into a parking lot and the driver announced, "Welcome to Lake Niasuk, the Caribbean of Ontario."

Lyric looked out the window. "Whoever gave this place that name has obviously never been in the Caribbean."

Despite being nothing like the tropical paradise some obviously drunk dolt compared it to, Lake Niasuk was still very pretty. Autumn trees surrounded the small body of water that reflected the slowly setting sun. Colorful cottages dotted the land around the lake and canoers could be seen moving across the water. Lyric took in the scenery and tried not to be angry at her grandmother, Fiona.

"I think your 'gift' will come in handy here, Lyric." Fiona said as she, her friend Joyce, and Lyric climbed into the only Lake Niasuk taxi and rode to a small church.

As they approached the church graveyard, Fiona grabbed Joyce by the arm. "Joyce," she shouted. "Why didn't you tell us?"

"I did tell you."

"No, you didn't. I think I'd remember you describing a crater-sized gap next to the church."

"The town calls it erosion," Joyce said as she stepped out of the cab. "They want to fill it in but I told them I was going to bring an expert."

"I'm the expert?" Fiona shouted.

"Why, yes you are, Fiona. You and I both know this isn't erosion. This is caused by the spirits we buried decades ago in jars with your mother. Right at the center of it, can't you see?" Fiona tried to remember the spell she, her mother, and Joyce did to capture the ghosts that were terrorizing the church at the time. She tried to imagine the ghosts at the bottom of the crater she was looking at.

Fiona couldn't see them but she knew Lyric could. Lyric decided to hide behind the cab. The cabbie looked at her. His arm hung out of the door as he tapped the side of the cab to the music on the radio. "Sweetie, it's not that bad. A few tons of top soil and it will be right as rain."

It wasn't the huge hole in the ground that scared Lyric. It was the dozens of ghosts swirling around inside it. Lyric shut her eyes and said to herself. "When I open my eyes, they'll be gone." Then she opened her eyes. They weren't gone. In fact, they were incredibly close, like a crowd who's come to stare at someone who's passed out. There were all kinds of people—or ghosts, rather—in various types of dress from various eras. There were men, women, and children staring intently at Lyric with concerned looks. Lyric closed her eyes again. She felt like she was going to pass out for sure.

Someone was shouting from the back of the crowd. "Give the child room. Let her breathe, for God sakes."

Lyric hoped the voice was human and opened her eyes to a tall, male ghost with long, gray hair and a handlebar mustache. She wasn't sure what era he was from but it was a long time ago. The ghost bent down and looked Lyric in the eye. "You all right, Missy?"

"No, sir, I'm not all right. There are too many of you. Why are you all showing yourselves to me? Usually, I only see one at a time."

The tall ghost stood up. "My dear, we're not showing anything. We're just here. We didn't mean to scare you."

"Thank you. I usually don't see so many."

"I guess that would be overwhelming. Let me introduce myself. I'm Mayor Stuart Bradley. What is your name?"

"I'm Lyric. Lyric Moon."

"Is that your mother talking to Joyce?"

"No that's my grandmother. How do you know Joyce?"

"Joyce has been taking care of this church for nearly forty years."

Lyric felt a little better. This old guy was kind. She peeked over the hood of the cab and saw even more ghosts. They were everywhere. Most of them running all over the graveyard. In the center of it all was a deep hole. In the center of the hole was a large, broken jar with a candle in the middle.

"She's the one who started it all," the mayor said, pointing a ghostly finger in the direction of a young girl in a pink dress with lace at the collar and hem. Lyric tried to find the "she" the mayor was talking about among the throng of spirits in the decimated graveyard.

"He's talking about me." The ghost was not a young girl. She was a large, angry girl who had blown herself up to look like a Macy's Thanksgiving Day Parade balloon that had been in storage way too long and was way too angry. "Everyone's always talking about me," the ghost yelled, looking around at the revelers. All the ghosts stopped what they were doing and stared at the inflated spirit. "That's right. For fifty years now, you have all been talking about me behind my back. There's nowhere to hide now." The ghost flew over the graveyard and, as she did, she shrunk down to the size of a ghostly eleven-year-old girl.

Lyric was frozen by fear. She turned white and stared at the scene, unsure whether she could move at all, let alone run. The ghost came at Lyric like a screeching cyclone, knocking her down. Then she actually passed out.

***

Lyric crossed a road to get to a little, blue house on the other side. Some sheer, white curtains had blown out of the windows and were dancing merrily in the wind. Lyric was mesmerized by them whipping around the tiny, blue cottage. Then she was inside. Everything was covered with sheets and she heard someone humming. She walked toward the sound.

A girl was playing on the floor with some old dolls. The ghost from the graveyard. She was wearing the same pink dress but it wasn't torn up and disgusting. Her blonde hair wasn't ghostly, but perfectly curled as it surrounded her pretty face. Lyric gasped. She was frightened but she wanted to face her fear. She approached her.

"Who are you?" she asked. "Why are you trying to scare me?"

"I'm not trying to scare you. I'm trying to scare everyone else." Then she turned to Lyric. "I want to be your FRIEND." When she said friend, her mouth got very large then shrank back into a sweet smile.

Lyric walked backwards a step or two but was less afraid of the girl in this place. "I'm not afraid of you."

Lyric sat down next to her and looked at the old and broken doll the girl was holding. Its red hair matted against its cracked face. The girl was looking at the doll as if it were the most beautiful thing she'd ever seen. She began to hum again.

"Why are you so mad at me?" Lyric asked.

The girl looked away from the doll and up at the ceiling. The anger barely contained within her skin.

"I'm not mad at you. I'm mad at your grandmother. She locked me in a jar and buried me in the graveyard for fifty years." The girl's face was starting to crack and a blue light began to seep out.

"I'm sorry that happened to you. I don't think she meant to hurt you."

The cracks on the girl's face began to seal up and she looked lovingly at the doll again. "How do you think witches are made?"

"I don't know. Genetics, I guess?"

"It's not genetics, you fool. It's a choice. They make a choice to use powers. They manipulate the world the way they want it. I hate witches. You're not a witch, are you?"

"I don't know. My grandmother is."

The girl looked at Lyric. "You could make a choice. You could be on the side of honesty, instead of the side of DECEPTION." With the last word, the girl threw the doll across the room.

"What do you mean?"

"I mean the only thing that saved me from going CRAZY in that jar was a gate under that graveyard. A gate to the most glorious place in the world. But I need magic to open it. You could do that, couldn't you?"

Lyric was stuck on "saved me from going crazy." Then asked, "What do you mean, a gate? A gate to where?"

"A garden. A garden full of delights. A happy place. Please help me."

The girl looked so sweet and helpless. Lyric just wanted to reach out and hug her. She opened her arms and the girl accepted the embrace.

"Thank you. You are right where I wanted to you. Now I can take you where I want to go." Lyric was out of her dream and the ghost was dragging her up a grassy hill. "You're going to like it. Trust me."

"You've taken me against my will. This is kidnapping or a supernatural version of kidnapping. What is your deal, anyway?"

"Come on." The ghost pulled Lyric's arm. A large gate came into view.

"Is that it?" Lyric asked.

"Yes. Isn't it beautiful?"

What Lyric saw wasn't beautiful but was a black gate covered in fog. It looked like it was the gate for a graveyard, not a gate to a garden.

"Are you sure we're in the right place? This doesn't look like a garden."

What the ghost saw was a beautiful garden with a golden gate. Flowers were blooming in all different colors. Woodland creatures were coming to the gate as if they were waiting for her.

"Isn't it beautiful?" The ghost's face lit up. She looked more human.

Lyric saw something different. The black gate covered in fog was in front of a barren landscape. She could just make out dead flowers, trees, and animals as fog rolled over the ground.

"Everything is dead here. This isn't ..." Lyric stopped herself. She realized something. She looked at the girl and saw how happy she was. Dancing up to the gate she was talking to all the dead animals but to her they were alive and talking back.

"You belong here," Lyric said as she stood about six feet away.

"I know that, silly. I want you to come too. I want a friend."

"I don't belong here. We see two different things. You see something beautiful. I don't. Everything I see is dead and rotten. This is all for you, not for me."

The girl turned toward the gate and all the creatures looked at her imploringly. "I don't know how to get to the other side. This is always as far as I go." The girl looked sad. "I thought you could help me and we could go together."

"I can help you. I don't need to go with you to do that. All you need to do is let go. Let go of earth. Let go of the graveyard and what my grandmother did to you. Let it all go and you'll be on the other side of that gate." Lyric wasn't sure where the words were coming from but, somehow, she knew what to say.

The girl shut her eyes tight. Then she shouted. "I can't! I'm just so angry."

Lyric shouted back. "I'll do it with you. I'll close my eyes and we'll speak together. Say the words 'I'm releasing my anger and moving forward.'"

The two girls began to chant together. "I'm releasing my anger and moving forward. I'm releasing my anger and moving forward. I'm releasing my anger and moving forward."

Both of them began to fade even more. "I think it's working," the ghost said. "Thank you. Goodbye." The ghost looked calm. She waved goodbye to Lyric. It was the last thing she saw before she was back in the graveyard watching the crowd of ghosts fade away in front of her eyes.

"Thank you," they said in unison.

GAME CHANGER

BY PETER TALLEY

I never was a fan of screaming into the void. Okay. I realize how ridiculous I'm sounding in front of this group of investors. They're playing on their phones and pretending to listen. How does that old saying go about taking a horse down to the water? They aren't going to support this project. I'm wasting my time.

Marjorie, do this. Marjorie, do that. I'm used to working hard for the family company but I'm tired. My flight came in late and the hotel didn't hold my reservation. Why not? Well, because my life has been pretty fucking stupid since I took this demotion. Yeah. I gave up a job at a Fortune 500 company to work for a tanking family business. The only thing going right for me is that I'm back in the will.

They said we are in a board game renaissance. The truth is that most of these assholes haven't played a board game since they were in grade school. I'm certain the guy on the far side of the conference table is playing a game on his phone. I can see the screen reflecting off his glasses as he tries to beat a high score. It's better than the pervert on the left side of the table who's sexting up his secretary. We all heard the rumors about the midlife crisis. She's just the new flavor of the month. My point is that I am trying to sell a new concept to a group of men who couldn't care less.

The jerk in the bow tie interrupts the presentation. He's rude but I'll be the one paying the price for coming off too snarky. I get in his face by making a joke at his embarrassing fashion sense. He sheepishly sinks into his seat and lets me get back on track. I used to be nice. I was the favorite grandchild, for fuck's sake.

What the hell do I care if this stupid game ever gets developed? It would take a miracle for the company to make enough to keep us open another three years. My brother says we should sell our shares. I wanted to. Hell, I even tried. No one gives two shits about this company.

We end the meeting with fake laughter and false promises to meet up next quarter. I won't hear from them again. It's fine.

On the way out of the building I'm met by a strange, little man who can't look me in the eye. I recognize him as Toby Turner. He's a game developer and former friend of the family. You might've heard of him. He's the guy who made that game about dancing raisins. He sued the shit out of us when Gramps didn't give him enough credit. They were supposed to be best friends. It was a bogus lawsuit and we all know what it was really about. Toby slept with my aunt. He knocked her up and refused to propose. Nine months later I had a ginger for a cousin. Gramps was furious and nearly beat Toby to death with a copy of his own game. The lawsuit came after that and the business never recovered.

"Hey, Margie," said the wheezy little fart. "It's good to see you again."

I don't answer him. There's no fucking point in pretending. I try to hail a taxi but Toby keeps waddling behind me.

"I'm sorry about Mick," said Toby. "I wanted to go to the service."

"You know what, Toby? Fuck off."

It's not fair that I have to play family liaison to this asshole. He steps back, looking as if he's going to cry. It makes me feel happy for one second until I realize I just cursed him out in front of plenty of witnesses. Knowing how things are going, I figure I'd be next to get slapped with my own lawsuit.

"Is that any way to talk to your godfather?"

"You aren't my godfather," I say. "You have me mixed up with Sharon." I roll my eyes at him and say, "Jesus, Toby. What the hell can I help you with?"

"I saw your name come up on an email," Toby says. "I wanted to see if I could help. I know Beckman and think ..."

"You want to help? Give us back our money."

"I did it to prove a point," stammers Toby. "I thought we were going to settle out of court. After Mick died it just seemed so ..."

"Pointless? Yeah, that's the word you're looking for," I say. "You fucked us over real good."

"When did you become like him?" asks Toby. His words cut deep. "You used to be the nice one."

Thankfully, I catch the eye of a passing cabby and step toward the curb. I slam the door shut and pretend I can't see Toby's face through the window's smeared glass. It is going to be a slow ride to the hotel in this traffic and all I want is to drink.

I think back to the day Grandpa died. I was fresh out of college. My boyfriend and I were settling into our new condo when my brother, Jake, called. He told us the news about the accident. We were supposed to attend an emergency family meeting. I didn't plan on going. Mom still sent a car. When I didn't show up, it caused a shit-storm that nearly got me disowned. Dad was furious and I was told in no uncertain terms, "You're either in the game or out of the will."

I lived through the holidays without hearing from any of my family. It was a shitty thing to happen. Not even the unwanted, red-headed, black sheep wanted to take my calls. Valentine's Day came next and I found myself dumped. Clint said I was drinking too much and that I wasn't fun anymore. What he meant was that he wanted to fuck one of his coworkers.

How did I crawl out of this gigantic hole of suck? It wasn't easy. I was drinking too much. You know what? I still am. What got me back in the family's good graces was being scared to death by the image of my dead grandpa.

I was haunted by the old man. You heard me right. Haunted. It wasn't any mixture of pills or alcohol. My grandpa made it his mission to drag me back into family politics kicking and screaming. I went to a therapist but she thought I was losing it because of the isolation. It became a chicken-or-the-egg kind of session. Was my life shit because I made bad choices or was it my shitty life that made me make bad choices? You know what? I wasn't in the mood for a mind fuck. It also didn't help that, when we took a break, I saw Grandpa in the mirror of the women's restroom.

I was splashing cold water on my face and, when I opened my eyes, Grandpa was there. He hadn't appeared in public before. He stood behind my reflection and growled. He actually tried to communicate with me! I felt his anger. It was worse than when he dragged me out of bed by my hair or when he almost shoved me through the condo's balcony door!

"They're going to commit you," warned Grandpa. His ghost was yellowish and smelled like shit. "You're the last one I can count on! What about my legacy?"

"You made stupid games!" I shouted. "Fuck you and fuck your legacy!"

I don't know why I thought he couldn't hurt me. Like I said, he did knock me hard enough into the balcony door to spiderweb the glass. I was just lucky he didn't manage to push me all the way through the door and over the balcony.

I felt a cold forceful grip around my neck. I remember feeling my feet lifted off the floor before being flung backwards into a stall partition. I slid to the floor and screamed. When I tried to crawl away, I felt my body flip over and get slammed into the tile floor. My vision blurred and a ringing in my ears made my head spin.

The therapist's secretary found me unconscious on the floor. It was said that I slipped on the wet floor and banged my head on the counter. I wasn't going to argue. The accident got me out of the rest of the session. After they checked to see if I had a concussion, I was able to reschedule my next appointment and go home.

I check my phone and see that I missed a text from Jake. He wants to know about the presentation. I type out a response and immediately delete the message. Whatever I send will start another argument that I don't care about. I'm tired of fighting and being the family scapegoat.

On the way past the hotel desk, I'm told the elevator is out of service. I'm not walking up nine flights of stairs. I glare at the clerk and decide instead to head straight to the shitty hotel bar. I order a vodka cranberry before scrolling through my social media accounts. It's another disappointing distraction of fake smiles, bullshit positivity, and horny, shirtless try-hards. I hate being online but those are the only relationships I have outside of work.

After a few more drinks, I find myself in the stairwell. I don't remember how I got to the fourth floor. I stop climbing the steps on the next landing so I can take off my heels. I stumble like an idiot and cling to the railing for support. I'm surprised I haven't seen any other hotel guests when I hear a door slam from below. At first I don't think anything of it until I hear a scratchy voice say my name. I then hear the clomping of feet scrambling up the stairs faster than anyone should be able to run!

It's hard to breathe. I'm temporarily frozen from fear. Part of me wants to take off running up the stairs. The less-drunk part of my brain says I should try to escape into a hallway at the next landing. I hear the footsteps getting closer. The voice keeps calling out my name. By the time I reach the door, I fumble with my room card. The tiny light glows red on the security lock. I try it again. It doesn't work.

"Marjorie," says the scratchy voice again. Whoever is saying my name is on the stairs behind me. When I turn to look, I see myself staring back. She looks like she's been put through hell. I see desperation on the bruised face. Her makeup and hair are a mess. I try to make sense of it all when she starts to vomit up grayish sludge.

"What the fuck?"

"Marjorie!"

"Stay away from me!"

It calls out to me again. I press my back against the locked hallway door and scream. It doesn't stop her from crawling toward me through the sludge she just puked all over the landing. I kick her in the face with my bare foot. I try to run away, slip in the vomit, and fall forward onto the stairs face first. I bite into my lip and taste blood. My hands reach upward to climb the stairs on all fours. It doesn't help, because I can hear her following me.

"What the fuck do you want?" I say through the tears and snot. "What are you?"

I'm now above it by a few stairs. I look over my shoulder, turn onto my back, and kick it again with both feet. This time I'm successful! I hear a crunch as I dislodge her jaw. She falls backwards down the stairs, landing lifelessly in a heap by the hallway door.

"What. The. Fuck. Are. You?" I ask, trying to stand up. My knees are scraped and unstable. I lean against the wall and wait for an answer.

Her wide eyes stare back at me. I hear raspy breath but she doesn't move. I'm expecting at any second for her body to flinch and continue the chase.

The skin on her face bubbles. My stomach churns as the thing at the bottom of the stairs melts into a yellow and gray puddle. It doesn't take long before it no longer looks human.

My fucking phone rings. I feel piss run down my thigh from being startled. It is my brother calling again. This time I answer. Jake doesn't give me a chance to say anything. I make out a few of his words before the call is dropped because of shitty reception. I could tell by the tone of his voice that something was obviously wrong. He was angry that I'd been avoiding him. Hadn't we spoken earlier?

A text message appears as I'm trying to decide what to do next. I figured it was Jake still trying to reach me. When I try to read the message all I see is a picture of a tortured fat man. It is Toby Turner. He's lying on a hotel bed littered in paper play money. Another picture appears of Toby. It a close-up of his face. His eyes are bulging out of their sockets and a wad of wet, fake bills is sticking out of his mouth. A third message appears on my phone. It is a single word. I don't know what it means.

"What the fuck is 'Criion'?"

The walk up the last few flights to my floor is surreal. I no longer feel drunk. I pass by a couple in the hallway who can't help but stare at me. Yeah, I look like shit. If I weren't so stunned I would've said something bitchy. I just didn't have the energy.

My hotel room is colder and darker than it should be. I hesitate to go fully into the dim room, for I know I didn't leave a lamp on. I see two hairy legs hanging over the edge of the bed. I already imagine I know who they belong to.

"Toby?" I ask. "Are you okay?"

I hear a gurgling sound from around the corner where his head should be. I creep in closer and feel a soggy piece of flimsy play money stick to the bottom of my foot. As I peel it from my skin, I can smell urine and I gag.

A half-circle is carved into the hotel wall above the bed. No. It's a backwards letter C. I see the word Criion spelled out and feel nauseous. I've seen all of this before. I was here last night.

I'm missing a day of memories. No wonder Jake was saying he'd been calling me since yesterday. I want this to make sense, but all I can hear is my grandpa's words and the rolling of dice. I did make it to the bar. After that I went upstairs to sleep. I took a warm shower and that's where everything went wrong. I heard chanting from the main room. My thoughts pulsated and I couldn't control myself. I tried to reach for a towel but instead walked absentmindedly to my phone. I stood in front of the mirror, dripping wet and very confused. I remember feeling my fingers dialing a number, hearing Toby's voice answer, and knowing I really wanted him to see me. It was important to be the nice one.

I must've stood there blankly for an hour listening to the dice roll. I didn't care about anything until I heard a knock at the door. Grandpa told me to answer it. The next memory is of me tearing off Toby's shirt and fucking him until we both passed out. I was congratulated in my dream by a muscular being wearing a black crown of writhing tentacles. He said I was winning and that we had more rounds to play. He said he'd give me an advantage to even my chances. Before I got any answers, I felt a pain grow in my gut. It burned and forced its way up and out of my mouth. The grayish sludge formed into my twin. I lost part of my soul.

Why was I chased up the stairwell? Was she trying to help? Did I kill a part of me?

Oh shit! What have I done to Toby?

"Toby? Can you hear me?" I brace myself against the wall when I see the dead, naked body in my bed. His eyes are still open in terror. Inside his disjointed mouth is a wad of play money. "What the fuck were we doing?"

"He was playing your game," said Grandpa. "The ceremony has come full circle." The door I left open to the hallway slams shut. "I'm glad you came back. We've been waiting for you."

The next morning I walk into the boardroom of my family's business. I know what has to be done. Waiting for me is a copy of BLEAK. It is a new game that will revolutionize the board game industry. I smile at Jake. He's secured the deal while I was away.

"Good job," I say. "I was slightly concerned after your call."

"Did you doubt me?" asks Jake. He doesn't wait for me to answer and says, "We can have it in stores by the end of the month. I don't know how they're going to manage to manufacture so many copies that fast, but the numbers are on track and looking great!"

"I'm sure it took some sacrifice," I say, taking my seat at the head of the table. "Have you called in the investors like I requested?"

"Hell, yeah. They are thrilled," says Jake. "The only complaint is that the dice feel too heavy." He flips through his open copy of the game and examines the unusual components. "It says on the box that they're supposed to made from real

300

bone." He can tell I'm not happy but continues anyways by saying, "It's a great gimmick but I think people aren't going to like that feature."

"It's nonnegotiable," I say.

"Kind of like this creepy fucker?" says Jake. He lifts up a black plastic miniature with tentacles and scrunches his face. "I'm surprised it made it past the play testers. Who the fuck is Criion?"

"He's the God of Gaming. Don't you think he'll make a good lead character?"

"Yeah, but I don't want it to hurt sales. Are you sure we should go this far off-brand?"

"What do you mean?"

"We're known for making family-friendly games," says Jake. "What do you think Grandpa would think about us changing up his legacy?"

I smile at the boy and say, "I'm sure we have his blessing."

"Really? I guess that's why you're known as the nice one."

THE MAD MONK

BY THOMAS CANFIELD

Andrei stood before the Prefect of Police, Oleg Speransky, with his cap in his hand. He had removed the cap not so much as a sign of respect but, rather, because it gave him something to do with his hands. Even so, he shifted from foot to foot, uncertain of himself and of how to explain what he had seen. Speransky was senior officer for the District and if anyone would know what to do, it was he. He sat behind his desk and his broad face and burly form projected calm and an easy, unforced confidence.

"Well, Andrei Petrovitch," he said. "What is it this time? Has the neighbor's dog been making noise again? Do you need help procuring a permit? What?"

"Nothing like that, your honor. I wouldn't come to see you over anything so trivial. In fact, I hesitated to come at all. Only I didn't know where else to turn. I'm at my wits' end. If a man such as yourself cannot help, well, then help is not to be had."

"Quite so. Unburden yourself, my friend. Whatever is troubling you, it cannot be so difficult or so intractable as all that. Come, speak."

Andrei shifted his cap from one hand to the other. He glanced around the office, examining photographs and citations, looking everywhere but at Speransky.

"The mad monk, Rasputin," he began and, having committed himself, the rest followed in a rush. "He has returned to St. Petersburg. I was walking along the Neva, you see, heading home after a few drinks, when up he climbed out of the river and clambered onto the bank.

"His face was streaked with mud, his beard and hair matted and tangled. A gash across his forehead and a bruise along one cheekbone lent him a sinister appearance. I do not know how he sustained these injuries—perhaps from the beating administered prior to his assassination. How long he had been immersed in the water I can't say. He stared at me and instantly I knew who he was, knew beyond any shadow of a doubt. It was Rasputin, and no other."

Speransky looked at Andrei and his expression was fixed and wooden, almost threatening, "You do realize, Andrei, that Rasputin is dead. The man you saw, perhaps he bore some faint resemblance to Rasputin. But it could not have been him. Rasputin is long dead, drowned in that very river. That is what brought him to mind, undoubtedly. The dead do not return to us, not even such a man as Rasputin."

"It was he," Andrei insisted. "I swear upon all that is holy and good. Do you think that I imagined it? I looked into his eyes and he into mine. He did not speak; he had no need to speak. Within those eyes resides such torment and pain as few could bear, the unshed tears of an entire nation. I could never mistake those eyes as belonging to another."

Speransky remembered those eyes, remembered seeing photographs of them—haunting, hypnotic eyes, filled with some dark emotion, some terrible secret. They overflowed with a restless, turbulent spirit that was as vast and limitless as the empty Siberian steppe. They were windows into the soul of one who would never know contentment or peace, who would never secure a place in the community of men.

"It was not he!" Speransky sprang to his feet. "How dare you suggest such a thing! He is dead and burns in hell, chained and shackled, encumbered with iron that he might never escape, might never breach the barrier between that world and this. Satan will not suffer him to open his eyes, lest he, too, fall under their spell. He knows fear, Satan does, because of such a man. We can only hope that he flays and torments Rasputin no end. Only thus shall a measure of revenge be exacted for all of Rasputin's many crimes."

Speransky's face was flushed with anger. His chest heaved. He balled both hands into fists and stared at Andrei as though he would attack him, as though he had never before known such hatred toward another human being. Then his shoulders slumped and the blood drained from his face. A grey pall settled over his features. Defeat permeated the membranes of his eyes.

"So, Rasputin has returned." Speransky's words constituted a form of surrender, an acknowledgment of a truth too self-evident to be denied. He groped for the chair behind him, collapsed in a boneless mass. The hard line of his jaw had dissolved. The decisive, confident bearing had leached away. He waved one hand in the air in a feeble effort to regain his composure. "What did he want? Why has he returned now, when Russia has finally regained some measure of stability? And why reveal himself to you, and not someone in a position of authority?"

"Before God," Andrei placed one hand over his heart to demonstrate his sincerity. "It is not something I wished to happen. I am blameless in the matter. I did not seek him out. It was he who called to me. That is, I believe he called to me. I don't remember hearing his voice. I found myself standing next to him, there on the bank of the river. I was greatly afraid. He smelled of wet clay and of death. He was a bigger man than I had imagined. His shoulders ..." Andrei stared off into the distance, shuddered. "A man such as he might crush stones in his fists, might shatter bone with a single blow."

Speransky nodded. "Half a dozen conspirators attempted to cut him down—and failed. No one man would dare attack Rasputin alone. The night of the assassination they lured him to a dinner party and plied him with alcohol. They had laced his drink with poison but he betrayed no sign of being affected. They shot him instead, would have left him for dead, but he rose up and ran. They pursued him and shot him again. But he would not die, this dark spirit, this conjurer, this unholiest of holy men. The assassins threw him into the Neva and he sank down into the depths where, by rights, such a man belongs. And yet ..." Speransky's face contorted in horror. "He has come back!"

"He was a terrible sight, that I can tell you." Andrei shuttled his cap back and forth between his hands. "More ghoul than man. His cheeks were hollow, his flesh spongy and water-logged. Claw-like hands, the joints swollen." Andrei bit his lip. "His head unnaturally large and grotesque. Had I the strength to do so, I would have run away. And yet, I detected no rage in him. I sensed no anger."

"It was not Rasputin, then." Speransky grasped at this as a drowning man might. "It was anger that sustained him. His hatred was directed not at one man or one individual but at entire peoples and nations. Who has brought more sorrow to Russia than he? Who has dragged her deeper into the mire?"

"Perhaps his anger was hidden, then. He had concealed it, as he concealed much else. I remember him leaning toward me, almost touching his lips to my ear. His voice trembled and shook with the effort of speaking. His words—at first I did not understand them." Andrei lifted his shoulders in a gesture of helplessness. "He expressed a wish, a desire, to be granted an audience with the Czar."

"He what?!" Speransky lunged forward, gripping the edge of the desk.

"Requested an audience with the Czar. He appeared—such was my impression—not to be aware of anything that had happened subsequent to his death. He knew nothing of the fate of the Czar or of his family, did not perceive that time had moved on and left him behind."

Speransky ran one hand over the naked pink dome of his head. "The Czar is something of a tall order," he remarked at last. "I do not know that it can be arranged. Not in this world, anyway." Speransky stared at Andrei a long moment. "And how did you, Andrei Petrovitch, respond to this request?"

Andrei wet his lips with his tongue. "You must keep in mind that I was scared. Mist was rolling in off of the river, the city appeared to have dissolved. I heard footsteps on the pavement above but could see no one. None of it seemed wholly real." Andrei rubbed his forearms as though assaulted by a sudden chill, as though the mist had followed him here into this very office, into the presence of the Prefect of Police. "I offered to act as a go-between, spoke of the Czar as if he were a living man—as Rasputin had spoken of him. I would have said anything, done anything, if only Rasputin should return to the river and leave me in peace."

Speransky nodded. "That was wise. Agitating Rasputin, contradicting him, would have been a mistake. Let him believe what he liked. The truth would have served no purpose."

"He handed me this." Andrei reached into an inner pocket of his jacket, withdrew an object wrapped in a silk handkerchief. He set it on Speransky's desk. "He asked that I return it to the Czar. He clutched at my jacket, his eyes filled with such anguish as the living shall never know. His sin, as the Good Book says, had found him out. Not for nothing had he insinuated himself into the confidence of the Czarina, exploiting

306

her weaknesses and so hastening her ruin. Perhaps, at long last, he perceived just how grievous was the injury which he had inflicted."

Speransky made no move to touch the object on his desk. "What is it?" he demanded.

A light kindled in Andrei's eyes. He settled his cap back on his head. "Ah, your honor, you will recognize it, surely. Whether Rasputin stole it, or extorted it, or came by it through some other foul deed, who is to say? Properly, it belongs to the people of Russia. It is a part of their inheritance and to them it must be returned."

Speransky reached out and unwrapped the object. His thick fingers seemed awkward and unwieldy, unequal to the task. At length, a luminous glow emerged from beneath the silk and spread across the top of the desk. Speransky peeled away the handkerchief. His jaw dropped in stunned disbelief.

"But how is it possible? My eyes must be deceiving me!" Speransky's voice was hushed, almost reverent. "It is as you say—a miracle! Did you know that, to this day, eight of the collection remain missing. There are none other like them in all the world."

The Fabergé egg was an object of ravishing beauty. Its art and craftsmanship blended together with such ease and naturalness that the piece might have sprung into existence whole, just as it was. Blue and white enamel fused with a pattern of gold filigree to create an effect that was incomparably rich and luxuriant, yet somehow uplifting. The piece radiated a sense of magic and enchantment.

"Rasputin!" Speransky's eyes were wet with emotion. "Even he could not carry the weight of a crime such as this. Even he is capable of remorse. After all these years, the heirloom is finally returned to where it belongs." A gentle smile of reverie played over Speransky's features.

"There's only one problem, your honor." Andrei made an awkward gesture of apology. "Rasputin has returned as well. He is here, in St. Petersburg, only waiting upon the mist to emerge again. Who is to say what designs he harbors or what villainy he now contemplates? One has only to look into his eyes," Andrei shuddered, "to know that the darkness resides in him still. He remains as cunning and ruthless as ever.

"And this time, heaven help us all, he will not be so easy to kill as before."

PULL BACK THE CURTAIN

BY CAMILLE DAVIS

Alaw looked at the room she found herself in, wondering how it could be foggy inside a house. She looked to the right and saw large, mostly-glass doors. They were closed tightly with no gaps between glass and door, so it couldn't be poor construction at fault. She looked to the right and saw an out-of-place, dark wood bar near the wall, like it had been imported for a party and never taken out. Everything else in the room was carefully tended for but cheap in design.

"Where am I?" she asked. She'd meant to think it, but the words had come spilling out of her mouth before she could stop them.

"Who are you?" a woman with a deep voice asked from somewhere behind her.

Alaw whipped around to look at her, the room spinning as she felt unsteady on her feet. "Did you kidnap me?" The words trembled, tumbling out the moment she thought them. She had never had this problem before; she could hold her tongue around her parents and the church officials, but not now.

"Uh no, you showed up in my sitting room. Uninvited, I might add, not that it matters."

"How am I here if you didn't kidnap me?"

The room started to settle, but it was still like looking through a thin layer of fog. The woman had close-cropped dark hair and light brown skin, and she was wearing a bright yellow shirt. It was hard to guess height or any other features through the interference, and Alaw wondered if she was as distorted in the woman's eyes.

The woman sighed, and it looked like she was reaching up to rub a hand over her short hair. "I'm Kiki. What's your name?"

"Alaw." Her voice turned frightened as she asked, "What am I doing here?"

Kiki started to walk closer to her. "I know this is going to sound ridiculous to you, but you're … a ghost."

"Ghosts aren't real," she said automatically. There were other creatures—other beings—that she believed in, but ghosts weren't included. They weren't real. That's all there was to it. "I can't be one because they don't exist." Kiki was close enough that she could reach out and put a hand on her shoulder if she wanted to. Alaw could see brown eyes and full cheeks over a square jaw as Kiki looked up at her, and it was more like looking through dirty glass now. Alaw could see her features because she was so close, but the room was as shrouded as ever.

"Have you looked at yourself since you got here?"

"How can I see anything through this fog?"

Kiki shook her head, looking sad. "There is no fog. Look at your hands, Alaw, and then try to tell me that ghosts don't exist."

She didn't want to. She had nothing to prove to Kiki, who was a stranger that had maybe kidnapped and drugged her—that would explain the fog part, wouldn't it? There was a growing pit of unease in her chest, and that was her reasoning for why she held her hands in front of her and looked down. Alaw froze, eyes going wide with terror. She barely had hands. They were thin wisps of white, like strained clouds stretching across the sky. Her hands nearly didn't have form, and there were no fingers to speak of. She tried to clench them into fists, but nothing changed. It was absurd because she could feel the change through her arms, but her hands didn't respond in kind. "What?" she whispered quietly, desperately.

"I'm sorry," Kiki said.

Alaw looked back up at her. She wanted to cry, but she was too terrified to get tears gathered in her eyes. "If I died, why am I here? Ghosts can't be good." She'd always wanted to be good. She'd tried, for twenty-five short years, to be good. She had failed, and the weight of that failure was crushing.

"You're not bad," Kiki said, attempting to comfort her. She didn't touch her, probably because her hand couldn't make contact with Alaw, and Alaw appreciated that because it only would have made her feel worse. "Besides, you're a vapor, not a fully-formed ghost."

"It doesn't matter." She was spiraling, feeling worse and worse with every passing second and with each panicked breath she tried to draw in. The motion didn't help because she couldn't breathe, but that realization only made it worse.

"Alaw!" Kiki yelled, and it was clear that it hadn't been for the first time, even though Alaw wasn't aware of any time passing. She snapped her mouth shut, chest feeling like it was heaving. "You came back for a reason."

"I did?" She was shaking from head to foot. If she had feet, that is; she was too scared to check. Right now, it felt like she still had them, and she wanted to continue having that delusion.

"You clawed your way back to some part of the world to share information. Maybe you don't remember what it was yet, but it was important. Don't you think if you were evil, you would have stayed in the afterlife, where it's peaceful?"

"I—" Alaw stopped. She wouldn't be able to deal with anymore shocks today; she couldn't. "I think I'd like to go back now," she said faintly.

"I'm sorry," was all Kiki had to say, and Alaw's mood plummeted further. "Look, just … you can float around here for a while until you remember something, okay? Don't worry about it. I don't want you to wander off and have someone call an ouster on you."

Alaw knew that she wouldn't like the answer before the question made it out of her mouth, but she still had to ask. "What's an ouster?"

Kiki's expression turned pained. "Just. Stay here. I'm not good company, but at least you'll be safe." She paused, waiting for Alaw to confirm. When she didn't, Kiki prompted, "Okay?"

"It's not as though I have a choice," Alaw whispered, unthinkingly trying to put her hand through her hair. The sensation was unfamiliar, but similar to how it had been when she was alive. She tried for a smile as she dropped her hand back to her side—as it were—but mostly it made the urge to cry much stronger. "How do you know all of this?"

Kiki tried a smile of her own; it looked as pained as Alaw's own must have. "I guess you could call me a lightning rod for the Beyond."

CRAFT & CHAOS

BY JD KETCHAM

Dinner had started innocently enough. My wife, Caitlyn, and I were both surprised at the invitation from our neighbor, Maria. We'd lived in our house for nearly six months now and had probably said less than 10 words to her between the two of us. But here we were, with just enough light small talk for everyone to get to know each other.

"We appreciate the invitation," Caitlyn said. "We're sorry we didn't invite you over to our place, but things have been so busy at the restaurant—"

"Restaurant? Oh, you must be the couple that bought the Main St. Cafe!"

"Mom? I told you that weeks ago," Alana said with a practiced eye roll that can only be accomplished by girls between the ages of 14 and 25.

"Did you? Oh, I must've forgotten. Silly me," her mother replied, her voice trailing off while she reached for her glass of wine.

"So, is it just the two of you?" I asked, hoping to move the conversation along.

"Hrmm? Oh, yes. Alana's father—"

"—Is gone." Her daughter finished for her and proceeded to storm off.

"I don't know what I'm going to do about that girl. I'm reaching the end of my rope," Maria said sharply. Her eyes were getting shimmery, but no tears fell. "But it's like she's two different people. During the day, she's a perfect angel. But she's up all night; sometimes I hear voices from her room. When I confront her about it, she talks back and storms off, like now."

"Maria, it's a teenage girl's job to run her mother ragged. We all go through that rebellious phase. If it's alright with you, I can try and go talk to her." Cait was always good at this part. Being gracious, without being dishonest. It was probably all her years as a bartender. Of course, being a natural medium and empath helps.

"Would you? I know we don't know each other very well, but it would mean a lot," Maria, said, her brave face slipping. Tears started to fall as my wife went up the stairs.

"Can I get you some tea or something?" she asked. It was apparent that she was trying to rally.

"No, thank you," I replied. Then, desperate to break the awkward silence, "Can I show you a magic trick?" I asked, pulling a deck of cards out of my pocket.

"You know magic?" she asked.

"You could say that. Here, shuffle these."

The trick was simple, using 21 cards, in progressive rows of three, you use math to predict their card. The structure of the trick allowed me to get three different divination layouts, and by having Maria shuffle the cards, I could do a reading without her even knowing.

I didn't have any real natural talents, like Cait, but I'd picked up odds and ends about magic. All kinds of magic. Stage magic works not because it's designed to fool people, but because it creates a situation in which people want to be fooled. Real magic—skills like divination, channeling, and sigils—

314

those work the opposite way. People want to believe, but when you show them the truth, they think you're fooling them.

I take note of the first three cards, a 2 of hearts, 5 of spades, and queen of diamonds. I immediately see her relationship with her daughter, the 2 of hearts being the card for connections and balance, and the 5 of spades normally for action. However, the spades are inverted to represent a disturbance in communication and thought. And the queen of diamonds is a female authority figure. I repeat the process two more times, each time getting similar divination results, and having Maria point to the row with her card. Just as I lay down the last card something strikes me.

"Maria? Was this your card?" I pick up the king of spades and turn it to show her.

"Yes. Wow, that's amazing. I suppose you're not allowed to tell me how it works."

"Sure I can," I say, "It's magic."

Looking down at the card in my hand, I knew that Maria and Alana had much bigger problems than teenage rebellion.

"I think I'll take that tea now," I said, as Maria left for the kitchen I looked at the card in my hand. Just then, Caitlyn came down the stairs.

"She wouldn't let me into her room. I tried talking to her but she wouldn't open the door," Caitlyn said. Then, noticing the cards on the table, "What did you see?"

"Reading was typical mother-daughter relations, 2 of hearts, queen of diamonds, inverted 5 of spades. I mean it's not uncommon for a teenage girl not to talk to her mom, is it?" I relayed.

"Then what's wrong?" Caitlyn could tell something was bothering me.

"This was the card Maria drew." I showed her the king of spades. Caitlyn looked at it a moment, her brows furrowing. I could tell she was trying to remember what I'd taught her about interpreting the cards. "An evil dark man; here comes the king of spades," I reminded her. "But it gets worse." I turned the card over.

I collect playing cards. A habit I picked up from my family. Caitlyn knows that I always gravitate toward the classic red deck with a symmetrical image of Cupid riding a bicycle on the back. The card Maria selected had a black back with archangels in a triple circle layout with white borders.

"I take it that card wasn't originally in your deck?" Caitlyn asked, already knowing the answer. In response, I flipped over the first column of cards from Maria's layout, Vegas style, showing their red backs.

"That's not good."

"What's not good? Did you speak to Alana?" Maria asked, returning from the kitchen with a pot of tea and a plate of cookies.

"No, her door was locked," Caitlyn replied.

"Alana's door doesn't have a lock," Maria said. As she did, I could see the color start draining out of her face. Caitlyn looked at me and then the card. Without a word to each other we both took off up the stairs to the second floor with a bewildered and terrified Maria behind us. Caitlyn stopped at the second door on the left. It was decorated in the usual teenage ephemera, band posters with boys far too pretty, pictures with friends, and a dry-erase board with markers. Maria pushed past me and tried to open the door.

"This doesn't make any sense, there's no lock—" When the knob wouldn't even turn she started pounding on the door. "Alana Cynthia Wilkie! I order you to open this door."

My wife put her hand on Maria's shoulder. "It's not locked, Maria," she told her in a soothing voice. "It's warded." I was sure the last bit was as much for me as it was for Maria.

"Can you break it, Cait?" I asked.

"If I had a black candle, a cauldron, some bog water, and a full moon, maybe."

"Okay, I'll take a crack at it." I pulled a marker off the board and proceeded to imagine the world OPEN in my mind. As I did so, I started drawing on the door next to the knob. The black marker didn't show up much on the dark-stained wood but it didn't matter. It was the symbol that was important. I imagined the four letters of the word superimposing over one another, into a single image. Their lines blending, some vanishing in lieu of others to create a single symbol. I drew as perfect a circle as I could manage, bisected by a vertical line. Off the center of the line, I drew another to the right connecting it to the circle. From the bottom of the center line, I drew a line moving up and left at an angle. Upon finishing the final line, there was the faintest spark of static electricity from the door to the marker, and the door opened slightly.

"Alana, I don't know what you think—" Maria stormed past us but stopped short. The scene in the room would have been breathtaking had I not known the danger involved. Alana was sitting cross-legged on her bed. She was looking up at something hanging in the air over her bed. It was transparent and indistinct, but I could just barely make out the shape of a man. On the bed, just in front of her knees, was a board made of old wood. Even from across the room and through the fog of spiritual energy, I could make out the letters on the board and the off-white planchette, almost yellow with age.

"What is that?" Maria asked breathlessly, confirming that she too could see the spirit in the room.

"It's Daddy," Alana answered her, though she never took her eyes from the spectre in front of her, and her voice sounded strangely far away.

"That's impossible ..." Maria said. Over and over. She just started repeating, "That's impossible." Then Caitlyn took her by the shoulders and said, "Maria, I'm going to need some salt."

"S-salt?" she asked, looking up at my wife. The mundane nature of the question blissfully took her out of her shock.

"Yes, salt," my wife replied, then added, "And do you have any candles?"

Things started to happen quickly. Caitlyn started gathering supplies: salt, candles, and some dried sage from the pantry, with a very confused Maria following behind her. Caitlyn started preparing the ritual. She drew a line of salt in a circle around the bed. Maria had given her a package of birthday candles from the kitchen and Cait placed one at each cardinal point on the circle.

Stepping inside the circle, my wife knelt in front of Alana. Gathering her thoughts and her will, she reached out and rested her hands on the planchette. With a very deliberate motion she thrust it at the bottom left of the board, pointing at the word "Goodbye." In an unnaturally loud voice, she called out, "Spirit! Leave now."

"No, don't make him leave!" Alana protested. I stopped Maria from going to her daughter just in time to keep her from breaking the circle. Just as I pulled her back, the spectral image flared into blinding azure light.

"Spirit! Leave now or be ousted." This time Caitlyn lifted the planchette and slammed it down on the board, still pointing at "Goodbye."

"No!" Alana screamed.

"Let me go! I have to get to my daughter!" Maria struggled against me.

"Spirit, I command you a third time, LEAVE." This time she picked up the planchette and, instead of slamming it down, she ran it through one of the candle flames. At this, the

318

shapeless spirit flashed again, this time scarlet in color before finally vanishing in a burst of haze.

Both my wife and Alana slumped down to unconsciousness. I carefully blew out the candles, and broke the salt circle with my foot, releasing the ritual. With my finger, I traced another sigil in some spilled candlewax at the foot of Alana's bed. This one for the word SAFE. My wife and I walk very different paths on the Winding Way, but I pitch in where I can.

"That board on Alana's bed. Do you know where she got it?" I asked a dazed Maria, who was tucking her daughter into bed.

"My grandmother's old talking board?" Maria asked. "I can't imagine where she would have found it."

"These things have a way of finding their way to those who are susceptible," my wife added. She had just started to wake.

"But that was just a parlor trick Grammy used to scare us kids," she said, looking down at her daughter.

"Maria, I think we all know that's not true," I said.

"That wasn't her father."

"How do you know?" Caitlyn asked.

"Alana's father isn't dead."

THE NEW YEAR'S ANGEL

BY E.E. KING

The first time Able saw Ana he mistook her for an angel. Maybe it was because, with her back to the light, her entire body seemed outlined in gold and glowed like a halo. Or possibly because the smile on her face was so radiant, Able thought it must be more than human. But probably, it was due to the large, white, feathery wings that were strapped to her back.

It was a New Year's masquerade. There were gods and goddesses, and devils, and mermaids, so he shouldn't have been surprised to see a woman dressed as an angel. But the wings fluttered so realistically that for just a moment, Able thought she had fallen from the skies.

Able was dressed as a troubadour in tight, black pants flecked with silver; a tall, felt hat that drooped over one eye; a black mustache; a mandolin slung over his shoulder; and a black and silver mask.

It might've been the mask that gave him courage because, without even stopping to straighten his tie, he walked right up to the angel and asked her to dance. It was awkward, waltzing with a hat covering one eye and a mandolin swung over his back. It was difficult not to bump the other dancers with the angel wings. But, despite the challenges, Able could have sworn their feet didn't touch the ground, and later, when he asked for a New

Year's kiss, she gave it to him without hesitation. Her lips were as soft as rose petals. She tasted of orange blossoms and dreams. Able was so filled with joy he could have died happy, but now there was too much to live for.

They were married a month later, in February, when the Monarchs were just waking from their winter sleep. The butterflies mate in mid-air. Afterward, the males die almost immediately, drifting down to the mossy ground, littering the forest like orange confetti. The females flutter north toward Canada and Alaska, resting on the first milkweed they can find to lay their eggs. Then they die too, leaving their unborn young to continue the journey. Millions expire. That is why the afterlife is so full of butterflies.

As with the female Monarch, so it was with Ana. In just a few months, she grew heavy with child. Her belly was as round and hard as a small planet. Able, who had thought she could not become more beautiful, discovered he was mistaken. She was so radiant he had to put on sunglasses before he kissed her. She was so filled with joy, no one in a twenty-mile radius could feel sorrow.

Though males were not allowed in the birthing room, Able screamed every time Ana had a pain. And when at last the child was born, pulled yelling into the world after three days of labor, Able and Ana both collapsed as though they'd been bled dry.

Able's mother cared for the baby while the parents lingered, drifting like moths between light and darkness.

Ana had the will to live but not the strength. Able had the strength, but after Ana passed, he lacked the will. He survived, but surviving is light-years distant from living. He worked hard, raising his daughter, Adelina, with love and care, supporting his mother as she grew old. But inside he was empty as a corn husk.

Each year he and Adelina built a beautiful altar for Ana, framed by giant white wings. Each feather was a gardenia petal, pasted onto a frame of lemonwood, so that butterflies gathered around the altar, kissing it with their feet.

Though Able was still young and handsome, and many tried to tempt him with sweets and smiles, he never gave anyone a second glance. After wedding an angel, he refused to court a mere woman.

Adelina grew up, left home, and got married. The night after the festivities, Able went to Ana's grave. "She made a lovely bride," he said, "Though not as lovely as you. He's a fine young man. I think they will be happy."

It was chilly for October, but Able didn't feel the cold. He rested his head on the tombstone and closed his eyes. Something soft brushed his cheek. And, when he looked up, he saw an angel perched on top of the grave. At first Able thought it was a trick of light, a shadow cast by the branches of a nearby tree, an illusion made by a moonbeam filtering through the leaves. His heart had been hurt too badly to give way to hope so easily.

But, as the breeze picked up, a feather fell from the angel's wing and drifted against his hand. It was as tangible as love, as real as heartbreak. Raising his face, he opened his arms to the angel. She bent down and kissed him. Her lips were as soft as rose petals. She tasted of orange blossoms and dreams. All night long he lay cradled in her wings. And when they found him in the morning, frozen and slightly blue, there was a smile on his face and a long white feather clasped in his hand.

FAMOUS LAST WORDS

BY AJ KNOX

"This building can't be haunted because there's no such thing as ghosts," said Joyce Thomas, laughing at Zeke Edwards.

"Famous last words," Zeke said, referencing "no such thing as ghosts."

"I'm telling you," he continued, "the conference room is the scariest place I've ever been to. When I'm in there, I'm not alone. I feel like something is out to get me." Zeke looked her in the eye with such conviction that she believed him.

"Maybe you just spooked yourself into thinking it's scary. It's just a big, empty room with a table and chairs."

"I'm telling you. Come see me after midnight, and you'll get the scare of your lifetime!"

"I think you're just trying to get me all alone," Joyce laughed.

Joyce and Zeke were part of the overnight cleaning crew for one of the largest buildings in the city. The conference room, whose cleaning Zeke oversaw, was on the highest level. Joyce oversaw the lobby and surrounding area on the ground floor. She rarely had cause to go upstairs, but that never stopped Zeke from asking. They had been friends long before being coworkers, and Joyce knew that Zeke liked her.

She had worked here since their high school graduation a couple years earlier, and helped Zeke get his job. Her mother had died in a car accident, and she stayed home to help her father raise her younger sister, Claire. Joyce had worked to become the supervisor of the cleaning crew, so she was able to choose the floor she was responsible for. She preferred the ground floor because of its proximity to life beyond her cleaning cart—to Dad and Claire.

Joyce knew that Zeke had been arrested for drug use, but he had promised to quit if she hired him. He had started working with her crew just a couple weeks earlier. In showing up to work on time, and sober, he seemed to be a man of his word. So, she had forgiven him for his past mistakes, that was all she could ask for.

The top floor was relatively new to Zeke. It came with rumors of being haunted, but he was not originally a believer in ghosts and such. He considered them clever pranks that became online videos. He had watched many supposed real videos, none of which had changed his mind.

Until one night in the conference room. He experienced weird things that he could not explain, and the next night he experienced more. There were intense cold spots, which would be there one moment and gone the next. There were strange noises, flickering lights, and the door to the restroom opening and closing of its own volition. He felt he was losing his mind and needed a trusted person to convince him otherwise, to explain it. Therefore, he wanted Joyce to come up and experience this as well. To rationalize the experiences as just scaring himself, as she had suggested.

"I'm serious, Joyce. I need you to come up and show me that I am not crazy, experience these things with me. Help me rationalize it. You know I never believed in ghosts and goblins ... things that go bump in the night. Help me see that I am just scaring myself," he begged.

"All right," she laughed. "I'll see you at midnight."

***

The top floor was not that large, consisting of just the conference room, a bathroom, a small lobby, an even smaller hallway, and a utility closet. The elevator and a stairwell off the hallway were the only entrances.

The elevator had a loud "ding" noise, so it was impossible for anyone to come onto the floor without Zeke knowing.

DING

He nearly jumped out of his skin. Looking at the clock and seeing the time as ten past midnight, he took a deep breath. The elevator slid open to reveal Joyce, smiling slyly.

"Did I just hear you scream?" she asked, flashing an eyebrow as she stepped into the hallway.

"Hey, this place is freaky. You'll see!" Zeke guided her to the table in the conference room.

"So now what?" she asked, making googly eyes.

"I swear, this isn't me trying to hit on you."

"Good, because we're waiting for one more."

As if on cue, the elevator dinged and slid open to reveal a young girl who was obviously carefree in spirit. Zeke recognized her right away, unsurprised that Joyce had invited her.

Aurora claimed all the time to be open to the spirit world and managed to fit it into every other conversation. She strolled into the room like she was one with the wind.

"Zeke, Joyce ... I can feel the energy between you."

"What does that even mean?" replied Joyce, her googly eyes forming a roll.

"Not from within. It's an energy in the room ... a presence is with us."

Joyce tapped Zeke on the arm. "Does that make any sense to you?" He shook his head.

Aurora sat at the opposite end of the table.

"So, this room is haunted, and the ghost is with us?" Zeke asked.

"Essentially, yes," Aurora answered.

"There's no such thing as ghosts," Joyce maintained.

"Famous last words, I'm telling you!" Zeke shot back.

Aurora pressed her palm on the table and lay down her head, effectively taking control of the room. She knelt this way in complete silence for a long moment. Eventually, Joyce smiled and shook her head.

Aurora began to hum, and Joyce eyed Zeke, mouthing "Really?" Zeke shrugged and asked quietly that she wait an extra second.

Suddenly, Aurora stood and opened her eyes. "I am calling out to the spirit in this room. Can you hear me?" Reaching, she took Joyce's and Zeke's hands into her own, and indicated that they should also link.

"The energy doesn't approve of you, Zeke. It doesn't like that you have a crush on Joyce. It knows Joyce does not reciprocate your strong feelings for her."

"This is bullshit!" exclaimed Joyce. She released both of their hands and made for the elevator. "What is this, Zeke? A way to guilt me into going on a date with you? Did you honestly think this would work? Did you both talk about getting me up here for this?"

"That's not what this is!" Zeke called out. "I didn't know she was going to be here!"

Joyce was a step away from the hallway when the conference room doors slammed shut with a loud WHAM!

Joyce spun to face Zeke. "What the fuck is this?!"

"I swear I don't know!"

Suddenly, the lights went out.

"We must recreate the circle," Aurora said, coolly.

In the pitch blackness, Zeke reached out and felt hands meet his. Confident that he had both girls he smiled.

When the lights came on, he was horrified. Instead of Joyce and Aurora, the hands belonged to one being dressed in long black robes. Zeke couldn't see the face or determine its gender. The being squeezed his hands with a vice-like grip. The walls had changed from off-white to charcoal black, and the doors were peeling back to reveal a long, cave-like pathway.

The robed figure held Zeke's hand and led him down the path. Zeke tried to pull away, but the cold grasp was too tight. For each question Zeke asked, he received no answer, and he eventually stopped asking. He felt they had been walking for years when the path finally ended at a river bend. His captor took him to the entrance to a large ship, a war galley. A long line of men and women were boarding the ship.

Zeke tried again in vain to shake his hand from the grasp of his abductor. He tried to rationalize what was happening. He decided this had to be a bad dream. As the line shortened, Zeke realized the people were handing a ferryman a gold coin before boarding the ship.

"Hey," Zeke called to his silent dark captor, "I don't have a coin! I'm not supposed to be here!" His words were again met with silence as they waited.

When their turn came, the dark figure released him, then did something Zeke was not expecting: It removed its hood. Zeke had envisaged a confrontation with the Grim Reaper of legend. He expected a skull, a skeletal figure, to be beneath the robes. He was shocked and ashamed when the figure revealed herself to him.

"Melody, I am so sorry," Zeke said recognizing who it was that had taken him.

"Your words have no meaning as you do not mean them in your heart," Melody Thomas said to him. "You have left my husband a widower, and my children motherless. Joyce gave up her future because of your recklessness. You never even told her that it was you driving the car that killed me. You thought you had gotten away with it."

Melody grasped a small pouch on her robes, retrieving one golden coin. "This is for you. It is your token to cross the river Styx with Charon."

"I don't want to," Zeke said, breaking down in tears. "I am sorry. I am so sorry. I wish I could take it back. … I've been doing so much better."

"You cannot take it back. And in doing better now, you cannot undo what once was done."

Charon stood at the entrance to the ship. He also wore a flowing black robe; however, his did not entirely cover his long, bony arms. His frame was very skeletal. He held a long staff that had a glowing lantern on the end. The shadows around him danced as if he were one with the night.

Melody handed the coin to Charon. He took it with long bony fingers. He gazed at the coin with his dead black eyes. Charon looked at her, then at Zeke.

"Whose voyage is this?" he asked in a deep, guttural voice.

Zeke bowed his head and admitted that it was his passage. Charon led him onto the galley. Zeke turned to look back at Melody, but she was gone.

***

The lights came back on as soon as Aurora grasped Joyce's hand. They were both taken aback for a moment, startled by the light. Both girls screamed when they saw Zeke sitting lifeless in a chair.

The paramedics arrived in typically quick fashion. They determined that Zeke had suffered a heart attack from fright and probably died instantly when the lights had gone out. Joyce arrived home early enough that morning to take Claire to school. Claire was so excited to see her. Jack, their father, had asked Joyce if was okay after her shift. She assured him she was, and he kissed them both on the foreheads then headed off to work. Joyce insisted Claire finish their breakfast before they left.

"Joyce!" Claire said, "I had a wonderful dream last night. Want to hear about it?"

"Sure do," Joyce said, grateful to take her mind off the events of the evening.

"I dreamed Mom visited me in my room last night. She told me everything was going to be okay. Isn't that nice, Joyce? I believe her. Do you believe her?"

Joyce smiled at her little sister. "Of course I do. That was a good dream." Joyce took her younger sister in a warm embrace. From a corner of the room, out of sight of the girls, Melody Thomas watched as her daughters hugged, then faded away.

HAUNTING REVENGE

BY MATTHEW MEYER

Terry stumbled into his living room after working another long shift. He wasn't part of a grueling repetition on an assembly line, nor was he constantly answering to a bunch of assholes through a small, rectangular window. He was an insurance agent, working behind a desk in a nice, air conditioned building where the local radio station religiously played classic rock from eight o'clock a.m. to ten o'clock p.m. He always had some radio hit cycling through his head.

Terry headed toward the bathroom and splashed cold water on his face. When he looked into the mirror, staring at the streaks of water now running down his face, he thought he saw the smiling face of Ben Clarkson. The smile seemed sadistic. He could make out the thin face with pointy chin, hollow eye sockets, and sunken cheekbones. Terry blinked and splashed some more water onto face—and Ben's face disappeared. Ben had been an acquaintance of his since he had started working at Global Relief Agency. Terry wouldn't necessarily call them best of friends. What kind of friend would provoke the other friend to present a knife to their abdomen?

After the bathroom Terry went to the kitchen and pulled out his favorite late-night remedy—a bottle of Jack Daniels. It was a repeated habit, especially since the whole incident occurred six months ago. It was so repeated that his peers had suggested he go to a few meetings. Terry was far from calling himself an alcoholic. It aided him in drowning out horrid memories. If turning into an alcoholic was what it took to live a peaceful life again, then pop the top again.

It was well past midnight when he awoke from his slumber. He was still in his recliner, the television playing the late-night news. The room was spinning and he felt like he needed to get off the merry-go-round or else he might spew chucks all over the other kids. He staggered to his bedroom, undressed himself from his dress shirt and suede pants, and tucked himself into bed without brushing his teeth. He would wake up in six hours anyway; his teeth could wait until then.

The nightmares began the moment he drifted back to sleep. He had been at the bar, Patty's Lounge, having what he had that night: overcooked burger, fries, and a glass of brandy. He hadn't been hurting a soul. Ben had come up to him first. He was shit-faced, holding true to a reputation of ten years. Ben had claimed that there were some rumors going around of Terry making advances toward his sister, who was a fitness trainer at their local YMCA.

Politely, Terry told him that he was out of his mind. Yes, it had been true that he had recently divorced his wife, and he was known to flirt around town with various women, some of whom were a good ten years younger or better. He had only been to the YMCA once since the ugly divorce, and Ben's sister hadn't even worked that day.

Ben wasn't hearing him. According to Terry, Ben wasn't hearing anything but his own delusional thought processes, powered by the influential juice that caused the gears to slow and jam on occasion. He started calling Terry every name in the book. At first, Terry remained calmed, finishing his food and downing his liquor. Even the bartender was telling Ben that his time was up.

Ben followed Terry outside and wouldn't let him get into his vehicle. This was where the nightmare got ugly. Ben threw the first punch. Terry wrestled him to the ground and managed to pin him, but Ben broke out a knife from God knows where and started swiping at him, managing to cut a thin sliver in Terry's left leg right under the kneecap.

Even in the nightmare, Terry could feel the anger rush to his face. He pressed his foot on top of Ben's wrist, causing him to loosen his grip on the knife. The vision of the knife entering Ben's abdomen always played back in Terry's mind. It was the most frequent of the memories, seeing the pain on Ben's face and hearing his agonizing cries. It always stopped him dead in his tracks.

The bartender had called the cops when they had first started fighting and, by the time Terry had stuck the knife into Ben, the flashing red and blue could be seen running up the street. Of course Terry was thrown in jail, and it was in jail when the news was broken to him that Ben had died in the hospital.

The trial was a long period of about six months; all that time he was pacing the cell floor. Fortunately he had a respected lawyer who had drained the self-defense law dry, making Terry dodge the forty-years-in-jail bullet. He couldn't thank his lawyer enough. It had been almost a month now since he was found not guilty, and Ben's family was still banging on his door, hoping to get a chance for a re-trial.

The time on the clock when Terry awoke read four in the morning. It was a Saturday, and he was off. He laid back on his pillow but his eyes were open wide. In the darkness, he thought he could make out Ben's smiling face again, stretching out from the plaster of his ceiling. He blinked, and the face disappeared.

I'm losing my mind, he thought.

The phone rang, startling him. He stumbled out of bed and went downstairs to answer it. Nobody he could think of would be calling him at that hour.

"Hello?"

There was no answer. He answered again, but the other end was dead. He slammed the receiver back down on the dock.

He turned around and his heart nearly burst out of his chest. Sitting in his recliner was the figure of Ben. He was smiling that same sadistic smile.

"Hello, Terry," the figure said. "It's been a while."

The body of Ben stood up and started in his direction. Even though it made walking motions, it also appeared to be floating. Terry was frozen in place. His mind was telling him to move but his body wouldn't obey. In less than five seconds they were nose to nose.

"When I died," the body of Ben started, "I was stuck. Something was keeping me from crossing over. For a long time I tried to figure out what I needed to do." The smile returned to his face. "Then I realized what it was. In order for me to cross over, I need to kill you!"

"No." It was all Terry could utter, and it came out soft and weak. Before he knew it, Ben's hand held a knife. It was the same knife Ben had pulled on him that fateful night; the one Terry used to commit his murder.

"See you on the other side." The pain came quicker than Terry ever thought. It was a burning pain that started in his abdomen and expanded toward is chest, his arms, and eventually his legs. He collapsed onto the floor, and the ghost of Ben faded away.

BEYOND THE LEVEE

BY PETER TALLEY

The summer of 1988 was my first real taste of freedom. I had a great bike and plenty of friends in the neighborhood. It was a different age. We could get away with playing until it got dark out. We rarely traveled all that far from home but it always felt like a grand adventure.

Life was pretty great for eleven-year-old me. I had allowance money for the Ding-Ding Man's ice cream truck and quarters for the local arcade. We'd spend our mornings at the junior high school pool. After drying off, we would eat lunch and have the rest of the day to mess around. We talked about cartoons, played with action figures, or hung out at the park. When we really felt daring, we would ride our bikes out to the levee. We played army with toy guns in those woods between the river and the old waterworks ruins. These were magical times. Sadly, though, they also included some terrifying moments. I'm not talking about the poison ivy, sand burs, or nettles. The only place that was off-limits was under the swing bridge. Back in those days it was still used by the railroad and operated by a grumpy man who was rumored to shoot kids with a pellet gun.

My best friend back then was David Lewis. His family lived catty-corner behind my house. We were both in the same grade but he went to private school. I introduced him to the other kids the previous year after our parents invited the Lewises over for a cookout.

David was a quiet kid. I'm not saying he was weird. He just listened more than he spoke. I didn't mind it because we were mostly into the same things. The difference was that he collected baseball cards because of his older brother. I didn't know until much later what happened to Brian. All I knew was that David thought the world of him and that he was no longer alive.

It was late on a muggy afternoon in the middle of July when David and I came up with the following day's plan. We spoke over the fence in our backyard about wanting to go fishing with Scotty and Wayne. My idea was to catch a matinee or see if we could pick up comics from the grocery store. I was fine with being out-voted because it meant we could also work on our fort.

I was proud of that fort since it was my idea to build it. It wasn't much to look at because we had limited tools. I'm amazed at what a group of kids could scrounge together down by the river. People used the area as a dumping ground even though it wasn't legal. We scored a backseat to a car that we used as a couch. It wasn't as gross as it sounds. We also made a kick-ass lookout tower up in a tree.

Dirt bike trails ran through the woods. They made it easy to navigate our kingdom beyond the levee. I didn't like sharing our woods with the bikers, but they mostly kept to themselves. The worst part was hearing the very distinctive sound of their bikes starting up. I used to imagine they were giant, pissed-off hornets.

We didn't catch anything on our fishing trip. Wayne said it was because of the train going over the old swing bridge. We all heard the whistle from around the river's bend. Thinking back now, I can't remember ever catching any fish at that location. I was just happy to be out of sight from the bridge operator's booth.

The sun was going down and our parents were expecting us home hours ago. I remember it being a Thursday night because it was leftover night. I was excited for mom's twice-baked potatoes. We were about halfway back to the waterworks ruins before Wayne said, "Oh crap!" He'd forgotten his dad's hammer back at the fort. His old man was a real asshole. We knew leaving that tool behind could get Wayne beaten.

Wayne was the toughest kid on my street. I still wasn't going to let him go back into the woods alone. Scotty and David argued about getting home. I didn't blame Scotty; he'd just been freed from being grounded. David, on the other hand, was being a coward.

"We all go home or nobody does," I said in my best Sergeant's voice.

"That's not how the quote goes," said David.

He was right but it didn't matter. I got my point across and, after saying goodbye to Scotty, the three of us headed back into the the woods. We ran most of the way to make up time. I knew getting home late was going to get me into trouble. It would be worth it, though. Wayne needed to know we soldiers stuck together.

I should never have suggested a shortcut after retrieving the hammer. It was getting dark and the mosquitoes were bad that year. The path back wasn't well marked. I had found it a week earlier when I was trying to hide from a dirt-biker. I hadn't done anything wrong. I was just working on my jungle survival skills.

We all heard about Brady Stark. It was a big news story that year. His disappearance gave teeth to the urban legends. We all heard the stories of the hook hand by the lovers' lookout and would tell each other the latest gossip about a bobcat on the loose. What made things real for us was when we found Brady's body for the first time.

I felt like I was being watched. I thought it was just my nerves until I heard Wayne tell me to stop running. A few yards to our left was a kid sitting on a log. He looked damp and tired. He was around our age but I didn't recognize him from school. Then David told us it was the missing kid from the news.

What happened next almost made me piss my shorts. Brady Stark stood up and pointed at me. I asked if he was okay. His mouth opened and hundreds of lightning bugs flew out from within the log! We were surrounded by the greenish glow and unable to move. Brady's skin took on a waxy glow and I realized he wasn't solid. He ran past us, through the woods, and back to the levee. I wasn't sure what happened but was surprised to see Wayne following after the boy.

We closed in on the clearing where the gravel access road led to a levee pump house. My heart raced and I was nearly out of breath. I missed it at first. David pointed out the soiled blue cloth. It was in the lower drainpipe that we found Brady Stark's ball cap. A few feet behind it was the kid's body.

I was the first to run. I didn't look back. I just hauled ass as fast as I could to where we stashed our bikes. When I got to my bike, I realized we'd lost David. Wayne was with me, hammer in hand, and looked like he was going to throw up.

I left my friend on the wrong side of the levee that night. It was a mistake that's haunted me through life. What's worse is that, when the deputies found David, he had curled up with Brady's corpse. I was told he was talking to it like it was his brother Brian.

***

It didn't matter which story you believed about Brady Stark's death. Innocence was lost and it affected the entire community. Paper routes were quit, kids couldn't go the parks, and parents whispered out of earshot of their children.

I, at least, was able to play in my backyard. I'd see David watch from his second-story bedroom window. He wouldn't smile or wave back. I couldn't tell if he was pissed off, embarrassed, or shell-shocked. I missed my friend but doubted our friendship would endure.

Scotty's mom let us have a sleepover party over Labor Day weekend. I was hoping it would be my chance to make things right with David. Wayne and I were the only two to show up. We ate pizza and watched videos that Scotty's dad rented for us. It wasn't until we were climbing into our sleeping bags in the living room that I had the courage to bring up what happened that night with David.

"We saw a ghost," said Wayne.

Scotty dismissed our conversation and pretended to sleep until I asked whether he believed us. He rolled over and said, "You're making it up. Go to bed."

"My mom says it happens all the time," said Wayne. "Ghosts are all around us."

"We're not supposed to talk about what happened," said Scotty. "My parents might be listening. Can we just go to sleep?"

"You told your mom?" I asked Wayne.

"She knows witchcraft," he said. I couldn't tell if he was bragging or trying to make a joke. "Brady wasn't my first ghost. We did a séance where I spoke with my uncle."

"Bullshit," said Scotty.

"Screw you," said Wayne. "I spoke with my uncle. He was in our kitchen as close as I am to you." He crawled out of his sleeping bag and said, "I don't care what you think."

"I don't believe in any of that satanic crap," said Scotty. "Ghosts aren't real."

"Believe what you want, asshole," said Wayne. "This isn't about Satan. Ghosts exist and they are like normal people. Most are pathetic little bitches like they were in life."

"You're full of it," said Scotty.

"And you're a pussy," said Wayne. "You wouldn't know what to do if you saw a ghost."

"Where ya going?" I asked.

"I have to piss."

I waited until Wayne was down the hall before I said, "I think he's telling the truth."

"He's lying," said Scotty. "It's like the time at recess when he said his dad built him a jet-pack for his birthday. He does it for attention."

"But I saw it too," I said. "Brady's ghost led us to his body."

"Whatever, dude," said Scotty. "I'm going to sleep now."

The toilet flushed and I saw Wayne a few seconds later in the hallway. He wiped his eyes and blamed it on allergies. I knew better. I was sure he'd been crying. It wasn't a secret that his family life was different than most of ours. He was a good friend and I didn't care that they were on food stamps. Everyone in class knew it. They just were too scared to openly tease him. So what if he had to tell a little lie to feel better about himself? I didn't mind. Wayne protected me from bullies and was a loyal friend. He didn't deserve how shitty his life was going to turn out.

***

Middle school was a real bitch for all of us. I'm talking more than the awkward phase most people face. My parents divorced and I spent most of eighth grade in counseling because of stress. I started having nose bleeds and anxiety attacks. Scotty moved across town, changed schools, and learned his mom was having an affair with our softball coach. Wayne ended up in a children's home for destruction of property. He apparently set off fireworks in a mailbox. David ran away from home. The police found him down by the river hiding in the drain pipe.

It wasn't until high school that I saw everyone again. Oddly enough, it was a homecoming football game where I noticed David across the field. He was playing in his school's band. I tried to catch up with him afterward but he pretended he couldn't hear me. I watched him climb into his parents' minivan and drive off.

It was good to catch up with Scotty now that we went to the same high school. We didn't hang out much besides having the same math class. He was big into sports and I was still fighting with anxiety that kept my grades too low to do any extracurricular activities.

Wayne, surprisingly, kept his shit together well enough to be allowed back into real school. We all thought he was destined for the alternative high school. I'm just glad he didn't drop out. I'd see him in the halls but we mostly ran with different crowds.

Halloween of freshman year was when David finally talked to me again. I'd never have guessed he'd be the one to bring the group back together. I was at my mom's house for the weekend and saw him through the kitchen window. We made eye contact, I waved, and he actually waved back. By the time I got outside, he was already over the fence, waiting in my backyard.

"I'm glad you saw me," said David. "My parents aren't home. I've been hoping we could talk."

"How've you been?" I asked.

"Good," said David. He looked at this feet and said, "I'm sorry. I'm sorry they wouldn't let me be your friend."

"Why not?"

"They say you're a bad influence."

"Well my mom didn't like us hanging out with Wayne either."

"What? Oh," said David. He scrunched his forehead. "I wasn't talking about my parents."

"Well then, who?"

"I was talking about Brian and Brady," said David.

I let out a nervous laugh. David shrugged it off and smiled. I didn't feel comfortable with how he stared over my shoulder.

"They say I can't trust you."

"What the hell are you talking about?"

"I told you," said David. His face became red with anger. "Brian and Brady." He grabbed my shoulders and shouted, "They say you're going to get me killed!"

I didn't expect him to come at me like a crazy person. The intensity in his eyes reminded me of every deranged psycho I'd ever watched at the movies. I pushed his arms away and stepped back and said, "Get off me, asshole! What the fuck's wrong with you?"

David's expression went blank. His arms dropped to his sides and his jaw hung open. I called out his name. I raised my hand up, swiped back and forth, and asked, "Can you hear me?"

He suddenly reacted. I felt his hand crushing my wrist. I couldn't pull away.

"Fuck off, nerd!" said David. His voice was cold and filled with evil. "You shouldn't have run!"

His grip was so tight that I feared he was going to snap my wrist. I tried again to pull away but David held on. He leaned in close. His breath smelled like rotten cheese. I couldn't figure out what was happening. All I can say is that I felt I was being surrounded. Thankfully, before anything else bad happened, we heard his parents' electronic garage door open.

"Why's your nose bleeding?" asked David. There was no sign of the angry young man from seconds before. He let go of my wrist and shook his head in confusion. "What did they make me do?"

I wish I would've said something. I was too scared. My wrist stung and I felt a dribble of blood on my upper lip.

"I didn't mean to hurt you," said David. "Stay away. Just stay away from me."

I remember watching him run back to the fence line. By the time David got back to his yard I could see his mom in the window. She looked terrified. I saw her close the curtains and fade from sight.

***

It was our senior year. The party down by the old swing bridge was underway. It had been years since I dared go beyond the levee. I was hesitant when I heard about the party. I only went because Beth asked me to go. We'd been dating since junior prom and life was good. Drinking beer, smoking weed, and making out sounded like a fun way to celebrate our upcoming graduation.

The location was next to perfect for my classmates. They'd planned to use a cornfield but had to change plans when we thought an underclassman tipped off the cops. It was Scotty's idea to use our old stomping grounds. We parked our cars and carried the cooler down the gravel access road.

I always hated that fucking bridge. At night it looked even more creepy as it peeked out above the trees. Its triangular superstructure was like the bones of a giant, rusted skeleton. On this side of the river was the mobile half of the bridge. It was turned due to spring barge traffic so it wasn't connected to the portion that extended from the other riverbank.

"We should climb it," said Matt Clark. I heard a belch when he asked Scotty, "Didn't you use to live around here?"

"We sure did," Scotty smiled mischievously. He was probably on his sixth beer. He looked at me but his eyes were glazed over. I had a bad feeling about what he'd say next. "Why don't we see if we can both get into the operator's booth?"

"There's nothing up there," I said. "I think there was an electrical fire or something."

"Let's find out," said Scotty. "Come on, Beth. You should come too."

It wasn't hard to climb up the giant gears at the base of the bridge. We easily got onto the railroad tracks and walked to the steps that would take us near the operator's booth. I felt like a little kid again being that high off the ground.

"Do you remember the old bastard who used to run this thing?" asked Scotty.

Beth answered before I could and said, "He was a child molester."

"That's right," said Matt. "Didn't they find a kid in his shack?"

"No," said Beth. She pointed to the pump house. "You can't see it now but there's a drainage pipe over there."

"That's fucked up, you know that?" said Matt. "Your girl's kind of a freak."

Beth elbowed me in the side, "I did a local history paper on the murder last year for Mrs. Fredrickson's class. The operator's name was Gerald Burrows. The police thought he was responsible for murdering Brady Stark. They never tried him though."

"Because he didn't do it," I said. "They interviewed him but the lawyers didn't have enough evidence."

"He got away with it," said Beth. "Everyone in town was super pissed about it."

"I heard he blew his brains out," said Matt. "You only do that if you're guilty."

"Or if people don't leave you alone," I said.

"I'm with her," said Scotty. "Burrows hated kids."

I shrugged. "You were the one shot in the ass with the pellet gun."

Scotty ignored me. "We're in luck. The door's busted open!"

"Did you check for bums?" asked Matt. "I don't want to get knifed by a …"

"You are so brave," teased Beth.

Scott was about to say something when we heard a moan from within the operator's booth. He looked over his shoulder at me and laughed. "What if it's a ghost?" I knew he was getting me back for the pellet gun comment.

"Wayne did say the bridge was a ghost magnet."

"Fuck that loser," said Scotty. "That's make-believe kid shit."

"It was the wind," said Beth. "Can we hurry up? It's getting cold up here."

"Let's carve our initials and get back to the party," said Matt. He pulled out a pocket knife and offered it to Beth. "You go first."

344

"You do it," said Beth. She handed me the knife and whispered, "Just our initials, okay?"

I hesitated for a moment before placing the blade into the wall board. I didn't like the feeling of nausea that crept into my stomach. It reminded of when David grabbed my wrist. Strangely, my wrist began to ache. I looked over at Beth and the guys and tried to speak. It felt like the bridge was starting to turn.

"Snap out of it, dude," said Scotty. "You've only had one beer!"

I finished putting our initials into the wall and handed Matt the knife when we heard noise from outside the booth. It was our classmates shouting to run. The cops found out about our party.

"We should stay put," suggested Beth. "They won't look up here."

"You don't know that," said Matt.

"Cops are lazy," whispered Scotty. "Sit down and shut up."

I kept watch as our classmates scattered into the woods and over the levee away from the bridge. There was no way the police were going to catch everyone. I only got nervous when the occasional flashlight shined upward to where we were hiding. We all held our breath and waited. It felt like an eternity before the area below the bridge cleared out and we were left alone inside the booth.

"Nobody better narc on us," said Matt nervously in the dark.

"They're out for themselves," I said. "Anyways, I think the coast is clear. We should climb down. I have to get Beth home."

"Oh, I'm already in deep shit," said Beth. "I lied and said I was staying the night with Erica."

"And she was caught. I saw a cop grab her by the access road," said Scotty. "Better come up with a new story."

"Can we get out of here?" asked Beth. "It's been fun but I really don't want to spend the night up here with you jerks."

We descended the stairs back to the railroad tracks. The river was so far down I started to feel dizzy. Then I saw a familiar face staring at us from the far end of the bridge. It was Brady Stark.

I woke up with the giant beams of the superstructure looming overhead, as if I'd been eaten and was now held within a giant stomach. I was between the railroad tracks and had the worst headache of my life. Beth knelt by my side and cried. She held my hand to comfort me but it did little good. I was hurting, confused, and thought I might've broken my spine.

A burst of lightning bugs filled the sky. I tried to sit up. The pain was incredible in my lower back. I looked around for the guys and found them at the end of the bridge. They were transfixed on the woods and hadn't realized Beth woke me up.

"There's something out there," whispered Beth. She snuggled under my arm and helped me to stand. "We're scared to climb down."

"Brady Stark," I said. It hurt to speak. "I saw Brady Stark on the bridge."

"Is that why you passed out?" asked Beth.

"We were the kids who found his body," I admitted.

The lightning bugs swarmed around us. Beth hugged me and I tried not to shout out in pain. Matt and Scotty swatted at the glowing insects until I heard Matt scream. He turned around and ran back toward us. Scotty soon followed but, for some reason, stopped short of returning to the middle of the bridge. He looked up and behind us at the operator's booth.

"No fucking way ..." said Scotty before he was interrupted by the soft plink of a pellet gun. We watched as Matt took the shot between the eyes, stumbled, and fell off the side of the bridge into the river.

When I think back to that night I can still picture my classmate falling in slow motion. The lightning bugs parted as his body passed through them. I remember seeing Scotty's fear turn into foolish bravery as he followed after Matt. I suppose there's a reason he's done so well in the military. I always admired Scotty but this was the first time I saw him as a hero.

I wanted to help but I was too slow. Beth was by my side. She was screaming at a faceless man in a plaid shirt who stood armed with a pellet gun. Gerald Burrows took aim with his weapon and fired at my girlfriend. The pellet struck Beth in the jaw which caused her to violently wrench her neck. She spat out blood along with a tooth.

"Get off my bridge!" shouted the ghost.

***

We have different ways of remembering the night of the party. I, for one, try not to think about it. The lucky ones ran off into the woods with a story to tell. A few others received minors-in-possession charges and did community service. Matt Clark wasn't so fortunate. He and Scotty wound up in the hospital. Scotty fully recovered and refused to speak of the incident. Matt, however, grew unstable and was put on medication. It wasn't how any of us wanted to remember our senior year.

Beth and I broke up shortly after the party. I wished things had worked out differently. Her parents wanted to sue my family for my part in her drinking and being injured. Thankfully that didn't happen. It felt like I was reliving the mistake with David all over again. Being beyond the levee cost me yet another friendship.

You still want to know how Beth and I escaped? I grabbed her and we jumped off the side of the swing bridge that was near land. I still have a scar on the back of my head from where a pellet hit me.

I spent the rest of the summer working and being stuck at home. My parents cancelled my graduation party, gave me a curfew, and took away my car. I had to walk to the ice cream shop where I made shit money and had to stand on my feet for the entire shift. I suppose it was fair for all of the trouble I caused. When I look back now, I'm ashamed to think how my selfishness hurt so many people. I was a real dick and am glad my folks loved me enough during that tough time.

I'd hadn't turned my life around by college. Sadly, I was still an asshole that blamed others for my mistakes. I didn't last long away from home. After a year away I moved back into my mom's house. I promised I'd go back to school in the fall. What I didn't tell my parents was that I was going to enroll in the local community college. I just wasn't cut out for the university.

Fall arrived and I did as promised. I was able to transfer my credits to the community college. I found myself bored by the classes but was happy that I met some new friends. I also ended up having a class with Wayne. For better or worse, we watched a lot of horror movies and talked about role-playing games.

Life was good but not great. I partied more than I should've. I could blame it on my time with Wayne but he never forced me to drink or do any drugs that I didn't want to try. I dated some. It never lead to anything serious. I pretty much was fine with letting my life continue this way until I got a call from my dad. He asked if I'd seen the newspaper obituaries. You could imagine my response. Only the old read obituaries.

Beth and David were dead.

I didn't attend either funeral. I didn't even know they'd been dating. I still have trouble picturing them together. If I had to see them dressed up in coffins, I probably would've lost whatever sanity I had left. Apparently they tried to outrun a train. From what it sounds like, there wasn't much to bury.

I don't recall much of the weeks following the tragic news. I drank heavily. I stopped going to class. The only person who didn't give up on me was Wayne. I'd sleep on the couch outside of his bedroom. He still lived at home but had set up the upper part of his family's house like an apartment. I avoided getting too caught up in his drug dealing, but it was hard not to realize we were both heading for dark times.

It was on a rainy night that we started talking about the old days. We reminisced about riding our bikes around the neighborhood and what happened to people we knew. When Scotty's name came up, the mood in the room changed for the worse.

"How many times did that asshole ditch us over the years?" asked Wayne. "That fucker always thought he was better than us."

"Not true," I said in our absent friend's defense. "He's a good guy. A real hero. I hear he's already up for a promotion!"

"You don't know shit about him," said Wayne. "I should've kicked his ass when he said I stole that kid's bike."

"But you did," I reminded him. "You totally stole Jared's bike."

"I'm talking about the other kid," he slurred. "Skip. He said I stole Skip's bike."

"I don't think so."

"I know so," said Wayne. "I took five fucking whacks from my old man's belt and I didn't even steal the fucking bike."

"Oh shit," I said. "I see what you're saying. Different bike."

"Yeah and that asshole always thought he was better than us."

"You just said that."

"He called me a liar," said Wayne. "Why'd we hang out with that dick?"

"I dunno," I said. "We were just kids."

"We saw some shit, man. We saw some shiiiit."

"Well, yeah," I agreed. "We saw a lot of shit."

"What the fuck are you doing here?" asked Wayne.

"Drinking beers?"

"No, man," he said seriously. "What the fuck are you doing with your life?"

"I'm still figuring it out."

"Nah," said Wayne. "This is my life, man. You had your shit together." He took the beer out of my hand and chugged it down. "You've always been a good friend."

"Thanks ..."

"Shut up, dumbass. I'm not finished," said Wayne. "You have to get your shit together again. I can't have you sleeping on my couch. I mean, you're always welcome to hang out, but dude." He stared me down and said, "We're always going to be brothers."

"What are you talking about?"

"I'm talking about you making something of yourself. I've been doing a lot of thinking and it's not good, man. We're running out of time."

"Dude. We're young."

"Men in my family don't make it past forty," said Wayne.

"That's bullshit."

"It's not," said Wayne. He readied his bong and took a long hit. "I don't make the rules. Two uncles and one cousin are already gone. My grandpa and his dad also died well before the big four-oh."

"Well, fuck," I said. "Is it a medical thing?"

"Some say it's a curse," said Wayne. "Like I said, We're running out of time. There's still hope you can make your life into something good. What do you really want to do with the time you have left?"

"I don't know," I admitted. "Why are you busting my balls?"

"Because I don't want you to stay like this," said Wayne. "I want to do something for you. Do you trust me?"

"I'm not dropping acid."

"I want to tell you about the future," said my friend. He went over to his dresser, opened the top drawer, and pulled out a purple velvet bag. "Here's my deck."

"Tarot?"

We'd talked about it before. Wayne's family was into weird shit. I even drove him to a New Age store to buy his mom's birthday present. I liked looking at the books. The shop smelled of incense and the girl working the counter was hot. I would've liked to go back but Wayne got called out by the store's owner for having a black aura or some shit. At the time we thought it was funny. It cost me getting the girl's phone number but it wasn't a big deal.

"It's cool if you don't want a reading," said Wayne.

"It's not that," I said. "I'm just surprised is all. I didn't know you had a deck."

"It's was my uncle's. He wanted me to have it," said Wayne. We shuffled the cards and Wayne motioned for me to split the deck. "They went to me since he didn't have any kids."

"My family doesn't have any traditions like that. Was this the uncle you told us about? The one you spoke to at a séance?"

"Uncle Stan was deep into the supernatural. Deeper than the rest of us. He used to read fortunes and commune with spirits. My dad said he was an ouster. It's like an exorcist but less churchy."

"That's cool."

"No, man. It's fucked up," said Wayne. "You've seen how people look at my family. My relatives settled this town. We should've been rich because of railroad money. Instead we're treated like trash because of a dumb legacy."

"You don't have to be like them," I said.

"But I want to," said Wayne. "It runs in my blood. Ghosts are real and some of them are nasty fuckers. Sometimes it's people. Sometimes it's places. Mostly they're like really thick memories tied up in knots. They need our help to find peace. I don't have a choice, man. I'm fucked no matter what. That's why we're having this talk. You have a chance."

I picked a few cards and arranged them in the way I was told. Apparently it matters which way you turn them face up. I felt good about my choices even thought I didn't have any idea what they meant.

"Interesting," said Wayne. "Every card you drew was from Cups."

"Is that bad?"

"No, man. There are four different suits. It's unusual to draw in that way."

"Should we shuffle again?"

"Nah. Give me a second though to read them." I waited patiently and soon he spoke again. "Water and instinct. Fluidity and imagination. All of these are represented in the cards. It makes sense, dude."

"What makes sense?"

"Do you see how this card's reversed?" asked Wayne. "It speaks of vulnerability. It also means hope and promises a returning."

"You're getting all of that from a card?"

"Yeah," said Wayne. This means stagnation. Your soul seeks opportunity. They're telling you to detach. The only way to find completion ... no, that's not it ... satisfaction. You have

352

to embrace change by moving on. Remember these cards focus on water."

"I do have to pee," I joked.

Wayne laughed, pointed down at the spread, and said, "You have to leave everything behind. That's your future. If you can do this, you'll be happy."

"What am I holding onto?"

"Ghosts," said Wayne. "You let the past fuck you up."

***

I took to heart what Wayne said. The next morning I woke up and decided to make significant changes. His words gave me the courage to try something new. I found my way back to sobriety thanks to that Tarot reading. It doesn't matter whether you believe in the magic or not. It worked for me. I'd witnessed the unexplainable before. Who's to say the cards didn't tell me exactly what I'd been waiting to hear?

I graduated from college, found a decent job, and decided it was time to move on. It turned out that marking "open to relocation" was the smartest thing I could've done for my career and love life. My life radically changed after meeting Jodie. I met her while attending a conference in Boston. We got married after a long engagement, bought a house, and decided to start a family. Before I knew it, I was in my thirties, the kids were starting school, and I'd opened my own insurance office. There was very little reason for me to think about the past. We'd go back for the holidays to see my folks, but that old river town no longer felt like home.

So why was I standing on the long levee at night? It was because of friendship. I knew it was a dream. I saw Wayne in the distance. He waited for me at the water pit that sat in the middle of the waterworks ruins, where we would throw rocks down into the old, flooded tunnel system. There wasn't much to see at this time of night, and the ruins were mostly slabs of concrete that had been reclaimed by shifting dirt and the growth of vegetation.

"Hey, man," said Wayne. He wore the same black leather jacket and blue jeans. What bothered me, though, was how much older he looked. He seemed tired and, for some reason, that reminded me of Brady Stark.

"It's been too long," I said.

"I heard you were back," said Wayne. He lit a cigarette and started walking eastward on top of the levee. "Try to keep up, fatty." He looked over his shoulder with a shit-eating grin and said, "You know I'm fucking with you, right?"

Wayne was right, though. I had put on weight. He still was rail-thin. I increased my pace and soon was by his side. When I looked down the straight path of gravel, it appeared that the levee went on forever. It wasn't how I remembered the way to the swing bridge.

"You know they're tearing down the woods," said Wayne. "It's a damn shame. The mayor wants to make it into a gated community."

"Who'd want to live on a flood plain? That's fucking stupid," I said. We both laughed at the idea. "I wonder if there's anything left of our fort."

"Like me?" asked Brady Stark. The dead boy with the blue baseball cap walked out from the woods below the levee.

I woke up startled by the sound of my cell phone alarm. Jodie was already downstairs making coffee. I heard the kids finishing their morning routine. It was time to start what should've been a usual Thursday. When I went to the bathroom to take a piss, I saw an additional reflection in the mirror. Brady

Stark placed his clammy hand on my shoulder. A painful chill spread through my body before I blacked out.

The doctor said it was a minor heart attack. I don't remember anything from the time between being in my bathroom and waking up in a hospital bed. It all happened so fast. I thought there were supposed to be warning signs. I didn't believe whatever happened was because of poor health. Brady's ghost did this to me.

I went to rehab, took time off of work, and planned to eat healthier. I did all of this for Jodie and the kids while secretly wondering if I was going crazy. It wasn't until I heard that Wayne died the night before my heart attack that I knew the shit was real. I hadn't escaped the past. The ghosts were still holding me back.

I wanted to go to Wayne's memorial service. I wasn't able to, though, because of the stint surgery. I did promise to make it back home to see his mom. It took a couple months for me to get around to making that visit, but it was great to see her again. We didn't talk about how Wayne died. The details were sketchy which lead me to believe it was perceived as a suicide. I didn't want to consider that possibility. I knew Wayne lived a hard life and, in some ways, I was surprised that he made it to his thirty-eighth birthday. I also wasn't entirely sure that he wasn't murdered.

I was tired of running away from what I didn't understand. Why were my friends meeting terrible ends? How did this tie into our childhood and that old swing bridge? I needed to find answers and the only other two who would believe me were Matt and Scotty. Unfortunately Matt was in prison and Scotty was overseas.

I found myself at the swing bridge for the last time on a rainy afternoon in May. It hadn't weathered the elements or tests of time very well. It was retired from service and left to rust after being deemed too costly to repair but too damaged to use. A new pump house had been installed nearby due to the recent flooding. It seemed out of place next to the antiquated behemoth.

I felt embarrassed of my fear as I walked to the edge of where the now-abandoned railroad tracks used to connect to the bridge. I took a deep breath and let it out slowly. Where I stood, I had a perfect view of the skeletal superstructure that had haunted my dreams for almost 40 years.

"What is it about you?" I asked. "Why did you have to fuck up my life?" I laughed at the ridiculousness of talking to a bridge. I was about to question it again when I realized my nose was bleeding.

"Hello?"

I turned to see a bald, elderly man with a walking stick. He smiled warmly from the access road and, as he came closer, he asked, "Were you talking to me?"

"No," I said. "I'm sorry. I thought I was alone."

"Are you okay?" he asked. "It looks like you could use a handkerchief."

"I'm fine," I said. "Thanks, anyway. It's just allergies."

"It's clean," said the elderly man. In his hand was a folded-up piece of white cloth. "Here. You can have it."

I took the cloth and placed it against my nose and said, "Thank you. You're probably not going to want it back."

He smiled and shook his head no. "I've plenty more at home." The elderly man planted the walking stick into the ground and sighed at the bridge. "Isn't she something?"

"You could say that." I said wearily.

"A breathtaking beauty, don't you think? I've read there's three left counting her, and she's the largest of them all."

"What else do you know about her?" I asked.

"That you shouldn't stand too close to the end of the tracks." The man chuckled and stepped back from the edge. "I used to come out here all the time when I was a child. You should've seen her in her glory. She was a gateway for both of our towns. When she turned, the sky would go black with smoke and you could hear those gears all the way down the river!"

"I saw it turn once when I was a kid. It was kind of a big deal. Hard to believe something so big could move like that."

"My boys loved coming out here," said the elderly man. "We continued the tradition with the grandkids. We'd have a steak fry and afterwards take a hike to the levee to walk off the beef. Those were fine memories. The youngest really loved train-watching."

"I guess I never thought of her that way," I said. "My friends and I used to play in the woods. We tried to avoid the bridge. We were scared of the operator's pellet gun."

"Gerald wasn't so bad," said the elderly man. "I worked with his son at the canning plant. He just wanted to keep people from getting hurt out here."

"So you don't believe the stories?"

"Not one bit," said the elderly man. "He was wronged by the newspaper. Gerald Burrows might've been a drunk, but he wasn't a monster."

"How can you know for sure?"

"Because it was an accident," said the elderly man.

Before I could respond I felt a blow to the back of my head in the exact spot I was shot by the ghost. I stumbled forward, trying not to fall off the train trestle. The elderly man then used his walking stick for a second time to shove me over the edge.

The swing bridge started to moan with movement for the first time in decades. I heard the gears overhead as they began to squeak and turn. I looked over my shoulder and saw the ghosts of David, Beth, and Wayne. They stood underneath the operator's booth as the gigantic superstructure slowly swung into place over the river.

I was on my knees in the bone-colored gravel. Locusts chirped louder as the blue baseball cap appeared over the tall grass. Brady joined us below the bridge. His skin was missing in places and I hated the smell of moisture that surrounded his soiled clothing.

Brady looked at me and then up to the elderly man. Tears formed in his eyes. "I'm going home," said the dead boy. His rotted skin repaired itself with each step he took away from the bridge. "I'm going home!"

A shot rang out from the operator's booth. Gerald Burrows howled in frustration at missing Brady. I watched the ghost as it aimed and fired again. This shot struck Brady Stark in the back of the head. I saw the dead boy's eyes widen as his body dematerialized into vapor.

"No!" screamed the elderly old man. He shook his walking stick in defiance at the opening of the skeletal superstructure. "Not my grandson!" He yelled out again before he attacked the bridge with his walking stick.

The swing bridge shook and I felt extremely queasy. On the far side of the bridge I saw a burst of silver light. It made me think of the train engines that used to travel across here at night. When I looked for the elderly man I realized he too was a ghost.

"Get off my bridge!" shouted Gerald Burrows. It was the same image Beth and I saw the night of the party. It acted out its role as if it could do nothing else until the elderly man's walking stick struck the bridge again. The pathetic ghost regained its face for a split second and looked down from his booth with annoyance.

"Come down from there," said the elderly man. "I want the truth! What did you do to my Brady?" He waited for the booth operator to descend from the stairs before shouting, "What the hell did you do?"

The scene ended abruptly before my eyes as the two ghosts faded away. I expected to see a confrontation but was instead left with the ghosts of David, Beth, and Wayne. They too vanished as wisps of black smoke at the arrival of a new entity.

"He's right," said Brady. "It was an accident," I saw the dead boy sitting in the shadows under the swing bridge. "You shouldn't have come back."

"I need answers."

"You won't find them here," said Brady. "The bridge is hungry for your soul. You should run while you still can. It's what you're good at." He blurred briefly as he stood up and shouted, "Help me! Help me! I'm down here!" A grim laugh escaped from the dead boy's lips. "Isn't that what you dreamt I said inside the drain pipe?"

"Stop fucking around and tell me what you want!" I demanded.

Brady winked at me and replied, "I'm your fear." Black smoke swirled and the dead boy shifted before my eyes. Its limbs extended as it twisted into a new form of mist, flesh, shadow, and bone. It wore the gray face of a bitterly desperate man. Around its neck was a thick, damp rope tied into a noose.

"Who am I?" asked the specter.

"You're not ... Brady Stark?"

"Who am I?" asked the specter, louder than before. "Remember me!"

"How am I supposed to know? Let me help you!"

The specter charged forward. I wanted to shove it away but instead passed through the image as it dissipated into vapor form. I landed hard in the rock and mud. What I hadn't expected was that this is what the ghost wanted. It was now inside of me. It entered my body while I foolishly defended myself. This is what must've happened with David in my backyard. This ghost could control the living.

Over a hundred years' worth of memories flooded my mind with images of the swing bridge and those who visited this place stuck between the dead and the living. In times gone by, many a fledgling automobile, train, and hiker crossed its span above the Missouri. It was a gateway for so many before falling into ruin.

"What do you want me to see?" I asked.

"My death," said the specter. "Tell me why I was forgotten!"

I watched through a drunken man's eyes as he stumbled his way to the bridge in the early hours of the morning. An unbearable sadness filled his heart. He'd lost his wife and son to illness earlier that winter. He wore no coat. In his right hand was a bottle, and in his left was a heavy rope. His body would be found later that morning hung from a lower beam of the bridge's superstructure. His death wasn't reported. The man was cut down and thrown into the river below.

"Oh, fuck," I said as the ghost left my body. It stood inches from my face and stared into my eyes. "You were the first person to die here."

"And some asshole covered it up," said Wayne. "It doesn't let you off for being a fucking cocksucker."

"Leave me be," said the specter.

"Make me, asshole." said Wayne. "My uncle was trying to help you."

"No," spoke the ghost. "He was trying to destroy me!"

"What the fuck, Wayne? What did your uncle do?" I asked, only to realize my words weren't being heard. This was another of those thick memories tied into a knot.

"Ousters are to blame," said the specter. "Your family ..."

I felt sick as guilt and responsibility swelled inside my chest. It was an overwhelming weight that filled my heart. I wanted to run. The emotions were too strong.

"You've damned us all!" shouted the specter as it attacked Wayne. My friend wasn't ready for the unleashed ferocity. Wayne tried to fight back. I watched helplessly as he was lifted and tossed around like a rag doll.

"Tell me my naaaame!"

"Go fuck yourself," said Wayne. He was beaten but defiant. I closed my eyes as the specter leaned over and entered his body. Upon opening my eyes I could tell the memory of Wayne's death was finished.

"I made him take those pills," laughed the specter. "I will be remembered. Tell me my name!"

For a moment I considered his words. I thought about all of the other lives this ghost was responsible for taking. Soon more ghosts arrived from out of the woods. I was surrounded by what felt like the entirety of the town's deceased who wanted to gather at the swing bridge.

"Tell me my name!" shouted the specter.

"Where's my family?" asked another.

"I want my mama," cried a little girl dressed in white. "Help me find my mama!"

"Get off my bridge!" commanded Gerald Burrows' faceless ghost.

I then heard Matt Clark scream. He wore an orange jumpsuit stained with blood. His hand reached out for mine. Our fingers touched briefly before he pulled away in horror to cover the stab wound in his stomach.

"Him too?" I asked, sadly. "Why?"

"Dude," said Wayne compassionately. He appeared at Matt's side with David and Beth. "We've said our goodbyes. Get the fuck out of here! You gotta move on."

"I don't want to leave you behind!"

"You don't have to," said Wayne. "You just can't keep carrying us with you." He smiled, placed his arms around Beth and David, and said, "I'll take care of them until we meet again."

"Stay," said the specter. "You must stay. The bridge is hungry." He floated near and reached for my throat. "Stay or I'll come for your children. This isn't over. You owe me my name!"

"You can't save us," said Beth.

"It's okay," said David. "We know you tried."

"We can't make it to the silver light. We're trapped because half of the bridge is made of iron. It won't let us cross over," said Wayne. "It's ghost science. I know because my relatives helped build this bridge."

The silver light from within the stationary half of the swing bridge pulsated. The weight of emotion lifted and I heard the train whistle from my dream. All of the ghosts stirred impatiently as they lined up one by one at the mouth of the superstructure.

"I don't understand," I said. "I thought your family wanted ghosts to find peace."

"We do," said Wayne. "But there's an order to things. That asshole has to go first! He's been blocking the gateway since he died."

"And he won't leave until he's remembered," I said.

"Tell me my name!"

"We all know it," said a meek voice from within the crowd of lingering spirits. A boy wearing a blue baseball cap pushed his way from out of the mob. "You dropped this the night you died." In Brady's hand was a tarnished wedding ring. He tossed it to me and said, "Read the engraving."

"Where did you find it?" asked the specter.

"The riverbed," said Brady. "It's been down in the mud this whole time."

"Read it!" shouted the specter. "Tell me my …"

"No," I said. "Go fuck yourself. You put us all through enough hell. The least you can do is give me time to say goodbye."

Brady smiled as the specter held its position.

"I think your grandpa would also like to know you're alright," said the elderly man's ghost. He leaned heavily on his walking stick and approached the dead boy. "I should've listened more closely," said the elderly man's ghost. "What happened to us?"

"It used tragedy to get what it wanted," explained Wayne.

"I only wanted to scare the boy," said Gerald's ghost. "I aimed low but something took control of my hand. I didn't mean to raise the gun. Brady hit his head on a rock after I shot him. I thought he'd be fine after resting but he never woke back up." The ghost glowed a dark shade of green before it admitted, "I panicked and put him in the drainage pipe. I know it was the wrong thing to do but I swear it was an accident. I only wanted him off my bridge."

"Why didn't you tell the police it was an accident?" asked Beth.

"By then I was called a child molester. Nobody gave a shit about what I had to say."

I nodded and said, "We've all had rough lives. Some were shorter than others. What matters now is that we find you a way out of here." Wayne smiled as I looked at the inscription inside the ring and spoke the name aloud, "Benjamin Westfield."

A strong wind blew through the river valley under the swing bridge. I felt the silver light at the far end of the superstructure grow larger and saw my friends float up and onto the abandoned railroad tracks.

"It feels safe to cross," said Wayne. He addressed the mob of ghosts on the shoreline and said, "Get your asses moving. We don't know how long this portal's staying open."

I watched as the ghosts lined up underneath the triangular, skeletal superstructure. At the head of the line was the ghost of Benjamin Westfield. His eyes were set on something beyond what I could see in the silver light. A smile formed on his weathered face as he stepped through the gateway.

"Wait!" shouted Wayne. A dastardly grin appeared as he blocked the next ghost from stepping into the light. "The fucker had it coming."

We heard a scream come from within the silver portal. It sounded as if whatever greeted Benjamin Westfield on the other side was not kind or gentle. The mob of ghosts frantically tried to rush back to my side of the bridge. What they didn't realize was that the mobile side had already started to turn.

"She chose us," said Wayne as he climbed the stairs to the operator's booth. He shrugged at the chaos below as the restless dead continued to panic. They scrambled and screamed but were unable to leave the triangular superstructure. "She won't let us forget." He leaned against one of the rusted beams and laughed. "You hear that? She's still hungry. If I give myself up, the rest can move on."

"What the hell are you talking about?"

"I'm making a deal," said Wayne. "A deal only an ouster can make. Get the hell out of here and don't ever come back."

I tried to argue. I wanted to understand. I didn't get the chance. Wayne stepped into the remains of the operator booth as a new portal opened in the middle of the bridge. Through the silver light I saw beings made of fog. They each held large scythes and links of heavy chain. The little girl in the white dress screamed. Beth, David, and Matt stared helplessly as the

Fog Men stepped through the portal opening and onto the tracks.

"Stop! They don't deserve this," shouted Wayne. "A tithe has been paid!" His voice echoed from within the operator booth. "You have no claim on these souls!"

Gerald aimed his pellet gun and fired into the Fog Men. "Get off my bridge!" He readied another shot but missed as a scythe sliced through his ghostly form. An explosive force of energy was released as Gerald split in two. I was knocked backwards and landed on my ass. I watched in awe as dozens of ghosts became bright bursts of light that drifted up and over the woods where my friends and I used to play. When I looked up at the bridge all I could see was Wayne standing alone on the tracks.

"We did it," said Wayne. He seemed exhausted and ready to collapse. "You gotta go."

"What did we do?" I asked. "Where are the ghosts? What happened to those …?"

"It's over, man. I made a trade. I stay with the bridge and everyone else gets to cross over."

"We all go home or nobody does."

"Not this time."

It was always about the bridge. The old bitch chose to haunt us for a reason. It hungered for our attention. Wayne warned that places could become ghosts. I watched as my friend disappeared, leaving me to ponder his fate. My anger turned into courage. It was time to put childhood fear behind me. I had to break whatever anchored us here.

"It wasn't about Brady, Gerald, or Benjamin, was it? It was about you becoming irrelevant to the community," I said knowingly. "You're a place of misery. You're the specter." I walked to the edge of the railway trestle and spat up at the malevolent superstructure. "You've possessed enough lives.

You used these ghosts to bring me here. Well, here I am! Fuck you. You deserve to be lost amongst the weeds. I hope you rust, fall into the river, and are forgotten. I'm done feeding you with my fear. Starve, you miserable bitch."

I could feel the bridge's overbearing presence. I kept my back to her and for a moment I swore I heard Wayne calling out my name. I refused to look. It was the bridge using his voice. An invisible grip held onto my shoulders and nearly forced me to swivel around. I bit my lip and kept walking.

My mind wandered to fonder times as I took the gravel access road back to my car. I wanted to return to Jodie and the kids. I missed them. Memories of my family emboldened each step and soon the old swing bridge was further behind me. Part of me expected to be shot when my old scar flared up on the back of my head. It lasted for a second and the pain faded away. I thought of Brady's final words before he died. I too was going home.

I can't explain a lot of what happened over the years but I've found a sense of closure. I'd like to assume Wayne and I had a part to play in solving a great mystery and that, somehow, this righted a great wrong. From what I've heard, the old bitch is still out there. I've read she's scheduled to be demolished for safety reasons unless the Historical Society can raise funds to restore her. I hope that, whatever happens, it will be enough to bring peace beyond the levee.

AUTHORS' BIOS

Peter Talley, at various times in his life, has worked as a high school speech team coach, newspaper advertiser, hospital emergency manager, investigator, and funeral home assistant. Born in Ohio, grew up in Iowa, and spent the majority of his time working in Nebraska. He currently resides in Hartington with his wife and son. Peter enjoys writing short fiction and is busy at work on a series of urban fantasy novels. PeterTalley.com

J. Tonzelli is a writer, film critiquer, and Halloween enthusiast who currently resides in rural South Jersey. He authored the anthology *The End of Summer: Thirteen Tales of Halloween* under his own name and co-wrote the horror-adventure series *Fright Friends Adventures* for younger readers under the shared pen name The Blood Brothers. When not obsessively checking the weather report for thunderstorms, he continues his appreciation for all things creepy while making too many jokes about skeletons. He loves autumn, abandoned buildings, the supernatural, and films by John Carpenter. You can catch up with all his writing projects at JTonzelli.com or read his cinematic musings at DailyGrindhouse.com.

Lauren Bolger will talk about music, movies, and books until you make snoring sounds or walk away. Previously, she's written about music. Now, she writes horror shorts and poetry, and is taking steps to complete her debut horror novel. She lives in a suburb sort-of near Chicago with her spouse and two young kids.

She's on Twitter: @renBolger | And here's her website: weirdseashell.com

Kyle Dump is a husband, father, and writer living in Lincoln, Nebraska. In his spare time, he loves wrestling with his toddler, making the baby laugh, and singing songs before bed. When Kyle grows up, he wants to be an author, but for now he enjoys being a short-story tinkerer and press release writer.

Born and raised in Michigan, **Richard D. Brown** is a young, up-and-coming author who is hard at work paving a path for himself. He already has a few books under his belt and looks forward to expanding his arsenal over the next couple of years. When he's not writing, Richard is either sleeping or working on his mental and physical health. His favorite genre to write in is poetry.

Matthew Meyer is a writer who has had an interest in writing since he was in third grade. His favorite books growing up were the *Goosebumps* series. After high school he acquired his Associate's Degree in Graphic Design, and since has had an interest in creating graphic arts. Matthew also has an interest in acting, drawing, and making videos. He has self-published a children's book series entitled *Raising Hare*. All of his publications can be found on his website at matthewmeyerauthor.godaddysites.com. When he's not writing he enjoys reading, playing video games, and spending time with family. He currently resides in Iowa.

A native of the Midwest, **John Timm** has lived on both coasts and several places in between in his dual role as college professor and radio broadcaster. John writes short fiction in several genres, but his taste runs to fantasy, short horror, and crime. He holds a doctorate from the University of Wisconsin – Madison, and when not reading or writing, teaches an occasional course in language, literature, or communications at a university in Phoenix, Arizona.

Marshall J. Moore is a writer, filmmaker, and martial artist who was born and raised on Kwajalein, a tiny Pacific island. He has traveled to over twenty countries, once sold a thousand dollars' worth of teapots to Jackie Chan, and on one occasion was tracked down by a bounty hunter for owing $300 in overdue fees to the Los Angeles Public Library.

Mark Thomas is a retired English and Philosophy teacher and ex-member of Canada's national rowing team. He resides in St. Catharines, Ontario, Canada.

Daniel Kruse is a guitarist, writer, songwriter, and LGBTQ advocate. He's a quirky kind of guy and he resides in Hartington, Nebraska.

Chris Dean travels the American West as a truck driver and this writer adores Yellowstone, the Klamath, and anyplace the sequoias brush the sky. A Chicago native, Chris currently resides in Iowa.

Barbara Avon is a multi-genre author. She has written since she was young, pursuing her dreams and vowing to write for as long as she can. She has worked at several different media publications and will continue to publish novels until "her pen runs dry." In 2018 she won *FACES* Magazine's "Best of Ottawa" award for female author and *Spillwords'* "Author of the Month." She believes in paying it forward and you can read about this belief, as the theme is given voice in most of her books. Avon lives in Ontario, Canada, with her husband, Danny, their tarantula, Betsy, and their houseplant, Romeo.

Born and raised in the suburbs of New York city, **Wendy Wilson** left the flatlands of Long Island for the mountains of the Shenandoah Valley in the '80s. There she settled on a small farm and raised a variety of children, goats, sheep, cows, and pigs. She has worked in a library for most of her adult life and now, in retirement, has turned her love of reading books into a love of writing them. In December 2018 she won second place in the online magazine *Beneath the Rainbow*'s Christmas contest with the short story, "Wishes Can Come True."

"To Be or Not," a story based on her published novel "Eternal Diets," was accepted into the *Hellfires Crossroads 7* anthology now available.

https://www.amazon.com/author/wbwilsonau

Jessica Thomas is a writer, children's illustrator, and artist living in Cambridge. She divides her time between writing, making art, and going for long walks in the countryside with her dog. She has a Master's of Creative Writing and an M.A. in History from the University of Auckland. She is currently working on an illustrated fantasy series, based on her academic research into medieval medicine.

Peter Palmieri is a retired physician and the award-winning author of three novels. He was raised in the eclectic port city of Trieste, Italy, but now lives in the Texas Hill

Country where he spends much of his time churning artisanal gelato, reading, and writing.

AJ Knox lives in Upstate NY with his wife and two teenage daughters. He has worked for the local power company for the past 25 years. In his free time, AJ enjoys writing stories of either science-fiction or supernatural influences, sometimes both. He recently self-published his first novella on Amazon Kindle and has other stories in the works.

Kylee Gee was born in Minnesota and raised in Silver Creek, Nebraska. After graduating from the University of Nebraska at Kearney, she married her husband. They continue to live in Kearney. Kylee enjoys writing short stories in her spare time and is currently working on a YA mystery novel.

Cari England is a screenwriter and author hailing from the Southeast. Growing up on a farm where the night's silence took on a life of its own, she strives to recreate that tension in most of her work, pulling people into the heightened senses that only darkness can summon. She has placed in several screenplay competitions, as well as published works across a myriad of anthologies.

Lauren Stoker is a native Californian and survivor of U.C. Santa Barbara, transplanted to New England for the thrills of skiing on ice and owning a snow blower. Lauren enjoys playing loud music, ranting about anti-environmentalists, and collecting beer coasters, while drinking a fine British ale. Since the tender age of 15, she has struggled with the written word (and sometimes won). Lauren's short stories have been published by *The Hedgehog Poetry Press* (U.K.), *The Arcanist* (a contest winner), *Page & Spine, 50-Word Stories,* and *Quantum Shorts.*

Her story, "No Substitutes Allowed," will appear in Thurston Howl Publications' anthology, *Difursty*.

Alex Blank, after moving to London in 2018, has been experimenting with various forms of writing. Through prose poetry, journalism, fiction, and so on, she's continuously finding and refinding her voice. While trapped and infuriated within the city's crowds—or in lockdown, within her own mind—she likes to explore the themes of identity, loneliness, and one's relationship to time and space. She's the culture editor and writer in *Roar News*, and her work has also been published in *HuffPost UK* and *Heliopause Magazine*.

Danielle Bissonnette has at times worked for a Medical Examiner, a funeral home, been a park ranger, a ski patrolman, and a nanny. She was born in Seattle, Washington, and grew up on both the east side and the west side of the Cascade Mountains. She holds a B.A. in Anthropology from the University of Washington as well as a certificate in Creative Writing. She has a great love of folklore and Pacific Northwest Coast Mythology. Danielle enjoys writing novels, short stories, and painting.

Paul Worthington lives happily in the South Wales valleys with his partner and two children. Manual worker by day and creator of short fiction, scripts, and novels in any other spare time he gets. Reads and writes sci-fi, horror, and post-apocalyptic fiction.

After bouncing back and forth between Florida and the Northeast for several years, **Thomas Canfield** settled in the mountains of North Carolina. His phobias run to politicians, lawyers, and TV pitchmen. He likes dogs and beer.

Rich Hosek is a television writer whose credits include *Star Trek: Voyager* and *The New Addams Family*. He currently lives in the obscure Chicago suburb of Stickney, readying his first novel, *Near Death*, a collaboration with his television writing partner Arnold Rudnick and parapsychologist Loyd Auerbach, for launch in fall of 2020. In his free time, he enjoys developing websites and teaching his sixteen-year-old son how to drive. You can learn more about his past and upcoming works at http://RichHosek.com.

Sophie Baker has been published in many journals and anthologies, and is co-founder of the Mermaid Poetry Collective, with ties to both the East and West Coast, and taught memoir writing for thirteen years. Sophie is profoundly intrigued with all worlds seen and unseen, and communicating between the two.

Ivy Miller's first writing gig was as an advice columnist for her Catholic middle school. From there she had many jobs, including, video and film producer, selling flowers on the street, and accidentally working at a restaurant that was a Mafia front. She has master's degrees in Communications and Library Science. She used to write reviews for *School Library Journal* and *Kliatt*, specializing in non-fiction and fantasy fiction titles. Currently, she is the mother of two awesome young adults and the Library Director for college preparatory school in northeastern Pennsylvania. She does her best writing on the couch in the wee hours of the morning. She loves to write speculative fiction short stories and novels with strong, female, older protagonists.

Pam Bissonnette, retired after thirty years managing cities and large public utilities in the Pacific Northwest, divides her time between living in Seattle and her cabin retreat in the Cascade mountains. An avid skier, hiker, vegetable gardener, and former orchardist, she shares the love of the outdoors with her two daughters, Danielle and Nicole. In Pam's first novel and in several short stories, she likes to explore the future of humankind and its evolution toward the supernatural, super-consciousness, and ultimate reality.

E.E. King is a painter, performer, writer, and biologist— she'll do anything that won't pay the bills, especially if it involves animals.

Ray Bradbury called her stories, "marvelously inventive, wildly funny and deeply thought-provoking. I cannot recommend them highly enough."

King has won numerous various awards and fellowships for art, writing, and environmental research.

She's been published widely, most recently in *Clarkesworld, Flame Tree, Cosmic Roots and Eldritch Shores*, and *On Spec*. One of her tales is on Tangent's recommended reading 2019. Her books include *Dirk Quigby's Guide to the Afterlife*.

Her landmark mural, *A Meeting of the Minds* (121' x 33') can be seen on Mercado La Paloma in Los Angeles.

She's worked with children in Bosnia, crocodiles in Mexico, frogs in Puerto Rico, egrets in Bali, mushrooms in Montana, archaeologists in Spain, butterflies in South Central Los Angeles, lectured on island evolution and marine biology on cruise ships in the South Pacific and the Caribbean, and painted murals in Los Angeles and Spain.

Check out paintings, writing, musings, and books at www.elizabetheveking.com

https://twitter.com/ElizabethEvKing
facebook.com/pages/EE-King
https://www.instagram.com/elizabetheveking
https://whatsinanafterlife.wordpress.com/

JD Ketcham is an author and an online personality. He's produced imaginative fiction in comics and prose. He's a regular reviewer and contributor to the *Two-Headed Nerd Comic Book Podcast*. He runs Planet Fiction Productions, a website dedicated to exploring the lengths to which fiction and storytelling can enrich all parts of the human experience. Otherwise, he's been a professional musician, barista, bartender, and musical instrument repairman. He's an unabashed geek and aficionado of all things comic books, dogs, genre fiction, good coffee, and Irish whiskey.

Beth Stillman Blaha lives in the foothills of the Adirondack mountains with her son, husband, and rescued Labrador retriever. She earned a doctorate in Clinical Psychology in 2008 and has worked with children and families ever since. She is working on getting a fantasy novel traditionally published and running a faster half-marathon.

Leonor Bass lives in Chile, with her mother, in a little town called Curicó. She's been writing since she was 15, mostly fan-fictions, until her creative brain asked for more and her first novel and later her short stories were created. She absolutely loves drinking huge amounts of coffee while reading a good mystery book, especially with a powerful woman kicking butt and taking names. Leonor is also fluent in Spanish, though the majority of her stories will surely be translated into her mother tongue.

Camille Davis was born and still resides in Arkansas, where she works on her writing every chance she gets. Camille writes both urban and high fantasy short stories and novels.

Ian M. Ryan, a student-athlete from Trinity International University, began writing at a young age. Ryan, who was diagnosed with diabetes, depression, and social anxiety at young ages, realized that writing took major stress off of his mind and allowed him to be himself. He is an aspiring young author and baseball player who hopes to find success in both areas.

Justin Alcala is a novelist, nerdologist, and Speculative Literature Foundation Award Finalist. He's the author of three novels, including *Consumed* (BLK Dog Publishing), *The Devil in the Wide City* (Solstice Publishing), and *Dim Fairy Tales* (AllThingsThatMatterPress). His short stories have been featured in dozens of magazines and anthologies, including "It Snows Here" (*Power Loss* anthology), "The Offering" (*Rogue Planet Press* Magazine), and "The Lantern Quietly Screams" (*Castabout Literature*). When he's not burning out his retinas in front of a computer, Justin is a tabletop gamer, blogger, folklore enthusiast, and time traveler. He is an avid quester of anything righteous, from fighting dragons to acquiring magical breakfast eggs from the impregnable grocery fortress.

Salinda Tyson has ducked under a library table during the Loma Prieta earthquake, marveled at ancient Roman aqueducts in France, strolled along Hadrian's Wall in the North of England, enjoyed double rainbows in Germany, and walked 500 paces around banyan trees in Florida. A lifelong fan of mythology and fractured fairy tales, she has a weakness for ghost stories.

Chisto Healy has been writing since his brother handed him Dean Koontz's *Servants of Twilight* at age 9. His hero and favorite author is Simon Clark so go read him right now. He's got a lot of great stuff of his own coming out and you can find all the details at https://chistohealy.blogspot.com/ which he does his best to keep updated. He lives in North Carolina with his wacky fiancée, her chill mom, three of the most creative and awesome kids the world has to offer, and a plethora of kickass pets.

Ross Young was born in Newcastle Upon Tyne in a hospital that no longer exists. Despite living in an array of countries and interesting locales, he remains uncultured and relatively ignorant. He lives in the French countryside with his wife and daughter. In moments of peace he writes novels, short stories, and anything that else that crawls out of the chaos to land on the blank page.

David Antrobus is a freelance writer and editor whose origins lie in northern England and who currently lives in the Vancouver area. He has published two books, both nonfiction, and has written numerous dark yet lyrical tales scattered among various anthologies and websites, including but not limited to *Storgy Magazine*, *Woven Tales Press*, *Dark Moon Digest*, *Pidgeonholes*, *Mash Stories* (third-place finish in their seventh flash fiction contest), *Indies Unlimited* (twice winner in their flash fiction contest), and *Ripen the Page*.

Made in the USA
Columbia, SC
17 September 2020

20048837R00226